LADY OF THE LAW

A MAUD OVERSTREET NOVEL

MELODY GROVES

WOLFPACK PUBLISHING
— EST 2013 —

For
Erin and Haley
&
Chris Enss

ACKNOWLEDGMENTS

Thanks to:
Judy Avila, Joyce Hertzoff, Phil Jackson,
Dennis Kastendiek & Kathy Wagoner

Special thanks to:
Myke Groves

LADY OF THE LAW

CHAPTER ONE
FOREIGNERS?...

SEPTEMBER 1872—DRY CREEK, CALIFORNIA

IF I'D BEEN A MAN, I'D PUT MY FEET UP ON THE desk here at the sheriff's office, lean back in the chair and sip this second cup of coffee. But I wasn't. And if I'd tried resting my legs like that, more than likely my skirt would bunch up and I'd fall backwards to the floor. Normally, the crash might bring people running, but since this was Sunday morning, most of Dry Creek's 372 citizens would be in church and not hear a thing.

And with my kind of luck, I'd be picking myself up the exact moment Seth Critoli, the handsome mayor and my sometimes beau, would come strutting in. He'd snicker, maybe guffaw, and I'd be mortally embarrassed. No, better to keep these laced-up shoes on the floor, and the skirt covering my ankles.

Now with the sun not yet all the way up, light gray intermingled with rose and gold. The streaks playing peek-a-boo with daylight was my favorite part of the day. Clouds, when the drought allowed some, sparkled lilac and crimson. And, most importantly... it was quiet. I reveled in solace, knowing calm wouldn't last long. Not that I had much to do, being sheriff. For the most part, people behaved themselves, but the town could get rowdy, especially when school was out. A couple of the boys tended to steal pies cooling on windowsills. A privy was overturned a few weeks back.

On Saturday nights, especially paydays, cowboys from the surrounding ranches and farms whooped and hollered into town. Letting off a little steam, they flashed their manly prowess with horse racing down Main. Arm wrestling competitions and of course, poker games and faro in our five saloons, kept them busy. Fortunately, for the most part, they behaved themselves and I rarely locked up one or two.

Generally, the town plodded along peacefully.

I drifted at the desk, a hot cup of coffee emitting wispy streams of delicious aromas. I breathed in all the heady smells a good pot of Arbuckles brings. Eyes closing, troubles melted right out through the toes, and a silly grin made its way up my face, I knew, because the skin stretched. A good kind of stretch.

Since pinning on the sheriff's badge a few months back, a joke played by the town council which backfired with an actual election this past July, Dry Creek settled into accepting I was sheriff—and a woman. As for myself, I'd at long last grown accustomed to the title: *Sheriff* Maud Overstreet. I no longer turned to look behind me when someone called out "Sheriff." Sure, we'd had our bumps along the way—I'd had to learn how to shoot, ride a horse, chase after bank robbers and handle saloons. In fact, some happy memories revolved around a saloon. And for the most part, I'd figured things out. Of course, Pa helped, along with the three town council members and the hunky mayor, and my almost-deputy, and the school marm and the postal office founder and... Well, I thought and sipped. Nearly everyone had helped me stumble my way through this law business. And in return, I'd done the finest sheriffing job I could.

Through the office window, streaked with dirt, hand and nose prints, which needed to be washed, I reminded myself, my gaze trailed across Main Street to Macey's Sew-N-Sew millinery shop. Behind the shop up the hill and down the other side were orchards. Lots of them. Trees tinged with gold and yellow hinted at fall, which would be apple time, which would mean... whiskey. The stills would be coming out by the dozens soon. Dry Creek home brewers produced some of the most desirable apple whiskey around northern California. I'd been told their "brew" was legendary. Since I'm of the female type, I didn't normally imbibe, except when absolutely necessary for the job, of course.

I sipped coffee, enjoying the warmth sliding down my throat and into my chest. Why did they have to produce shine so close to town? Why didn't they take their stills somewhere else, where I wouldn't have to worry about them and the trouble they bring?

Tap. Tap.

I jumped at a knock. Coffee sloshed over its brim, dotting my blouse. Great. I brushed at the drops and Mayor Seth opened the thick wooden door, breezed in like it was the middle of summer. His smile was wide, friendly, welcoming. Butterflies tickled my insides. Today, I liked Seth.

"Thought I'd invite you for breakfast, Maud." Seth dragged a chair around to the side of the desk. Its scratching and screeching across the wooden floor made me wince. "You haven't eaten yet, have you?" He sat, glancing around the tidy office like he was expecting piles of dirty dishes.

"I'm here enjoying the first, no, second cup of coffee. I'd love to have breakfast with you." My stomach grumbled and rumbled. Eggs, hashed browns, bacon and a toasted slab of sourdough would start the day off right.

Seth leaned back, not something he would do if he were heading off for food. Obviously, something else wobbled around in his brain. Something I wasn't about to like.

"Things going well for you?" I tried making my voice nonchalant. What I really wanted to say was, "No prisoners locked up back there in the cells. I'm free. Let's go. I'm starving." But I didn't.

Seth crossed one leg onto the other and ran a finger down the seam in the boot. I'd seen him do this before and it usually proved to be the harbinger of unwelcome news. He shifted in the chair. I sipped, a much longer swallow followed that one. I needed all the fortification within reach.

"Remember the Chinese fireworks over the Fourth?" He cocked his head toward outside.

"Course I do. I went chasing bank robbers while you and everyone else oohed and aahed over the festivities." Where was he taking this? "And?"

"There's more."

He made no sense. "More what?"

"Not *what*. Who." After finishing his boot inspection, he thunked it onto the floor. "Two whole families of them moving in. And I don't think the town's gonna like it."

"Them who?" I clutched the cup tighter than necessary. Besides having a charm about him I found usually irresistible, he also tended to back into topics. At times he was maddening. Like now.

"The Chinese. Haven't you heard?" He spread his hands out palm up. "More Chinese are coming and they're bringing all their relatives. Soon we'll be overrun. Dry Creek'll be called 'Celestial Creek.' We'll all be eating rice with chopsticks and bowing to each other. Heck, Maud, we'll all be speaking slant eye."

I blinked so hard my eyelids hurt.

"Besides," he continued, "we've got enough foreigners as it is. I mean, look at—"

"What? Foreigners? Your ma and pa came from Italy. Born there." Did my voice sound as shocked as I felt? "You're a fine one for talking."

Seth sat back, his mouth closed for once. His gaze traveled over me, the desk, the gun rack and landed on the door.

When he grew smart enough not to continue his rant, I pushed my way in. "How about Rune McGuire at the telegraph office? From Ireland. Took him a year after he landed in New York to locate here. Had to go mostly by oxen caravan." I was on a roll. "And Ian MacKinney?

One of *your* town councilors? Scotland. Same thing."

Seth wagged his head as if trying to roll the marbles in there into the correct holes.

"And for Pete's sake," I was on a rant and had more ammunition. "My housekeeper, Mrs. Tran... off the boat from China. Lovely woman. We're fortunate her family chose to make Dry Creek their home. She brings so much culture and... and... diversity to town. I love talking to her, although I don't understand most."

He opened his mouth, but closed it.

I continued. "When you think about it, we're all foreigners of some kind." His hang-dog downcast gaze gave me pause. Kind of felt sorry for him, but he had it coming. The only foreigners I didn't want in Dry Creek were the outlaw types. They weren't welcome, no matter their country of origin.

I sipped long on the coffee, finishing it clear down to the grounds. "How about that breakfast you mentioned?" If I didn't push him out of the chair right away, he'd probably sit there all day, pouting. "I'm starving."

He perked at the mention of food. Seth nodded, stood and held out a hand. "Sorry, Maud. I get carried away sometimes. You're right. We're all foreigners." He flashed that charming politician's smile—always melted my heart. "It's... well... I've been over talking to Pearl."

Pearl McIntyre, school marm. My friend, business associate, nemesis. She'd kept company with Seth a while back, and if rumors were correct, she'd been wanting to again. I was in no mood for talking about Pearl. Prettier than me, daintier, younger. All the things I wished to be.

"I'll fetch the gun and bonnet." Months ago, I would've laughed when putting those two words together. Nowadays, I didn't give it another thought. 'Gun' and 'bonnet' were items I never left without. And this morning, with no prisoners to guard, I was free to roam around town and not worry about feeding them or making sure they didn't escape. I was in no mood to round up a posse and give chase. Not when cold weather was coming. But I was curious about the Chinese families moving in. Mrs. Tran hadn't said a thing. Or maybe she had. And what did they have to do with Pearl?

CHAPTER TWO
MY HEART'S ON FIRE...

A BIT EARLY, EVEN FOR A SUNDAY, CHURCH WASN'T out yet. Only one other couple occupied chairs. Seth and I made our way past tables to the back of the Shoo Fly Restaurant. Here we could sit and talk without being overrun by citizens asking questions about all sorts of town matters or making speculations as to our relationship. I had enough speculation myself. We weren't exactly seeing each other romantically, but we had met for supper a time or two. More like business partners and, at times, sparring partners.

We ordered coffee and food from Jacob, our waiter and a youngster in the last grade of school. He'd made it to tenth, considering he was close to sixteen and an average student. His mama was a friend of mine and she kept me apprised of his doings. Most were good—he worked weekends and after school—and so far, had stayed out of my jail. Always an admirable trait. I'd heard through the town grapevine he was sweet on a girl older than him. I made a mental note to ask Pearl about this. Guess my prying nose needed gossip. After all, I reasoned, as sheriff of Dry Creek, I had to always be prepared. I had to know what was happening. Especially when it was juicy gossip, bordering on scandal.

Seth leaned back in the chair and slurped too-hot coffee. I sat up straight stirring mine. As much as I wanted to know why Seth had invited me out for breakfast, I didn't want to know. It was pleasant simply sitting, enjoying the early-morning quiet. Our plates showed up with eggs, ham, potatoes and flaky sourdough biscuits. A small jar of orange marmalade on a white linen tablecloth completed the stomach-rumbling breakfast. Homey aromas swirled under my nose, tantalizing my senses. Cloth napkin in hand, I patted the corner of my mouth, hoping to catch the drool. My stomach rumbled as if it could see what was about to come its way.

I salted the eggs, forked a mound of scrambled heaven, brought it to my mouth.

Clang! Clang! Clang! The fire bell.

I dropped my fork, stood so quickly my chair scooted back, tipping into the next table. Seth did the same. Fire was never welcome.

We bolted through the restaurant, elbowing our way past the gawkers crowding outside the door.

"Fire! Grab a bucket!" Other orders flew through the crowd.

I snagged the nearest tin bucket I could find—hanging on pegs next to the restaurant's door, always kept ready. Its round bottom gave me pause for a second. Then I remembered. Round bottom buckets wouldn't sit flat, which kept people from using them for anything besides putting out fire. The one I held was painted bright red with the word FIRE stenciled on it.

Acrid odors made me sneeze. Dark gray smoke roiled into the sky, blotching the early sun. Seth, bucket in hand, bolted into the street. I followed, head on a swivel, dizzy from searching for the source. There. Smoke rose from the north end of town. My heart thundered. The school!

Skirt in one hand, I hiked it above the tops of my shoes, not caring if someone might spy my ankles, and made a run for it. Seth's legs, longer than mine and not encumbered by a skirt, covered the distance quicker. Town folks passed me, running all out, many with buckets.

I trotted up Main Street, around the corner. Seth, way out in front, led the pack. Along the way, the smoke thickened, growing blacker. I coughed, my eyes watered. Around a final corner, past two fir trees, the school roared ablaze in demonic glory. Flames licked the roof and down one side. Nearby bushes flared from dropped cinders.

Men and women with buckets formed a brigade scooping water from the nearly dry stream several yards away. I sidled up as close to the building as possible, hoping no one was inside. I tried to look, but flames, hot as the hubs of hell, pushed me back. A window popped, glass erupting like it'd been shot. I jumped.

"Seth." I grabbed his arm and pointed. "It's a complete loss. Concentrate on keeping the trees from catching fire. Otherwise," I snapped my fingers, "it's the whole town."

With Dry Creek sitting in the middle of a forest, we were asking for trouble. When they built the school a few years back, they'd cleared a perimeter around most of the area, but it wouldn't take much for flames to jump from tree to tree and then wham! The town would be gone.

People handed tin buckets down two lines to the ones near the school who then dumped water on the flames. They tossed the empty buckets to waiting kids who ran back to the nearby stream.

From the front, I counted twenty, maybe thirty men and women, a few older boys, passing buckets, throwing water. Had anyone checked the back? I tossed my bucket to an empty-handed kid and raced around the school, dodging heat and flames and skidded to a stop. Over a hundred feet away, orange curls danced on the privy's roof. Fresh embers jumped and spread ever higher until the entire structure was engulfed in a blazing, explosive inferno.

My worst nightmares were coming true. The privy, set near a tree, sent sparks flying into the canopy. Within seconds, the dry limbs caught, bursting into an orange and red ball. Then another tree exploded into brilliant colors. Ash clogged my nose. I sneezed.

No one else had discovered the privy now crackling down into a pile of burning wood. I scampered to the school's side and pointed. Hollering above the creaking timber and the growling fire, I shouted. "Back here." I wheezed, pulling in spurts of air. "The privy. Trees. Can't save the school.

Concentrate on the trees." I shaded my watering eyes, caught a sneeze. The stand of pines off to the south were not ablaze—yet.

I grabbed a full bucket from a woman about ready to hand it off to someone else and sprinted back to the privy. Shadows danced against the tree trunks, bringing the whole forest alive while the spindly fingers of the trees reached out as if grasping for another breath.

I tossed water but, as if in defiance, the flames leaped and danced as they consumed, queerly beautiful in their destruction. Then piece by piece, the privy crumbled to the ground. Crashing, puffs of dust spewed skyward.

Men, axes in hand, chopped tree trunks, felling what was left into the schoolyard. The bucket brigade moved in, dousing limbs and undergrowth.

Pitiful groans at my back spun me around. The school, once a sturdy, yet inviting icon of a promising future, popped and moaned as if alive. It swayed with a rhythm all its own. I stood, mesmerized by the colors, sounds, odors. Pine scents swirled, mingling with burning wood, its smell at once both pleasing and terrifying.

Dry Creek's citizens doused, tossed dirt, cursed, chopped and tossed more water until the monster of red, orange, and yellow died out, compositing into nothing but deathlike grayness floating in the air. It sputtered, refusing to give up its life but at long last succumbed. Wisps of silver-gray smoke curled and danced its way through the haze. Sweat lingered in the air.

And then... the final flame hissed, like a broom on wet wood, at last wheezing out.

Lumber creaked. Glass shattered. The building leaned

right, bits and pieces of the roof sailed off, splatting and shattering into the mud.

"My school." Pearl McIntyre, skirt held up—the tops of her shoes clearly visible—raced around the corner. Mud making the dirt slicker than... well, darn slick, Pearl slid several feet and careened into Seth. Of course.

I coughed to clear my smoke-clogged throat, dragging the back of a sooty hand across my nose and mouth. People wiped grimy hands on their water-wrinkled clothes while the makeshift fire brigade muttered and mumbled as they wandered away, their hard work done and a soapy bath in order. I turned to Seth and behind him, in the distance heading toward town, a man escorted a woman wearing a beautiful orange and red skirt, reminding me of the colors in the fire.

Had I seen her before? Maybe. But my thoughts centered around the fire, the cause, not about a stranger in town.

With the smoldering ruins too hot to poke around, my research into its cause would have to wait at least until tomorrow. I stood, shoulders drooping, hands on hips, and immediately ruled out lightning. Not a cloud in the sky. Which left accident... or arson. My mind wanted accident, but my gut told me otherwise.

Pearl sobbed into Seth's wide chest. "What happened? My school." Her tear-stained face gazed up at him. "What'll we do without a school?"

Good question.

Seth held her tighter. "Tell you what. Join Maud and me for breakfast and we'll figure something out." He turned to me and ran a hand across his own face. "Got soot there on your face, Maud," I nodded, certain I looked more like the black-faced singer I'd seen in a Sacramento minstrel show. I waved a tired hand at his face.

He used the back of a hand to smear more soot around on his, then shrugged. "Our eggs are probably cold."

That wasn't the only thing gone cold, but I had to be a grown-up and accept the fact I was a public official.

Couldn't have personal feelings, apparently, when you're sheriff.

"Excellent idea," I said in my most friendly officer voice. I patted Pearl's shoulder. After all, she was sort of a friend and I hated to see her so distraught. Plus, my stomach growled in earnest. I was starving.

But first, I'd wash my hands. And face.

CHAPTER THREE
IT'S A FINE MESS...

MONDAY MORNING STARTED AS A TYPICAL MONDAY, whatever that was. Usually, my days began quietly and within an hour or so my sometimes deputy, Pokey Johnson, would wander by, stay long enough to sweep the floor or drink all my coffee, only to waltz out again. He helped out part time at Otis' Mercantile and in partial payment slept in a room in the back. Pokey's real name was... well, it wasn't Pokey, but despite my mental head scratching, I couldn't remember what it was.

With the fire yesterday, I hoped the school's remnants would be cool enough today for me to sift through. Maybe I'd find the reason it started. But first, I'd have another cup of coffee, shuffle new wanted posters and peruse the mail our new postal office had delivered Saturday. Pokey drove the wagon three times a week clear to Dutch Flats, over twenty miles one way, hauling back all sorts of bundles, including packages, newspapers, regular and official mail. Took all day, but he was paid fairly well. Dry Creek was happy we were getting regular service.

I should have known better than to relax. My cup was still half full when the door flew open and in strutted the three town council members. All the air sailed right out of my lungs when I looked up. I felt like a big ol' balloon unknotted. It wasn't that I disliked these men. Each could be charming in his own way, but together they were more like a big pile of goofy puppies, each vying for attention, seeing who could yip the loudest. Earlier this year, they were the ones who'd talked me into acting as a fill-in sheriff for two-three months, simply until election time this past July. Turned out I liked the job and was elected sheriff officially. That was probably the proudest I've ever been of anything I've done.

From my roost, I was eye-to-eye with Ian MacKinney, ankle high on a June bug, half owner of Otis' Mercantile, the first and largest general goods store in the area. When agitated, his brogue turned so thick, even he couldn't figure out what he'd said.

Towering over Ian stood saloon owner Slim Higginbotham, nothing slim about him. If he wasn't overweight, then he was more than a foot and a half too short. Of the three, I liked Slim. He'd ridden with me in a posse I led chasing bank robbers. Got them, too. His calm demeanor and clear head kept me out of dire predicaments more than once. Plus, his Tin Pan Saloon had become one of my favorite hangouts, when I got to hang out.

Harvey Weinberg stood at my desk, one boney hand on his hip. At least where I imagined his hip would be under the big, black coat. Harvey owned the Dry Creek Mercantile, not as large as Ian's, but he stocked any kind of weapon imaginable—mostly surplus revolvers and rifles from the War Between the States. He'd personally reconditioned each of them making him something of a gun expert. Jewish, with curls hanging down each temple, he reminded me of pictures of Rabbis I'd seen—long dark beard below a narrow-brimmed flat hat, aquiline nose with small red lines running up and down like tiny roads, narrow shoulders, narrow hips as well and wearing clothing one size too large. He shuffled around always a bit disheveled.

Before I could say "Good morning," Harvey set the tone.

"What are you doing about it, Miss Overstreet?" He corrected himself. "Sheriff."

I glanced from man to man. "About what?"

Harvey pointed behind him toward the edge of town, where the school had stood. "The fire. What kind of *schlub* are you? The *fire*. How did it start?" His cheeks flared red over his olive skin. When that happened, I knew he'd blow.

"What have ye done 'bout it, lass?" Ian, all four-feet-nothing of him, stormed to my desk, pointed his shaking finger up at me. "'Tis bad for business, it 'tis. Why, no one's buyin' nothin' today, they are. They're all scared. Hidin' in their *dachaighean*, their homes."

"What?" I must have blinked a hundred times as the recent swallow of coffee inched down my throat in a hard ball. "What're you talking about? You were closed yesterday and opened up less'n an hour ago today."

"Aye, lassie." Ian brought himself up as far as he could. "An' not one person has been in my place in that time. Not one."

"And," Slim looked at his fellow town leaders for back up. "People are talking. They're scared. They're sure it's an arsonist and their house or business will be next."

"But—"

"You've got to do something!" Ian tugged at the ascot around his neck.

"He's right." Harvey balanced on one foot alternating with the other. "We've got our eyes on you. Do your job, Sheriff."

I set the mug down hard, brew sloshed over and landed on a wanted poster. Both hands on the desktop, like smoke, I eased up from the chair. My heart thudded in my throat. Hands clenched, relaxed, clenched. How dare they threaten my job when it was no longer theirs to give. I'd been elected by voters of the entire county and only they could remove me. However, the town council held sway over the area, and they could, in actuality, take my badge.

I hissed through clenched teeth. "Matter of fact, I was

headed out there right now." I yanked my bonnet from the hook behind me.

"Another thing." Slim crossed his arms, uncrossed them as he *ahemed*. "Looks like the town's expanding. More and more men... and women, come in every day. Gold panning you know... timber..."

"That's a good thing, isn't it?" I hoped he'd come to a point with all this rambling.

"Seems to me, you all stand to benefit from new people in town. Buying more goods, drinking more."

"Aye, 'tis." Ian's gaze swept over my desk. "But there's a *staing*... a difficulty." He splayed his hand, pudgy fingers stuck out like cobs. "A wee problem."

"A problem?" Why were these men so difficult to understand?

Slim jumped in to interpret. "A few families of... Orientals... Chinamen are moving in. More Celestials than what we got already." He blinked at Ian, Harvey and turned to me. "You know what that means."

Tension in the room sucked out all the air. I straightened my shoulders and gave my practiced glare—narrowed eyes and significant frown—to each man. "No. What *does* that mean?"

"Crime." Ian tapped his fingers on my desk. "Steal everythin' canna be nailed down."

"Can't understand a word they say. *Nit farshteyik!*" Harvey paced and threw up his hands. "Sure, they bow and move out of the way when we walk down the boardwalk, but you know the whole time they've got chopsticks aimed at your back."

I stood stunned. "The Chinese I've met have been law-abiding citizens. Never had one locked up, even overnight."

"And they don't drink." Slim shrugged. "They're not good for my business. I think they kinda take up room."

"Get out!" I shook a pointed finger at the door.

Harvey leaned in so close I thought he'd bite my

outstretched digit. "Watch them good. Mind our words. They're trouble. *Schlecht*."

"Out." It was all I could do not to bean one of them with my coffee mug.

* * *

MY HANDS WERE full that week with idle children out of school. Most parents kept them busy doing chores, sending them on errands, but a few imps took the opportunity to create as much mischief as they could. Pie pilfering occurred two or three times a day. Hen rustling—snatching chicks from one farm and blending them with another flock—caused all sorts of mayhem. Too bad pullets weren't branded. Would have made sorting them out much easier.

Back at my desk, another long slurp of coffee brought my thoughts to what I'd done to investigate the fire.

No one had seen anything. And I'd about talked to everyone. Nearly four hundred fine citizens reported nobody suspicious lurking around the school. Many of the students I'd spoken with were simultaneously outraged and joyous it had burned. I reassured them that soon, they'd have some place for their lessons. Until that moment, I'd never realized eyes could actually creak when they rolled up to the tops of eye sockets.

The past week Pearl McIntyre had been busy trying to talk the good people of Dry Creek into opening their homes or finding room in back of their businesses to school the younger citizens. Only until a more permanent facility could either be found or built, she'd assured them. So far, she hadn't much luck. Today, I'd try my hand, using my badge, to impress the citizenry they needed to step up.

Downing the last of my coffee, I pushed back, vowing to wash that grimy window before wandering downtown. The office door banged open. Cullen Magruder stormed in, his unshaven face scarlet, waving his arms around, hollering in something other than English. I think it was Irish or Scottish or something like that, maybe a mixture, but he wasn't making himself clear. He paced back and forth in my office, gesturing toward his farm on the edge of town, muttering, sputtering. He whipped off his hat, slapped it against his thigh, the doorjamb, and then the edge of my desk. Dust and hay flew with each strike.

At first, I was amused but soon realized he was about to explode. I stood, towering over him by a good four inches. I wasn't as tall as most men, but definitely taller than the women. Standing like this, our height difference was almost comical. I didn't laugh and neither did he as he stared up into my face.

"What're ye going to do, *Sheriff*?"

That part I understood. As he calmed, his English bloomed.

"About?"

"Me barn. I already told ye." He jerked his thumb over his shoulder. "Me buggy."

"What about them?"

He marched from my desk to the door, the entire time with arm outstretched, fingers pointing outside. "Me buggy. Some *gurrier* put it on me barn. A mickey dazzler!"

Had I heard right? "*On* the barn?"

Words tumbled from his mouth in no sort of order. I listened hard, only catching one or two.

"Let me understand." I actually wanted to, but clearly, I'd not heard right. "Somebody took your whole buggy, everything except the horse, and placed it on top of your barn?" A smile threatened to climb up my face.

He let out what I was sure was an expletive.

By the time he'd calmed enough to describe his situation, the more I wanted to see for myself. I'd never ever think to do something like that. It didn't hurt anyone and as a prank, it was right up there with moving the privy back three feet in the middle of the night. Visiting that in the dark... well, it would be funny happening to someone else.

"Come see, Sheriff." Magruder held the still-open door and gestured for me to step out. With still no prisoners to watch, I grabbed my gun and bonnet and walked with him to his farm.

Fortunately, it was only a mile or so and the walk gave me time to chat with him. His wife, he said, was home watching for those "bowsies" as he called them, to come back and try something else. Silently, I mused whoever did this wouldn't do anything like that again. But they were apt to try something a bit more exciting soon. I'd have to keep my eyes peeled.

There it was. Indeed, a one-horse, black carriage adorning the top of the barn much like a weathervane. Only this one didn't spin around with the wind. Set directly in the middle of the peaked part of the roof, the rig straddled the high part. It appeared secure so I wasn't too afraid it would fall down on our heads.

"Any idea who did this?" I stood back taking my time, before moving in as close as I could hoping to see better.

Magruder narrowed his eyes at me. "Bet it was them no-good Italian boys. Enrico and... and..."

"Lorenzo?" I stepped back. Those boys had never caused trouble. I knew them from church. "The Pellegrini brothers?"

"That's them. Two oldest. Damn wops." Magruder spit. "Don't trust 'em. Can't understand a word they say. Damn I-tie Dago foreigners." He spit again.

He continued mumbling while I stood there blinking. What? First Seth and now Cullen Magruder, himself a foreigner.

Jennie Sue Magruder, born and bred Kentucky native she'd claimed, joined us staring at the buggy. She held a baby, not more than four days old by my reckoning. But what did I know about babies? This one was wrapped in a soft blanket, Jennie Sue rocking it back and forth. Normally I would be begging to hold it, figuring by at my age, I'd have had a yard full of kids, but presently I wasn't seeing a baby in my immediate future. Or a buggy. I saw angry red dots swimming in front of me.

"Whadda ya think there, Maud?" Jennie Sue's Kentucky drawl was almost as thick as Magruder's Scots-Irish accent.

School couldn't get back in session soon enough, is what I deep-down thought.

Jennie Sue wiped one hand on her not-so-white apron and used it to shield her eyes. "How d'ya suppose them boys hauled it clear up there without us noticin'?"

"Was it there last night at suppertime?" With all the commotion a large family creates, they probably didn't hear anything. After all, there were already five children in the house, this one made six. I struggled to push out of my mind the image of the two of them busy making baby seven. Probably could have driven one of those new steam engines into the barn and nobody would've notice.

Magruder huffed into his mustache. "Nae, Sheriff. Our sabhal... the barn had no such adornment when we prepared for the night."

"Why do you think it's the Pellegrini boys?" I'd calmed down enough not to want to choke the life out of Cullen Magruder.

He eyed me skirt to bonnet. "Came by the other day wantin' work. Askin' if there be chores need doin'. Imagine the nerve." He waved toward the barn. "I run 'em off is what I done. Don't want the likes of no Dagos on my land." He nodded toward his wife. "Told 'em stay off from me family."

I'd heard enough. All the fun had run out of this. "I'll talk to the boys, ask around." A peek at the baby made me smile. My heart softened. Nodding, I started off, the walk back to my office would help clear my head. "Good day, now."

"Wait, Sheriff." Magruder grabbed my shirt sleeve. "Wha' about me buggy?"

I looked up, smiled at it sitting on top of the barn, much like a proud peacock. Pulling my sleeve out of his grasp, I leaned in. "Might hire some boys to help bring it down. Maybe the Pellegrinis."

* * *

BY THE TIME I returned to my office, I couldn't contain my smile. I beamed. My gracious. That was one righteous prank.

One for the history books. I poured a cup of coffee, plopped into my chair and stared at a note, written in shaky penmanship, on top of a pile of wanted posters in the middle of my desk.

My heart thudded in my throat. *Don't interfere*, it read. *Or else.*

Or else what? Interfere with what? Who wrote this? What did it all mean? I glanced around expecting to find someone lurking in the corner, pen in hand, evil glint in their eye. Empty. All four corners and the cells. Even the supply room was devoid of people.

Frowning, my forehead wrinkled. Was this a threat? I'd need to treat it as such. Would I tell anyone? Maybe it was a joke the kids were playing on me, now they had time on their hands.

I'd go with that one. Yep, idle kids. I slid the note into the top desk drawer when the door squeaked open and in walked Mary Beth Malroon and Elizabeth Covington, Elizabeth known fondly as Sadie.

Mary Beth was about my age, been married, widowed and married again. Her three children attended school every day, rain or shine, sick or well. Sadie could have been Mary Beth's older aunt. Her four children were grown, busy having lives of their own. The two of them coming into my office was one of the things I liked most about my job and one of the things I liked least. I never knew from one moment to the next what was going to happen.

I stood. "Ladies. Welcome." I pointed to the two chairs in front of my desk. Usually Pokey or Seth occupied them, so it was a treat having women there. "Coffee?" I held up my cup.

"No, thank you," said Mary Beth.

"None for me." Sadie arranged her skirt over her ankles as she sat.

Small talk centered around weather, men, and children until it sputtered to an uncomfortable pause. The room echoed silence until Sadie cleared her throat and patted her hair peeking out from under a satin and felt hat. It matched her outfit to a T. I briefly wondered what she thought about bright orange and yellow skirts.

"We have an idea, Maud." Sadie leaned forward, her hands folded in her lap.

"And we think you'll love it." Mary Beth's blueberry-colored eyes gleamed. Her obvious enthusiasm crinkled the skin near her eyes as she smiled.

I looked from woman to woman. "And..."

"Well, you've been a true inspiration to us, Maud. A true inspiration." Sadie unfolded her gloved hands and flapped them at me. Was that rouge on her cheeks or was she excited? I couldn't tell. However, no proper woman would wear rouge. That was reserved for actresses and other trollops.

"It's something our growing town needs. Within a year we'll be downright sophisticated." Mary Beth straightened her hat, although it didn't need it. I did notice the pink flowers around the crown matched the pink in her dress.

"And...?" All right, they had my curiosity piqued.

The women looked at each other and back at me. As if they'd practiced, they said in unison, "We want to open a charm school."

"A what?"

"Charm school." Sadie pulled her already straight shoulders back, lifted her chin and produced a lovely, wide, warming smile. "You know. We'll teach manners, poise, civility—"

"I know what it is." I nodded. "Sounds delightful."

Mary Beth beamed. "We knew, absolutely *knew* you'd love it! After all, you're the inspiration."

So they'd said. "How's that?"

Like all the wind had been taken out of their sails, the women deflated in front of me.

Mary Beth offered the explanation. "You're sheriff."

"Right." My word was drawn out, soft.

"Unquestionably, Maud," Sadie added, "if *you* can do it, *anybody* can." She reared back in her chair as if I'd stuck her with a fork. Her hand covered her mouth. "I didn't mean... I meant... It's..."

Instead of taking offense, but still not understanding completely, I laughed. A good, long, honest laugh.

"Oh, thank Heaven." Sadie fanned herself and looked at Mary Beth. "I only meant with you being a woman—"

"And so successful as a sheriff—"

"Any woman could run her own business." Sadie glanced out the window, which still needed cleaning. "We're not waiting for any man to give his approval." She raised both eyebrows, leaned forward and dropped her voice to a severe whisper. "It's not a man's world anymore."

CHAPTER FOUR
DON'T ROCK THE BOAT...

I SPENT HALF THE DAY SIFTING THROUGH ASH, blackened primers and readers, rickety desks and dead-cold piles of burned lumber. The tin roof had fallen in, managing to slide off to the side of one wall. Laying exposed to the elements, what was left of Dry Creek's schoolhouse sat like a ship set ablaze and run aground by its mutinous crew.

"What a mess."

Seth's baritone voice spun me around. Hand over my heart it thumped as I sucked in air. "Scared me half to death." A longer-than-needed look at his body as he stood across the debris kept giving my heart reasons to throb. Today he was wearing a freshly pressed jacket and shirt. Down his trousers ran a creased line that only professional cleaners do. My creases, which for Pa's line of work as the bank's president needed to be precise, usually ended up sideways. Even as far away as he stood, I could tell Seth had shaved this morning and surprisingly, trimmed his mustache, which tended to grow out in spikes. For part of a moment, I wondered what the occasion was, but then decided not to overthink.

He ambled toward me. "Figure out anything yet? Any culprits come forward?"

I stooped to pick up part of a United States map, the

edges charred. "Nothing. It's a mystery. But has to be human caused, right? I mean, there was no lightning in the sky, no rain, no wind..." I was babbling. It had to stop or I'd embarrass myself even further. Sometimes Seth brought out the worst in me.

He hooked his thumbs in his vest pockets and stood, surveying school residues. What thoughts were fluttering in his brain? I couldn't detect, so I turned my thoughts to the matter at hand.

Tired of the town council and several parents pushing me to start school up again, I decided since Seth was mayor, part of this was his problem. Maybe more than part. "We gotta find some place for a school." I picked up a blackened wooden ruler and thought back to a time when one like it had rapped my knuckles, only because I'd poked the boy beside me or kicked someone in the playground. Nothing serious.

"Nobody's come forward offering a space?" Magically, Seth stood at my shoulder. I wondered how he'd made it across the yard without my following his every step. I breathed in bay rum after splash and hoped my sigh was muted.

"Nary a soul." Was I talking like a pirate? Darn that Seth. "However, don't know if you've heard, but Sadie and Mary Beth plan to open a charm school. Soon, I think."

Seth burst out laughing, doubling over, holding his side. When he surfaced, his lightly tanned face glowed pink. "A charm...?" He straightened up completely, his copper-colored eyes squinted with amusement, an inner glow of mischief flashed with them. He drew in a long breath. "Oh, that's rich."

"They're serious."

"I'm sure they are. But women don't need to *learn* how to be charming. They're born knowing." He held up a hand and ticked off with his fingers. "Charm men out of their money. Charm men into marriage. Charm men—"

The punch to his arm turned out to be stronger than I'd

intended. But he had it coming. He stumbled back massaging his bruised arm and, most likely, bruised ego. Then "Seth magic" happened. He leaned in and kissed me. Right on the mouth. It wasn't hard or lingering, not like I'd hoped, but the memory would be lasting.

With my fingers touching my lips, I froze. What had just happened?

Seth turned, kicked at a charred board. "Have you asked Swede Swensen over at the livery stable if we could use his back room? Only until this gets rebuilt?"

A flush of excitement surged through my body, diluted by confusion. Had he really kissed me? And why? Maybe it took an impressive whack on the arm to bring him to his senses. Or not. I played along.

Drawing in a deep breath so as not to stutter, I tapped the butt of the gun in my holster hoping to bring my head back into being sheriff. It worked. "I don't think parents would go for a livery stable. We'd have to clean it up and maybe then we'd have to convince them it's good enough temporarily."

Seth had wandered across the ruins again. "Maybe we can talk some of those boys into helping move some of this blackened timber."

"What's wrong with girls helping?" Was I starting to sound like Sadie and Mary Beth?

"Girls?" Seth looked up, stick in hand. His bushy eyebrows narrowed. "Guess there's no reason why not. Just didn't think of it."

Of course not. He was about to be educated. "I've been thinking, Mr. Mayor." I figured when I called him that, he knew this was not a social event. No more kissing... for now. "We need a fire department. Got a postal office, now we need fire protection."

"What?" Seth removed his hat, ran his fingers through brown hair, set it back on and sighed. "No money in the town's budget, Maud. Not one penny extra. It would have to be all volunteer."

"I figured as much, except maybe the leader."

He kicked at a pile of ash, a cloud of dark gray covering his shoes. "What's wrong with what we've got already? The town showed up and put out the fire, as you know. The system's already working."

"For now. But seems like the town's almost doubled in size since last year and growing. What happens if there's two at once? Or more than one building? Or—"

"Got it." He held up a hand. A slender, well-manicured hand.

"At least support me when I talk to the Three Wise Men." I glanced behind him. "I mean town councilors. Maybe they'll see a way to find money."

He nodded. Finally, I had won. Sort of. "Let's go talk to Mr. Swensen. See if we can have us a school by Monday."

I started off but Seth stayed gazing into the pile of rubble. Had he found something? Something important? I waited then wandered back.

He rubbed a hand over his smooth chin. "Got election time coming up next month. Town councilors won't like me asking for money right now. Can't afford to rock the boat. If anything, I gotta save them money. Let's wait 'til after I'm re-elected."

Immediately angry, I stomped my foot and pointed toward town. "You mean to tell me you're running scared of three men? You won't fight to get a fire department? What happens if your almighty town burns down before you get *re-elected*? Huh? Huh? And what if you lose?" The pitch of my voice was more like somebody poked me with a stick, but I was on fire. "You're the mayor, for crying out loud. You're supposed to do something for the citizens. For the town!"

Instead of his kowtowing to me, knuckling under and coming to his senses, he laughed.

Again. He held his arms out wide as if hugging the world. He choked laughter while his eyes glistened.

I stomped again. "This isn't funny."

Sauntering toward me, his smile disarmingly generous. "No, it isn't funny." He held my shoulder. "And I'm not gonna lose. Nobody's running against me. But you... you're hilarious. The way you stomped your shoe and the gray ash poofed up... and your bonnet hung to one side... and your hair..."

I'd heard enough. I tramped back to my office and got to thinking about obstinate men and zealous women and fire departments. I had me an idea.

* * *

BUT FIRST A SCHOOL. I checked with my charm school ladies busy setting up one room of Sadie's house. After wiping my feet on the throw rug on the porch, I knocked. Let in, I stood, feeling out of place. I thought my house, which Pa and I shared, was large. In comparison, this was enormous and without a doubt big enough for a few students. It was an ideal place to learn how to set a table, how to sit with proper posture and to... well, I wasn't exactly sure what one learned at charm school, but I knew it was good. Maybe I could drop in on occasion.

"Is your school going to teach reading, writing, ciphering and such?" Maybe we could have regular school here as well. No need to clean out a livery stable.

Mary Beth held one hand up like she was fending off a bear. "No, absolutely not. We've got Miss McIntyre to do that. A certified teacher."

Confused, I glanced around again. Obviously, I was missing something.

Sadie waltzed over to me, a cup of tea in hand. She offered it and an explanation. "We plan to offer Saturday classes. For girls mainly, but boys are welcome, too." Was that a titter? Boys needed manners. I struggled to envision muscle-bound, buggy-hefting Enrico Pelligrini daintily seated on a settee, knees together, balancing a China teacup and saucer on his lap while sitting up straight, making polite small talk. Right. That wasn't going to happen.

"When do you plan to open? As you know, school hasn't started back up yet." I sipped the delicate, yet delicious tea.

Busying herself repositioning a gold and green brocade sofa, Mary Beth stopped. "This Saturday. Three days from now. We've already enrolled four students."

The teacup froze mid-air. I hadn't seen any handbills at the mercantiles or heard any announcements in church. Of course I hadn't been to church recently, but still, as sheriff I should've heard something.

"Of course," Mary Beth said, "we've been in touch with Miss McIntyre and she's given her blessings to our new business."

Where had I been all this time? Why didn't I know? I returned the cup and saucer to Sadie, felt my shoulders sag. Bringing them back up, it wouldn't do to slouch in a charm school, I nodded to the women and let myself out. I probably muttered a thanks or good day, but maybe not.

Mulling over what to do next, who to talk to next, what Mrs. Tran would make Pa and me for supper tonight, and why didn't I know about the school, I ambled down Main Street not actually seeing the town. People, buildings, horses blurred as I stepped around sleeping dogs, squealing children and gossiping women standing in the middle of the boardwalk.

I spotted my office and decided to go there. My sanctuary. Real coffee instead of tea would help clear my head.

"Maud. Sheriff Maud. There you are."

I spun around like an off-kilter ballerina only to spot Pokey Johnson running toward me.

He was in his mid-twenties I knew, but I couldn't help think of him as an overgrown teenage hound dog. His feet were too big, arms too long; he tended to knock things over, but he was good company. I liked him.

While he was not on the skinny side, his roundness showed he hadn't missed many, if any, meals and he enjoyed a good belch now and then. His sandy brown hair, hiding under a narrow-brimmed black hat, always seemed to stick out like a scared mop. Pokey's too-short blue vest hitting well above his waist, made him look even shorter, although he had an inch or two on me.

He held out his fist. "Looky what I got." Opening it, his eyes widened, and a grin soaked up his entire face.

Sitting on his callused palm was a dollar-size bronze token with funny writing on it. Round, it had a hole in the middle where I guessed you could tie a string and wear it as a necklace. I picked it up, turned it over. More strange scribbling on the back. A closer look revealed figures I'd seen the local Chinese write.

I returned it to his outstretched palm. "That's... terrific, Pokey. What is it?"

While his smile faded a touch, his eyes continued to sparkle. "Knew you wouldn't know." He leaned in close. "It's a good luck charm. Got it from Liu Yu just now."

Why was I so confused? "Who's Liu Yu? And why'd he give it to you?"

Pokey blew out a deep breath and when he did that, I knew it would be a long story. Before he got two words out, I interrupted. "Let's get some coffee at the office, and you can tell me all about it."

CHAPTER FIVE
TAKE LUCK...

"YOU MEAN TO TELL ME, THIS MR. YU BEFRIENDED you and gave you that good luck charm?" I leaned forward at my desk, one elbow propped, the hand holding a coffee cup halfway to my mouth. The other elbow, also propped on the desk, pointed east, toward a hill growing into an area known as Chinatown. "Why would he do such a thing? What are you going to do with it? And how do you know it's good luck?"

Pokey's wide-eyed, excited face melted. I guess I'd hurt his feelings. But I was curious. And intrigued. And more than a little suspicious. It dawned on me I'd kind of taken Pokey in under my wing, so to speak. I'd become a surrogate ma, even though I was only about ten years older than him. Both of his folks had been killed some time back in a buggy accident and with no kin of his own, I think he'd adopted me. Naturally, like a plucky mother hen, I wanted to protect his feelings.

His eyes lowered so far I swear they landed on the desk-top. Shoulders, which had been held back straight and proud, now drooped. Holding the amulet, his hand closed and opened like it was hot, then cooled off. Hot. Cold.

Not able to stand the silence and I'm sure what was his disappointment at my lack of enthusiasm for his prize, I offered some solace. "It's real nice, Pokey. Maybe it is a good luck charm. You gonna wear it around your neck?"

I figured he'd give an emphatic no, necklaces were for girls, he'd never, ever be seen around town wearing one and what was I thinking anyway? But he produced half a smile and raised a limp shoulder.

"You'll need a string to put through that hole." Mentally, I ran down a list of possible strings and such laying around. I came up empty handed.

"There's some rawhide at the store thin enough. Think it's supposed to go over to Mr. Swensen to make peggin' strings on a saddle. Maybe I can buy some."

"Good idea!" I wanted to sound as enthusiastic as possible. When Pokey was sad, it broke my heart. "So, tell me again, slower this time, how you got involved with Mr. Yu."

Pokey brightened. He sat back, gazed at the amulet, ran his finger over the raised Chinese writing. "I've been kinda sweet on Mae Yu ever since she come by the store last week. She invited me to supper last night—with her ma and pa's permission of course—and afterwards, Mr. Yu brought this out and give it to me." He held up the amulet, turned it toward the light streaming through the street window that still needed a good washing, and produced a smile brimming with well-being.

Maybe this good luck talisman really would bring fortune to a fella who needed a break in life. He'd had a rough time and could use providence. And a girlfriend? As far as I knew, he'd always been single, never speaking with a girl more than fifteen, twenty seconds. Pokey was shy, extra-shy. Maybe his luck was about to change.

I finished off my coffee, pushed back cringing at the squeaking as the chair legs tried to slide across the rough wood. Maybe I could wax the floor. As I stood, Pokey turned his full attention on me.

"Miss Mae told me about her family and the fact only the boys go to school, when there is one."

"Well, they're new here. Moved in a few weeks ago. Give them time to adjust then I'm sure they'll send everyone."

"No, she said only the boys. Always been that way." Pokey rubbed the charm, nestled it into his vest pocket and stood. "Fact is, she's never been to school herself. And she's... she's... well, I'm not sure how old she is, but gotta be over eighteen. She's worked in her family's laundry more than eight years she said."

Pieces of the culture puzzle pulled themselves together. "You know, thinking on it, Mrs. Tran said the same thing. Girls don't go to school. Said they don't need that kind of learning. Reading, ciphering, writing is a waste of time, she said." I glared at Pokey. "Can you imagine? I wonder why they think that."

He started for the door, turned back. "I wonder, too. I'll ask Mae's parents. They don't talk English to where I can understand much, but they invited me back tomorrow night. They're lookin' to open up a restaurant." Pokey produced a smile that reached clear to my heart, wrapped itself around it and tugged. "A real Chinese restaurant. And their food is good. Sticky white rice and fresh chopped up vegetables like carrots and onions and the likes I've never ever seen. Even got some kinda sue-y sauce they put over it." He licked his lips as he walked out.

With his flavorful description, I licked my lips, too. After he shut the door, I stood, broom in hand, thinking about school and girls and good luck charms. And then like a being hit with a bucket of cold water, it hit me. I knew exactly what needed to be done. Get a regular school up and running again, talk to the new—and old—Oriental families in town, get those girls in school. Create a fire department. And somewhere in there, I knew Mary Beth's and Sadie's charm school would come into play, but exactly how I wasn't sure. Charm school. Pokey's new charm. I regarded the broom in hand. Coincidence? I thought not.

And of course, half the town would not like the idea of Chinese being educated alongside their precious non-

Oriental children. But too bad. They'd simply have to get over it and accept people for who they are.

I sighed a long, hard, determined sigh and realized while one hand gripped the broom, the other was firmly planted on my hip. This was *going* to happen.

* * *

FIRST THINGS FIRST. I washed that danged window. Inside and out. While I rinsed, rubbed and polished, I considered who to talk to, what to say, how to answer insane questions and wondered if Mrs. Tran would have any insight about good luck charms. I'd hate for Pokey to be setting his hopes and dreams on a round stone with writing on it.

With so much to do, I couldn't keep up our house with the cooking, cleaning, mending and also do my sheriffing job with the fire, schools, misplaced buggies and such. Not enough hours—or energy—or coffee—in the day. I mentally thanked Pa, again, for hiring such a wonderful woman to keep house. Maybe Mrs. Tran was *my* good luck charm.

I put the cleaning rags away then went outside on the boardwalk to admire the handiwork. That window sparkled. No more dirt, rain-splattered mud, nose prints and other globs I was loathe to identify. Oughta hold for quite a while.

Dusting off my hands and doing a mental back pat, I glanced around hoping someone would wander by and offer congratulations. Instead, I spotted Mayor Seth and school marm Pearl McIntyre walking arm in arm across the street toward me. Were they an item again? Boy, these on and off again relationships made me crazy—and dizzy.

Pearl waved. I waved. Seth guided her across the street where I waited for them, my teeth gritted. Would they notice my clean window? Probably not.

"We've got exciting news, Maud." Eyes glowing, Pearl glanced up at Seth. "You wanna tell her or should I?"

Oh, swell. I steeled myself figuring wedding bells would peal in the not-too-distant future.

Seth opened his mouth, but Pearl continued. "We found a school! It'll be just right until we can rebuild."

"A school?" Two tons of trouble lifted right off my chest. I couldn't help but smile. "You did? Where?"

Seth and Pearl spoke as one. "The church!"

"What? The church?" Why didn't I think of that?

"Reverend Jenkins stopped by the office yesterday." Seth pointed down the street toward the white-clapboard church. "We chatted for a stretch, and I mentioned needing a school. He immediately offered the sanctuary."

Turning toward the church and finding the three of us facing the same way, I bobbed my head. "School during the day, five days a week. Sunday used for services. Saturdays for weddings." I let out a long exhalation of relief sending a thank-you skyward. "When do you start up?"

"Seth and I talked about that. I'm thinking Monday. Give us time to get the word out. Pokey's bringing extra school-books donated from Dutch Flats during his mail run Friday."

Pokey already knew about this? Where was I? Didn't I see him yesterday? Him and his Chinese amulet?

I tuned into the two of them chatting like school kids on their first day. "... and won't have to build a morning fire since the Reverend takes care of heating the place."

"No blackboard, though." Pearl pursed her lips stroking them with one dainty, lacy-clad finger.

"Maybe Otis' Mercantile has a map like the one got burned and at least something big to write on." Seth produced his heart-stopping politician's smile as he leaned close to me. "Now *we* won't have to clean out Swensen's barn."

We? I let it go, a bit grateful for avoiding the unpleasant, even though I wondered why Seth thought of me when talking of mucking out stalls. I pushed that thought away. "Before you go, Pearl, you know the Pellegrini boys?"

Head tilted sideways, eyes narrowed, she gave a quick nod.

I held up a hand. "Got a complaint about a prank Magruder thinks those brothers did. You heard them talk about Magruder or his buggy or some such?"

Seth ran a hand over his curling mouth then pointed east. "They the ones put that buggy up—?"

"I have no proof. Just wondering."

Pearl shook her head. "No. Those boys are good kids. But when I see them again—"

"Thanks. Magruder needs help getting it down," I said. Seth's mouth turned upward, a grin hidden under his mustache. I turned my full attention to him. "Wanted to talk to you about the Chinese in town. In particular, the two new families."

Seth threw his shoulders back pointing a long forefinger in my face. "See! I told you you'd be worried about those Orientals." He waggled the finger. "Causing trouble are they?"

Immediately, my outrage surrounded me like an army around its besieged general. "No trouble." I muttered, vowing to keep my temper, although Seth was close to being choked. Or kicked. I looked at Pearl, hoping her good nature and nurturing qualities would tame him. "I understand the girls don't attend school. Never have. We need to do something about it."

"Not at all?" Pearl uttered an indrawn gasp. "Ever?"

"Apparently the boys can, but—"

"We need to do something." Pearl tugged Seth's arm. "These are the citizens of tomorrow. Our future. They're the ones going to build our great nation. Without them educated, able to read and write, cipher, what'll become of them? Our country?" She shuddered. "I hate to think."

"You know..." I leaned against the wall, next to the window, its cleanliness forgotten. "The church is plenty big for everybody. Chinese, too."

Seth scrubbed his face. "Ohhhhh... boy."

CHAPTER SIX
GET ME TO THE CHURCH ON TIME...

VISIONS OF MY IMAGINARY WEDDING—WHITE dress and veil, Pa at my side as we walk down the aisle— paraded through my head and heart as I stood in front of the church. Inside, up at the altar, my husband-to-be, Elijah J. Goodman waited, that charming boyish smile on his face as his eyes ate me up. A gold band, two-bedroom house, complete with white picket fence and a yard full of kids were in our future.

But it wasn't meant to be. Several months previous, and after five years of waiting for Eli to come back from wher- ever he'd gone, he returned only to rob the bank and break my heart. I'd arrested him. Life simply wasn't fair.

I turned thoughts back to the present. The church's whitewashed siding glowed in the afternoon sun and its stained-glass windows were cleaner than my clear one. As much as I had wanted to be the one to find a suitable place for a temporary school, I had to admit the church was more than suitable. There was even a yard in the back where the children could eat their mid-day meals and play at recess. An added bonus was with the church located closer to town than the burned school, parents could stop by easily to check on their little darlings or chat with Pearl. Looked like a win-win in my mind.

Opening the door, I stepped inside. Nothing fancy but the wooden pews lined up nicely and a sage aroma permeated the room. Clean, inviting sage. However, I knew within a matter of an hour or two the church would smell more like active boys running through mud puddles. I didn't think frogs and lizards had odors, but when chasing girls with them, boys would probably get stinky. Quite possibly the reverend had forgotten what it was like being a young man.

Up at the front, Reverend Josiah Jenkins and councilman Slim Higginbotham were in conversation. Both looked over as I walked in. "Just talking about you."

"Maud!" Slim waved.

This couldn't be good. "Howdy!" I strode down the aisle resisting images of a white dress and navigating through cheering guests. I nodded to both men and waited for the other shoe to kerplunk.

The Reverend, his face a gorgeous battlefield of wrinkles, produced a wide, warming smile. "I think holding school here is a tremendous idea, Sheriff Overstreet." He nodded. "A tremendous idea. If anything, the youngsters who don't regularly attend Sunday services will at least become familiar with the inside of the church. It won't be scary to them."

"Never thought of it like that, but maybe you *will* see increased attendance." I wasn't quite sure where he was headed with this part of the conversation, but I was all right with it. So far he wasn't threatening me or warning me or...

"Maud, the other town councilmen aren't happy."

Kerplunk.

Slim dipped both wispy eyebrows. "Haven't caught the arsonist yet, have you? Who knows? He could be out there right now ready to set another fire. And you haven't found him. People are on edge. Scared. What're you doing about it?"

Jenkins pushed into the diatribe. "Give her time, Slim. She's been busy. Got a lot going on right now." He eyed the councilor, then slid his dove-gray gaze to me. "Hate to say this, Maud. But in part, he's right. First the school. Who knows? Next it very well could be the church."

"Not on my watch, Reverend." My shoulders straightened themselves. "Not when I'm in charge."

* * *

I MOSEYED up the street toward the office, a clot of cold pumped in my throat. What if the arsonist had a thing about schools? Maybe somebody'd had a bad experience with a teacher? Somebody with a grievance? Possibly been expelled for devilish reasons? I ran through a short list of other possibilities and came up with: *someone had to be crazy to do such a thing*.

Was Reverend Jenkins right? Would the church be next since it would now be a school? With the encounter of each person on the street, I wondered if he or she was the culprit. I ruled out almost everyone as members of the church, strong business leaders, or women with too many children to worry about... the list went on. I couldn't find a single, solitary individual who was truthfully suspicious looking. I'd have to dig further and... harder.

Behind me, a deep rumbling on the street reminded me today was coach day. Once a week, we had stage service from Sacramento. I always tried to remember to meet the coach since its arrival was, well, a highlight of the week, but also to see who entered our little town. Usually I was a welcoming committee of one, so I waited for the elephant-sized Concord to pass, its wheels churning up dust and the driver reining in "Whoa" to the horses. Hiking my skirt, I scurried up the street.

By the time I arrived at the telegraph office, our official stage stop, the stage was already offloading passengers. Correction: passenger. Singular. And what a passenger he was. I stood mouth open, agape. Actually, *gawking* would be a better word. I pulled my eyeballs back into their sockets, closed my mouth and swallowed what I was sure was drool.

There stood Adonis. At least what I envisioned that stunningly gorgeous creature of mythology to be. Tall and straight, yet incredibly rugged, his coat sleeves strained to cover his muscles. He was a remote, majestic figure in splendid boots. The quintessential Western man. I stood on the boardwalk feeling as awkward and shy as a young schoolgirl, and then... he turned his handsomely chiseled face to me. Aristocratic eyebrows rose when he spotted me while half a smile dimpled his cheeks, which had been shaved yesterday. A full mustache, warm brown matching his hair, adorned the upper lip. Although I was sure he'd ridden all day, he wasn't rumpled. Not an inch on his trousers, shirt or jacket showed wear nor tear of such a long trip. He wasn't even dusty. Daresay, was I straightaway in love?

The grizzled jehu who had driven this stretch for years tossed a carpetbag off the stage's top then climbed down.

The heart-stopping passenger offered his hand to the driver. He flashed a picture-perfect smile. "Thank you for a most comfortable ride."

Outstandingly handsome and courteous, too? Was I dreaming? A quick pinch of my wrist told me no. Was he too good to be true? And then it hit me. Of course. With my luck he was either a bank-robbing outlaw, or already happily married with scads of children who adored him. Then again, maybe not. I'd go with "not."

I pulled in two deep breaths, cleared my throat, checked my knees to be sure they'd hold me and stepped forward. His gaze swept me skirt to bonnet, lingered on my badge and finally rested on my face. I hoped breakfast parts didn't cling there. I stuck out a hand, stood up straight and about died when he took it. Soft, warm, welcoming. Reminded me of snuggling under a fuzzy blanket on a cold winter's night. His touch was that wonderful.

"Howdy, Sheriff." His voice. Could it be any lower or smoother?

"Howdy," I said back, but I'm not sure anything came out.

He relaxed his hold while his mouth curled on both ends. "Lady of the law? Don't think I've ever met a female sheriff before." He tilted his head to the left, not enough to make him look lopsided, but enough to show polite humility. "Not that I've had many run-ins with the law, you understand."

Steady, girl, steady, realizing he still held my hand. I used my other to thumb toward the office. "I've been sheriff for months now—you'll find Dry Creek quite the progressive town—we're even opening a charm school tomorrow and since our school burned down, now we'll be holding classes in the church—can you imagine, a church?" And I stopped. What was I doing prattling on like a love-sick calf? I was much too old to be a flighty female, as Pa used to call me. Apparently, the stranger realized my nervousness and relaxed his star-studded smile.

He let go much too soon and tipped his hat. "Allow me to introduce myself properly, Sheriff. I'm Aldridge Armstrong, schoolmaster. I've come seeking employment."

Oh please, knees, keep me upright. Another breath pulled in and parts of the town within his aura came into focus. I recognized the telegraph office next to me. "Maud Overstreet, Sheriff." I grimaced. He already knew the sheriff part. "Welcome to Dry Creek."

"Pleased to make your acquaintance. And thank you." His gaze swept up and down Main. I knew because I followed every move he made. "Is there a reasonably priced hotel close by? And then some establishment for a hearty meal?"

"Across the street, Mr. Armstrong. The Gold Strike is ace high... and only hotel in town."

He put two fingers to his hat brim and ducked his head ever-so-slightly. "Thank you, ma'am. I'm hoping they have space for one tired traveler."

I wanted to tell him Pa and I had an extra bedroom, but

clamped my jaw shut before the words spurted out. "I'm sure they'll have room for you." Did I bat my eyelashes at him? I pointed down the street toward the Shoo Fly Restaurant. There's only two choices. You can get steak and potatoes there. I eat breakfast there often."

"Breakfast? Perhaps we can dine together, some time."

Heart fluttering like a captured butterfly, I nodded, words having left the ol' noggin. Before I could make anything more function in my head, a young boy tugged on my skirt. Apparently, I'd missed seeing him run up.

"Sheriff? Sheriff?" Jimmy Hatsford stomped his bare foot until I looked down at him. "Mayor Critoli give me two whole pennies to tell you."

"Tell me what?" He had my full fuzzy attention.

"He says you gotta come to the office. He says it's, er... herg..."

"Urgent?" Mr. Armstrong finished Jimmy's sentence.

Jimmy nodded and tugged on my skirt to follow him. "Says it's im... por... tant!"

I turned to Adonis. Flirting forgotten, at least lessened, I raised one eyebrow at our new visitor. I hated to go, but well, after all, I was sheriff. And I had to show Mr. Armstrong I put duty first. "Sorry. Have to go. Nice meeting you. Again, welcome to Dry Creek."

I let Jimmy grab my hand and lead me down the street as if I didn't know where Seth's office was. A quick glance back revealed Mr. Armstrong retrieving his bag and starting for the hotel.

CHAPTER SEVEN
SOMETHING SMELLS...

SLIGHTLY OUT OF BREATH, I KNOCKED, THEN opened the door to the mayor's office, fully expecting a harried, out-of-sorts mayor, pacing window to desk, muttering under his breath, arms waving as if conducting an orchestra. Instead, I found Seth perched on the edge of his desk, chatting with two women sitting in chairs in front of him. Seth slid his rear off the desk, glanced at them, at me and nodded.

"So glad you could come, Maud." Seth waved his hand at an empty chair next to a woman I recognized, but her name eluded me. "We've been talking business."

"Business? What kind of business?" I arranged my blue calico skirt around my ankles carefully, so if I stood quickly, I wouldn't trip.

The woman closest to me turned partway in her seat, her words easy to understand despite a heavy German accent. "Ester and me are tinking of opening beezness, here in town. We taut mahbe da mayor could give us good pointers."

Ester. I put the name with the face. Ester Sibley. Her husband worked for my pa down at the bank. I tight grinned at her. "What kind of business are you thinking?" They had my full attention. Even though we seemed to have enough, Dry Creek could use more commerce.

Ester leaned forward, her eyes dancing. "Bakery. I can make cakes, cookies and such, but Hilda, here, knows the mouth-watering recipes for German goodies."

"Ya. I cook much back in da old country." She ticked off on one hand. "Strudel, lebkuchen, Bremer klaben, vanillekipferl..."

"Stop. Enough." Seth held up a hand, licked his lips. "I don't know what you said, but I can smell it already. I'll help, I'll help."

My stomach grumbled thinking the goodies were already baked and I'd denied it the sweet sensation of German cooking. Growling again, louder this time, my stomach's complaints turned Seth's head. I scooted around in the chair and I'm certain my cheeks turned red. Curiosity possessed me and I leaned in. "So, what made you decide to go into business?"

Both women sat back and gasped. Hilda's eyes grew wide. "You, Sheriff. It was you."

I'd never suggested to anyone a bakery would be a good idea. In fact, right then I chided myself for not thinking of it first. "Me?"

"You becoming sheriff, Maud." Ester held both hands palm up. "You showed us women can do as much as—"

"If not more—" Hilda glanced at Ester.

"Than a man." Ester turned to Seth. "I'm sorry, Mayor, but we've needed someone like Sheriff Overstreet here to lead us in the right direction. Not another... *man.*"

She pronounced "man" like it was something to be stepped on, like a bug.

My shoulders sprung back, pulling me upright. Lead. They want me to lead. Exactly like the charm school ladies said. Maybe women businessmen... women business *owners*... was a good idea. No, a great idea. Together, we'd show the men of this town, in particular the Three Wise Men, not to dismiss women when it came to running a business. The more I contemplated, the more I firmly decided these women *would* be successful. They would show the world women were worthy and valuable and so much more than homemakers and mothers.

"Where're you thinking of opening this bakery?" I swear the aroma of baking apple pies wafted under my nose.

Seth cocked his head sideways. "They're looking at the far end of Main."

"As far from the restaurant as possible." I smiled knowing old man Tillery, who owned the place, sputtered at any mention of competition. Recently, there had been rumors of another eatery, other than the Café, opening up but mysteriously, the idea had been dropped overnight.

"First," Ester said, "we'll be cooking in Hilda's home. Selling out of there. Only until we have enough funds to lease—"

"Or buy," Hilda added.

Ester nodded at her partner. "Or *buy* a store." She high palmed her hand across both women indicating her imagined storefront sign. "*Dry Creek Sweet Shop.*"

I imagined it too as my stomach gurgled and grumbled. "So, you're not looking to get a loan from the bank?" I looked at both women. "I'm sure my pa and your husband could work something out."

"Never." They spoke in unison.

Hilda shook her head so hard I swear I heard rattling. "Dis is *our* beez-ness and no man ist goin' to tell us how ta get monies. We're making dis by our own."

Ester bolted up to her feet like she'd been poked with a cattle prod. "Or not at all. You, Maud, of all people, should know that."

I looked to Seth to jump in and help settle ruffled feathers. But there he sat, now behind his desk, a wry smile hidden under an umbrella of a mustache, still neatly trimmed. Eventually he picked up on the cue. "Ladies." He scooted back his chair, eased to his feet and placed both hands on the desktop, leaned in. "I'll do whatever I can to help, as will Sheriff Overstreet. You have our full support."

In some way, I felt compelled to explain exactly how becoming sheriff wasn't my original idea or intention, but then thought better of it. No need to tell them the town council had badgered me until I'd given in and agreed to fill in for our old sheriff who'd decided to go fishing and forgot to come back. Plan was I'd be sheriff only for the few months until election time.

Instead, I offered, "With a lot of hard work, I'm sure you'll do fine. And, as the mayor said, I'll do whatever I can to help."

"Thank you." Hilda and Ester again spoke as one.

Hilda stood, smoothed her green, lightly ruffled skirt, adjusted her hat and made her way to the door. Ester was next. I followed behind both women, Seth on my tail.

Ester turned at the doorway. "Thank you again for the encouragement." She used a forefinger to push up round glasses threatening to slip down her nose. For the first time since knowing her, I noticed her high cheekbones accentuating country-green eyes. She must have been a real beauty as a young adult. Now, soft age lines cascaded across her forehead. Not enough yet to make her look old.

They stepped out into a soft California fall breeze.

The door clicked shut, I turned to Seth. "Bakery. Yum. I'll most likely head over there every day."

Seth eased his rear onto the desktop again. "You know." He turned his eyes on me. "This is the third time a woman has come to me with business ideas." Ticking off fingers, he wagged his head. "Charm school, bakery and... blacksmith." A smile flirted with his mouth. "Smithing probably won't work, but they're all saying it's because of you."

Shifting my weight, not sure where he was going with this, I produced my heart-fluttering smile. Not too wide, not too flirty, no teeth showing. "Glad I can help."

"I don't get it," Seth said. "I thought I understood women. How hard could it be? You all want to grow up, get married, have kids and a house. Grow old. Have dozens of grandchildren to dote on. Nothing complicated there. Simple."

"Not every woman's cut from the same cloth, Mayor Critoli."

He drew in a long breath, patted his chest. "I've decided a woman's natural state is a mystery."

I opened the door and stepped outside. Before closing it, I whispered, "That's what we think about men."

CHAPTER EIGHT
WHAT'S COOKIN'?

SUPPERTIME WITH PA HAD ITS UPS AND DOWNS. WE didn't eat together every day, what with me the sheriff and him the bank president. We both were busy, but more often than not, we managed to share one meal a day. This evening at the dining table, Pa across from me in our usual seats, all I could do was think. I pushed the fried chicken and new potatoes around on the plate, smells of frying grease intermingled with thyme and basil. Chin in one hand, fork in the other, I poked at the meat while thoughts of a million other things took center stage. I had no appetite, even though Mrs. Tran had fried the chicken like I'd shown her. She's added more herbs and spices than usual. Pa glanced at the folded newspaper by his plate. Conversation tonight was not much more than grunts.

What was Aldridge Armstrong doing right now? His first day in a new town and somebody should be showing him around, making him feel welcome. If I hadn't had to come home and eat with Pa, that somebody would've been me. Dining alone wasn't appealing, so right then I vowed to find him in the morning and make sure Dry Creek hospitality was in place. Besides, if he wanted to be a teacher, maybe he and Pearl—I jerked upright. My Lord, not Pearl. She'd get her claws into him, and he'd never see the light of day again.

He'd succumb to her female wiles—with which she over-flowed—and next thing I'd know there would be wedding bells. What was I thinking letting him out of my sight?

I forked the chicken with a vengeance like it was trying to escape, shoved it into my mouth, gulped down the glass of buttermilk, wiped a white mustache and stood. "Gotta go to work, Pa."

He glanced up, grunted an appropriate response and within a minute I had my bonnet on my head and door open. Nobody would come between me and my new man. I saw him first.

As I marched downtown, I thought about my man. All right. He wasn't mine, but he absolutely was a man. And if things worked out like I hoped, Adonis would indeed be *my* man. But first, I had to find him.

I searched all the usual places—restaurant, saloons, hotel, even the church. Nada. Nothing. Nowhere. Where could he be? Mentally, I ticked off all the logical places discovering I'd covered most of them. With more than Pearl and Mr. Armstrong on my mind, I decided to take an evening stroll toward the edge of town where the apple orchards were busy providing the town with fruit. Apple pies, cakes and anything else that could be made from apples were finding their way into stores and houses. This time of year, the farmers had jingle in their pockets. If they didn't sell the fruit themselves, they leased a portion out to distillers.

Ahead, in one particular grove, warm apple juice smells wafted strong. I stopped. A deep sniff. A still. If memory served, there were several in the orchards. Guess it made sense to set up the kettles and tubs and such near the source. If anything, they provided whiskey to the saloons and true apple cider to the restaurant. My thinking was if no one objected, stills were good for business. On numerous occasions the town council had agreed, and, to my surprise, it turns out those three were some of the distillers' top customers.

As sheriff, I figured inspecting the stills' operations would fall under my job description. Besides, safety for the town was important and if one of the tangle of wires and pots blew up, it could catch the area on fire and then the town... I *really* needed a fire department.

Halfway along the trail winding around trees and clumps of bushes, I spotted Aldridge Armstrong walking toward me, small canvas bag in hand. He slid to a stop.

His hooded eyes, flirty silver gray, hid behind sweeping black eyelashes. They rested on mine. I couldn't breathe. Or swallow. So I stood, transfixed.

"Sheriff Overstreet," he purred. "I am pleased to see you again. And so soon." He smiled a rich, heavenly smile.

Say something. Anything. Instead, I smiled back and bobbed my head. *Idiot.*

Awkward silence filled the orchard. I swear even the birds stopped chirping, waiting for me to say or do anything meaningful. He looked at me. I looked at him.

Finally, he held up the sack. "I've been craving fresh apple cider. The hotel clerk recommended the still right behind me." He shifted his weight.

I blinked trying to get air back into my lungs. All I managed was to bob my head again.

Mr. Armstrong came to the rescue. "Would you care to share a cup of cider with me? I'd enjoy the company."

Of course I would. Inside, I shouted "Hooray!" while I pulled in more apple-smoked air. "Thank you." I spoke. "I'd be delighted to have a cup with you tonight and show you around town tomorrow when there's more light, because it's kinda hard to see anything in the dark, even though we have the modern gas lights up and down Main Street, it's easy to get lost, or run into somebody or find your way back to the hotel—" I froze. There was no doubt now, I was in love.

That disarming smile took up most of his face. "How about we enjoy this cider over supper. I haven't eaten yet."

"Restaurant's still open for a bit." Butterflies stomped in

my head. I wanted to tell him all about the fried chicken and how every Sunday we have chicken for supper although today wasn't Sunday... but I didn't. He'd probably heard enough already. I pointed toward town.

We walked side by side back and I prayed with each step I wouldn't trip over an upturned root or rock and fall. I'd never, in all my lifetimes, be able to face him again. Luck stuck with me while we strolled down the street. No missteps over cupped wood on the boardwalk, no tripping over my skirt. I also managed to make complete, short sentences as I pointed out various businesses. In reply, he asked appropriate questions.

Sun set early this time of year and the town glowed with strands of orange and deep yellow as the sun plunged behind the hills. Shoo Fly Restaurant, at the far edge of town, served until full dark. Again, we were in luck. I'd been right. Still had an hour or two left before they closed.

We took a table near a wall where he ordered two steaks with all the fixings. I assumed one steak was for me, but I doubted if even one bite would go down.

Waiting for our order, Mr. Unbelievably Handsome leaned forward in the wooden seat.

"So, you've been sheriff a while and know what's going on around town." He paused the right amount of time between sentences. "How secure is the bank?"

My hackles went up and warning signs marched in front of my eyes. It was more than obvious. He was a "sweep-me-off-my feet" bank robber come to investigate what he considered to be easy pickings from a small town. Again. Well, if that was true, he had another think coming. I'd show him we were not to be fooled with. I sipped his apple cider, which turned out, had a kick to it.

"My pa is the bank president and I can assure you, your money is more than safe in there. The vault is the newest and finest money can buy. No one can open it without Pa's permission."

And then I froze. Had I said too much? If this gorgeous,

scintillating man was indeed a crook, I'd just told him to capture Pa and force him to open the safe.

"Are you all right, Sheriff?" Mr. Armstrong held my elbow. "You've lost some color there and you groaned." He leaned close. "Is it the cider?"

I held up a hand. "Why'd you ask about the bank?"

Leaning back, he flashed a heart-stopping grin. "I get it. You think I'm a brigand, casing out the place." He laughed. Actually laughed, loudly. His shoulders jiggled as he searched the ceiling. "My fault. All my fault. Guess you never ask a sheriff about a bank."

I failed to see the humor, but my shoulders relaxed as well as the hair on the back of my neck. Maybe he wasn't a thief after all. I waited for him to finish chuckling and with the timing of a saint, the waitress swooped in with plates in both hands.

She set them at our table. "Here ya go, Hon." Speaking to me, she went on. "Greatest steaks in town. Cooked just 'til the moo's gone."

I recognized her from the many times I'd eaten breakfast here. Margaret, I think her name was. "They smell delicious." And they did. My stomach growled. She whisked away before I had a chance to thank her.

"This is a real treat, Sheriff," he said. "I loathe eating alone. I miss my daughter."

I must've sagged clear into my seat and puddled on the floor. I knew it. Knew he was married and off the market. I mentally kicked myself and regarded the fork in my hand. Should I stab him or myself? "Your daughter?"

"Emma's seven. Her ma died last year and I miss the simple things, like sitting down to a meal together."

Whew. I patted my mouth imagining it was my forehead. "Sorry to hear that." And I was. But it was also good news, in a perverted sort of way. "So why come here?" I figured he'd say he was passing through, took the wrong stagecoach, had a moment of insanity... some drivel.

"I'm from San Francisco, born and raised. Emma, too.

But I don't like the big city life anymore and don't wish it for my daughter. I'm seeking some place quiet, relatively crime free. You know, some place nice to raise a family. I asked around and Dry Creek was mentioned. Thought I'd come take a look."

Whew and double whew.

Suddenly, my steak tasted extra good. I dug in like I hadn't eaten in days. As much as I tried not to, I spoke over the food in my mouth. "Said you're a school master?"

He nodded, being polite not to speak while eating.

I didn't wait for his response. "I'm not sure we have any openings at the moment, but there's a possibility, and only a slight one, we may be starting a school for Chinese girls."

His face lit up and his eyes sparkled. "I've had experience teaching the Orientals. Only the boys, but there's probably not much difference between boys and girls."

How could he be more wonderful? "Tomorrow, I'll introduce you around. Let you get a feel for the town. Perhaps you could speak with Pearl McIntyre, our school marm."

"Absolutely." He held up a porcelain cup, filled with delicious coffee. "How fortuitous to have met you. Here's to you for being so helpful. And... so delightful." His face beamed. "Cheers."

"Cheers." We clanked cups, my body melting like warm molasses.

* * *

LIFE FELT good in all the right places. While I was here in the office, at home our housekeeper dusted and swept and cooked and cleaned better than I ever did. She was like having Ma again, only without me having to tell her where I was going and who with. And she never lectured me on proper table manners. Mrs. Tran was my version of heaven.

Beams of early light danced along the office walls, twirling down the wanted posters tacked up on the board. The rays pirouetted across the desk, weighted down with neat piles of paper. Like a rainbow, the end of the sun rested on the potbelly stove in the corner, the coffee pot waiting, full of freshly brewed joe.

Hammer in hand, small nail between lips, on tiptoes I reached for the single empty space on the message board to tack up the latest poster. This fella, saddled with the alias "One Eye Pete," was clearly a desperado, wanted for about every crime except murder. That was always a plus in my way of thinking.

"Howdy, Maud!"

I about toppled off my toes like a ballerina gone flat, and almost swallowed the nail. I spun around. Pokey. A longer look at him and I swear he brought the sun in with him.

He covered the office from door to me in a few long strides, took the hammer out of my hand. I gave him the nail and in two taps, Ol' "One Eye" took his place among other miscreants.

"Thanks." I stood back admiring the board. Satisfied, I retrieved the hammer. "You're happy this morning. What's up?"

Pokey selected an empty enamel cup hanging over the potbelly stove. He blew into the cup, puffs of dust making their escape. He poured coffee, sipped. His eyebrows dipped as if contemplating the galaxy, then sipped a second time.

Gaze traveling from the cup to me, he beamed brighter than the sun in summer. I couldn't help but smile too. "'Member that good luck charm Mr. Yu give me?" he said.

I had no clue where this was going, but with Pokey, conversation was always an adventure. I extended a hand toward the chair he was already lowering himself into. "Sure do. Pretty."

He patted his vest pocket, indicating, no doubt, treasure lived in there. "It's not 'pretty', Sheriff Maud. It's striking. It's handsome. It's—"

"Striking? Handsome?" I sat up straight. "Pokey, where'd you get such a large vocabulary?"

Tinges of red pinked his cheeks followed by a shy grin.

"Miss Mae uses big words. Guess it kinds of rubs off on a fella."

"Looks like it sure does." More coffee swallowed and I felt more like my old self. "Since you're my part-time deputy, you find out anything about the school fire?"

He wagged his head while trying to sip his coffee. The cup must have been attached to his lips since not a drop spilled.

I didn't wait for him to finish his slurp. "Gotta find out who did it." I leaned forward. "'Tween you, me and the fence post, I keep waiting for that alarm bell to go off again. Another fire. Maybe this time, somebody gets hurt."

Pokey plunked his cup on my desk. "No need to get all bothered. My good luck charm'll protect the town. Don't worry so much." He pulled the talisman out of his pocket. "My luck's changed since I got this." He ticked off on his fingers. "First, I met Mae. Then I got a raise from Mr. MacKinney, then I ain't had a broken wheel or such on my mail run, and..." He looked at me with those bright eyes. "Fact is. I think you need one of these."

"I don't—"

"I'll talk to Mr. Yu today." Pokey turned the amulet over and ran a meaty finger across the Chinese characters. "Might just give me a chance to see Miss Mae."

It had been a long while since Pokey seemed so happy... and in love. But I had my doubts about an Anglo-Chinese union. Townspeople put up with their relationship, what there was of it, out of respect for Pokey. He was well liked and quite the hero to many. He'd help capture the bank robbers a few months back and actions like that were hard to forget. The town's funds were once again tucked safely in the bank. But would that fact withstand prejudice?

"And while you're talking to Mr. Yu, go back to the school." I picked up my cup and leaned back. "See if you can find where the fire started." I'd sifted through soot so many times the tips of my shoes were permanently black.

I glanced from my shoes to the window. Three silhouettes marched past. Before I could warn Pokey, the door screeched open and like monkeys in a barrel, the three town councilors tumbled in. I groaned loud enough Pokey looked at me, his eyes narrowing as if in confusion. We both sat up straight, shoulders snapping to attention like a general had burst into our barracks.

Slim Higginbotham, the friendliest of the three, eased to the front of my desk and shook my hand. Then he took Pokey's. "Maud," he looked at me and Pokey, then back to the other two councilmen. His gaze returned to me. "Sheriff," he corrected himself. "We've been discussing this fire issue."

"*A Dhia*, Slim! Stop beatin' around the bush." Ian MacKinney, all four feet of him, marched up to my desk and stood shoulder to ribs next to Slim. He trained his forest-green eyes on me, the lids at their usual half-mast. "Maud, ye got ta do somethin'. Find out who set fire to tha school." His forefinger pointed at me then toward the door. "Now!"

I pushed myself up to my feet, the chair scooting back. "I *have* been. Nobody's seen anything suspicious, or anybody suspicious. I've been doing my job—"

"Not well enough, it seems." Harvey Weinberg, owner of Dry Creek Mercantile, moved in closer. I took a long step back, the back of my legs running into my chair, which banged into the wall. "The town is talking, Sheriff Overstreet. And it's no good. *Feh!*" He turned to Slim and Ian. "Told you not to appoint her."

"Now wait a minute." Pokey eased out of his seat and stood. "She ran for office and won."

Slim pursed his lips at Pokey and nodded. "That she did. And up 'til now, doing a fine job."

"Up 'til now?" Anger, frustration and disbelief pressed on my chest. I could hardly believe what I was hearing. From Slim? Then, on the other hand, I shouldn't be surprised.

Holding up a hand in peace, Slim raised one shoulder. "Not too many street fights. Maud, your jail sits empty most of the time." He rushed his words. "Which is good. Town doesn't have to pay for their feed."

Something inside me snapped. I leaned forward, my desktop pressing against my thighs.

"If all of you would help, instead of blaming me, maybe we'd get this figured out. Pokey and I've done all we can. Talked to people, sifted through the ash... nothing. Maybe with more eyes and ears, we can get this solved."

For once the three men were quiet. They'd not heard me talk back to them before. "And another thing." Since I had their attention, might as well go for it. "While we're on the subject of fire, I've been doing a lot of thinking. We need us a fire chief. Someone who commands attention. You know, someone to oversee a group of volunteers."

The men huffed, stammered and looked at each other. Eyes blinked and mustaches twitched. I almost laughed.

Slim glanced at the other men. "We'll talk about it and get back to you."

"No sir." I fisted one hand on my hip. "We need to discuss it now. Do I get a fire chief or not?" I looked from face to face. "I'm thinking fifty a month sounds about right."

Slim choked. Ian stepped back two feet like he'd been kicked. Harvey marched across the room muttering in what I assumed was Hebrew.

I waited for them to reel in their outrage and come to their senses. It took a long three minutes while Pokey and I exchanged glances.

At last Harvey stopped pacing. "Tell you what, Maud. Forty a month and not a penny more."

"And no raise for at least a year." Ian waggled his pointer finger at me and then Pokey.

"Gotta be someone trustworthy. *Mór agus làidir.* Big and strong. A man ta be reckoned with."

"I'll take all that into consideration, gentlemen." I nodded my way to the door and opened it. "And I accept. I'll let you know who you're going to hire as the new fire chief within a few days."

The three councilors grunted and mumbled their way out the door. After closing it, I beamed at Pokey. "I won!" And twirled a little dance.

Pokey and I sank into our respective chairs. We sat both silent for a good minute, then Pokey finished his coffee, stood and stepped toward the door. "You were awesome, Maud. Imagine... asking those fellas to turn loose of a dime. And you did it."

"Can't wait 'til I find a chief."

Pokey thumbed over his shoulder. "You'll be needing that good luck charm first off, Sheriff."

He sailed into the day like a puff of smoke. I peered into my coffee cup, reading the black grounds as if they could divulge the future. Maybe an amulet around my neck wouldn't be a bad idea, after all.

CHAPTER NINE
LIGHT MY FIRE...

ENOUGH WAS ENOUGH. I WAS TIRED OF THE FIRE hanging over my head. Who were *they* to imply, no come right out and state, I hadn't been doing my job? And whose job was it, exactly, to figure out how it started? Obviously, it would be my job to hunt down the criminal and arrest him, but who... I seethed. How was I supposed to know how it started? Pa, who sat in the bank all day doing whatever the president does, had been no help when I went over my "findings" with him—a bunch of burnt timber, books and shattered glass.

Walking down Main, I thought about choosing a fire chief. Someone who'd get the immediate nod from the councilors. Who? Words from the new bakery owners and charm school ladies flew around my head. I was an example, they'd said. Women could do anything, they said. Couldn't they? Then why not a female fire chief? I stopped in the middle of the boardwalk. Why not indeed?

I wracked my brain trying to figure out which of the women I knew would make a good chief. My brain finally landed on one—Penelope Plunkett. I didn't know her well, but she was young, mid-twenties and full of spunk. Some people in town secretly questioned if she was all girl, her being so strong and such. In my mind, I had no doubt because she and I sometimes saw each other at church and discussed the lack of available bachelors. She drooled over the same ones I did. Fat lot of good that did either of us.

Penelope stood eye to eye with me, but she could hoist a tree trunk without breaking a sweat. I'd never want to be in a fight with her. Changing course, I made a quick U-turn, marched back up the street, changed directions close to the end of town and headed south toward her family's farm. They raised some of the fanciest chickens I'd ever seen, feathers of various colors—some brown and white, some yellow—and their eggs were the tastiest. In fact, they sold most of their eggs to the restaurant, netting a nice tidy sum.

I buttoned my cape, glad to have its warmth this morning as the weather had turned toward the rainy, chilly side. I wondered where I'd find Penelope. In the house cleaning up breakfast dishes? Mending? Sewing a new dress? Making a pie? The closer I got to the farm, the more I recognized a figure in the distance, way out in a field, plodding behind two mules pulling a plow. Of course. She was the son her pa always wanted. Not sure about her ma, but her folks must be pleased having her around. Less work for her pa.

I clomped around the barn yard, skirted behind the privy and picked my way over the furrows in the field until figuring I was within shouting distance. I hollered and hollered. Moving in closer, I hollered again, this time the nearest mule flicked one ear toward me. That was all it took. Penelope glanced over her shoulder, pulled the team to a halt.

Wrapping the reins around a plow handle, she pulled off her gloves, shook them out and extended a hand. The grip about put me on my knees. Hopefully by tomorrow I'd regain feeling in my right hand.

"What brings ya out this way, Sheriff Maud?" She ran her callused hands down both sides of her riding skirt. I figured she probably wouldn't wear pants—no proper lady did—but then not many proper ladies plow the north forty.

This was a terrific use of a split skirt. I couldn't tell the original color, this one being mud spattered.

"Maud?" She ran the back of her hand over her forehead managing to push up her hat along the way. "Everything all right? My folks?"

Holding up both hands, I glanced toward the house realizing how this must look. "Your folks are fine. No emergency."

A smile sailed across her wide, tanned face. "Whew. There for a minute, I thought—"

"Sorry. I have me this idea and wanted to run it past you." My gaze followed the acreage to where it seemed to melt off the edge of the earth. No trees close by, so the meeting would be either in misting rain or we'd have to trek back to the house. I chose here and now, for the essence of time.

How should I word this exactly? I'd thought about what I expected from a fire chief, and with her standing in front of me, turned out I was tongue-tied. I stammered.

"Got a funny look on your face, there." Penelope leaned in. "Feelin' all right?"

I nodded. "Fine." I mentally pulled up my britches, although I never wore any, and started. "Remember the school fire about ten days ago?"

She pulled herself upright, her head bobbing. "Course I do. Talk of the town." Her triangular eyebrows dipped. "Find who did it?"

"Not yet, but Pokey and I're working on it." I looked behind her at all the plowing she'd done and the acreage she had yet to do. Maybe she wasn't the ideal choice. But I was here. I'd ask. "I'm looking to start a volunteer fire department with one paid chief fireman."

"Sounds like a good idea." Her honey brown eyes lit up. "Maybe we won't have no fires no more."

Rain dripped onto my chin, my hat keeping it out of my eyes. I'd need to hurry before I was soaked. "I'm thinking *you* would be a great fire chief. Town council's offering forty a month."

"Thought you'd want a man for that job." She stepped back, eyes roaming over me as if sizing me up as a competitor.

"It's come to my attention that women can do what men do. Why not a woman fire chief? Who knows? Maybe all the volunteers will be women, too." My shoulders involuntarily shrugged. "Or all men, or whoever you choose. A mixture."

Penelope stood still, only her head swiveling, her soft eyes looking over the fields. What did she see? Waiting, I shivered wishing I'd thought to bring gloves. I had to get back to town or end up with a bad cold.

A full minute ticked by before she moved and spoke. "Forty?"

I nodded again... and shivered again.

"How much time'll it take away from my chores?" She looked across the half-plowed field. "Pa—"

"Hopefully not much. Only when there's a fire." And I sincerely hoped those would be few and far between.

She flashed a full smile. "I think it's an honor and a privilege. Maud, I'll be Dry Creek's first fire chief." She extended a hand. "And I'll do ya proud."

Hesitating to take her hand again, instead I rubbed mine together, blowing on them. "Terrific. We'll turn Dry Creek on its ear."

I took one step away, and she bear-hugged me so tight it squeezed my breath right out. Fighting out of the embrace, I smiled. "I'll be in touch when I know more." Placing one foot in front of the other, I'd gone maybe a yard when she patted my shoulder.

"This'll be fun. Thanks, Maud!"

Her "pat" catapulted me two feet. Regaining my balance, I waved goodbye. "Be thinking who'd you like as volunteers. Make it clear they don't get paid."

"Alrighty. Got it." Penelope waved. As an afterthought,

she yelled, "Got one in mind already. That good-lookin' hunk calling himself Armstrong. I'd be his boss any day."

I slid to an immediate halt. She'd seen my man? He'd been in town what, two-three days? Turning, I'd have to make ownership abundantly clear. He was *my* almost beau. I picked my way over to her, lowered my voice and tried not to glare. "What about him?"

Her oval face softened, the lips smiling and parting a bit. "He's dreamy. So big. So strong. So—"

"Much too old for you. Besides," I pulled out all the stops. "He's got a daughter and doesn't have time for courtship what with him setting up a job and maybe a school and findingtime to rent a house and he's new in town so he doesn't know what he's doing and..." I ran out of air but the rest I said under my breath. "I saw him first."

Either she wasn't paying attention or she ignored me. Penelope nodded. "Yep, he'd make a great fire man." Her eyelashes fluttered like new-born butterflies. As if coming back to her senses, she looked at me, less than two feet away. "I'm sorry Maud. What were you sayin'? Just thinkin' of him makes me mushy inside."

That was about the way I'd describe it, too. A long sigh escaped my chest. "See you soon."

Penelope waved again, picked up the reins flicking them over the mules' backs. "Step up now, Fred. Step up, Ernie."

I slogged across the field, dejected and yet more determined than ever Aldridge Armstrong would be mine. Not only was he yummily gorgeous, but he seemed to be *the answer*. The question on every little girl's mind—who'll they marry. We all had pictures in our heads of what *he* would look like as we grew up, and while I had to admit Eli, from a disastrous lack of judgment on my part a lifetime ago, seemed to fit the bill, *this* one, hands down, was ace-high, top of my list.

The sky played tricks on me and sliced open a dark cloud. Rain fell in large, cold drops, faster than before. Wind wrapped my skirt around my legs. I tried to bolt across the yard, but bolting turned into more of a push against nature. I managed to find the road. As luck would have it, a wagon approached from behind, heading toward town I hoped. I stopped, waiting.

And who should be driving? Pokey. Bless him.

CHAPTER TEN
SHAKE IT BABY...

HE DELIVERED ME HOME INSTEAD OF THE OFFICE. I made a mental note to keep an extra set of clothes there in case I ever needed to change in a hurry. Too bad Mrs. Tran didn't work today. Sure could've used her help. With Pa still at work, I pushed sticks into the stove, lit the kindling, set a kettle of water on to boil, shivering while I waited. While the fire did its thing, I slipped out of all my wet clothes, dried off with a towel I'd meant to wash and let down my hair, which, fortunately, wasn't too wet, thanks to my bonnet.

Warming up with new clothes head to toe and a hot cup of tea down my gullet, I carried a second cup into the living room. The green brocade divan called. I gave in, stretched out and did a mental listing of what to do. Fire Chief. Check. New beau. Check. Sort of. School for kids. Check. Chinese girls in school. Nope. Catch arsonist. Double nope. All the wind fluttered out of my sails. At first I'd been on a roll, patting myself on the back for accomplishing so much. All right, another cup of warm tea and then back to the office.

An hour later found me at my sheriff's desk, hoping not to find another threatening note which had me a bit jumpy. Nothing yet. I pushed around wanted posters and three written complaints. The grievances were about the amount of "road apples" on Main and how it was difficult walking across the street without getting "atmosphere" on skirts and pant legs. Those I shoved aside. "Watch where you walk" would be my advice.

Wanted posters were a different item all together. I carefully scanned those looking for anyone I recognized. Good. Nobody I'd seen around town. All of a sudden tired and a tad chilly, I hauled my body out of the chair, stoked the fire and put coffee on to boil. While waiting and smelling the brew, I swept the office, amazed at how dusty it gets even with the rain.

I opened the door to push the small hill of dirt onto the boardwalk and came face to ruffled blouse with Pearl McIntyre. Fortunately, I was slow with the broom and didn't coat her shoes. I tilted my head. Shouldn't she be in school? I checked the time. School would be out about now.

"Glad you're here, Maud." Pearl stepped over the collection of mud clods and dirt and waltzed into my office. She pulled in coffee-laden air. "Smells great." She pointed toward the potbelly stove complete with coffee pot. "You mind?"

"Only if you pour me one, too." I swept the detritus out, closed the door against a cold breeze. Pearl set a steaming cup on my desk, sipped her own cup then eased to the chair Pokey usually used.

We passed the traditional small talk of how-you-doing-today and isn't-the-weather-great/terrible. A few minutes passed before she got down to the reason for her visit. I wasn't ready to argue how soon a new school could be built, who was actually attending or if there were enough books. I felt achy and didn't care much.

She studied the inside of her enamel coffee cup for a long breath then raised her robin's-egg blue eyes to mine. We held the stare for a second or two. "I've got a notion, Maud, and I need your help."

I liked Pearl, most days, when she wasn't hanging onto

Seth, which come to think of it, wasn't so offensive now with Aldridge in town. "What's up?" My throat scratched as I swallowed. That couldn't be a good sign. I swallowed again. Yep. Scratchy.

Pearl leaned back then forward as if rocking. "You've inspired me, Maud." She chin-pointed outside. "First a charm school, then a bakery and I just heard about Penelope."

News travels fast, although my focus was more on my throat than the town. "And...?"

"I've put a lot of thinking to this, Maud. A lot of thinking." She pulled in a long breath, thrust out her chest. "I've decided to run for mayor in this fall's election."

Wow. I had not seen that one coming.

My mouth dropped open, I blinked like dust was in my eyes, wrestling my face and body under control. "Say what?"

"Feels different now that it's said out loud." Pearl's voice was light, trivial, like a thistle bloom falling into silence. "Like I said, I've given this hours of thought, and I want to do it."

"But Seth—"

"I know." Pearl stood, pacing my freshly cleaned office. "It's about time a woman ran this town. No more 'men this, men that'. *We* will make the decisions from now on. No more asking the men for money or, heaven help us, their opinion."

"But Seth—"

"Seth? I didn't ask him or even tell him I'll be running against him. He'll find out soon enough, once the posters are printed and up, all around town. Besides, he's been in office long enough. Time for new blood." Pearl stared out the window, her hands held up, swaying overhead like she was at a Revival meeting. "I'll make speeches, kiss babies, come up with campaign promises. Imagine, with me being mayor, people will move into town just to see what the fuss is all about."

"There'll be a fuss all right." I hoped to squeeze into this one-sided conversation.

"And think, Maud. What you and me and Penelope can do together. Imagine the dances, new businesses, better roads... as a team, you, me, Penelope would be invincible. We'll put Dry Creek on the map for sure."

This was all a little more than I could handle at the moment. I changed the direction.

"Seth is of the opinion he's running unopposed. Shouldn't you tell him first?"

"First? Nope. I told you first." She lowered her arms and voice, turned around to fix a stare on me. "And I'm hoping you'll give me your full support. As sheriff, your word wields a lot of weight. Your endorsement will get me elected."

I leaned back against my chair. Seth had been a good mayor, not always seeing things my way, but he had been in my corner when no one else was. On the other hand, Pearl had a point. Maybe the mayor's job needed to be taken out and shook on occasion. And it would get good and shook once *she* became mayor.

CHAPTER ELEVEN
WHERE THERE'S SMOKE...

THIS HADN'T BEEN THE MOST EXCELLENT DAY OF my life. It wasn't the worst so far, but then again, the day was only half over. On the bright side, I now had a fire chief and hopefully, by later this afternoon, she'd have wrangled enough volunteers to call themselves a department. However, my sore throat had increased to feeling like I'd swallowed a whole dried corncob. My body craved more blankets. Coffee didn't help chills or throat, but sure felt good coursing through my veins. Enough of this black brew and maybe I could fight off the demon disease.

I vowed to do as little as possible. Rearranging the wanted posters tacked on the bulletin board seemed a good idea. Tomorrow would be better I told myself. Another long study of the wanted posters brought no revelations. And then, there it was. Another note, this one tacked on the board, covering the face of an outlaw. I peered close before ripping it down.

Leave it alone. Your done.

Again, what? Who wrote this? Done with what? Or who? I shook my head as I put the note in the drawer with the other one. Should I start watching my back? Was someone out to get me? Should I tell anyone? Positively not Pa. He'd worry. Not Seth. He'd tell me I'm crazy. No, I'd keep it to myself for now.

A glance at the Regulator on the wall, along with a longer glance outside, told me it was late afternoon. I could go home soon, put my feet up and rest. Since the house-keeper had the day off, Pa would have to fix his own meal, or more than likely, go down to the restaurant. I perked up. Maybe he'd bring something back for me.

Stretching like a cat after a long winter's rest, and yet a bit uneasy, I let my back snap and pop through its symphony. Fortunately, with nobody locked up, I was free to go home. Pokey didn't need to stay the night, and he was about to return from his mail run and would be tired.

Securing my bonnet, I latched the front door, making sure it was closed tight, and strolled down Main. Pa's house was four blocks away and over a street, but the walk should do me good. I'd meet a few citizens and assure them the town was safe.

The distinctive clacking of large wagon wheels, screeching of brakes and Pokey's familiar "Whoa now, fellas!" brought a wide smile to my face. I veered over to the official postal office, serving also as telegraph office, to check on my favorite part-time, almost deputy.

Pokey wrapped the reins around the brake handle, jumped down from the high seat, ran a long sleeve across his forehead and nodded. "Good run, Maud. No trouble." He pulled the Chinese amulet from under his vest and held it up. "Couldn't have done it without this." He kissed it, returned it to its home.

"Uh huh." I peered over the wooden side spotting only two half-full bags of mail. "Where's the rest?"

"All there was." He shrugged. "Must be some problem in Sacramento." Reaching over the side, he tugged out one bag, I grabbed the other. "I'm sure the rest'll come in at once. Then I'll need *two* wagons."

We lugged them into the office, and I loosened the first drawstring.

Clang! Clang! That dang fire bell. My stomach clenched as I dropped my string and rushed into the street. People, eyes wide, pointed up the hill, which on the other side in a valley, were the collection of apple distillers.

As I ran, I figured one of them had exploded. Not uncommon when people didn't pay attention to the mixture and the pressure valves, I'd been told. It was the first I could remember here in Dry Creek. I prayed no one was seriously hurt. Hiking my skirt higher and not caring if anyone spotted the top of my button-up shoes, I sprinted toward the edge of town where, sure enough, smoke billowed half-way up a hill. Pokey ran beside me and men already ahead of me ran toward the smoke. From the sounds of grunts and boots and shoes scraping across the dirt, men ran behind me, too.

The ringing of the bell faded in the distance.

It wasn't hard to find. White smoke with hints of brown, roiled into the trees and mushroomed into clouds. Men shouted, hollering about water. Scrub brush clawed at my skirt while tree limbs whipped my face, but I pushed aside most of them and followed voices—panicked, worried, frenzied voices.

Pokey rounded a tree to my left. He pointed over his shoulder. "Penelope's right behind us."

A glance confirmed it, but my focus was on the fire. If it caught trees and the undergrowth, the town might be in its direct path. I couldn't let that happen. Smoke wafted my direction, stinging my eyes, assaulting my nose. I blinked back tears threatening to wet my cheeks, and a cough further irritated my sore throat. The smell of burning wood reminded me of timber camps near Sacramento and... what was the other smell? Apples? Burning apples? That brought back memories... my first pie.

The smoke thickened, more brown than white now, and I arrived at the scene out of breath. I'd never realized how far up into the hills these distilleries extended from the flat lands. Half dozen or so men and women used shovels to dump dirt on the fire; another few knelt by a man lying on the ground.

"All right, ladies... and men." Penelope's voice came from my right. "Let's get this fire out. Don't want it goin' to town."

I looked over in time to watch my new fire chief point and issue more orders. My thanks flew skyward for having the foresight to hire such a competent woman. A man may have done as well, but why question it?

My attention turned to the injured man. Or was he dead? I knelt by this charred individual and realized he had brewed his last batch of apple whiskey. I'd been told this could be dangerous work, but I always wondered, "how dangerous could this really be?" Well, now I knew. Deadly dangerous.

"Who is he?" I studied the face—his still-smoldering beard, wide brown eyes, singed eyebrows—no one I knew.

"Charlie." A man, whose soot-covered face was dotted with wet spots, wagged his head. "Charlie... Flattery. Just set up yesterday. Said he'd done this kind of work back in Ireland and was a top distiller."

"Guess he got careless," another man said.

"And paid the ultimate price," a third said.

Charlie's tattered pants and shirt were held together by thread. I blinked back whatever moisture clouded my eyes— the stench of burned hair and clothes turned my stomach. Standing, I checked on the fire.

Penelope and three women, looking more like teenagers, shoveled dirt onto hot spots and used their tools to swipe at burning branches. I walked the perimeter and grateful the fire was not only contained, but almost out. I would have breathed the proverbial sigh of relief, but the smoke jammed into my lungs. Coughing didn't help.

Pokey patted my back. "She done good, Maud. Penelope's about got this out."

Breath still refusing to return, I simply nodded, then pointed at Charlie. "Take him... town."

Pokey's voice rose above the others. "Get him down to the undertaker. Please. We'll finish up here."

Now that the crisis was about over, my body shook. Was that sweat on my forehead or fever talking? Probably a bit of both. I had to go home. To bed. Relief swept over my entire body when I realized someone else would take care of the fire cleanup, and Pokey would take care of the town. It wasn't all on me, for a change.

I started back down the hill and less than a quarter of the way, who did I run into? Aldridge Armstrong. My heart fluttered and then settled down for a nap. I didn't feel well enough to drool this evening. I was going home.

"Sheriff Overstreet!" Aldridge flashed a wide smile, his white teeth glinting in the fading light. "Everything under control?"

"Distillery blew up, man died." Even for me that was short. "Fire's out."

"My goodness. I'm so sorry. Anyone you knew?"

"No." I pointed toward town. "Sorry. Gotta go. Talk to you later."

Mr. Wonderful held my arm. "No need for me to get in everyone's way. Think I should walk you home. You're looking a bit... worn."

'Worn' was a good word. I nodded my thanks. We navigated the hill in silence until we got to the town's outskirts. People stood in the street peering toward the last wisps of smoke. Questions ranged from "Fire?" to "Anyone hurt?" to "What're you doing about safety for our distillers?"

Frayed beyond belief, I answered with one or two words as I pushed the way homeward. Three blocks from the house I spotted Pa standing in front of his bank, a clot of people waiting with him. He stepped out when he saw me.

"Everything all right, Maud?" Pa's iron-gray eyes traveled up and down my body. "You all right?"

"She's tired, Mr. Overstreet, and I don't think she's feeling well." Aldridge jumped in for me.

"I'll be fine, Pa." I glanced at Adonis, who had lost his luster right now. "Mr. Armstrong is seeing me home. Think I'm coming down with a cold is all. Smoke didn't help."

Pa gave me a quick hug, something he rarely did. Guess he was concerned about his little girl or wanted Aldridge to know he was protective. Either way, his embrace felt good.

"I'll have Maizie at the restaurant bring over some tea for you." Pa patted my upper arm then extended a hand to Aldridge. "Haven't officially met. I'm O. L. Overstreet, Maud's pa."

"Wonderful to meet you, sir." He shook with Pa. "Aldridge Armstrong, new in town a week or so."

"Good to meet you, too." Pa raised one bushy eyebrow, hints of gray pushing aside his dark brown hair. "When you get settled, stop by the bank. Open an account. Really settle into town." He winked at me. "Maud, I'll be home soon." With that he swiveled on his heels and headed back to his bank.

Aldridge nudged me, his hand now on the small of my back. It tingled. "Let's get you home." Several steps later we were on my porch. He stood back. "I'll see if there's a doctor or nurse who can come by. Meantime, get rest."

"Don't bother. Housekeeper comes tomorrow. I'll be fine." I opened the door, not wanting him to leave and yet needing him to go. Otherwise, he'd be putting me in bed and while that was undeniably some place I'd want to go with him, just didn't want to right now.

"I'll check on you in the morning." My hero stepped off the porch. "Go. Rest." He flapped his hand toward the door.

I stepped in and waved. He may have waved back, but if he did, I was already headed for bed.

CHAPTER TWELVE
THERE'S THAT VOICE AGAIN...

HALF OF ME WOKE REFRESHED AND RESTED, THE other half grumpy and sore. I rolled right and immediately regretted it. A beam of gloriously happy sunlight pried open one unfriendly eye. The cranky part of me recoiled, much like the vampires in the penny dreadfuls I'd read. I snorted, growled and flopped away. The refreshed part, which half of me hated right now, urged the entire body to get up. It was a new day. All of me had things to do.

Sitting on the edge of the bed, I tried out various body parts. I swallowed. No corncobs today, which was good. I've always hated having sore throats and this one was no exception. I rubbed my face. No soot came away on my hands so I must have washed before going to bed. Good. Stomach rumbled. Breakfast would help get both halves to declare peace and work together.

I eased off the bed and stood. My eyes watered, from the smoke, I figured. A sniff in my room reminded me I should wash my clothes today before walking down to the office. Or maybe Mrs. Tran would do it for me. I didn't have too many sheriffing outfits and this light blue calico, the smoky one, was a favorite. My bare feet practically giggled as they padded over the red and gold rug filling most of my room. I liked its cozy feel and tightly woven texture, not to mention the colors and pattern. Big roses covered the entire area. Pa had said they were too loud for a bedroom, but the dark pink hues made me smile.

By the time I'd dressed and found the kitchen, grouchy me was gone. Maybe not gone completely but subdued. A hot cup of Arbuckles would drown the rest.

"Pa?" I checked the living room, dining room and his bedroom. Gone. "Must've had an early meeting today." Speaking to an empty house? Where was our housekeeper? Probably at the market. This was Wednesday. And then the revelation hit—I had the house to myself. Glory be. I could put feet on the coffee table, slurp the coffee and scan last week's newspaper. Alone. No one to tell me otherwise.

I set the coffee on to boil, fried up two eggs, cut a wedge of rye bread Pa had bought at the new bakery and slathered it with jam. Coffee aroma drifted to my nose, but that brown brew took its time getting to a drinking stage. I waited and waited, drumming my nails to nubs on the counter, until at last it was ready. I poured a steaming mugful, took it to the table where my now-cold eggs and bread waited and dug in. Scanning the *Sacramento Bee*, I noted they'd had fires lately, too. Coincidence? Probably. Unfortunately, fire was all too common.

As I slurped and munched, I mulled over the latest fire and its causes. Today, I'd have to go back to the whiskey distillers and see if I could find any more about the mishap. Mishap? I chided myself for so lightly thinking about what got a man killed. This was more of a tragedy. At least Penelope and her department—I smiled at the term —didn't let flames reach town. I'd have to stop by and thank her today and see if the Town Councilors would give her an advance on her monthly pay. No doubt, she had earned it.

But first, another cup of coffee. I whisked my dishes to the kitchen basin, poured the brew and wandered to the living room. I could sit here and enjoy it as easily as at the table. My favorite chair in sight, I aimed for it right when a knock at the door jolted my nerves enough to slosh my coffee.

I grumbled opening the door and in marched Seth Critoli, mouth set in a tight line, eyes narrowed to slits, red tinting his cheeks.

"It's all your fault, Maud. All your fault." He surveyed the room as if an entire audience was present.

Closing the door behind him, I stood with my back against it, mug in hand as if to ward off evil. "And good morning to you, too, Seth. What? What is?"

"You know." Seth roamed around the room, peering through doorways, one leading to the kitchen, the other up the stairs to the bedrooms. "*You* know," he said louder with his back to me.

"Afraid I don't." I waited for him to stop pacing, turn around so I could see his face, perhaps tell if he'd been drinking. Probably not. Way too early for that.

His eyes roved up and down my body until I squirmed. The gaze, this time not one of lust or want, was of anger, resentment. I chinned toward Pa's chair. "Sit down. Want some coffee?"

Two, three deep breaths in and out, his wide chest expanding and contracting, Seth regarded the upholstered wing back chair as if it had materialized right in front of his eyes. He looked at it, me, it again and threw himself into the cozy confines. After he settled, he nodded at me. "Coffee would be good."

Wary he might lurch out of the chair and attack, I kept an eye on him as I backed into the kitchen where the coffee aroma wrapped its comforting arms around me. I poured a cup, set it on a saucer, added one teaspoon of sugar and shuffled my way to Seth. I handed it to him, I found my chair, surprised my mug sat on the table next to it.

He huffed and puffed while he sipped. His golden-brown eyes roamed the ceiling.

We sat in silence broken only by the ticking of Pa's mantle clock, a gift he'd given Ma as a wedding present. I'd always loved the gold filigree cupid holding the clock face, and as a child wondered how long that little angel could hold it up.

Too many tickings for me to count passed. I blurted out, "What's my fault? What d'you think I did?" I'd already gone down a mental list of possibilities and found nothing too heinous.

Seth sighed long, leaned forward and stared. "You're a... you're a... a... girl."

I laughed out loud, rather relieved. "Glad you noticed."

His face flushed a deep pink. He pointed his cup to the door. "She's running against me."

Ah, now I understood. Part of me wanted to guffaw at him, the other part, the smart one, held the tongue and merely nodded.

Drowning his sorrows in the cup, he polished off the coffee, plopped both cup and saucer on the side table and slapped his knees. "Well, that about covers it. Guess I'm done."

"With the coffee, the visit or life?" Confused, I glanced behind me at the door then at Seth. "You came all the way over here to tell me I'm a girl and Pearl's running for mayor?"

Without taking a breath, he sprung to his feet. "How can she do that?" His eyes narrowed and daggered into mine. "Why? Why can't she be content teaching school? Kids love her. She should be happy doing that. Why be mayor?"

"She probably—"

"Mayor of all things." He turned his back and marched across the room toward the hall. "Why not be a doctor? A lawyer for Chrissake." His arms flew upward. "Or hell, president? Huh? Why not?"

He spun around, marched forward, aiming for me.

I put my mug down and stood, careful not to get tangled in my skirt. "Why—"

"All because of you. You."

Right then, the humor I'd seen in his rant drained. "Now

wait one minute there, mister." I pointed a finger at him, my voice louder than I'd planned. "I had nothing to do with Pearl's decision. Nothing whatsoever. She came to me and *told* me. Didn't even ask. So, whatever bee's crawled into your bonnet, better squash it right now. I didn't do it."

"You influenced her. And the others... Trying to be men." Sarcasm coated each word. "All because of you." Exasperation oozed out of each of his pores. I could smell it. If I hadn't been so outraged, I would've felt sorry for him.

"Back up the mules there, Seth." I hadn't been this angry in years and in some perverse way it felt great. Liberating, even. "You and the mighty town council came to me. You came to *me* asking for my help. I didn't want the position, but you assured me I was the number one person for the job. So don't tell me it's my fault. Any of it. These women are free to do and be what they want. And as long as they don't break the law..." I pulled in my horns and lowered my voice down to a snarl. "I'm behind them a thousand percent."

Whoa. I'd never given a speech like that before. I stood there, barely breathing, heart racing. Was I shaking? No. Guess I *had* grown since pinning on the badge. Maybe I really was an influence on the women in town. A good one, I hoped.

My shoulders straightened, chest puffed out a bit more, I nodded. "Now that we understand each other, I want you to know I'm not endorsing either of you. You're both good people and while you've done a great job, Pearl might do a great job, too." I dagger-eyed at his open mouth, wide eyes, raised eyebrows. "Please know I'm not taking sides."

We stood like that, two cougars face to face, growling over an imaginary piece of meat. Neither of us flinched. Were we involved in some kind of game of chicken?

Melting, Seth dropped his shoulders and cocked his head. Faint beginnings of a smile slid up the right side of his face. He shifted his weight, eased toward me. I held my ground. This was my home and he'd insulted me. Insinuated I had something sinister on my agenda. I froze. And watched. And waited.

He stopped in front of me, so close I smelled his bay rum aftershave, liberally applied. We were close enough to kiss. But I wouldn't kiss him. Not today. Today I was angry.

Wordlessly, he reached for my hands, held them to his chest. Under my palms—a small bird fluttered. His heart beat as hard as mine. My hands rose and fell with each of his breaths. The surging power of his presence extinguished my own breath.

His hands moved to my waist, pulling me closer. My eyes closed. The woman inside me came alive, reveling in the moment.

Blithely ignoring the voice of reason that screamed "stop!", I wrapped my arms around his neck and settled into his kiss.

CHAPTER THIRTEEN
I WILL NOT YELL, I WILL NOT YELL, I WILL NOT...

MORE THAN LIKELY I'VE HAD BETTER WAYS TO start a morning, but right now I couldn't remember any. We'd quit kissing, cuddling and saying we're sorry so low it came out more like deep breaths, but my knees shook. Literally. I had to sit until some semblance of reason circled my brain and nested there. Seth admitted I was the finest kisser ever and he'd always remember this one.

And then he was gone. The door clicked shut and I sat there basking in the glow.

Apparently, I made it to my office because here I sat at my desk, wanted posters and two sheets of paper, messages —more like complaints—from citizens, sprawled over the wooden top. A pencil in hand instead of a cup reminded me I needed more Arbuckles. Vaguely wondering if I'd taken the coffee pot off the stove at home, I shrugged. The stove fire would go out eventually, or Mrs. Tran would appreciate she didn't have to build the fire this morning.

Still without cup in hand, I sat mulling over my morning, desperate to make sense of the kiss and to figure out the rest of my day when Pokey waltzed in, the door closing behind him. Without uttering a sound, he made his way over to the stove, poured yesterday's cold sludge in a mug and stood sipping.

Maybe this morning he'd been severely kissed, too.

Watching, I sat frozen like a deer, thinking maybe he hadn't seen me. Thinking, too, this was Wednesday, mail collecting day. Soon, he'd be in that wagon trotting off to Dutch Flats for the newspapers and parcels and such. He wouldn't return much before dark, now that daylight came to an end sooner than I preferred. Spring and summer were my favorites parts of the year—plenty of sun and lovely, warm air.

Pokey sighed long and loud then turned his puppy-dog eyes to me. "I don't get it, Maud. Just don't get it."

"Don't get what?" With Pokey, one never knew where the conversation would lead. I guessed it was about his Chinese lady, but with him, it could be anything. When he continued to survey the inside of his cup, I asked, "What's wrong?"

"Oh, you know."

That was the second time today. It was getting old. "No, I don't know." I put down the pencil, swiveled in my chair. "Tell me. Please."

His gaze swept outside, through the window to the buildings across the street. I followed the path. He saw things I'm sure I didn't. He breathed in and out twice followed by a long sigh. "Ian MacKinney..." he turned to me. "Well, you remember he owns half of Otis' Mercantile? Where I work? Well, Mr. MacKinney told me to stop seeing Mae Yu. To stop going to her side of town. Stop having supper with the family. Said it was hurting business."

Without warning, my stomach clenched as tightly as my jaw. How could MacKinney be so blind? Pokey was in love and no amount of differences in last names, eye shapes or language would stop him. Nor should it.

The nerve. The gall. The audacity. I jumped to my feet, the chair teetering back. "I'm gonna go talk to Ian. This isn't right. It's not fair and it's not right." Maybe I was on a roll today. First Seth, now the town councilor.

Plucking my bonnet off the hook by the door, I reached

for my gun belt and froze. Would I need a gun simply to talk to Ian or the other councilors? A glance at Pokey and he probably thought the same thing with those wide eyes and lowered eyebrows. All right. No gun.

"Stay here. Have more coffee 'til you have to leave." No way did I want him talking to

Ian or Slim Higginbotham or Harvey Weinberg or even Seth, for that matter. Pokey was too much wrapped up in all this and a clear head was obviously needed. Not sure I was the 'clear head' right now, nevertheless, I marched through the door and out into society hell-bent on setting prejudice on its sit-upon. After today, the various groups would live in peace.

While I marched, I realized what a fancy it was. Maybe I couldn't change everyone's mind, but I'd grind away at Ian's. That would be a good start.

I found him behind his desk in a corner office of the mercantile. I did not bother with the nicety of a knock. I shut the door behind me. Hard. The glass rattled.

Middle aged Ian MacKinney looked up, flashed an awkward grin and waved to an empty chair in the corner. I glanced around. The office was so small only two chairs fit, Ian's and the empty one.

I pulled the wooden chair as close to the desk as possible. "I'm here on business, Mr. MacKinney." No need for pleasantries or beating around the bush. This day seemed to be one for plain talk.

"Madainn mhath. Good to see you again, Sheriff." He lowered the papers in his hand. "What kind of business?"

"Two things." I decided on the easier one first. "After yesterday's fire up in the apple orchard, Penelope deserves to get her pay now, instead of waiting until the first of next month."

He pushed his bottom lip forward as in thought. "Said we'd pay her, did we now?" His Scottish brogue turned thick. "I taut she volunteer *an as gaidh*. For free."

Oh brother. I'm sure my eyes rolled. I sighed. "No. Not

for free. You and the others agreed to forty a month. Remember?"

Scratching his chin, Ian looked everywhere but at me.

I sallied forth. "And she should get it *now*." I pointed my finger toward the hills. "She was there within moments and kept the fire from spreading to town. She deserves her due. Today." I wanted to stamp my foot, maybe even hold my breath, but the six-year-old inside of me was surprisingly restrained.

"Yer aff yer heid." Ian leaned forward, his eyes narrowing. "Crazy, ye are. And I tink she waits until pay day, the first of the month."

"Why not—"

"We *all* wait for pay day. Just like ye. She won't get paid every time flames shoot."

He had a point. All right, I'd give him that argument. "Fine." I gritted my teeth, steeling myself for the next. I rose from the chair and leaned over the desk, both hands white knuckled gripping the edges. "What's this about not allowing Pokey to have a girlfriend?"

"Come cryin' to ye, did he?" Ian's raised eyebrows touched the hair covering his forehead. "What'd he tell ye?"

I glared at Ian and vowed not to lose my temper. This had already been a trying day, one of conflicting emotions, and I didn't need to fuel the fire. "You said his going out with Miss Yu was bad for business. And you didn't like him going to dinner over at her parents' house."

Ian's hard eyes bored into mine. The air seethed with tension.

Then he leaned back and laughed. More of a chortle than laugh. His cheeks, although hidden by fashionable sideburns, puffed out and pinked. "I did say all tha'. He eats o'er thar, coomes ba' and sleeps. Doozn't work as hard as he should."

Some of the wind in my sails withered.

"And," he continued, "the Celestials ha' their own

mercantile. Pokey buys from them. Instead of bringing business here, he takes it yon."

Now I saw the picture. It wasn't so much that she was Chinese, it all boiled down to money—who gets the coin.

I let out an audible submissive sigh. Looked like the egg was on *my* face. I'd have to explain things to Pokey and let him stew on it over his mail run today. I forged a tight grin. "Thanks, Mr. MacKinney. Sorry for the brusqueness. I'll let Penelope know about her pay. And talk to Pokey." I reached for the door handle.

"One mair ting, Maud." Ian cleared his throat. "Sheriff."

Waiting for the other boot to drop, I figured whatever it was, would be the topping on a crazy day. I waited, hand on knob.

"We canna have a woman mayor. 'Tisn't done. A cat canna be a doog. You're freens with Miss McIntyre. Tell her to quit this foolishness and announce she's no longer running. She'd be makin' Dry Creek a laughin' stock, she would."

My fuse was re-lit. "A laughingstock? Of what?" I released the doorknob and used my long finger to point at his chest. "What's wrong with a woman being mayor? Does she threaten your... your..." I'd wanted to say manhood, but that was way too forward. I struggled for something else.

Before I came up with the exact word, Ian marched around his desk and leaned against it. "Wimmen runnin' the town 'tisn't done. She canna know how. She's a lass. With no experience, she has. If she were to win, there'll be riots in the street, drunken cowhands and miners running up and down Main, hoolies in the saloons. And who'll teach school? We'll have kinder running amuck." He shook his head. "Nae. It'll nae do."

Calm down I told myself. Calm. I took a deep breath. "I had this conversation with Seth just this morning."

"Good! Then we underst—"

"If Pearl McIntyre wants to run for mayor, I'm all in favor

of it. I think she'll be good for the town, not that Mr. Critoli hasn't been."

"But—"

"But she has the right to run and in fact, think I'll help her." Right then and there I knew my life would change. What did I know about being mayor other than what I'd seen Seth do? Another thought wobbled in my brain. I'd be Pearl's campaign manager! No, no, no, no. Said I wouldn't take sides and I meant it.

Campaign manager did have a ring to it, though.

Ian's eyes went wide. "Yer bum's cot the windae! Yer off yer nut if yer's goin' to help her. Bring nothin' but heartache and disaster to our fair town." He pointed his finger up into my face. "Mark my words. T-r-o-u-b-l-e."

"I'm glad you can spell, Mr. MacKinney." I hated the sarcasm in my voice, but this had already been a tough day and from the looks of things, wasn't going to get better. Maybe a long walk down Main and out to the apple distillers would help.

"Ye need to talk sense into her, you do. If a' wimmen stick fae their talent, the coos wi' be well milked. Convince her to stay teachin'. *That's* a woman's job."

I opened the door and stood in the doorway. "She's free to do what she wants, and I won't try to stop her." I produced what I hoped was a polite smile. "I'll be leaving now. Got my own job to do."

As I closed the door, Ian's parting words made me laugh. "Awa' an bile yer heid."

I wasn't totally sure what he meant, but I got the gist.

The cool, bordering on cold air replaced the heat coming off my face. If I was going to make sense and see things clearly, I'd have to calm down. I stepped across the street, pulling in a lungful of dust. The world melted into colors instead of the black and white of Ian's office.

Sunlight, mottled by white, puffy clouds, bathed me in its glory. Warm, not too hot, slight breeze to cool my skin, a promise of a breath-takingly gorgeous evening. I stood on the boardwalk soaking in the pleasantness. Two women sashayed past me, nodding a friendly hello. I recognized them and nodded in return, but names were out of reach for the moment.

First, I'd need to tell Pokey what Ian said, find Penelope and finally scout around the blown distillery. Hopefully, it was clearly an accident. No need to think otherwise. I'd have to talk to others in that profession, see how it's done. I laughed inside. Up to a few months ago I'd never tasted whiskey, or beer for that matter. Even now, that event wasn't too often. And I usually chose beer. But many men preferred the apple whiskey, according to the bartender at the Tin Pan Saloon, if amount of consumption was any indication.

I strolled up Main, hoping Pokey was still at the office so we could discuss things. I had plenty to say and no doubt, he would too. I'd traveled half a block when a familiar, deep voice behind quickened my pulse.

"Maud... er... Sheriff Overstreet. There you are."

I turned to find Aldridge Armstrong trotting up the street. *In* the street was more accurate. He ran behind a line of horses tied at the hitching rails.

He waved and hollered again. "Wait up."

Of course I waited. Seeing him again made me tingle. Almost as much as Seth's kiss this morning.

Cold, icy chill washed over my entire body. What kind of woman was I? A woman who let the mayor kiss her like that and yet gets weak kneed around a stranger? What kind of woman, indeed?

But I couldn't help myself. Something about him excited yet confused me. I'd like to get to know him better.

He caught up and nodded, touching the rim of his hat. "Been looking everywhere for you. First your house, then office, then the mercantile and now..." Adonis's face rearranged itself into a grin exuding friendliness. "How're you feeling?"

There were so many ways to answer that, but I assumed

he referred to my sore throat and fatigue of last night. "Throat's much better, thank you. I appreciate your concern."

That grin of his blossomed into a full-fledged smile. "Terrific. I was worried."

"No need." I grinned back. "I'm a healthy gal."

"I... uh... that is..." He shuffled his boot across the wooden walkway. We stared at each other for a few seconds until he blurted out, "Wanna go out with me tonight? For supper?"

I didn't have to think for even a moment. Of course I did. But I decided to play a little harder to get. I glanced down the street to take up time. I gave in. "I'd love to."

"Great. I'll pick you up at your house, now that I know where you live." Mr. Wonderful stopped fidgeting. "Want to invite another couple? Four is always a good number."

A bit disappointed but also a tiny bit relieved, I nodded.

"Great," he said again. "How about the mayor and the school teacher I've seen him with? She and I could talk education."

"Oh, not a good idea. No, no, no." I shook my head hard.

"Well, then. How about your deputy and that Oriental woman I see him with? They make quite the pair. I'd like to get to know them better."

"Also not a good idea." For this I felt the need to explain. "Problem is, Chinese aren't allowed in the restaurant." I held up a hand. "Don't know why. They just aren't. It's unfair, I know."

Aldridge gazed up and down the street. "They have their own restaurant? Some place they go out to eat?"

He had me there. I had no idea. "I'll have to ask Pokey. He'd know."

"Would you be willing to go there, instead? I mean, if they'll let *us* in?"

Now that was an idea I'd never considered. Why not, indeed? It would be fun. I thumbed over my shoulder toward my office. "I'll ask."

CHAPTER FOURTEEN
BURNING THE MASH...

OF COURSE BY THE TIME I MANAGED TO FIND MY way to the office, Pokey was long gone, so I couldn't ask him about supper plans. I'd spent way too much time flirting with Mr. Amazing and not enough time doing my job. Whatever that was, exactly. On second thought, I'd *been* doing my job—connecting with Dry Creek's fine citizens. While standing on the boardwalk, I'd nodded to and spoken with about half the town. And now, thinking on it as I sat at my desk, perhaps the fine men and women of this little burg hadn't just "happened" by as they'd said, but intentionally wandered past to take a closer gander at the sheriff and her new beau.

Then again, possibly they did have "errands" to do on Main and I was merely in the way. Pushing a wanted poster aside, I decided it was coincidence. People had way too many other pressing matters than spying on my love life. What there was of it.

And what there was of it right now was darn complicated. Why had I let Seth kiss me like that when I knew Aldridge Armstrong the Magnificent was my man? I stacked a poster on top of the other one. Seth and I were simply friends. That's all. Nothing else.

Then why did I tingle at his touch?

I pushed back and the screeching of the chair legs brought my attention to the office.

A strong slurp of Arbuckles would help sort things out and then a walk to the distilleries would clear my head. If I couldn't get my thoughts straight doing all that, then I'd be a hopeless case for sure. I brightened at an idea—on my way back from the hills, I could find Pokey's girlfriend, Mae Yu, and ask about Chinese restaurants. I'd bet they had one and had no objections to us coming in to eat. I frowned at the thought. Would they? Why? We were respectable, law-abiding citizens *with money*. Why would they turn us down?

As I stood at the potbelly stove sipping my rather cold coffee, I thought about our own restaurant here in town. Why would they turn down respectable, law-abiding people with money simply because their first language was not English? Because their eyes slanted more than most of us? Because they performed jobs many others would not? Were those good enough reasons?

Having no answers to any of the questions, I downed the remainder of the coffee, plucked my bonnet and gun from their hangers, closed the office door and started for the distilleries. I passed a few people who waved and within minutes I had walked up into the hill north of town. The trail was well traveled, no big rocks or tree snags to fall over. Nothing that would reach out and make me embarrass myself. I made it to the first distiller within half an hour.

The man's face was hidden behind a bushy beard, untamed mustache and chin-length sideburns. Hair hung from under his hat. He reminded me more of a shaggy dog than a human being. But when he spoke, no doubt he was a man. His voice, deep and gravelly, sounded more like he should be on a pulpit rather than behind a six-foot round, rusty, copper kettle.

I stuck my hand out. "Howdy, sir. I'm Sheriff Overstreet and—"

"Know who ye are." He took his time extending a hand, shook with me, and within seconds, retracted it. He wiped the palm down his shirt front. His drab brown eyes bulged, reminding me of toads I'd seen after a heavy rain. One eye wandered up and to the right while the other seemed to inspect me skirt to bonnet.

I was real tired of being looked at like a piece of meat, or an oddity from one of those traveling shows, or even a female who's pretending to be the law. Why did I feel I had to prove myself?

Probably because I did.

"What cha need?" He shoved pudgy hands into his vest pockets, turned and ambled back to his kettle. On the way, he stopped at a pile of sticks, selected two, each a hefty inch thick. He held one in each hand and turned to me. "Didn't catch what ya want." He cocked his head toward the dying fire under one of his kettles. "Ah'm busy."

Taken a bit aback, I soldiered on anyway. "I'm sure you are. Have a few questions about the distillery blowing up yesterday."

He shoved one stick into the flames and held the other against his shoulder, more like a club than firewood. He eyed me again. "Like what?"

Before answering, I surveyed the area. Nothing suspicious or out of the ordinary, whatever that may be. I'd wanted someone to explain the process to me, mainly to determine if the explosion had been an accident... or not. But from the looks of this fella, I figured he wouldn't be too forthcoming as to the ins and outs of whiskey making.

"Wondering if you knew the man who was killed. He a friend or acquaintance of yours?"

I kept the kettle and fire between us. No telling if he would try to come after me with that stick. "And I never did get your name, sir."

"Nah. Ain't li'ble ta neither."

Alrighty then. If I couldn't get his name, there was no way I'd get any real help. I nodded to him and aimed for another still. The second encounter resembled the first.

The third man was a bit more agreeable than the other

two. He, at least, didn't spit my name when he spoke. And he was clean. Relatively so. No grease smeared down his shirt, pants weren't torn and filthy. And he'd shaved, probably last week.

"It's simple," he said, pushing a twig into the fire. "Flames heat up the kettle, steam comes up the pipe here, corn bobs around in there for a bit, then hundred proof comes out here." He pointed at various contraption pieces. As much as I followed his finger, nothing made a whole lot of sense. Perhaps Seth or Aldridge would know. Would Pa?

"So tell me, Mr. Wolcott, d'you think yesterday's explosion was an accident?"

He peered at me for several heartbeats. Wagging his head, he spoke into the forest. "Coulda been."

"But you doubt it?"

Nodding, he scratched his chest. "I knew that fella from before. Careful."

Funny, prickling sensations danced down my back. I was on to something. "If you and I looked at the site, you think maybe you could help me figure out if it was an accident or not?"

A long sigh, he glanced into the forest then nodded. "Sure. He was a good man. Least I can do."

We poked through ash and copper and parts and pieces. It all looked charred to me and I couldn't help keep looking at where his body had been. I'd heard the undertaker had made the trek up the hill and had help taking the man to the morgue. Not a job I'd ever want. Seeing the body was bad enough.

"How does all this work?" I hoped he'd be willing to share. I figured he wouldn't consider me a threat to his enterprise as I wasn't up here to arrest him or to set up my own still.

Mr. Wolcott rubbed his graying stubble of a beard, eyed me, then pulled in a deep breath.

"Since you've asked twice, I'll try to tell you in a few words. There's an art to not burnin' the mash."

Burning the mash. I stored that in my brain for future use.

He licked his lips, began. "In producing whiskey in a turnip still like this one here, you fill 'em with ground corn, rye or wheat, apples when they're in season, water, barley malt, yeast and sugar."

"You can get all this in town?" I mentally pictured the mercantiles rubbing their hands with glee at all the distillers.

"Sure do." He nodded. "Now, the mash ferments—takes a few days. A foam, called the "cap" forms during this time and when it disappears, we pour what's left into the pot and build us a fire."

Fascinated, I asked, "This where it might burn?"

"Yep. A steady cooking temperature's mighty important. Steaming alcohol gases move up into this here tube. We call it a worm." He pointed to what looked like a long hose. "Then them gases come back into liquid and trickle out the end of the worm stickin' out the bottom. It squirts into a jar, jug or bucket."

"And you've got alcohol." Who figured out how to make this? I was amazed and stunned at the same time. Why couldn't I have dreamed this up?

Mr. Wolcott squatted by the end of the worm, inspecting various connections and parts he hadn't named. "Huh."

I waited for him to say more, but he gave a softer 'huh' and crooked his finger at me. I squatted next to him.

"See that piece right there, Sheriff?"

Squinting at what I assumed had been part of the boiler, I nodded.

"No, right here." He thumped the side of the copper. "Looks like something was jammed in the end. Something that weren't supposed to be there."

More tingles raced down my back. "You mean... you think someone deliberately caused this still to explode?"

He rocked back on his heels and stood peering down at the jumbled mass of copper and wires and "worms." A soft wind moved pine branches sending their earthy smell under my nose. A meadowlark cawed over who knew what and a small critter of some kind dashed under leaves. I waited for my expert to pronounce his decision.

Both eyebrows raised, he ran a hand across his chest then looked over at me. "Sheriff, I do think this was no accident." He nodded at the wreckage. "Think it was on purpose."

Breath caught in my chest while black and white curlicues swam in front of my eyes. Could that be possible? A longer look at his tense face and I resigned myself to the fact a murder had taken place.

After leaving the site, Mr. Wolcott returning to his still and me aiming for town, I ran over a list of possible suspects. He'd told me almost every man up in the hills could've done it. But, why? He'd said everyone made a decent living making whiskey and this fella hadn't been around long enough to make true enemies. Not that he knew of.

So, back to square one. At least now I knew it was murder. I shuddered at the word.

* * *

I HADN'T FORGOTTEN about eating Chinese food tonight, but the thought had naturally been pushed to the back of my brain. By the time I arrived on the outskirts of town, having wandered through "Chinatown," as people now called it, I remembered about supper. Shocked I could forget such exciting plans, however, could I even be pleasant company tonight? Too much on my mind. Choosing not to bother the Yus, Pokey's adopted family, I went straight to my office, hung up my gun belt and bonnet. Silence and an empty cup on top of the stove, greeted me.

Standing there, staring at the cold, black potbelly stove in the corner, my world felt almost the same way. Bleak, unfeeling... bitter. What I needed was a drink.

I actually giggled out loud. A drink? Me? In the middle

of the afternoon? I sobered a bit and realized yep, a shot of whiskey would be the ideal elixir right now. I'd pretend to go in to inspect the saloon and have a swig to be sure it was safe for consumption.

I giggled again. Yeah, like that would fool anyone. No, I'd simply step in, step up and down one. I deserved it.

Should I go it alone? Maybe Seth wasn't busy and would join me. Then again, I considered, maybe he'd think I was wanting more of this morning. My chest warmed at the vision. Not a bad idea. Not a good one, either, but an idea. Wouldn't hurt to try. Besides, I needed someone to talk to.

* * *

SETH PUSHED PAPERS ASIDE, smiled at me and stood. He popped his bowler onto his head, bowed as I walked out the door first. We made quite the couple, I suspected. But this wasn't a happy occasion, although it might turn into one. As we walked, I remembered a few months ago when Pokey, Seth and I ended up in a burping contest in the Tin Pan Saloon. Not one of my finer moments.

We took a table near the back, our way of trying not to be too obvious, a jigger of whiskey and a mug of beer in front of each of us. Seth threw his shot back like a seasoned champ, but my throat rebelled. At least I could try to be ladylike about *something*.

While we sat, I recounted today's findings. Turns out, I was more upset about the murder than I'd thought. Tears welled when I was about halfway into my beer and Seth bought me another shot. I drank it down like a real pro. It stung like a bad sunburn in my throat, but I managed to breathe within half a minute.

"Let's see if Sam's got a notion of what's going on up there." Seth stood and threaded his way to the bar. I followed, grateful for the few patrons, which made navigating through the dark room relatively easy. No shoulder-to-shoulder men angling to get up to the bar. There was plenty of room.

"Heard any rumblings of trouble up on the hill, Sam?"

The bartender froze mid-air, a glass and towel in hand. He eyed Seth then turned to me. "Why? What's goin' on?"

Should I tell him or not? The man's murder would be common knowledge soon enough, so I came clean. "That still that blew up yesterday?"

Sam nodded and leaned closer.

"Murder. Someone stuffed cloth into the worm." If I hadn't been so upset, I'd have mentally patted myself on the back for knowing the terminology. "They blew up the still deliberately."

The glass slammed to the bar counter while Sam used the towel to mop his forehead. "You don't say?"

I shrugged.

"Yeah," Sam said. "I've heard some things from a few of the boys."

"Like what?" Seth swung his head side to side as if someone was eavesdropping. No one paid us any attention.

Sam inspected the glass. He swiped at one smudge with his shirtsleeve, then put the cleaned glass under the counter. "Heard somebody's trying to take over the hill. Trying to get rid of competition. There's talk... and it's only talk... that the mercantiles are considering raising prices to force out some of the distillers." He wagged his head. "But I never thought one of 'em would stoop to murder."

I swung my full attention to Seth. In this kerosene amber light, he'd lost some color in his face.

CHAPTER FIFTEEN
CHOPPED SOOEY, ANYONE?...

SETH AND I STOOD AT THE BAR MULLING OVER what Sam had told us. Was there a conspiracy between the two mercantiles? Judging by the shocked look on Seth's face, he'd never heard of nor considered such a thing. I had to admit I hadn't either. But here we were. Both dumbfounded.

Sam poured us another beer without our asking and moved on to a man leaning at the far end of the bar. Left on our own, we sipped and thought. Thought and sipped. My practical side said there was no indication prices were rising, yet my instinctive side said something was going on. Something nefarious. All right, that was my imagination. I had no hard evidence of anything untoward brewing under the surface. Or had I turned a blind eye?

I hated questioning myself, so turned to Seth. He was always easy to question—he'd open up like a tin can of sardines with that little handle—and besides, I needed to bounce ideas off him. A long draw of my beer and I started.

"You know Ian and Harvey better'n I do." I watched his face for an indication he'd protect the hard-headed, stubborn town council members.

He nodded—softly, almost imperceptibly.

"Think they would get together and fix prices just to

push out distillery fellas? Think they're in on a cut of the whiskey?" Now that part I hadn't thought about before. The question simply popped out. I cut my eyes sideways at Sam. Was he in on it, too? Who *did* he buy his whiskey from? And why couldn't you buy it at the mercantile?

Seth frowned into his beer. "Didn't think they would. Haven't heard word one about prices going up, but who knows? Maybe they'll do it slowly, carefully to where we don't notice until one day, a sack of sugar which used to cost one dollar now costs a dollar ten. Then a dollar twenty and soon *wham*! It's two dollars."

That was a sobering thought. I'd have to go investigate, compare prices.

Sam wandered closer our way, which gave me a chance to lean over and flag him down. With the lowest voice I could handle without whispering, I asked where he got his whiskey. From which distiller.

He raised one eyebrow, followed by a half quizzical, half "what a dumb question," look on his face. "All of 'em," he spread his arms wide. "This time of year, what with the apples ripe, it's prime." He leaned toward me. "Usually, I buy from the lowest seller, but this year they're all charging the same. So, I take the first what comes along."

I glanced at Seth then Sam. "They all taste the same?" I hadn't noticed any difference. I snickered silently and rolled my eyes. As if I do a lot of drinking. But if they did, then what was the point of having several up there?

"Nope." Seth and Sam answered in unison. Seth continued. "Some are sweeter than others, some more bitter."

"And some have a smoky apple flavor." Sam cocked his head toward a half-full bottle. "But I don't drink the bark juice myself. Same with beer."

"You don't?" Why had I never considered a bartender who didn't drink?

"Haven't touched it in years." Sam picked up a rag and headed down the bar.

I downed the last swig of my beer, for some reason

feeling guilty for drinking. Maybe I had been better off before I learned how to enter a saloon and belly up to the bar. Not like I did it often now, but I wasn't nearly as timid as I'd been earlier this year. Maybe my job was corrupting me.

While Seth finished his drink, I stood standing, thinking about my life. Had my values been tainted? Had I given up my morals simply for a tin badge? What had I done?

A light tug on my upper arm brought me back. Seth held it lightly and nudged me toward the door. "You all right?"

"Why wouldn't I be?" Had I said that in a rather airish tone? I cringed.

He let go of my arm, held the door open and we stepped into lowering daylight. "You seem a bit... preoccupied, is all. Guess you would be."

"It's been a jam-packed day for sure." It was at that awkward moment what I'd pushed to the rear of my brain earlier, sprung forward. Aldridge. That delicious supper invite was moments from happening and I had yet to do my part. How could I let Mr. Breathtaking down? I screeched to a halt. "Sorry. Gotta go find Pokey and the Yu family and change clothes and go tell Pa and lock the office, change bonnets on...put *away*... my gun..."

Seth pecked my cheek with his soft lips, his mustache tickling my skin. He nodded. "Enjoy your supper tonight. Or whatever it is you're doing." With that, he tipped his hat, turned and disappeared into another saloon.

* * *

RUSHING UP MAIN STREET, I passed women with bundles in one arm, an unruly child herded with the other. Men waved to each other while a few helped their wives carry packages. Busy place, I thought. Soon, most women would be home cooking and then getting children ready for bed. I, on the other hand, needed to get ready to go out for supper. A real treat.

First, I needed to make sure Pokey had returned from his mail run. Hopefully there had been no trouble and the mail was already being sorted. By the time I arrived at the far end of town, sure enough, inside the postal office, Pokey and a couple helpers sorted the last sack. I let out a silent sigh.

Pokey waved an arm around the room. "Nothing exciting, Maud. Just another run with no troubles. By the way, Jake over at the postal office in Dutch Flats sends his regards." He winked at me and lowered his voice. "Think he's kinda sweet on you. Asks about you every time I come by."

"Hope you tell him only the good things." I touched Pokey's arm. "Can I talk to you?"

"Well, sure Maud. Er... Sheriff Maud." He followed me out the door. "There a problem?"

"Sort of." There was no easy way to beat around the bush. "The Orientals? They have a restaurant?"

Pokey's shoulders jiggled. "'Course they do. Food's real flavorful, too." His forehead furrowed. "Why you askin'?"

"Think they'd be willing to serve four of us tonight? You, me, Mae and... well, a friend of mine?"

He stepped back one step, swung his head left and right as if surveying the street, looking to find the right answer. Moving in close, he cocked his head. "Don't see why not. They serve me, so why not more?" One of his eyes squinted. "Why?"

How could I put this? I decided the safest way was honesty. "My friend, Aldridge Armstrong, wants the four of us to go to supper. But Mae can't go into our restaurant. He's wondering if the Chinese would accept us. Let us eat there."

Silence enshrouded me. The boardwalk. The entire town. My heart beating was the only sound.

After what felt like months, Pokey pushed his bottom lip forward. "I'll ask the restaurant's owner, Mr. Kwan, but I'm sure we'd be welcome." His eyes swept the ground.

"Never considered they weren't welcome in our restaurant, since Mae always invites me to hers. Curious we could go to theirs."

"Doesn't seem fair, does it?" Relief sat on my chest. "Go ask Mr. Kwan right now and I'll finish up here."

"Better yet," Pokey said, his eyes trailing up the hill to Chinatown. "Come with me. You can meet Mr. Kwan and his family."

Before I had the chance to say no, I found myself surrounded by white tents smelling of laundry soap. Wisps of steam emanated out the back.

"His house is this way." Pokey tugged my arm and pointed to a clapboard sided house a short block over. It sat on a hill, backed into the dirt. Not sure what I was expecting, exactly, a house looking similar to mine surprised me. Maybe I figured there would be the upended swoop at the roof corners, a gong outside to announce visitors or maybe even a statue of a dragon out front. I just knew that whatever the house looked like, it wasn't this.

We approached the door, located traditionally on the south side, wiped our shoes on the mat and Pokey knocked. Within seconds, a slim, older woman opened the door. Her oval face blossomed into a smile that reached clear into her heart. She undeniably liked Pokey. That much was obvious. But then, most people did.

"Mr. Pokey! Delightful encounter!" She bowed at him and he returned the greeting.

He elbowed me, and I followed with what I figured was a deep bow, although I think it was more of a head nod. I'd have to work on that.

Pokey beamed at her. "Mrs. Kwan, this is my friend the sheriff, Maud Overstreet."

Mrs. Kwan flapped her hand. "Yes, I know. Welcome." She stood back and motioned for us to enter.

Something pungent assaulted my nose, kind of like sticking a thorny corncob up there.

My eyes watered. I froze. Then sneezed. Using my sleeve

I daubed at my eyes, tears now running down my cheeks. The room blurred as I turned to Pokey.

"Forgot to warn you. Incense." Like a true gentleman, Pokey handed me his handkerchief. He nodded to the woman then back at me. "Mrs. Kwan's family is good friends with Mae's."

Mystery solved, I wiped my nose, eyes, nose before things came into focus. Boy, if all Chinese houses smelled like this one, no wonder they stayed to themselves. The room was more what I expected to see. A red patterned rug took up most of the small area, a statue of a fat man with his hands overhead sat on a short table in the corner, a jar of smoking sticks at his feet. Must be the incense Pokey mentioned.

Embroidered tapestries depicting mountains in a mist hung on the walls. In the pictures, some sort of writing, Chinese characters like the ones on Pokey's amulet, framed the mountains. I caught myself turning my head sideways to read. Just swirly lines crossed with straight ones. A true mystery as to how they read this. Two low chairs, one long bench took up most of the room. Off to the one side stood a folding screen partitioning off another portion of the house, I assumed. Otherwise, it was bare.

Mrs. Kwan, a long tight skirt hobbling her steps, followed behind us. I turned and to my embarrassment, looked down onto the top of her head. She didn't even come up to my shoulder. Ian MacKinney was a giant in comparison. I'd seen short people older than twelve before, but not one this close. Was Mae this tiny, too?

"You want tea?" Mrs. Kwan pointed toward a short table with cushions set around it on the floor.

I shook my head envisioning my long legs wedging themselves under the table. I couldn't fold them enough to sit cross-legged on the cushion. No, sipping tea like that wasn't going to happen. And then a thought hit me. Would their restaurant be like this too? Pictures of Aldridge squeezing his legs under the table or even attempting to cross them, made my heart race. No, this would never do.

Bizarre thoughts and awkward pictures filled my head while Pokey asked about the four of us eating at the restaurant. He'd already broached the subject before I could stop him.

Mrs. Kwan bowed. "Of certain, Mr. Pokey. You come. Bring friends." She smiled widely, showing fewer teeth than most people had. She bowed to me.

I bent over hoping this was acceptable and met her smile. "Thank you. We'll see you tonight."

Once Pokey and I were outside and away from prying Chinese eyes, I grabbed his arm stopping him. "What're we going to do?" I made sure my voice was low. "We can't eat there."

"Why not?"

"I don't fit."

"Don't fit *in*? With the Chinese?" Pokey's face clouded in confusion. His eyebrows dipped. "But you said... I don't under—"

"I don't *physically* fit. I'm too big." I took a step back. Those words put together were foreign. "At the table. My legs won't go—"

"Don't worry, Maud." Pokey patted my arm. "I've eaten there before and there's a higher table. With chairs. You'll be fine."

All the worried wind out of my sails, my shoulders drooped. Whew. One problem solved.

And then it hit me. What to wear? Sheriffing clothes? Going out dress? Sunday finest? Hair up? Hair down? And shoes. Oh my.

By the time I decided to wear my hair down, Pokey was ten steps ahead of me. I ran to catch up. "I've got another question for you." I matched my pace with his.

"They're expecting us in an hour, Maud."

"No. What I'm wondering is... what do we order? How

do we know what to eat? I can't read their writing." Once again, I was genuinely worried. How would Aldridge react?

Pokey slid to a halt and turned to me. "Quit worrying. It'll be fine. Mae will be there to interpret and if you can't decide, order Chopped Suey." He gave me a quick, light hug and veered to the right.

Still confused, I called after him. "Chopped sooey? I didn't know they ate pork!"

CHAPTER SIXTEEN
SHALL WE...?

MR. MARVELOUS KNOCKED ON MY DOOR EXACTLY at six. I rushed to open it and counted his virtues—good-looking, polite, intelligent, thoughtful, heroic, empathetic, and now... punctual. The list simply kept growing. Could he possess even more charms?

I opened the door to a faceful of flowers. Daisies, roses and others I couldn't identify tickled my nose. Stepping back, I took the extended bouquet, curtsied. Curtsied? What was I doing? But that was all I could do. Breathing was optional.

My cheeks ached from the grin.

A hesitant baritone voice brought me to what sense I had. "Uh, may I come in?"

How long had he been standing there while I grinned like a catalogue woman who'd just met the man of her dreams? An hour? Two? I held the door wider. He waltzed in, whipped off his hat and pegged me with those velvety gray eyes of his.

Stuttering and stammering, I managed to get out, "I'll find a vase for these." Or something along those lines. Truthfully, I don't know exactly what I said, but I didn't care. Nobody had brought me flowers before, except Pa on my fifteenth birthday. And that didn't count.

He waited, hat in hand, until I placed the posies in Ma's biggest vase and brought it out to show. This was one of the grandest moments I'd ever had. Between my heart beating like the drums I'd heard in parades and my head twirling like a ballerina, I had no control over the rest of me. I held out the vase. Aldridge took the flowers and set them in the middle of the formal dining table. The arrangement looked more than stupendous.

Aldridge glided in close to me and before I could stop myself, I reached up and kissed him. Then he kissed back. My thudding heart silenced while my stomach performed handsprings. My world slid to a happy stop. Another light kiss then he leaned back and smiled. "If I'd known I'd get that kind of reaction, I would've brought you flowers sooner."

Pressure pushed behind my eyeballs. I dabbed at a tear in the corner of one. "Surprised me is all." *Surprised* being an understatement. "Thank you."

Pointing toward the door, he scooped up the wool cape I'd draped over the chair. "We should go. Don't want to be late." Like the true gentleman he was, he swirled the cover over my shoulders, straightening the corners. A gentle peck on the cheek. "Shall we?"

Oh boy, we shall!

Walking arm in arm down the boardwalk, the few men and women still out and about glanced sideways at us, but instead of staring, simply nodded a greeting, tipping their hats. Obviously, they approved of their sheriff being escorted around town by such a great example of manhood. But as we strolled, I cringed at the brashness of kissing this man of my dreams. How could I have let myself be so swept off my feet I ignored the modicum of society formality I usually kept? So far, he didn't seem to mind my breech, but the night was still young and maybe he'd realize I was a hussy in sheriff's clothes.

We met Pokey and Mae in front of the Chinese restaurant. I'll be the first to admit I was nervous never being inside such an establishment and not knowing what they'd be serving. But, with Aldridge at my side and Pokey at the other, I was game for about anything. This would be a meal worth remembering.

Although I'd seen Mae once or twice before, I hadn't taken the time to honestly look at her. Taller than most Chinese women by several inches, she was slim with shiny raven hair hanging straight, bangs framing her oval face. Ebony slanting eyes set off her sweeping eyelashes, which seemed to flutter when she looked at Pokey. Lips, which drew up into a bow, tugged me in as she spoke, which wasn't often or loud. No wonder Pokey was smitten with her.

After introductions, Pokey held the door for us and heavenly, foreign smells wafted from every direction. I sniffed, unable to identify them. We stepped in, all eyes turning to us, and what felt like millions of scowling faces scrutinized every inch of our bodies. Had I worn my badge? Not wanting to look down at my chest, I pushed that question aside, lifted my mouth into a slight grin and nodded to the crowd. Turns out it wasn't a million faces, probably closer to twenty, but men and a few women, all seated on pillows, legs crossed under short tables, simply stared. Conversations and chopsticks froze mid-air.

Pokey and Mae bowed. "*Ni hao*," they said in unison, greeting the diners.

Stunned silence followed. I swallowed, hard. Maybe this wasn't such a good idea after all. Certain I blinked more times than humanly possible, I finally pulled in enough air to clear some of the chopped suey from my brain. Leaning forward, bending at the waist, I bowed, hoping this was right. Why hadn't I checked with Pokey beforehand? I righted myself and a glance sideways showed him winking at me, his slight nod confirming my manners. Inside, I jumped for joy I'd done something right. Outside, I stood still searching for the table Pokey promised was here.

Standing next to me, Aldridge the Astonishing also

bowed, palms together and enunciated without hesitation, "*Ni hao*."

What was that? Then I remembered. He'd said he enjoyed teaching Orientals, so it stood to reason he'd know something about their customs. Why hadn't *he* clued me in? Sheesh. Between Pokey and Aldridge, one of them could've helped.

Like a silk-pajamaed angel from Heaven, a woman materialized from behind a privacy screen. She scurried over to us, bowed and muttered something in Chinese.

Mae's eyes glowed as she turned to the three of us. Flapping her hand, Mae signaled for us to follow. "She say 'welcome' and to come."

More relieved than confused, I followed Mae with Pokey and Aldridge right behind me. In the far corner, rather secluded but still in the large room, stood a regular table with four regular chairs. Hallelujah. One concern resolved. Now for the hard part. We circled the table like starving wolves then each chose a chair. I was first to decide. I selected the chair in the corner, my back to the walls. This felt more comfortable than not being able to see what was happening in the room. Mae chose the seat on my left and the men took what was left.

So far so good. Aldridge, the-impossibly-good-looker, seated on my right, leaned close, his rich voice low. "How'd you like it so far?"

"Good." And I meant it. Now that I'd been allowed in and actually taken a real seat with the diners more or less ignoring us, I relaxed. Tension drained from my back, and I slouched. Then, I sat up straight, like the proper lady my ma had tried to raise. "I'm glad you had this idea, Mr. Armstrong. I think it'll be a memorable evening."

That come-hither smile slid up one side of his mouth. "I'm sure it will be. Thanks for trying something new."

Heart thumping so hard I thought for sure my blouse was doing its own dance, I glanced down to see how badly I was embarrassing myself. No movement. Just gentle rising up and down with each breath. And sure enough, there was that badge. Guess it was a force of habit now. Then I rethought—I was sheriff full time, not when it was convenient. Of course I should have it on.

Another woman in pajamas, dark blue silk, rushed to our table, small porcelain cups on a tray. She set them down, one at each place. Without a word, she scurried away, tray in hand. I eyed Mae who nodded at the steaming cups.

"*Chá*," she said blowing on hers, sipping.

I studied the liquid and sipped. I wrinkled my forehead, a tinge of disappointment in my voice. "Just tea?"

Mae flashed a grin. "You like?"

I nodded. Feeling like a five-year-old allowed to sit at the grown-up table, I followed Mae's every move. I blew and sipped. I put down the cup and nodded. Sweet, pleasantly warm. The cup itself sported blue flowers that swirled around the sides.

Pokey held up his cup. "Here's to you, Maud, and Mr. Armstrong. Thank you for suggesting this." We "here here-d" and sipped. My cup emptied way too fast, but before I could ask for more, the same woman stood at the table, a bowl of steaming rice in hand. She placed it in the middle of the table and wordlessly scurried away.

The bowl, filled to the brim with plenty for four, sported similar blue flowers around it.

In his politest teacher-like voice, Pokey explained the process. "We eat family style. Everybody gets a scoop of various food. Rice is the main dish, everything else goes on top."

"Like what?" My curiosity was piqued, stomach rumbling at more delicious smells coming from the kitchen.

Mae took over. "Like steamed vegetables. And steamed fish."

Fish and steamed didn't go together in my book. But I was willing to try anything—once.

"How about chicken?"

Both Pokey and Mae nodded. "Chicken feet. Very good," Mae said.

I didn't want to be rude, but no way would I eat feet of chicken, especially since I knew where they had been. Turning to Aldridge for guidance, he laughed. Out loud.

"Don't have to eat it. They'll understand." He patted his stomach. "I'll have your part."

Eeewww. I reeled in my disgust. Before I could ask further questions, plates of vegetables appeared on the table, the same waitress laden with bowls. She set one at each place, then produced four pairs of chopsticks setting those in the middle of the table too.

Mae handed each of us the utensil, filled her bowl with rice, topping it with odds and ends of the rest. I watched her every move, sure I could do what did she. Finished, she pointed her chopsticks at the various dishes. "Rice, *lou mei*, razor shell with *douche*, fried noodles, steamed carrots, mushrooms and soybeans."

"Sounds delicious." And they did. Would I want to know what it was—exactly? No. A closer inspection—no chicken feet. Whew.

"Now you," she said in her sweet voice.

She scooped food into my bowl, loading rice with the rest on top. Aldridge scooped next, heaping his plate with all sorts of who knew what. I admitted the smell was mouth-watering and I couldn't wait to try it all. Pokey was last.

Finally, all the bowls brimmed with food. Pokey held up his chopsticks. "Dig in."

The three of them held the bowl with one hand, brought it to their mouths and shoveled like they hadn't eaten in weeks. I gripped the two sticks between my fingers and clicked them together. One sprung from my finger, bounced off my bowl and immediately somersaulted into my lap.

Hoping no one had seen, I grabbed the stick and tried again, this time more closely watching Aldridge. Before I had mastered feeding myself, the waitress brought four shot glasses along with a blue-flowered bottle. She set them down and rushed away.

A shot glass? I wasn't having any of that apple whiskey. No siree. Tonight was an adventure and I'd try something else.

"Ah, *baijiu!*" Aldridge distributed the glasses and poured a clear liquid into each one.

"Most popular drink in China."

I sniffed the liquid and discovered it was fragrant. Reminded me of the roses now sitting on my dining room table. All right. Since it was served in a shot glass, I couldn't drink much. I wouldn't get silly or giggly like I'd done before at the saloon. Probably didn't have much of a kick anyway, being that I'd never seen a drunk Oriental. And I'd be sure to have only one or two. I'd be safe.

I sipped the warmer than room temperature *baijiu*, which didn't take my breath, but its savory taste was stronger than I'd expected. It slid down smooth and warmed my chest. A second sip was easier. I liked it. I turned to Mae, our interpreter of the Chinese world. "This *baijiu*. Made here in Dry Creek?"

Mae shook her head but Aldridge explained. "If I'm not mistaken, it's imported from China." He looked at Mae. "But sources tell me they're thinking of starting to produce it here, locally."

Great. One more still to worry about. Changing my thoughts to food, I picked up my chopsticks, determined to get something to eat. Using my hands would be awkward and, downright rude.

Taking pity on me, Aldridge took my chopsticks. He held one up. "Balance it on your ring finger. Like this." He demonstrated on his own hand. "Now, put the other one in the valley between your pointer finger and thumb along the first one, but rest this one on your middle finger."

His hand on mine sent raised bumps up and down my entire body. I could hardly breathe.

Another longer pull of *baijiu* calmed me. I poured another shot.

"Now, use your thumb, pointer and middle fingers to grasp the second chopstick a bit more tightly." His hand encased mine. "There, like that." He sat back, smiling.

I sat there, chopsticks in place hovering over my food. "Now what?"

"Eat." He demonstrated, chopstick into rice, then into mouth. "Like this."

"Not hard," I said, my shoulders springing back. "Anybody can do it." I scooped rice onto the chopsticks, raised it to my mouth and every single grain and three noodles leaped off and splatted onto my good skirt.

Pokey and Aldridge smiled, Mae tittered. Another full shot of that drink—it went down smooth now—and I was ready to start again. Nothing would keep me from my meal. By now I was full-out hungry, and my stomach demanded attention.

I squeezed the chopsticks together creating a flat platform. Maybe I could scoop like a skinny spoon. Nope. More rice in my lap. More sideways looks and grins. All right. If not rice, then I'd attack the vegetables. At least those I could use my hands. But first, more *buy-juice*.

Vegetables now in my lap, I swept them off to the floor, refilled my glass and toasted the chopsticks. "Here's to you, you dumb little twigs." Were my words as clear as I heard them? Pokey raised his eyebrows at me. Mae smiled, and Aldridge shoveled in food.

Pushing up both of my long sleeves until they bunched at the elbow, I vowed to win this war. "You're not going to defeat me," I promised the one chopstick I held up. "You *will* let me have supper."

An idea hit me. Why not use them like forks? Holding both like spears, I managed to staba piece of meat hiding under carrots. I wrestled it into my mouth and followed it with more spirits.

Aldridge put his hand ever-so-gently on my arm. "Go

easy on that stuff." His chopstick pointed at my glass. "It'll sneak up on you and kick like a mule!"

I leaned against his shoulder. "That's all right. Nobody sneaks up on me." My words sounded slurred, but intelligent. "I got a gun."

"You left it at home." Aldridge pushed me upright.

"Oops, forgot." I grinned, mystery meat in my mouth. Proud of spearing supper, I leaned back and held up my utensil. "Ha! I figured it out."

Pokey downed his third glass, or maybe his fourth, and holding his chopstick like a sword, threw down the gauntlet. "Ah sa!"

I took the challenge immediately. My unused chopstick in hand, I leaned across the table and smacked his. "'Ah sa' back at ya!"

Back and forth, back and forth. On my feet now, I leaned way over and tried to poke him in the chest, but not being able to reach that far, his arm would have to do. I stabbed. Twice. Steamed vegetables flew as our weapons smacked the food. Pokey was stronger than I'd thought, and he managed to hit my sword hard enough it plunged into the dish of unknown origins. Pieces of carrots hit the table. My weapon of choice stood at attention.

I held up my other sword and hit Pokey's hard enough it flew into the table next to us, narrowly missing a man hunched over, rice bowl in hand. I leaned back, letting out a full-throated roar. "Ha! There! I win!"

"Na ah," Pokey leaned low across the table, his shirt scraping through noodles and veggies on his plate. "I still got a sword left. So there."

Fortifying myself with the last of the magical elixir, another bottle mysteriously appearing two glasses ago, I used my chopstick to flick rice at him. "Take that!" Rice sailed across the table, hitting Mae's shoulder and Pokey's vest.

Mae shot me a look, mumbling something in Chinese that resembled "round eyes" while brushing off supper.

Not to be outdone, Pokey flicked back.

"Put down your chopstick, Maud." Aldridge's voice in my ear meant nothing.

How dare he try to ruin my fun. "It's not a *chop* stick! It's a *flicking* stick!" I roared and waved it like a baton. "Look! I invented flick sticks!"

"I got one, too!" Pokey held up his.

A strong grip on my arm brought me to my feet. I turned my attention from Pokey to Aldridge, his face inches from mine. Confusion, embarrassment and a tinge of anger crawled across his face. "Time to go," he said, so low I almost couldn't hear him.

"Why?" I looked at the table, blurry plates empty, except mine. "We done?"

"You are." Aldridge-the-Party-Pooper led me through the restaurant, now as quiet as a church. Chinese faces stared, watching us leave.

Outside, I stopped and located Pokey behind me, Mae making him drop a handful of rice.

I pointed a wobbly finger at my deputy. "You done, too?"

"'Parently." He pointed at me, his long forefinger wiggling in my direction. "I still won."

"Did not." I used my pointy finger as a sword, striking his again and again.

Pokey fought back, then stopped, leaned over and lost his supper. Mae stood back until he straightened then ran a sleeved arm across his mouth.

I waited for Pokey to look at me. "That's not very lady-like," I said.

"I ain't no lady." He waggled a finger at me again. "Not like you."

"I ain't a lady, either. I'm a... sheriff." Fuzzy, hazy thoughts spun around my brain.

"See! Told you!"

"Am not."

"Uh hu—"

"Pay supper! Pay supper!" Shooting out of the restaurant, a woman in her pajamas fluttered a furious hand in our direction. "Pay now. Pay now."

"Oops!" I dug around for my skirt pocket, forgetting I had no pockets.

Aldridge held bills overhead. "Here. This should cover it." Handing them to the woman, she counted, then grunting in Chinese, spun on her slippered heels and stormed off.

"Cover! I get it!" I laughed long and loud, then burped.

Pokey burped back at me. I burped again, louder and moved in closer to him. "I win!" we said in unison.

"Do not!" Pokey said.

"Do too!"

"Do n..." My world spun, stomach roiled.

Aldridge gripped one of my arms, his hand on my back, and pushed. "We should go."

CHAPTER SEVENTEEN
IT'S ONLY WORDS...

Stirring coffee, the spoon clinking side to side, was about the only activity I could muster. An absurdly happy sun gleefully sent its obnoxious rays to assault swollen eyes. The beams glinted through the window like unwelcome visitors intent on "spreading the good word." I squinted and glared at the same time. Couldn't it be cloudy for once?

Not exactly sure how I had managed to wander into the office this morning, vague recollections of nodding to people on the boardwalk floated in the back of my mind. Sitting here, head nestled in hand, I struggled to hold the spoon in the cup and keep my head from falling off its neck.

The next task to accomplish—I'd already made coffee, poured it and sat, which, that in itself, should be enough for one morning—was to shove the brass band and its ear-splitting racket out of my head. Making the troupe in my stomach quit stomping the Virginia Reel would be a bonus. They all performed with wild abandon and never before had I hated music, dance and alcohol with such clarity.

I took a long gulp of the black brew, my self-pity turning into self-loathing. I cringed every second I recalled last night. What was I thinking? How could I ever face Aldridge again? How was Pokey? And Mae? Would she hate all round eyes? Or forgive Pokey at least? And what about the patrons, and especially the owner of that restaurant?

Could I simply shrink until completely disappeared? Could I die and bury myself somewhere no one would find me? Maybe a being from another dimension would come and sweep me away, all traces gone. I perked up at that thought. Spiritualism they called it. That would be the ticket. Did I know anybody practicing going to the "other side"? My head throbbed too loudly for more thought. I'd revisit options later.

Unable to hold the pounding melon upright, I tossed the spoon onto the desk, and, using shaky hands as a pillow, rested my forehead on the cup. Warmth from the coffee on my hands and face proved reassuring. Not too comfortable in this position, but it beat lying on the floor or using one of the cots in the cell. No telling which little critters lived in the mattress stuffing.

"Sheriff? Are you listening to me? I said, 'we have a situation'."

I flung myself backwards, hit the chair and sat upright. Something wet ran from the corner of my mouth. I swiped at it, blinked at least thirty times, realized the drum and bugle corps in my head had turned into an oompah band playing polkas. I blinked again and stared up into three sets of eyes. The town council.

Great. Could I will myself away into another dimension? Where were those séance people when I needed them? I wiped off the rest of the drool, gripped the coffee cup, glad it wasn't embedded in my forehead, and focused on each man. Or tried to.

"What's the problem?" My gaze started at Ian MacKinney, moved to Harvey Weinberg, and ended with Slim Higginbotham. Their blank stares, tinged with confusion, brought sagging shoulders back. Had they already heard about last night? More than likely.

"This town's going to hell in a hand basket, Sheriff. It up

to you to stop it." Harvey stood in front of the desk, leaned on it, one palm supporting his weight.

Having absolutely no idea what he was talking about, I shifted my gaze to Ian.

"'Tis truth he's be speakin'. Somethin' needs to be done, and with ye bein' the law an' all, ye're the one ta be doin' it."

I searched Slim for translation.

He spread his arms out wide. "You know, Maud. The newspaper. The *newspaper*."

Even with Slim's help, I was one hundred percent flummoxed. I blamed it on that dang Chinese liquor. "What newspaper? What happened? Didn't Pokey get it from Dutch Flats?"

Harvey smacked the desk. I jumped. "That's not what I'm tellin' ya, Sheriff! *Listen*."

Slim moved in closer to Harvey. "No, Pokey's getting the papers just fine. What Harvey's talking about is Mrs. Emily Penderton." He pointed over his shoulder. "She's starting up a newspaper here in Dry Creek."

"And you're to blame." Harvey pointed a shaking finger in my face.

"For what?" Could I be any more confused?

"Canna have such a thing, Sheriff. Na, canna." Ian's ruffled feathers paced from window to desk.

"Why not?" I considered pinching myself to see if I was still sleeping. This had to be a dream—bordering on nightmare.

"First of all," Harvey stood back, crossed his arms over his chest, glared at me like I was five. "She's a woman. That right there's bad enough."

"Soon this entire town will be run only by woman!" Ian stopped his pacing long enough to point behind him. "Imagine what'll happen. I canna."

The little drummer boy in my head marched onto the desk while the dancer in my stomach stomped to his rhythm. Together we would tell these windbags where to go.

"A woman can—"

"Of course, of course!" Slim, bless his heart, took lead on this current crisis. "Women are the backbone of our society." He eyed his fellow blow-hards. "It's just that... um..."

Harvey elbowed Slim out of the way to reclaim center stage. "Newspapers are bad for business, Maud. A disaster for this town. We don't need a nosey, busybody *woman* come digging into our business."

"An', what's worse, she'll write about it, she will." All of Ian's diminutive stature resumed marching from desk to door to window. His arms flew out like a squawking crow about to fly away. If my head hadn't been reeling from last night's soiree muddled with total confusion of this latest catastrophe, I would have laughed. But a grin? Not possible.

Two, maybe three deep breaths later, I pushed my body up to its feet, a trick I'd doubted moments before. Walking around the desk, one hand on the top just in case, I stood next to Slim and faced Ian and Harvey.

"Gentlemen, what is it you expect me to do? Exactly?" As if I didn't know.

Ian stopped, mid-flight. "Are ye cakey?" His green eyes flared, his round face twisting into a horrified expression of disbelief. He glanced at Harvey. "Told you she was doolally." Back to me. "Stop her. 'Tis simple. Tell her *no*. She canna do this business."

"That's right." Harvey pulled back his shoulders, stood large, taking up most of the space and air in my office. "Don't need such company around here. One newspaper, the one from Dutch Flats, is enough." He looked left and right. "Got enough trouble 'round here as is."

By standing, part of my head cleared enough for what I hoped was intelligent conversation. "So, let me get this straight. You three don't want a new business in town? You don't want to sell to the people who may come in because of it? Because of your advertisements?" I narrowed what I was sure was red-ringed eyes. "So, you're telling me you're against free speech? Guaranteed by our United

States Constitution? And you don't want to make more money?"

Screeches, gulps, mumbled harrumphs spiraled through the air. Each shook his head, either denying my accusation or trying to rattle some of the rocks to one side. Sometimes it could be hard to figure out which.

"Nah, nothing like that, Maud." Slim reached to pat my shoulder then retracted his hand, obviously reconsidering such a bold move. "It's just that, well, we think it'll cause trouble. Maybe people shooting each other. Killings. Trouble Dry Creek doesn't need."

"That's right." Curls on both sides of Harvey's Hasidic head bounced. "A story about say... the upcoming mayoral election, for example, might just get people riled up."

"Isn't that the point? To help citizens make the right choice?" A slight burning in my chest threatened to move up to the throat.

"We've had elections without it." Ian pegged me with his eyes. "Doin' fine I'm thinkin' without any overinflated facts. An', yer aff yer heid if ye think I'll purchase an ad from this dobber. Especially a woman dobber!"

Needing to sit and soon, I held the door open. "I'll give this some thought, gentlemen." I stepped outside hoping they would follow. They did. "Good day now."

Once they swaggered down the boardwalk, I hurried back inside, closed the door, thinking I should lock it and have the world go away. I poured more coffee and collapsed into my chair. More sips. I mulled over why these businessmen would not welcome a local newspaper. It seemed logical they'd want something that would not only advertise their goods but add to the town's reputation as an ace-high place in which to live.

Why not, indeed, unless... conversations in the Tin Pan sprung to mind. Maybe what the barkeep had alluded to was true. Maybe, possibly, Ian and Harvey and other mercantile owners were manipulating prices.

Or, just as importantly, was it because Emily was female?

I'd known her for years and was surprised she wanted to run a newspaper. But then again, her children were grown and gone, her husband away all day building houses. And, as I understood it, she had finished all ten years of school, which undeniably qualified her. Probably, she was ready for another challenge. And this would be the mother of all challenges. I liked Emily. She was strong, sensible, about my mother's age if she'd still be alive. I sat thinking things over, then came to the conclusion I couldn't imagine anyone else running our weekly news source.

As soon as the rhythm section in my body was tired and quiet, I'd call on Emily to see exactly what was what. The more I thought, the more excited I became. I ran my hand across the imaginary sky. *Dry Creek Clarion. Dry Creek News. Dry Creek Courier.* Oohh, I liked that last one.

* * *

A couple of hours crawled by. I drank coffee, pushing papers around on my desk until the door squeaked open. Apparently, I hadn't locked it. In strode my knight in shining armor. My dream come true. And then memories of the previous night smacked me in the face. Aldridge Armstrong, big as life, stood in the office, cloth bag in hand.

With pulse-pounding certainty, I vowed to sort out my thoughts, arrange them, impose order. Instead, I stumbled to my feet hoping, praying not to get tangled in the skirt and do a face plant on the floor.

He held out the bag. "Brought you dinner. Thought you'd be hungry about now."

Could this man get any better? My knees threatened to melt. "Thank you." Was that all I could mumble? How about: *where've you been all my life?* Or *clearly you aren't human. You've got to be a god.* But I remained dumb.

"It's just a sandwich." He cocked his head toward town. "Got it at the restaurant. Hope you don't mind."

Mind? Why would I mind? Then I realized I was still

standing, mouth open, waiting I guess, for coherent thoughts to form in the brain so they could exit through the mouth. Was that even possible?

At last, the various body parts pulled themselves together. I pointed to a chair in front of the desk. "If you brought two, we can eat here. Coffee's hot."

His shoulders relaxed and he blew out a slight breath. "Sounds wonderful. And yes, I've got two."

I poured coffee while he arranged the food. Suddenly, I was ravenous. Not just for food, but for him. He was the man I'd been waiting for my entire life. Was he too good to be true? I pushed that thought aside as I munched the sandwich, made exactly the way I liked. Toasted sourdough, tons of mayonnaise, lettuce and a thick slice of ham. Could life get better?

We passed the hour eating, me apologizing, eating, me apologizing, he forgiving me, drinking coffee, me apologizing. When no words were left, we sat quietly, basking in the glow of good food and even better company.

And then as if someone popped my balloon, Aldridge wiped his mouth one last time, pushed back and stood.

"I've got a meeting in a few minutes, Maud." He folded the bag. "Mae Yu and I are talking about opening a school for Chinese girls."

I froze. "What?"

He nodded. "We spoke this morning, and we've both decided it would be beneficial to the community. Not to mention the girls." Aldridge held up a hand. "We thought we'd work out a few of the kinks before coming to you and Mayor Critoli in an official capacity. And yes, we know there's a charm school, but this would be different."

So, turns out, my Mr. Wonderful was even more wonderful than possible.

As much as I hated him to leave, I understood. I had work to do, too. I covered sad disappointment by listing errands. "I need to go see Emily Penderton about her starting a newspaper. Then check in on the new bakery and stop by the charm school. Then talk with Pearl about running for mayor." I left off needing to figure out who burned down the school. And who murdered the distiller. That could be tomorrow.

Aldridge slid his arm around my shoulders, drawing me close. He kissed the top of my head, something I found to be oh-so endearing. "Take care of yourself, Sheriff. Don't let those bakery ladies get the drop on you." His chuckling bounced my shoulder.

"Don't worry. I always hit what I aim for." I patted my hip where the holster should be. "I've been practicing." Well, not really, but I'd planned to. Some day.

A long good-bye later, he stepped into the hustle and bustle of town. Vowing to get *something* done today, I stepped outside, closed and locked the door behind me, enjoying the lingering tingle of Aldridge's kiss. He waved as he turned right, toward Chinatown, then stopped, whirled around and flashed me a broad smile. Instead of rushing into his arms as my entire body pleaded to do, I waved back and turned left, toward downtown and Seth's office. I'd need his opinion on opening a newspaper before talking to Emily.

CHAPTER EIGHTEEN
WOMEN ARE PEOPLE, TOO...

I FOUND SETH IN HIS OFFICE, ALONE, STANDING AT the window, staring. I rapped lightly on the open door, waited for him to turn around, which he did, hunched and slow, turtle-like. His handsome face possessed the empty look of a withered balloon. I'd only seen this one other time, and that was when his father was dying. Immediately, my heart went out to him. Something was wrong. Beyond doubt wrong.

Approaching him like one would a hurt animal, I closed the door, eased over to the window, wrapped my arms around him. Usually, this would be a no-no in today's society, but we were friends and at times, more than friends. He needed a hug, and I would give him one.

He sighed into my shoulder, mumbled something, then straightened up. "What're you doing here?"

"Came by to ask your opinion, but... what's wrong?"

Running his soft hand across his freshly shaved face, he pulled in a long breath, brought his focus to me. "Just thinking."

"Doesn't sound like you." I lifted one corner of my mouth, not in a smile or a grin. Just a friendly gesture. "You don't generally think." That didn't come out right and a beat later, we both smiled.

"Sometimes I don't. You're right." Seth pointed to a chair in front of his desk. "Been pondering this election coming up. Maybe it *is* time to let someone else be mayor. Go back to being a real estate broker."

"What?" I leaned forward, wishing we could have this conversation over a beer. "Why'd you think that? You've been a terrific mayor."

He stepped next to the chair at his desk to look at the sepia picture hanging on the wall. In it stood his mother, father and gaggle of siblings. I'd studied this photo many times and considered how serious he looked as a younger man. Had to have been taken a good five, six years before. His father was in it.

I waited while he finished staring out the window, sank into his chair, and turned his attention to me. Figuring I knew what the issue was, I decided to let him go ahead and tell it. He sat. I waited. He stared. I rearranged my skirt. He stared. I reviewed my list of things to do now that my head seemed to be more in thinking order, the marching band quiet, apparently having worn themselves out. I waited.

At last, he sighed, chest rising and falling like my cakes usually did, and turned his copper brown eyes to me. "It's all my fault."

That was a new one. I pressed gently. "What is?"

He pointed toward the closed door. "Pearl." Another sigh. "Told her I love her. And look what she did." He rubbed his mustache. "Now she's running against me."

Fighting an urge to simultaneously look toward the door thinking Pearl stood there, and jump up and give him another hug, I studied my clenched hands. Wait a minute! He loved *her*? I thought he... Well, I wasn't sure what he thought. I knew my feelings ran deep for him, but *love*?

Seth picked up a pencil, holding it more like a pitchfork than a writing instrument. "How could she?"

I allowed my shoulders to lift and with them, my hands, palm up. "Maybe she thinks she can run the town from a woman's point of view. You have to admit, it's fairly one-sided around here."

"What d'you mean?"

Should I explain just how society revolves around men, or throw him one or two examples? I opted for the short version. "Men run the world. We have little say in the matters of life and it's just women are finally realizing we're people, too."

His eyes crinkled on the sides as he smiled. "People, huh?" He laid down the pencil.

I shrugged again, nodded. "And... we have brains." Was I going too far with this? Maybe. But the words were uncorked and popped out of my mouth. "And ideas. And wants and needs. Just like men."

Seth sat for long moments, fingers steepled. He brought them to his lips, down to his desk, back up to his lips. Nodding over them, his sensitive eyes locked on mine. "You're right, Maud. Again." His full eyelashes, rivaling any woman's—of which I was secretly jealous—swept up and down. "I need to start doing some thinking on this. Become... what do they say? More modern?"

Hallejulah! Could it be? Would Seth at long last break out of his male world and try to see things differently? Without wanting to scare him off or push too hard too soon, I decided to start small. "What would you think of starting a newspaper in town?"

Deep furrows raced across his forehead. He was actually thinking. Scratching an ear, he again peered out the window, or toward it at any rate. "Never thought about one. What would it say? There enough "news" around here to warrant a paper?"

"Sure is." I brightened, sat soldier straight. "What about apple season? We could run new recipes for apple pie. Or apple cider."

"We?"

Caught. I backpedaled. "Whoever edits," I stammered.

"And how about straightening out the rumors of the distillery accident? I'm sure there's a bunch of information out there that's utter conjecture." I was on a roll now. "And what about the school burning? Maybe someone will come forward with information. That would be so helpful. And, you know, maybe run an article on you being mayor and on Pearl running for mayor. How about an article on the new bakery? Or the charm school?"

Seth held up a hand. "Getting ahead of yourself, aren't you? Don't we need someone to run it?"

"Or helping to build a new school." I wasn't finished with my list, but the look on Seth's face told me he was convinced. Taking a long breath, I straightened my bonnet and cleared my throat. "Fact is, there is someone who's thinking of starting up a paper." I ran my hand across the imaginary sky, picturing the banner. "The *Dry Creek Courier*." So, I took liberties there. No harm done.

"No kidding?" Seth leaned forward. "You've spoken with him?"

"Not directly. Had a meeting today with the town windbags and, of course, they complained. Fact is, I'm beginning to think there's something they don't want known, publicized. Something a bit untoward... shady."

"Like raising prices so the distillers don't make as much profit." He snapped his fingers, then pointed one at me. "Like we talked about in the saloon. What's that called? Price fixing?"

I hadn't heard that term exactly, but I agreed. Suddenly, something smelled fishy. "If you think a newspaper's a good idea and I have your backing, I'll go talk to this person right now. Tell her it's a good idea."

"Her?"

Dang, caught again. I sighed hoping Seth's new way of thinking was still in place. "Mrs. Emily Penderton. She'd be ideal."

"Another woman running a business? *Another* one? Here

in Dry Creek? What're all the men supposed to do? Aren't we in charge of anything, anymore? First thing you know, the saloons'll be full all day with women off running the world. Telling us where to go, what to do." He stood, paced desk to window, mumbling, "Fire chief, bakery, charm school, mayor..."

"You forgot sheriff."

He wheeled around like he'd been jabbed by his own pencil. "Women. They're everywhere. Into everybody's bus—"

"And we're here to stay, Seth." I wanted to tell him he just better get used to it. Things were going to change from now on. But images of his red eyes when I first walked in made me pull in my horns. I softened. Finding myself now standing, I offered this bit of wisdom. "Half the world is women and, without us, you wouldn't be here."

He hung his head, all the wind out of his sails. "What'd I do about Pearl?" His words were so soft I almost didn't catch them.

Placing my hand on his forearm, feeling the muscles tense under the sleeve, I gently squeezed. "Depends on how badly you want to stay mayor. You've got a good chance of winning since only men can vote."

"You think?"

What I wanted to do was scream and throw a temper tantrum right there on his expensive rug. Women should be allowed to vote, too. Why not? Weren't we as good as men, maybe better? But instead, I nodded. What Seth couldn't see were my teeth grinding.

Before I teared up or threw a chair across the room, I decided now would be a good time to pay Emily a visit.

I said my good-byes and hurried up Main. A thousand and one conversations rattled in my head as I nodded to citizens and sidestepped one drunk coming out of the Tin Pan Saloon. I hoped Emily still wanted to run a newspaper. Now, more than ever I wanted her to. What a terrific idea! Why hadn't I thought of it first?

I remembered the way to her house because it was the first one on the block, three streets over from Main. It had always been one of my two-story favorites with its white gables, high wide porch with five steps and a darn picket fence making it idyllic. I'd envisioned having a house like that someday, a yard full of children. Why didn't I have a husband and children?

Before I knocked on Emily's door, I pushed down the hollow feeling and inattentively ran a hand across the badge. If I couldn't be a Mrs., I'd be a Sheriff.

Emily opened the door before I knocked a second time. She ushered me into her well-kept living room where no speck of dust would dare appear. My house, not even the office, was this clean. Or tidy.

After I eased down, ever so carefully, on her lake-blue satin striped sofa, Emily sat across from me, a short table in between. I broached the subject for my visit. Her reply was close to word-for-word what I'd expected.

"I'm sure you've experienced the same thing, Sheriff. Maud." Her fawn-colored eyes smiled, which I didn't think was possible. While her face was long, the mouth was small, too small to be in proportion, the crinkles around her eyes in some way made up for it. They didn't flash her age, which I guessed had to be fifty, instead brought more life to her face, the cheeks a light pink.

"What same thing?" I sipped the tea she had served moments before.

"Having too much time on your hands." She waved her hand around the room. "You can only clean, dust and cook so much. Besides, it's time I give back to Dry Creek. This has been a wonderful community and I want to show my appreciation by starting up a newspaper."

Made sense. And I definitely agreed with her. I thought back to standing at my front room window watching people trot off to work, wishing I was one of them. Pa made enough money to keep a nice house and as much food as we wanted. I didn't have to take in ironing or laundry as many women did simply to make ends meet. I didn't have small mouths to feed, only Pa's, and he was no longer a growing boy.

When too much silence filled the room, Emily chose to expound. "Thought it would be a weekly, like Dutch Flats', and I'd sell it for a nickel each issue."

"A nickel? Wouldn't a dime be better? I mean... five cents sounds cheap."

She held up her cup and pointed toward town. "I figured five, everybody could afford it. But if you think—"

"Gotta consider what it'll cost to print, then set the price accordingly. If you want to make any money." Now I was starting to sound like Pa, being the banker he was. "What do you plan to print?"

Her eyes lit up like Fourth of July fireworks. "Plenty of advertisements. Advice columns for cooking, the news of course, and... I was hoping to have a weekly column by you. Give you a chance to say whatever's on your mind."

"Me?" I nearly dropped the rose-decorated teacup. "You want me to write something? Every week?" I sucked in all the room's air. "What would I say?" Panic clenched my stomach. The room spun. Getting sucker punched with a flatiron skillet wouldn't have been as terrifying.

Emily stood, sat next to me. "Lost color in your face, Maud. And you're shaking. You all right?" She extracted the cup from my hand and set it on the table. "It was simply an idea. You don't have to if you don't want."

Whew. I sure as shooting didn't want. As room colors returned to normal and my hands relaxed, I considered. Maybe that would be a chance to let the fine citizens know what was going on. Possibly quell rumors. Then again, probably not, because rumors and gossip were the backbone of any small town.

"Let me think on it, Emily. I appreciate the chance to get the word out."

She unfolded her long legs, her China blue skirt draping nicely around them, and stood. "I take it you heard from the town council?"

Not quite ready to stand but knowing I should, I managed to get my legs under me without stepping on my skirt. It wasn't nearly as becoming as hers. "I did. They're not in total agreement with this newspaper venture, but you have the blessing of the mayor. He thinks it's a great idea."

She expelled a long stream of air. "Thank you for letting me know. I was going to him next. Now I don't have to." A smile reached both ears. "Found a small shop off Main I can rent cheap. I can get started today."

"Sure can." I headed for the door, then stopped. Unsure how to say this exactly, I searched for the right words. Facing her, I took in her beautiful home, handsome clothes and well-tended yard. I'd hate to see it all go up in smoke over misconstrued stories. "Emily, running a newspaper is more than ink and paper." I lowered my voice. "The wrong words can get people riled. Some might take stories the wrong way and cause all sorts of mayhem."

"I've thought about that."

"Think about it seriously. I'll protect you and your business as well as I can, but... you never know. Some don't take kindly to so many women running businesses now."

"Then they'll have to get over it." Emily held the door open. "I'll take your warning to heart, Sheriff. And thank you."

"Good to know."

A couple of steps down the porch, I remembered my biggest question. I stopped, yanked my skirt out from under my shoe, turned to find Emily still standing there, smiling. I absolutely had to know. "What're you gonna call your paper?"

She shrugged. "Thinking about *Dry Creek Citizen*. What do you think?"

Citizen wasn't bad, but I liked my idea better. "*Courier? Dry Creek Courier?*"

Tilting her head to one side, she tried it out. "*Courier*. I like that." Her eyes lit her entire face. "*Dry Creek Courier* it is!"

Ha! I'd take a victory wherever I could find it. I nodded, waved again and bounded down the remaining steps. I'd celebrate over a piece of pie at the bakery. I deserved it.

CHAPTER NINETEEN
SOMETHING ABOUT HIM...

ONE LAST BITE. I SAVORED THE RICH, YET TART apples hiding under the flakiest, lightest crust I'd ever tasted. Ma had been a good cook, but this pie, this apple-chokecherry pie was ace high. Maybe if I hung around longer, even though it was almost closing time, Ester Sibley here at the *Dry Creek Sweet Shop* would take pity on me and let me test a second piece. Half of me wanted the recipe, the other half thought I was out of my gourd. First, I'd never be able to recreate the perfection, and second, why would I want to cook if someone else would?

Since I'd come in so late, Ester and Hilda had a bit of time to spend talking with me. Both had admitted they could use a sit down.

Once they'd pulled out chairs, melted into them and tucked the hanks of hair back into buns, they sighed.

Hilda played with her half-full coffee cup. "This is much harder than I imagined," she said, her Swedish accent softened by years living in America. Her sapphire eyes looked tired, almost sunken. "Not only we cook, but wash the dish, sweep floor and keep account of all our monies."

"And order supplies." Ester's acorn-colored eyes hinted at a flame burning in her soul. Although her drooping shoulders mirrored Hilda's fatigue, something about Ester was on fire.

I regarded both women, wondering if they'd stay in business long. "I do know how tough it is to keep house and run a business." I started to smile then thought better of it. "At least I don't have to cook all day."

"Oohh..." Hilda threw up her hands and gazed at the ceiling. "Oohh, cooking. It is easy. I do it all my life." She returned sparkling eyes to me and placed her sturdy hands on the table. "When I was young, back in the old country. I always help Mama. My brothers, they don't help Mama. *I* do." She wagged her head. "It's all I know. What I love to do."

"And you're very good at it." I knew I spoke over my last mouthful, but I couldn't help myself. I chased crumbs around with the fork, then after crushing the last, I turned the conversation. "How is business? Are you making any money? And while I haven't heard anything, are the men of this town bothering you?"

Ester slid the quite-empty plate closer to her, I suppose getting ready to take it back to the kitchen to wash. I doubted I'd see another piece until tomorrow.

"If you mean 'bothering' that we're women running a business, no. Even the town councilors have been in." Ester's eyes sparkled. "In fact, they meet here every Tuesday morning for coffee and one of Hilda's strudels."

Mentally licking my lips at strudel, I considered the other half of the question. "Are men bothering you at all?"

Ester threw her hands up like Hilda had done. "Bothering us? Oh yes! Indeed they are. Men come in all the time asking for 'pie like mama used to make.' We've had to expand our recipes—"

"Such as meat pies," Hilda added.

Ester nodded. "Those, too. But we can't go wrong with apple pie or Hilda's strudel."

I leaned back, suddenly feeling full and a bit sleepy. After all, it had been one long day. "So, your business is going well. Is that right?"

Two bobbing heads accompanied by wide, tired smiles, told me everything I needed to know.

"It's all-in apple-pie order, Sheriff." Ester scooted her chair back. "I wonder every day why I didn't do this sooner."

Hilda groaned up to her feet. "Yes, thank you once more, Sheriff." Her hands swept around the four-tabled room. "You were inspiration." With that, she plodded toward the kitchen, retying the apron snugged around her waist.

Refusing to take my offered money, Ester also headed to the kitchen, my empty plate in hand.

As I sat in the newly opened bakery, finishing the glass of milk in front of me, listening to dishes clattering, I rummaged around in my brain for the next and most important concern on my plate. Who set the school on fire? Or preferably, *what*. I hated like blazes to think someone, one of the fine citizens of Dry Creek, deliberately put match to wood and burned down such an important building. I hoped it was instead a mouse, or some animal dragging a match across the floorboard, that caused the inferno. Cartoonish images popped into my head: a large rat, red phosphorous friction match in one paw, hopping across the school wooden floor, sadistically laughing at the sparks behind him. I could almost hear his squeaky, high-pitched voice saying, "That that, Miss McIntyre. Hate school! Hate you!"

I blinked hard, hoping to extinguish the images, and succeeded. If it *were* an animal, I'd hope it wasn't something like a rabbit. They seemed so... innocent. Finally done with my milk, and knowing no more pie was forthcoming, I tiptoed into the kitchen and handed my empty glass to Hilda. A quick look around showed a spotless set of pots and pans, all stacked on shelves. My own kitchen should look this bang-up. I said thanks and made my way out the back door and headed for a charred pile of debris.

* * *

AGAIN, for about the four hundredth time this month, I stood over the ashes of what had been a completely good schoolhouse and wondered. How could I figure out who did it? No one had come forward with even a hint of a clue, which left me... empty. Holding the proverbial bag. With nothing inside. No new ideas. Simply a void of facts.

I blew out a long stream of air, which turned into a white cloud. For the first time today, I realized Fall was upon us and major chill was in the air. I shivered. Would it actually snow at some point soon or be irritatingly cold for months? While I contemplated, I wandered over to the building's southeast corner. Here, what had been the cloakroom now sprawled like a dropped bundle of sticks. Thinking about all the children who'd stood here, removing jackets, jostling each other, wishing school was out for the summer, brought a smile to my face. I turned over charred boards. Puffs of burned ash flew up, clogging my nose, bringing on a big sneeze. The tang of salt and white vinegar wood smoke competed with a more woodsy, earthy smell.

The wood, its singed texture reminding me of pictures of alligator skin, broke in half when I kicked it. Nothing underneath but two more burned boards. And then... peeking out from under a knot of charred wood, what looked like... material? I knelt and ran my hand along the edge of a board and caressed a piece of fabric. Most of it was burned beyond recognition other than it was cloth, but one corner was intact. Muslin. Basic, plain cotton material. I'd recognize it anywhere. I'd learned to sew on muslin.

While I wasn't a trained fire investigator, I figured this could have been what started the whole mess. I carefully scooped up what I could and dug around. Within half a foot lay what looked like two or three thoroughly burned red phosphorous matches or parlor matches, the paraffin dipped types. The wooden ends were black, but intact. Could this be what started the fire?

Holding my findings almost as gently as I would a newborn, my shoulders sprung back, I looked around for someone to appreciate my efforts. Not a soul in sight. All right, I'd bring this back to Pokey and Seth to see what they thought. Before doing that, I studied the matches closely. No bite marks on the end. Probably not an animal.

As I walked back to town, I considered stopping by the mercantile to see who'd purchased this match and fabric. Within the next breath I realized many people buy parlor matches and it would be impossible to determine who and when. I stepped up onto the boardwalk. On the other hand, I could present my find to Harvey Weinberg at the Dry Creek Mercantile and show him I'd at least uncovered a tiny piece of evidence. Possibly, and I wasn't holding out much hope at this thought, *possibly* he would quit berating my efforts and help me. I needed somebody besides Pokey and Seth in my corner.

With my kind of luck in place, I opened the mercantile door and skidded to a stop. Across the room stood not only Harvey, but Ian and Slim, all three gathered around the potbelly stove in the corner, hands extended over the heat. Like over-weight ballerinas, they spun to see who'd rung the bell over the door. Inside I laughed at their lack of coordination and looks of consternation. Apparently, I was the last person they'd expected, or wanted, to see.

Slim recovered first. His smile was warm, welcoming. "Maud." He waved me closer.

"Come in where it's warm."

I hadn't planned to share the news with all three, but on a quick second thought, it would be the decent thing to do. Plus, I wouldn't have to make the same speech three times. Looking around the store, it appeared empty. More than likely all the customers had already gone home to start supper. Standing closer to Slim than the other two, I extracted the matches and fabric from my pocket and held them up.

"This, gentlemen, is the cause of the school fire, I

believe. Found them under a couple burned boards." I hoped my voice sounded as strong as I felt right then.

Slim plucked first the matches and then material out of my grasp, held them close to his face, then sniffed the material's blackened tips. His nose puckered as he croaked out, "kerosene." He then gave the matches a closer inspection. "Drunkard's matches."

I cocked my head and an eyebrow went up on its own. I hadn't heard that term before.

As if reading my thoughts, Slim rushed to explain. "Called drunkard's matches because see, right around here," he pointed to the blackened end, "they're dipped into paraffin. Helps keep people from burning their fingers when they strike it."

I nodded. Good to know. I'd add that to my list of relatively useless information, which I seemed to have in abundance.

Slim handed the material and matches to Ian who passed on to Harvey. Mumbles, harrumphs and throat clearing rumbled around the store.

Harvey strode to the door, locked it, turned the "Open" sign around, pulled down the curtain before returning. I wondered why he felt compelled to be so secretive, then realized it would be safest if no one else knew my discovery quite yet. No telling what would happen, which fingers would point where.

Ian nodded toward the culprit. "Canna believe some Johnny would set flame to tinder." He fisted a hand, the other held over the stove. "Why?"

"Why, indeed." Slim returned my find to me and I immediately tucked them into my skirt pocket. He frowned into the stove. "What's the point? What would they gain by torching a school?"

I looked from man to man, expecting, I suppose, the answer. When it didn't magically appear, I blew out a long, exasperated breath. "At least we know it was set." Part of an idea pushed its way into my brain, and I wasn't smart enough to stop it before it took wings. "I'll ask Penelope Plunkett, you know the new fire chief, to help me inspect things. Maybe she'll have ideas."

Nose whistles, grunts and hands shoved into pockets made me wish I'd kept quiet.

Harvey leaned closer to me. "It's women who cause trouble. This fire chief of yours," pronouncing "chief" like it was unfit to be included in his vocabulary, "what does she know about how fires start?"

Ian, not to be outdone by Harvey, pulled off his cap, ran short fingers through his hair. "Nay, canna have womans doin' man's work." He nodded to his co-conspirators. "First light, we go ourselves to see."

That was it. These long-winded gasbags wouldn't take over my investigation, especially not after a few days ago accusing me of not doing anything about it. I lowered my voice to the deepest timbre I could muster.

"Sorry, men." I held up a hand. "I don't want or need your help. I'll get this solved my way." After a deep breath, which I hoped they couldn't see, I continued. "Penelope and I will figure this all out. And when we do, you three will be some of the first to know."

Wild blinking from all told me I'd hit a nerve. Inside I gloated and started for the door. "Only reason I came by now was to show you what I'd found." I waited for Harvey to unlock the door. The bell tinkled as I stopped inside the doorjamb. I couldn't help myself and uttered, "Good day, gentlemen."

With the door firmly shut and locked behind me, I felt like whistling back to the office.

But I didn't whistle, a bouncy step being enough. I nodded to a young man busy lighting the gas lamps hanging on both sides of the boardwalk. Dry Creek was actually becoming well-heeled, I considered. We didn't have bonfires up and down Main like in the old days. We'd become modern, civilized with our gas lamps.

As I walked, careful not to trip over the cupped boards, a

rumbling to my rear caused me to stop. Sounded like the stage. This time of day? Or was it night? Closer to night, for sure. I turned and sure enough, the Sacramento-Nevada Overland Stage pulled up to the hotel across the street. Rarely this late, the stage had been known for its punctuality. Hoping nothing of grave misfortune had happened, I navigated across the rutted street, hoping not to step into any road apples.

The driver, or jehu some called them, was a well-muscled fella who went by "Bumps." Since his neck resembled a tree stump, I assumed the rest of him was just as substantial. Someday I'd ask about the exact reason for his moniker, but this wasn't the day. On the other hand, the name seemed fitting.

He scrambled down from the high driver's seat, tipping his hat to me as he landed.

"Howdy, Sheriff."

"You're late." I winced at stating the obvious. Plus, how lame was that?

Bumps thumbed over his shoulder toward his stage-coach. "Loose wheel. Had to stop and fix it." A snigger rumbled his wide chest. "Fella in there didn't take too kindly to helpin' out, but seein' as he wanted to *ride* to town 'stead of *walk*, he decided lifting part of the coach so's I could put the wheel back on would get the job done." His sun-whacked face cracked wide open with a smile.

"Guess you can be persuasive, Bumps."

"Part of my good-natured personality." One of his wide shoulders rose.

Two exhausted-looking women, their hats askew, skirts and blouses caked with dust, climbed out. One man, the one I presumed who'd been reluctant to help, exited last. He stood, brushing California from his canvas jacket. Something about him was familiar, but in this waning daylight, I couldn't pinpoint it. More than likely my imagination.

"Welcome, ladies, sir." I nodded. "I'm the sheriff here in Dry Creek." Before I could give more of a welcome speech, two men in a buggy pulled alongside and jumped out. The women squealed, throwing themselves in the men's arms. I turned to the man, now standing alone. He glanced down the street as if possibly waiting for someone, then shrugged.

Wanting to be a fine example of Dry Creek hospitality, I offered my hand. "Sheriff Maud Overstreet, sir. The hotel behind you has clean sheets and reasonable prices." He did not take my hand.

After studying the hotel, he turned to me. "Does this quaint village retain a boarding house? I may be staying in town at least a fortnight."

"We certainly do. Down the street, around the corner." I squinted at him, questioning his obvious disdain for Dry Creek. Quaint? Village? Please. I soldiered on, ever the welcome committee of one. "You mind giving me your name? Maybe tomorrow I could point you in the right direction of your business here."

Hesitating, he stuck out a hand. The grip was what I'd expected—weak and soft.

"Ford. Nathaniel Ford." He picked up a brocade bag from the sidewalk. "I'll let a room at the hotel tonight, then arrange further accommodations tomorrow." Starting off, he stopped and spoke over his shoulder. One finger tipped the hat brim. "Thank you kindly for the welcome."

Yellow gas lamplight played on his face. Something about him again reminded me of someone I knew. But who? The lanky man, taller and thinner than Pa, shorter than Aldridge, stretched, rubbed his back and opened the hotel's door.

I narrowed my eyes. Something about him prickled my stomach.

CHAPTER TWENTY
THAT'S ENGLISH
FOR YOU...

A GOOD NIGHT'S SLEEP MADE ALL THE difference. This morning, I was back to being myself—full of energy and ready to meet the day. But first, another cup of Arbuckle's which I had ground this morning at home. Coffee like that would make the world an even better place. I poured the steaming brew into the tin cup at the office and considered my day. I'd need to talk to Seth about yesterday's match discovery and, for some reason, after a night's rest, it didn't seem too significant. Maybe it was, maybe not. A niggling question at the back of my brain had sprung forward sometime during the night—why hadn't we found it sooner? After all, several of us had scoured the debris and come up with a big red zero. Why now?

Then again, should I look a gift horse in the mouth, as they say? And what was a "gift horse," anyway? Maybe Seth would know. I added a spoonful of molasses to the cup, stirred, all the while contemplating odd turns of phrase. Mulling over quirky English, I plopped at the desk and slurped cautiously, the brew scalding hot. Glad I already knew how to read and write our crazy language, I could not imagine having to learn speaking it, much less anything else.

Which brought my train of thinking around to my Mr.

Adorable and Pokey's Mae starting a school for Chinese girls. Those youngsters would have a long row to hoe. I stopped. There it was again... another saying.

Before chatting with Seth, I planned to talk to Penelope to get her thoughts on my find. Maybe she'd think it as odd as I did, or maybe she'd chalk it up to an oversight on everyone's part.

I pushed a few new wanted posters around, careful to study each one in case a scoundrel of the worst kind decided to come visit Dry Creek. Images of the man on yesterday's stage came to mind. I combed through all twenty or so posters, rechecked a few messages from the boys in Sacramento and Dutch Flats, and came up empty. Must be my wild imagination, or had I become suspicious of everyone I didn't know personally? Would wearing a badge do that? I hated to think it had come down to that, but the more I pondered, the more I decided this tin star was to blame. Not that I would give it up, but my way of thinking had for sure taken a different direction.

Before I knew it, the cup was empty and the posters stacked neatly on the desk's corner. Happy to have found no new threatening notes, I had no more excuses not to get out and about. Although the sun beat down like it was midsummer, the air refused to cooperate. A chill, bordering on downright cold, had set in recently which meant I'd need gloves, wool coat and possibly a scarf. Penelope's farm was a full mile or more out of town and since I didn't own a horse, I'd have to walk. Whenever Pa and I went somewhere far, we'd rent a buggy from Swensen's Stable. And the couple of times I'd had to go chasing after bank robbers earlier this year, I'd ridden a horse, which I'd never done before. But, as they say, "desperate times call for desperate measures," and quickly I'd learned to ride. Going to Penelope's today was no 'desperate time,' so no 'desperate measures' were necessary.

I buttoned the coat and stopped. More phrases. Crazy English. Go figure.

* * *

PENELOPE STOOD, hunched over on the tip top of her barn, the rooster weathervane, not a buggy like Magruder's, at her elbow. Even from a distance, I recognized her sturdy figure. I hiked in closer, her Pa walked outside from the barn toting a wooden toolbox.

He shaded his eyes as he hollered up at her. "Got longer nails and heavier hammer for ya. Anything else?"

Penelope mumbled something I couldn't quite make out.

"I'll tie a rope to this box and ya can haul it up!" He looped a rope through either side of the handle for stability and tied it with a vengeance.

Deciding to announce myself before coming within striking distance of a swinging arm or hammer, I cleared my throat. "Howdy, Mr. Plunkett!"

He spun around like I'd jabbed him with a pitchfork, glaring into the mid-morning sun. "Who...?" His wide shoulders relaxed a bit under his flannel shirt. "Sheriff. Gave me quite the start."

"Sorry. I tried not to sneak." I waved to Penelope who returned the greeting.

"What brings ya out this way?" Penelope's Pa, not a man to beat around the bush, always spoke his mind. No idle chit chat or pleasant conversation with him. In some ways, Penelope was like that too.

"Thought I'd run some findings past Penelope, since she's the town's new fire chief." I said rather loudly, figuring he'd be mighty proud of her. Instead, he huffed.

"She got better things to do than running around town, sticking her nose in places it don't need to be. Told her so, too, but she won't have none of my thinking." His gaze traveled up the ladder, now occupied with Penelope coming down. "Kids these days. Got no dang blame sense."

At least he didn't curse too badly, like I'd heard he could. I had a sneaking suspicion Penelope could swear like a cowboy in a stampede if need be, but I'd never seen that side of her. And frankly, I hoped I'd never have to.

Her boots touched ground the same moment she said, "Maud. Good to see you. Everything all right?"

Yep. To the point. Just like her pa.

I dug around in my coat pocket, extracted the burnt match, held it up like a hard-won medal. We gathered around peering at it as if that splinter of wood held the world's secrets. "Found this yesterday in a burned book." I glanced at Penelope and then Mr. Plunkett. "Hadn't seen it before, but I'm thinking this lucifer caused the fire."

Mr. Plunkett touched the match like it was still hot, then picked it out of my fingers. He squinted, holding it within inches of his eyes. He grunted, raised both eyebrows, which furrowed his forehead into rows of concern. Without a word, Penelope plucked it from him and mirrored her pa. She cocked her head, leaned in and smelled the match, then straightened up.

"Match hasn't been fired recently." Penelope wiggled her nose, taking half her face with it. I would have laughed if this had been a laughing matter. She handed the lucifer to me, her pa following its path with his concerned gaze. I put it back into my coat pocket.

"Where'd you say you found it?" Pa ran a meaty hand across his face, which needed a shave about three days ago.

"In the debris." I shrugged. "Nudged a singed book then noticed this stuck in it."

They nodded in unison. Pa pointed toward my coat pocket. "I'd say you found the culprit, Sheriff. Them lucifers, what with their white phosphorous, burn hotter than those new safety matches dipped in red phosphorous. This one, sure as shootin', could have started a fire big enough to take down a schoolhouse."

Penelope wiped her hands on her jacket. "He could be right, Maud. Makes sense." She nodded at Pa. "Guess I need to get to town and check the school again. Might find something else."

"Now? You goin' now?" Pa flapped his arms like he was trying to fly. "What about the barn?" He pointed to the toolbox all trussed up, ready to go to the roof.

"Won't be long, Pa. Besides, the town needs me." Penelope buttoned her jacket, shook out her skirt, which had been tucked into the top of her boots and started toward town.

"Back in two shakes of a lamb's tail." She stopped and smiled. "Wonder how long that is exactly?"

I wondered too, but again... that's English.

* * *

WE KICKED, toed, dug, moved ashes and lifted timbers until we resembled coal miners I'd seen pictures of. At least we were above ground, which counted for something, but managed to get this dirty. I'd need a proper bath, I figured, to return to my original color. Maybe Penelope and I could wash up at my house, since she had so much farther to go.

What we found was exactly what we'd found before—nothing of any consequence. So, why the match now? That exact question did a slow burn in the back of my brain, moving forward throughout the morning until it took over all other thoughts. My obsession had a stranglehold on rational questions such as: which pie to have today? Will I see Seth next? Or is Mr. Marvelous going to ask me out tonight? None of that mattered.

At times like this, I hated my brain. Turncoat.

I held up a gloved hand now richly coated with old leaves, dirt and soot. "That's it. We're not going to find anything else." I pointed toward the book where I'd found the single clue. "Guess we should be happy I located the match."

"Least we got that." Penelope wiped sooty hands on her coat kicking at one final blackened bench leg. "I agree with Pa. Think you found the cause."

Standing for a moment, studying the debris field around

me, I considered her words. All right. We've found how it started. Now... who? And then... why? Would we ever know?

We trudged toward town, Seth meeting us halfway.

"There you are. Been looking all over. Gotta come quick. There's a..." He thumbed back over his shoulder toward town. "A..." Stepping back, he eyed me, then Penelope, his gaze trailing head to toe, toe to head. He inched away.

"There's a what?" I moved closer.

The look on his face melted from wide eyes to squints as his head and shoulders jerked right and left as if he couldn't decide whether to run or laugh. "Got a bit of dirt there on you, Maud." He rubbed his own left cheek and addressed Penelope. "Uh, you, too."

All the sarcasm I'd ever known threatened to spew out and engulf Seth. But my brain had taken an obsession break and chose to be civil. "Thanks, Seth. I tend to get dirty when I've been *working*."

Was that pithy enough? Did he deserve it? Probably not.

Penelope jumped in like she'd rehearsed our routine. "Maud and I were comin' over to your office soon's we cleaned up. Got something important to show you."

Shaking his head, Seth, who appeared to have his sea legs under him finally, stammered and pointed again. "Quick, Maud. 'Fore it gets ugly."

"What gets ugly?"

He grabbed my coat sleeve and tugged. "Them."

Bolting toward town, he sputtered and stammered trying to answer a barrage of questions, Penelope and me navigating the dirt road, our skirts held in one hand while scrubbing our faces with the other. Our efforts more than likely smeared the soot around.

And then... I heard them before I saw them.

A sizeable clot of women and a few confused-looking men mingled in the center of Main, all holding signs above their heads. Voices, loud and strong, sailed down the street.

"A woman's place is in the home!"

"Down with women in business!"

"Who's minding her children?"

"She should be home cooking!"

Not in many lifetimes would I have seen this coming. How could women turn on other women? I'm sure I stood mouth open, eyes wide, head tilting, my entire body numb. I regained some feeling in my head while I counted at least eight women and three men, along with a variety of small children and dogs. Chickens, always roaming the street, had the good sense to run off and hide.

Signs, crudely written, reflected their chants. The largest proclaimed:

Business. No place for women!

Seth nudged me closer to the crowd, my feet unwilling to join the melee. Nevertheless, I stood near a woman whom I took for the leader, one I'd seen in the mercantile.

"Simmer down! All of you!" I hollered.

No reaction. I hollered louder. "Everyone! Stop!"

Nothing. In fact, their backs were to me, all faces pointed toward downtown. I pulled the Colt from the holster, cocked it, aimed at the sky, and pulled the trigger.

Bang!

They jumped and spun like a frog on a hot griddle. The herd all turned to me at once, eyes wide, staring and snorting like they were ready to run through the nearest fence. A few pointed their signs at me.

"It's all your fault!" One of them yelled. Others joined in, chanting. "Your fault! Your fault!"

Holstering the gun, I glanced at Penelope and then Seth, both of them smarter than me, who had stepped back from my side, now standing a yard or more behind. All right. I put on an imaginary wide-brimmed Stetson and polished my badge. I was sheriff. And in charge. Straightening my shoulders and standing tall as possible, I moved in. I didn't have far to go but stepping in showed my courage. I hoped.

Holding up both hands, I raised my voice. "What's going on here?"

One woman elbowed her way to the front. "Women don't belong running a business. They belong in the house."

"Yeah," another pushed her way through. "They're takin' men's jobs."

"Soon all the men'll be out of work!" A third one hollered.

"Then how are men gonna take care of us?" A woman in the back shrugged, her sign bobbing up and down.

"It ain't lady-like to be running a business." The first lady stuck her nose up high. "Gives us women a bad name." She turned to the person next to her. "Imagine. Doing a man's job!"

A woman jammed her hand on her hip. "It just isn't seemly!"

At long last a man in the crowd had the courage to speak. "Next thing ya know, they'll be wanting the vote!"

"And come in our saloons!"

That was met with a smattering of chagrin, mainly from the men who'd gathered around to watch the spectacle.

Penelope's long legs carried her up next to me. I guessed she'd had enough.

"Nothin' wrong with owning a business and being female." Penelope took a long breath in and held it. "We can do both."

Again, the crowd pointed their signs at me. "Your fault."

Knowing I had to get a handle on this bunch or the jail cells would soon be full, I stepped up onto the closest boardwalk making me about six inches higher. It would have to do. Seth stepped up next to me, bless his heart.

I held up my hands—again—waiting for the crowd to calm. Two of them did but the rest—dousing a fire with oil would've done the same thing. They erupted. Chanting, promises of boycotts, even threats of bodily harm bulleted toward me.

They moved in like a rabid pack. I swear I could see fangs dripping with drool.

"What's going on here?" Harvey Weinberg's booming voice echoed from down the street.

The crowd spun, now facing Harvey, Ian and Slim marching up the middle of the road.

"Just a friendly discussion with the fine citizens," I hollered over heads. The pack turned back to me.

Seth whispered in my ear. "Better get this broken up right now, Maud."

"And exactly how, Mr. Mayor?"

Penelope joined us on the boardwalk, her height a real advantage. She could see over most heads. "How about offering them something?"

And then I had it. I leaned down to where I was even with the leader, a brassy woman. "How about you and some of the others here, plan a dance? Hosted by the city, so we'll pick up the bill." I eyed the three town councilmen now within ten yards and pointed at them. "They've been wanting to host a dance all year, just never found the right person to make it happen. I think you'd be ideal."

"A dance?" She lowered her sign and looked around, probably deciding whether she'd bring her husband or not. "With me in charge?"

I nodded so hard my neck hurt. "You and a couple of your friends can pick the date and the place. The town'll get a band and I'm sure the new bakery could provide refreshments."

The crowd quieted, listening in on what we said. Murmurs of *dance* floated around the group. A few of the women now smiled, nodding.

Seth picked up on the strategy. "Bet Mr. Swensen would let us use his barn."

"And I know a fiddle player who'd come." Penelope pulled an imaginary bow over imaginary strings.

Ian, Slim and Harvey elbowed their way to the front.

"What's goin' on here, Sheriff?" Harvey scowled and mopped his face.

"The ladies are busy putting together a dance. A rip snortin' barn dance. Like you all've wanted." I eyed each councilman in turn. "And the town's footing the bill."

CHAPTER TWENTY-ONE
EYES ON YOU...

"A DANCE? YOU PROMISED THOSE OLD BIDDIES A dance?" Harvey's outstretched arm waved up and down, his pointed finger aimed first toward the closed door, then toward me. "What on earth possessed you to do that?" His Hassidic curls bounced like coiled springs on too much coffee.

"What were ya thinkin'?" Ian tapped his forehead so hard his finger left dents in his skin. "Not much, 'tis what it was."

We stood in Seth's office, Penelope, Seth, the three wise windbags, and me, which left little breathing room. Although Seth had enough chairs for everyone, we all chose to stay on our feet, each claiming our own corner of the world.

Slim Higginbotham, my posse-riding friend, the only one of the town blowhards to help me capture bank robbers, cleared his throat. He scrubbed his face like he had leftover breakfast applesauce on it, his gaze trailing from person to person. Taking two deep breaths, letting them out like a steam engine about to chug out of town, Slim began.

"What Maud did was right."

A hush fell over the group. I gave my full attention to

Slim, hoping what he had to say would put an end to harassment by the other two town officials.

"That could've been ugly, out there." Slim pointed where Harvey had. "Those... *women* were looking for trouble. It's surprising they're not all in jail right now." He turned his eyes on Ian. "If it wasn't for Maud's quick thinking, come next election you'd be voted out of office."

"They can't vote, Slim." Harvey's finger thumped on Seth's desk. "They can't do much damage."

"Maybe they can't vote," I lowered my voice. "But their husbands can." Frowns and harrumphs parade across the men's faces. Ian pursed his lips.

"But women shouldn't be ownin' businesses." Ian brought himself all the way to his full height. He looked up into faces. "Their place is in the home. Cookin', cleanin', raisin' babies."

"And they do." I couldn't help myself. I knew to stay quiet, let the men strut, but despite the voice of reason telling me to shut up, I spoke anyway. "They do all that *and* run successful businesses. They keep house, cook supper and bake breads and pastries. Some teach those 'babies' how to say please and thank you and how to run a successful home. And others will be helping those children read by printing a newspaper."

"It's bad for business," Harvey sputtered. "When they should be buying for their homes, they're busy elsewhere doin' men's jobs."

Not one to keep quiet, Penelope jumped in. "Buying what, Mr. Weinberg? Mr. MacKinney? Aren't the bakery women buying flour, sugar and lard from your mercantiles? More goods than ever before, just so Dry Creek can have sweets with their coffee? I'd say that's good for business." She faced Slim. "And you think men'll come into your saloon and read the newspaper over a beer or shot of whiskey?"

Seth, who'd been silent until now, edged closer to me. "Penelope's got a point. New businesses are good for Dry

Creek, and with Maud plotting a dance now, I don't see the harm." He leaned his rear end against his desk. "A barn dance is just what this town needs. What we didn't need were those women marching down the street."

Using all my muscles, I kept myself from hugging Seth right then and there. Instead, I smiled, wide enough my cheeks ached.

"Besides," Penelope soldiered on. "Those women will be buying new dresses, shoes maybe, even new material to sew fancy clothes for this dance. They'll be buying it from...?" Her poignant pause was just right. "*You*. Both of you. So, I think we should give Maud a round of applause for her great idea."

Penelope clapped and tossed in a few "here heres." Seth joined in, then Slim and finally a couple of lackluster congratulatory attempts by Ian and Harvey.

* * *

THE EUPHORIC FEELING didn't last long. On the way back to the office, my boots skimming along the surface, I spotted the fella off yesterday's stage. Carpetbag in hand, he walked up Main, tipping his hat to the women along the way and nodding to the men. Something about him simply put me off. He was up to no good, I could feel it, and I was determined to find out what. So, I did what any other sheriff who wanted to keep their town safe would do.

I followed him.

Keeping my distance, I wended my way up the board-walk, passing a clot of women standing in front of Ian's Dry Creek Mercantile, where I caught whiffs of *material* and *dance* on their conversation. I smiled inside but kept my eyes on Mr. Nathaniel Ford, if that, indeed, was his real name. He wasn't going to get away with any mischief in this town. No siree. I dogged his every step.

He stopped to chat with a man who then pointed toward the Dry Creek Café, our newest eating establishment, opened earlier this summer. In fact, it was only one of two places to get a meal, and from what I'd heard, was doing well. I ate there rarely, opting more for the older, homey Shoo Fly Restaurant, simply out of habit and because I knew the waitress.

Ford touched the brim of his hat, looked right and left, stepped into our dusty, rutted Main Street and managed not to get run down by a wagon full of hay and then by two horses whose riders nodded to him. On busy days like this, it was taking your life in your hands simply to cross the street. Gripping my skirt, hiking it up high enough not to trip on it or let it drag in the dirt, I followed this latest miscreant into the Dry Creek Café.

He took a seat at a table directly under the window facing Main and flashed a wide smile at the youngster who handed him a menu. A menu? Dry Creek was undeniably becoming progressive now that we had printed menus. In the other restaurant, the fare was written on an easel black-board resting on a table. They changed the meals often judging by the chalk smudges, making it hard to read whether it said pork sandwich or pork sawdust. Neverthe-less, it always worked well, no second guessing about what you could order, but deep down I admitted I felt so... so *fancy* with a paper list of offered cuisine.

I pulled my attention away from menus and took a seat two tables behind him. The young lady handed me my own menu and I spent way too long deciding on coffee. My stomach wouldn't entertain the notion of food right now. I was too excited, being on this caper. Besides, I'd need to keep attention on my quarry, not on how good the ham sandwich was or how the cook had added the right amount of herbs and seasoning to the mashed potatoes. No, I had to maintain.

Absently, I licked my lips when the waitress took the coffee order. Before she waltzed away, I couldn't help myself. I lowered my voice and ordered a steaming mound of mashed potatoes, admittedly a favorite food.

I couldn't tell what Mr. Ford had ordered, but he was served coffee when I was. He sipped, blew across the cup, sipped again. For whatever reason, I mirrored him. Sip, blow, sip. Cup down. A big breath in. Little one out. Cup up. Sip, blow, sip. Cup down.

Before I knew it, the waitress stopped at his table, set a plate with a sandwich and pickles on it, sliding it along. Another sip and my cup was empty, but a mound of mashed potatoes sat in front of me. The waitress poured more coffee as I kept an eye on how the stranger bit into his sandwich. Nothing sinister there, chewing like normal people. He wiped his mouth with a cloth napkin, took another bite.

Possibly not paying enough attention to feeding myself, I brought my forkful of potatoes to my mouth, stabbed my lip. The pain jerked me back in my seat.

"Ow!" Had I said that aloud? Apparently so, since the patrons, including Mr. Ford, turned eyes on me. He gave a slight wave before returning to his food. I rubbed my lower lip then thought to use a napkin. I daubed and silently cursed.

After what felt like days, customers returned to their own meals with me left feeling the fool. But I had to admit —despite a few lumps, those potatoes were tasty.

Finished with his meal, Ford pushed back from the table, stood, pulled out coins from his vest pocket and tossed them on the table. He placed his napkin on his plate, picked up his hat and bag, and stepped away.

And aimed right for me.

He stopped at my table. Using his hat to point, he nodded at the empty chair across from me. "Mind if I alight a while, Sheriff?" He flashed a wide smile. "Questions are vexing me and I feel you could adequately address them."

So, I'd been made. Here it was, my first time ever stalking a criminal, and I'd blown my cover. I nodded, words failing me.

Sitting with an air of authority, he carefully placed his bowler hat crown down on the table and nodded at the lone forkful of potatoes sitting in the middle of the plate. "Good?"

His sepia-colored eyes, lightly bloodshot, trailed over my face.

My head bobbed while full sentences played hide and seek with my mouth.

"Oh, I understand. How rude of me. Sorry," Ford said, his voice higher than most men's. "Impolite to speak with a mouthful of food." He leaned back in the chair. "So, I'm looking to open up a business here in town. Who should I speak with about that?"

What was it with businesses all of a sudden? Why did everyone feel the urge to become an entrepreneur? I held up my fork while chewing and thinking. How could I discourage such a low life man from starting a business here in town? A sip of coffee and I knew he was expecting conversation.

"What sort of business, Mr. Ford?" Maybe it would be something we already had or something we didn't need.

Ford dug around in his vest pocket, pulled out a small card and pushed it across the table. Dark black, fancy lettering read:

Nathaniel Ford, SPFA
San Francisco, New York, Chicago

So, I was immediately impressed. I'd never seen a real calling card before. Anybody who carried those must be important. Maybe I'd been wrong about this man, my badge devilishly getting the better of me. I decided right then and there I'd give him a chance to explain himself, even with his big, fancy words. If I didn't like what I heard, I'd lock him up or buy him a one-way ticket out of town. Besides, I had no earthly idea what SPFA meant.

"You been to all these places, Mr. Ford?"

"Indeed. Our offices are in many cities, but the size of

my card allows me to list only these three." One side of his mouth slid into a coy grin. "Have you?"

"San Francisco." Why was I allowing myself to be suckered into friendly banter with this villain? Despite his oiliness, something about him drew me in. Something, again, raised tiny bumps on the back of my neck.

"Beautiful city, San Francisco." He smiled full out, his mouth full of too-white teeth, then leaned closer as his face grew serious. "But don't ever call it 'Frisco'. People there hate that. For them, it's all or nothing."

Even *I* knew that.

Now with the plate clean, mashed potatoes swallowed, coffee mug half full, I pulled my shoulders back and sat taller. "What sort of business you looking to start?" Involuntarily, my eyebrows bunched. "We've already got just about any kind you can think of."

"That is true. And a delightful town it is." He slid the card closer to me. "I strolled around this morning taking in the bracing air and liked very much what I saw."

Where was he going with this? I agreed there was much to like about Dry Creek, but how could someone ascertain that in fifteen hours, most of which were more than likely spent sleeping?

"There is unquestionably one business lacking, Sheriff. In fact, this town is sorely in need of such." He leaned back surveying the inside of the café. "Lovely eatery."

"It's new." Now, why did I have to blurt that out? Why would he care?

His eyes lit up like sparklers. "You don't say. Then they most definitely need my services." He leaned across the table, lowered his voice like he was telling a secret. "As you can tell by my card, I sell insurance. Life, property, fire. A place like this, what with its wooden structure, kitchen with open flames, is prime for a fire. I'd genuinely hate like the blazes..." Another smile blossomed. "Sorry. 'Blazes' wasn't the right euphemism... hate like the dickens to see this fine establishment burn without any monetary recompense."

Big words. The man used outrageous big words and most I knew what they meant. But even if I didn't, I wouldn't let on. The one thing I did know was insurance was becoming a substantial deal, especially after that terrible fire in Chicago last year. I'd read over 300 people were killed and over half the city destroyed. He was right. I'd hate to stand around fiddling while Rome burned.

I couldn't help but grin. More English phrases.

While I pondered, I sipped the remainder of the coffee, now bordering on luke-warm, and puzzled over his words. This man, his business intention, was not something to be discussed over cold coffee. No, Seth or even my Mr. Handsomely-Marvelous and I needed to sit in a real office and discuss.

"Tell you what, Mr. Ford." If that was a real name. "Let's go down to the mayor's office. I'll introduce you to him and we can talk there." I stood, hoping I wouldn't stand on my skirt. I hated when that happened. *So* ungraceful.

"Grand idea, Sheriff." Ford plucked his hat from the table, stood and gripped his carpetbag. "Tell you what. I need to register at the boarding house, so I'll meet you at the mayor's. Direct me to his office and I'll join you promptly."

He opened the café door like a true gentleman waiting for me to sweep through like those queens I'd seen in picture books. We stood on the boardwalk while I pointed toward Seth's.

Nodding, he started off then turned back. "Sheriff Overstreet."

I hadn't moved, keeping an eye on him until this miscreant had strode off. He walked back the few steps he'd already taken, ending up standing close to me. So close, in fact, I smelled Bay Rum aftershave on him. The same smell Aldridge had. Immediately, I froze. Could it be? And then I remembered. Both Seth and Pa used the same cologne. It was by far the most popular sold, so it seemed logical Mr. Ford would use it too. I relaxed, but just a bit.

"I'm wondering, Sheriff." Ford glanced up and down the street. "How did a lovely creature such as yourself, become sheriff? I'm thrilled the town had the good sense to appoint you, but isn't it rather unusual for a woman to enforce the law?"

"I wasn't appointed, got elected a couple months ago." I wasn't about to tell him I'd been duped by the town councilors who thought my being a lawman—a *lady* of the law—would be good for business. Like a circus sideshow, it would bring in outsiders to gawk at the woman who would be sheriff. And they were right, men and women drove into town to buy items they didn't need or have a drink or two they claimed were necessary for their well-being. But the tables were turned when I actually caught a gang of bank robbers. Apparently, the town's citizens were pleased enough to keep me on.

"Unusual, indeed." Ford tipped his hat to me and a woman squeezing to get past, then turned. "Within the hour," he said over his shoulder.

CHAPTER TWENTY-TWO
WHERE THERE'S FIRE, THERE'S...

SETH AND I WAITED FOR THIS SUPPOSED businessman to appear by passing time chatting and catching up on the past day's events. We laughed at the expression on the three councilor's faces when I announced a dance. I allowed as we'd turned that riot's tide real quick and got the drop on the three ol' windbags.

"Truth be told, I *am* looking forward to the dance, Seth." I relaxed into my chair in front of his desk, thoughts of Seth's and Aldridge's arms around me as we swayed to the music flirted in my head. "Haven't danced in... well, maybe a year or two." Maybe a lot more than that, but I couldn't think back that far without hurting my head or heart. I'd planned to dance at the wedding of Eli and me, but that scoundrel decided to rob the bank, instead. Not only did he take the town's money, but he also stole my future. Until I became sheriff and met Aldridge Armstrong.

"... have been here by now." Seth checked his pocket watch. "Don't ya think?"

Attention back on Seth and the here and now, I figured he was talking about Nathaniel Ford. The *late* Mr. Ford. Then I reconsidered. I didn't want him dead. Think of all the paperwork and aggravation I'd have to go through figuring what to do with the body. No, it was better if he was alive.

"Just late. Probably stopped to chat with somebody, try to sell them insurance. You know those kinds of elixir pushers can't resist a chance to make a dollar." I was about to open my mouth to expound on the lack of virtues of such salesmen when a knock at the door stopped me.

Seth opened it and in stepped Nathaniel Ford. Part of my brain let out a silent sigh. No dumb paperwork to do after all.

Ford took the chair Seth pointed to, which was next to mine. I nodded a greeting as Ford opened his leather satchel and pulled out a thin stack of papers. Without much fanfare, he launched into his spiel, making direct eye contact first with Seth and then with me.

"And you can see by the insurance figures there," Ford tapped his finger on the papers he'd splayed on Seth's desk. "No doubt the fine citizens of Dry Creek need fire insurance, what with the beautiful but woody trees and shingled roofs and such." He sucked in a small bit of air and continued. "I mean, this town is beautiful, stunning really. And I'd hate—"

"To see it go up in flames." Seth finished Ford's sentence. "Got that. But just how does having insurance keep the church, for example, from burning? Or old man Elder's barn? Or Maud's..." He pulled in air and looked up at me. "I mean the sheriff's office? What you're offering isn't protection from fire."

"No sir, it isn't. Only God can offer that service."

I forced my eyes not to roll. He meant well and I couldn't help but marvel at his enthusiasm for his product, whatever that was. He hadn't gotten around to spelling it out yet.

"What I *am* offering, in case God isn't watching, is relief from total financial ruin in case of fire, flood or death." Ford pointed at the closed door. "Those fine citizens deserve to know that in the event calamity befalls them, at least they have a financial net to return them to their feet. Those hardworking, God-fearing town folk are entitled to being able to breathe easy at the end of the day knowing their efforts will not be in vain. Their labors will remain upright and yet, even if they do succumb to disaster, my company will be there to recompense their property loss."

Seth and I looked at each other, desperate not to burst out laughing. I'd never heard anybody, not even a traveling preacher we'd had come through last year, chew his words as fine as this Nathaniel Ford. If he'd been a politician, he'd without doubt give our own three blowhards a run for their money. This man was the finest yawn I'd ever heard.

Seth ran a hand across his freshly shaved face, his mustache falling neatly back into shape, sort of like a furry caterpillar draped over his top lip. The look from his sensitive eyes, which at times melted my toes, locked on mine. I knew what he was thinking. I had the same thoughts.

Seth slid his gaze to Ford. "How's that work, exactly?"

Ford puffed himself up. "For a minimal monthly fee, we guarantee to pay a percentage of the value of their property should something untoward happen."

Before I could jump in with a question, Ford rambled on. "There are certain limitations, of course. Such as an act of God. We can't cover those calamities."

"Act of God?" I'm sure my mouth flopped open. "Such as...?"

"Lightning." Ford held up one finger, then another. "Earthquake. Hordes of locust."

I laughed out loud despite my attempt to hold it in. "Locust?"

Ford raised one eyebrow so high it brushed the hair hanging over his forehead. "Young lady, all sorts of plague and pestilence happen. We can't insure what God deems necessary to help cleanse the earth."

Leaning forward, Seth used one finger to point at Ford. "So, you're proposing a business that plays on people's fears?"

"You're taking their money," I asked, "hoping nothing happens to their property, so you don't have to pay out?" Sure sounded like a racket of the finest kind to me. Dry

Creek didn't need nor want that sort of business. I knew I didn't.

"Life's a gamble, Sheriff." Ford shuffled the papers bringing one with a picture to the top. He held it up. "See this medallion here?" He showed it to me and then Seth.

An iron circle, about dinner plate size, sported an embossed red pumper fire truck in the middle with the initials F.D. Co. across the bottom. It also read 1835.

"Buildings that are under our company's protection get a medallion, much like this one displayed in Boston, to put on the front of their buildings. This helps the fire department know if they're insured or not. And helps us know, as well."

My mouth went dry, my heart filled my chest. "So, you're telling us, Mr. Ford, that our fire department should only put out fires of buildings you've insured?" I stood, gathering my skirt and indignation. "What kind of business are you running?"

Ford leaped to his feet, one hand held up, the other still clutching the picture. "No, wait. You misunderstand me." His gaze flitted from me to Seth and back. "These medallions are our way of advertising. That's all. Nothing nefarious of the sort. We sincerely wish no building to be harmed, none at all. But, with Nature and people being who they are, things happen. Accidents happen. All we do is offer the chance to rebuild if an unfortunate incident were to occur."

Yeah, right. I wasn't convinced, but the look on Seth's face made me back off a bit. He was considering and, for Seth, that was a big event. Usually, he simply reacted.

Silence engulfed the room. I remained on my feet as did Ford. After what felt like years but in reality was probably half a minute, Seth let out a long breath and rose. He stood behind his desk.

"Mr. Ford, I'd like you to speak with our three town councilors. They are all businessmen as well as city officials. I'd like to get their take on your business." Seth dropped his voice. "Of course, I can't prevent you from opening up shop.

After all, it's a free country. But maybe this new idea is worthwhile and maybe it isn't." He pointed toward the door. "I'll need to think on it. In the meantime, let's set up a meeting with the councilors."

"Would this evening be a possibility?" Ford shuffled his papers, stuffing them back into the satchel. "I'd like to get this fantastic opportunity for the public going as soon as possible."

"I'll see what I can do." Seth shook hands with Ford while I nodded. He returned my nod with a tip of his hat and left the room.

I stood for a bit watching the door close. Seth eased around the desk and stood shoulder to shoulder with me. We both studied the door.

Half a minute later, my shoulders bounced up and down with chortles wallowing around in my throat. I looked over at Seth. "What just happened?"

"Whatever it was," he said, "it was a daisy."

* * *

I STEPPED into the afternoon air glad I'd worn a warm coat. I pulled it tighter. My ears and nose tingled with cold, but the rest of me was toasty. Not a cloud in the sky meant nothing kept the warmth in. It would be cold tonight, probably the coldest yet this fall.

Walking down the boardwalk headed for my office, I checked off a list of things still left to do today. First, see how the newspaper venture was coming along. Second, find Pokey and talk to him about the mail and his Chinese girlfriend. Ever since the dinner disaster, I hadn't seen much of him or her for that matter. Third, I decided to talk to Pa about this new insurance business. Maybe his bank would be interested and maybe he'd know more about this than I did.

"Hey there, Sheriff."

I must've jumped ten feet while I spun around and

slapped at my pistol in the holster under my coat. Heart drumming in my chest, I grabbed for it while recognizing the source of the voice. Aldridge, my gorgeous gentleman friend, had come up behind me and whispered in my ear.

What I wanted to do was collapse in his arms, let them wrap me in security, then bathe me with his warm, passionate kisses. Instead, I stood still, smiling, like a simpleton.

"Sorry if I startled you." Aldridge gripped my right arm. "Thought you saw me coming."

Shaking my head, partly to end the rattling in there and partly to tell him I'd been too busy thinking to take notice, I pulled in a long lungful of air. "Good to see you. Sorry. I was a bit preoccupied."

"Guess you were." He released my arm. "I'd been searching all over for you. Again. You seem to be an expert at hiding."

I thumbed behind me toward the mayor's office. "Had a meeting—"

"That's fine. I know you're an important part of this community. It's just that it seems you're all over every-where." He held out one long leg. "Least I get good exercise by looking for you."

My thoughts were still back at Seth's with Ford and his business proposal. Maybe Aldridge would know something about insurance. After all, he'd been in San Francisco and Sacramento. Bigger towns than Dry Creek. I looked up at Mr. Wonderful. "Want to get some coffee? Something's come up, and I could use someone else's opinion."

Aldridge pulled a silver filigreed pocket watch out of his vest, opened it, cocked his head, then snapped it shut. "Got a meeting in less than an hour. But I'd love coffee and maybe a pastry over at the bakery?"

He had me at pastry. My sweet tooth was rarely sated and one of Hilda's Swiss strudels would be wonderful right about now. I couldn't help but lick my lips.

We ambled toward the new bakery. Aldridge mentioned

a meeting with Mae and two leaders of the Chinese community. We took the last two empty seats, ordering strudel and coffee, as we sat. Aldridge explained.

"It's moving forward nicely, Maud. The school for Chinese girls."

I perked up. This was something on my list I hadn't managed to get to yet.

"The leaders, Tan Po and Yuan Zhou, have been reluctant to send girls to school. In their country, girls didn't need an education."

"But," heat rushed to my cheeks. "They need knowledge in *this* country. If they're going to succeed in America, they—"

"I'm not arguing with you. I totally agree. This is what Mae and I will be telling them. Mae will give examples of how the Chinese community can grow with educated women." Aldridge's passion for the topic rounded out each word.

Hilda slid a cup of coffee, its heavenly aroma swirling under my nose, in front of me, followed by a wedge of flaky-crusted strudel. Apple, if the fruit peeking out was any indication. All conversation stopped as Aldridge and I each raised a fork. I slid the ambrosia into my mouth. My eyes closed. How could anything be this scrumptious? Not as scrumptious as Aldridge, of course, but close.

After the piece of heaven made its way down my throat, I opened my eyes and looked at my beau. His eyes were still closed. I smiled, then picked up the cup. While delicious, the coffee ranked second to the strudel.

We talked a few minutes about the insurance business, but at that moment, it didn't seem to have the urgency I'd experienced earlier. Apparently, the influence and confluence of strudel and Aldridge smoothed out the wrinkles of concern.

By the time our plates were scraped clean, coffee cups drained, it was time to go. We lingered out on the boardwalk in front of the bakery.

"Let me know how the meeting goes." I wanted to attend with him, but Aldridge had assured me my presence wasn't necessary.

"And," Aldridge tipped his hat. "Let's talk more about this insurance business. Seems like a good idea to me." With that, he gave an ever-so slight bow, turned on his heels and marched up the street.

Wheels rattled and horses' hooves thundered behind me. I spun around just as Pokey and his mail run trotted up the road. That wooden wagon, beige tarp covering the mail, slowed as it passed. Pokey, both hands busy with entwined reins, shouted.

"Howdy, Maud! Just got back!"

"Welcome home!" I hollered, but he was already too far away to hear. He'd pull up at the mail station at the end of town, jump down and unload the day's mail and newspapers. As much as I was curious as to what had come in, I was tired and ready to go home. Tomorrow was another day.

CHAPTER TWENTY-THREE
LUCK OF THE...DRAW?

AFTERNOON SUN LIT POKEY'S BACK AS HE OPENED the office door and stuck his head in. "Maud?" He then pushed his whole body on through, closing the door as gentle as if he were stroking a purring cat. "Maud?"

I spotted my sometimes deputy over the pile of papers on my desk. Apparently, they multiplied faster than any horde of rabbits ever could. These stacks hadn't been on my desk this morning. Must've come in on yesterday's mail run. Pokey's visit would provide a wonderful distraction from dreaded paperwork. Reports to fill out and file with the county; monthly reports to the town councilors; semi-annual reports to the state. Not to mention combing through the wanted posters sent by the boys over in Sacramento. So far, nobody had slipped in a note. By now, I figured, it was boys playing a joke on me. At least I hoped so.

Welcoming Pokey, I pointed to the coffee pot perched on the stove in the corner. "While you're getting a cup, how about one for me?" I hoped my well-honed, turned down mouth and fluttering eyelashes would get me a cup without having to actually get up myself.

"Course, Maud. Glad to."

Pokey's nod and half smile made me suspicious. What was he up to that he was so happy? Not that he ever denied me my coffee. He was a good soul and a dependable right-hand man. But I'd not seen him this happy, contented in a long time. I'd have to credit Mae and, deep down part of me had to think that good luck amulet he always wore around his neck had something to do with it. He believed in it, so why shouldn't I?

After setting the steaming tin cup on my desk, he chinned toward the papers stacked on each corner. "Sorry 'bout that. I brought 'em over this morning, but you weren't here." He eased into a wooden chair in front, his usual place to sit. "Looks like you got your hands full."

I blew then sipped. "Sure do. Wanna help?" The coffee slid down my throat, warming my insides and my mood.

"Sure would like to, Maud. Sure would." He set his cup down on papers covering the desk, studied one, then his eyes trailed over the entire desk and at long last, up to me. "I would," he said, "but I got a terrible lot to do myself." He aimed his cup toward town.

"Like what?" Part of me was aggravated, the other part understood. He had the mail run, his job sweeping up at Otis' Mercantile, and Mae to court, which was a full-time job on its own, seeing as she was Chinese. Pokey walked a fine line in both cultures, and it couldn't be easy. Then again, I had Mr. Amazing to court. Without a doubt it was keeping me busy, what with going to dinner and having coffee and strudel. I started to lick my lips, hoping the taste was still there somewhere when Pokey answered my almost-forgotten question.

"This good luck amulet sure is working!" He leaned forward and pulled the talisman out from under his vest. He studied it. Love and admiration and a touch of awe radiated on his face. "Just got me a promotion." He looked up at me. "Mr. Otis put me on full time. Gave me a raise, too!"

While a bit shocked, I was possibly more stunned. Gunnar Otis didn't give anything to anybody. He was an

honest businessman who liked to support the community—
as long as it didn't cost him anything. Allowing Pokey to
sleep in a room at the back of the store was above and
beyond what I'd expected of him when we first met. My
suspicions were Mr. Otis related to Pokey by some means.
Possibly reminded him of somebody he knew. Or maybe of
himself. With Gunnar, one could never be sure.

"He gave you a raise?" I plopped the cup on the paperwork, a couple drops of brown liquid landing in the middle
of wanted man's forehead. "Full time? That's wonderful,
Pokey. Simply wonderful!" What I wouldn't call a dark black
cloud, more medium gray, parked itself over my head.
"What about the mail run?"

"We talked about that. As you know, I drive three times
a week." Pokey held up three fingers as if I wasn't sure how
many we were talking about. "He said one of those he'd
consider my day off, the other two I could work evenings
when I got back."

So unlike Gunnar Otis. Was something amiss? I'd have
to talk to him about this turn of events. I pressed Pokey for
answers. "Why'd he need you full time? Is business
booming?"

Both of Pokey's shoulders rose and fell. "Seems to me
more people are comin' in, but it's alright with me. I can
save what he pays me, spend what the town gives me for the
mail, and maybe in a year or so, ask Mae..." Red attacked his
cheeks. He studied his lap while his fingers intertwined with
each other, making something of a Gordian knot.

Stunned a second time, I leaned forward ever so slightly
until I was almost lying on the desk. I lowered my voice like
everyone was listening. "You're thinking of getting married?
To Mae?"

"I really like her." Pokey untangled his fingers but still
spoke to them. "And her folks seem to like me."

"But she's..." I couldn't find the right wording. "And
you're..."

"I know. But we can make it work."

Tons of reasons it wouldn't paraded across my brain. Pokey, a white man of low to moderate income, marry a Chinese girl whose father, something of a leader in his community, runs a restaurant? What could possibly go wrong there? Inter-racial marriage flat wasn't heard of, or tolerated in many towns. Dry Creek seemed to turn a blind eye to their courting because Pokey was a popular fellow, but marriage was a whole different ball game. And what if they had children? I shook my head. Oh my.

"You think it's a bad idea, Maud?" Pokey's voice had risen in pitch, grew defensive.

"Maybe we'll just run away. Or move to China."

"Hold on." I held up a hand. "I didn't say it's a *bad* idea. You just need to tread lightly. There's plenty of time to talk about this. Have you discussed it with Mae, yet?"

Pokey shook his head. "I want to save enough money and surprise her. Think she'll say yes?"

What could I say to that? "I have no idea. She's obviously fond of you. But you've only been courting, what, a few months? Give it time." All of a sudden I sounded like a mother hen protecting her chick. Was this what getting old felt like?

"All I know is," Pokey eased to his feet, cup still in hand, "is I think she's swell. And I'm gonna work hard to show her and the town. I'll make money." His honey brown eyes flared with passion. "I'll make enough to buy us a house. Right here in Dry Creek if she wants. And money to open up a store. Like Mr. Otis's."

To say I was more stunned than before would be wrong. Shocked, maybe. Taken aback, possibly. What happened to the old Pokey I knew? That sweet kid whose goal in life was to belong to a family and get enough to eat? I rethought. At twenty-five he wasn't technically a 'kid,' but something about him was young and innocent. Maybe you change like that when you fall in love. Had I changed as well? Not that I'd noticed, but then again, my infatuation with Mr.

Wonderful was young yet and I was older than Pokey by ten years. Plus, Pokey and Mae had a good month or two on us. I changed my line of questioning.

"You think you'll have enough time for Mae if you work full time and drive the mail coach?"

Pokey's cheeks, which had just returned to their normal tanned light pink, flushed again.

His gaze swept the floor, the walls, the door and then me. His head bobbed. "Got a couple nights free. And we're going to that dance."

Uh oh. I hadn't seen that one coming. It would be interesting to see how the town, especially those self-important biddies, would react when Pokey came sashaying in with Mae on his arm. It would be a test like no other this town had seen for a while. In a way, I felt sorry for him. Pokey had no idea what could happen, what a hornet's nest he'd poked. But, on the other hand, if their relationship were to continue and thrive, they'd have to face facts. People were prejudiced. Some more than others.

"Maud, I gotta go." Pokey threw back the last of his coffee. "Just wanted to come by and tell you the good news." He plopped the cup on the desk as he pushed up to his feet.

I bolted from the chair and gave him a tight hug. "I'm so pleased for you."

If his cheeks could have glowed, they would have. He beamed enough to challenge the sun. Opening the door, he then stopped, holding out his good luck amulet still around his neck. "I just gotta get you one of these."

With that, he nodded, stepped out, closed the door with confidence.

I sat back down, mulling over his visit. While he gave the amulet credit, I figured it was Pokey, the man. He worked hard, was honest, had a solid head on his shoulders and would make Mae, or whoever, a fine husband. Fleetingly, I wondered if I could be as lucky.

Maybe there *was* something to that amulet, after all.

* * *

Two HOURS into the paperwork marathon, I pushed my shoulders back, pulled in several deep breaths and found my feet. Twisting, my back popped so loud at first I thought it was the chair falling over. I rocked my head side to side, the neck complaining the entire time. Paperwork.

Ugh. Enough for one day, besides twilight was lengthening the shadows and, with no prisoners in either of the two cells, I could spend the night at home. I wondered what Mrs. Tran was fixing for supper. She usually cooked vegetables in a wide pan called a wok, but she was learning how to fry a steak as well as chicken. Whatever she cooked was divine. Pa and I ate together, hashing out the day's issues. Mrs. Tran would serve, then go home to cook, I assumed, for her family. In her absence, my job was to clear off the table and stack dishes. She would wash them in the morning.

Hopefully, tonight Pa and I would talk about insurance. And about Pokey. And a school for Chinese girls. And...

Maybe I should simply relax and enjoy the end of the day. All those concerns would wait for tomorrow.

Coat wrapped around my calico skirt and blouse, bonnet tied under my chin, I opened the door and a folded piece of paper slid to the ground. I assumed it had been stuck in the jamb. My heart beat harder as I opened the missive.

Final warning! Bak off.

Despite the misspelling, my shoulders pulled themselves back, my stomach clenched, and panic closed my throat. Third note. This was getting serious. I studied the letters. Different handwriting from the last two. A glance right and left up and down Main. No nefarious characters hiding in the shadows, no weasel slinking off, tossing a backward glance over his shoulder. Only a couple of men wandering into a saloon at the end of the block.

I stuck the note in with the other two, then closed the office door, locking it, this time. The *click* reverberated down the street. Quiet for this time of day, but then again, it was almost complete dark. Most people were home eating supper by now. I hoped to be one of those people soon.

On the way, as usual, I stopped in every store that wasn't closed. Generally, the shopkeepers were turning their 'open' signs around or trying to shoo out the customer who couldn't decide which shovel to buy. The bakery had been closed a good two hours by now, the charm school would have closed early afternoon, and the newspaper office sat dark.

Actually, I wasn't sure Emily was printing yet. I hadn't seen a paper and I was sure I would. It would be the talk of the town. I made a mental note to chat with Emily Penderton tomorrow, see how things were going.

For a town only now close to four hundred strong, we had five saloons, each doing a whale of a business I'd been told. Not that I went in often, especially just to have a drink. But I did stop by on occasion to make sure nothing too nefarious was going on. Dry Creek had no 'red light' district, at least that I knew of and, I was supposed to know everything, but every so often a woman of questionable virtue would frequent a saloon. The owners employed what they called bar girls and hostesses, but the only work they did was on their feet—delivering ordered drinks, laughing at ridiculous jokes and giving men a softer perspective on life. And from what I'd been told, a man or two had intended to take a bar girl upstairs, but the owner, as well as the woman, nixed that idea in short order. Faro and poker games kept the men busy and, for the most part, patrons behaved themselves.

The first four saloons I peeked into on my way to supper

were not full at all. Several tables sat empty, but the men who were in there were minding their manners. I sauntered down Main, thinking of the lack of customers. It dawned on me for a Saturday night, saloons were much too quiet. Which was fine. Quiet since gold hadn't been discovered nearby—again—and nothing especially interesting was going on. This was a typical, small-town night.

Relaxed and already mentally tasting pot roast with gravy and creamed corn, I pushed open the doors to the fifth one, Slim Higginbotham's Tin Pan Saloon. I stepped in and froze. Customers were backed against the walls, while in the center two men stood toe to toe, glaring at each other. The drawn revolvers in their hands must have been .44s as they seemed to fill up most of the room. I stared first at the guns, then at the bartender's rounded eyes. He stared back at me.

Attention now on the two men itching to kill each other, I thought I recognized one of them. Rudolfo... Garcia or something like that. The other I'd not seen before. Someone needed to do something before they pulled a trigger. More than likely somebody other than the one they aimed for would get hit. Possibly even killed. I looked around for that person to stop the gunfight.

That would be me.

With that realization, curses flew around my brain before I managed to wrangle them out of my head. What could I say or do to stop these men?

Unbuttoning my coat so I could reach my own gun, I held up my left hand and took one uneasy step farther inside. Eyes turned to me, all eyes except Rudolfo and the other fella. Their stare remained glued on each other.

"Hold everything, men." I hoped and prayed my voice was tough, imposing, confident. I hoped, also, the men would literally hold everything and not shoot. Although my body urged me to turn around and run, my feet inched forward. "Put down your guns. Let's settle your differences like gentlemen."

"He no gentlemen!" Rudolfo hollered. "Talk dirty 'bout *mi esposa!* He need killin'."

"You damn, toothless Mexican greaser!" The other man raised his revolver shoulder high. "Got no right to be in here. Go drink with your own kind."

"Cabron!"

Bang! Bang!

Rudolfo stumbled backwards, strangely managing to stay on his feet.

Bang! A streak of orange shot out of Rudolfo's gun. The other man stepped back, grabbed his upper leg, the pants material turning crimson.

Rudolfo dropped his weapon, the metallic thud on the wooden floor echoing around the hushed room. He sank to his knees and groaned.

I must've blinked a million times before my head cleared enough to make sense of what had happened. Both men on the floor, I rushed to Rudolfo, pushed his gun out of the way. The bullet had torn a hole in his coat, and when I pushed it aside, blood seeped into his shirt.

"Get the doctor!" I yelled to a man standing near the door. "Hurry!" He backed out into the darkness, to get Doc Monroe, I hoped.

The bartender edged from behind the bar, knelt by the other man. "Maud, he took a bullet in the leg."

"Get his gun, Sam."

Sam did as requested, handing it to another man standing close.

"Fred's been shot, too!" A man I sort of recognized hollered from the side. "He's bleedin' bad."

Great. Three bullets, three men. What were the odds? And where was the doc? I gazed down at Rudolfo, now in my arms. Breaths wheezed and he shook like an earthquake. I'd never seen anybody hurt this bad and, I had to admit, it scared me. Where *was* the doc?

Two or three men inched closer, one kneeling on the other side from me. I opened Rudolfo's coat revealing a blood-soaked shirt. It was bad. Sam tossed me a rag and I pressed it against his chest. At least the bullet was on the right side, so possibly it hadn't hit his heart.

Where *was* the doc? I looked around. Men milled, a few finished their drinks, some pushed through the doors into the cold night air. Rudolfo sighed, closed his eyes. Was he dead? I hoped not. Putting my hand on his chest, I felt his heart beating. Mentally, I took a deep breath. I scooted out from under him, then coerced my shaking legs to get my body upright.

Pushing through the growing crowd now coming out of the shadows, I rushed to where Fred lay, two men by his side. I knelt next to him. One of them looked over at me.

"He's dead, Maud. Not fair. He wasn't doin' anything. Just standing. Next to me." The man's bewildered blue eyes trailed up to me. His face, totally blank, confirmed exactly what I felt. How could this have happened?

Then it hit me. How could I have prevented it? I should have prevented it. Should have known what to do, what to say. It was my fault Fred died and maybe Rudolfo, too.

"Somebody get the undertaker." Had I said it out loud or mumbled like my brain said I had? Apparently I'd said it loud enough that someone announced they'd go and prod the doctor. I didn't, *couldn't* respond except for a nod.

"What's going on, Maud?" I looked up at Seth standing next to me. "Heard shooting, and then somebody ran down the street yelling about a gunfight."

He offered a hand while I regained my feet. There was nothing to do for Fred. Heaviness sat on my chest, my heart a clod of mud, my head full of confusion.

"I'll ask again." Seth leaned in closer. "What happened?"

Pressure pushing against the back of my eyes, I turned away from the mayor, struggling to make sense of it all. I pulled in lingering smoke, rubbed my eyes then choked down regret. "Two men, Rudolfo and this other fella, shot. Bullet hit Fred."

Seth slid an arm around me, pulled me close, then

released me. Like a thump on the head, I realized I was still sheriff, I still had a job to do, I still needed to be strong. I was the law and had to act like it.

The doors flew open. Dr. Smith Monroe rushed in, black bag in hand. "Who's shot?"

I pointed to all three.

CHAPTER TWENTY-FOUR
HELP WANTED...

PA AND I SAT UP MOST OF THE NIGHT TALKING AND hashing out the shooting. I reheated the mashed potatoes and chicken Mrs. Tran had put away and picked at it while we sat across from each other at our dining table. I rambled, asked questions looking to him for support and advice. He gave some and at long last, pointed to the Regulator on the wall.

"We both have a long day tomorrow. Think I'll go to church early." He stood, gathered my mostly full plate and headed for the kitchen. "'Bout time we both get some sleep. It's two."

"In the morning?" My brain denied that two came twice a day. Could I sleep at all? Most likely not, but I'd try.

We said our goodnights and I changed into my warmer flannel nightgown since nights were cold now. I blew out the candle by my bed, snuggled under the covers and closed my eyes. I wanted sleep, needed sleep, but it wouldn't come. Counting sheep didn't help, rehashing a plot of a boring book did nothing, even going over what I should write in my report didn't help. I tossed and turned, threw off the covers, snuggled back under them, tossed some more. Images of Rudolfo and Fred and the other man paraded through my mind and heart. Blood splatters on the floor, their clothes and my hands... my God, my hands! I hadn't noticed until I got home and Pa pointed out they were covered in a dried, but sticky red-brown mess. Even though I washed them multiple times, but like true nightmares, the feeling wouldn't leave.

I ran my hands down the tufted covers, lightly first, then stronger and faster. The blood refused to be wiped away. To be cleansed. Rudolfo's eyes looked into mine. He moaned.

I threw back the covers again and bolted upright. No way could I pretend to sleep when so much grief had happened. A glance into the window revealed morning wasn't even thinking of appearing yet, but it was clear sleep was not going to happen before the sun came up. In fact, I wasn't sure I ever wanted to sleep again, not with those images lurking in my head.

I wrapped a robe around me and wandered into the kitchen where I pulled out the plate Pa had stuck in the ice chest. Taking it to the table, I sat and stared at the tender chicken. Was I hungry? Thirsty? Sleepy? I answered no to all those questions and wondered why I'd bothered to go to bed last night and then wondered why I'd gotten up.

Soft, deep *bongs* resonated in the dining room. I counted five emanating from the wall clock, which meant Pa would be up in an hour and the sun would make its appearance not long after that. Knowing I had to be in the office earlier than usual, I started a fire in the cookstove, set coffee on to boil and headed for my bedroom. Had to get dressed for the day, even though no amount of rouge could conceal my fatigue, erase the light purple half-circles under my eyes when I looked in a hand mirror.

A deep yawn or two, the squeak of a wardrobe door opening told me Pa was up. Neither of us would be ready to face the day, but we had little or no choice. Rudolfo dying was one of my greatest fears and the doc's would be the first order of business, after coffee. At least one cup, maybe two would get me on my toes and out of the house. Maybe.

I sat next to Pa at the dining table, him forking the eggs

and the diced leftover chicken. Me, I sat, stirring and staring at the coffee, its blackness sucking me in, taking me down to a world I didn't understand. Spiraling me down to a scary, dark place.

Several pats on my arm brought me back. Pa's worried eyes studied me. He didn't say anything and didn't need to. That look—his warm, fawn-colored eyes hidden under bushy, graying eyebrows, which dipped low—made me feel things would be alright. I remembered that same look after Ma died, the two of us standing at her grave, hand in hand after everyone had left, struggling to make sense of life... and death. I stopped stirring and staring, laid my head on his shoulder. He pulled me close and despite attempts not to, I cried.

Tears flowed for a minute or so, then I sniffed. He handed me his good linen handkerchief. First I dabbed, then blew. "Thanks. You always know what I need."

"Hey," he said, tenderness in his voice reserved just for me. "You're my little girl."

With that, more tears. Then I felt silly. After more dabbing and blowing, my head had cleared. A look at the coffee. It was merely black coffee, nothing malevolent. Nothing that would take me down to a nasty underworld. I chided myself for those thoughts.

Pa slid his arm from around me, picked up his fork and finished his breakfast. We sipped our lukewarm coffee, each lost in our own thoughts. And then like an old married couple, we finished together and stood at the same time.

I smiled for the first time in what felt like years and wrapped my arms around him. "Thanks, Pa."

"Maud, I'm proud of you," Pa whispered.

I squeezed him extra hard, then released him. He picked up his dish and fork and headed for the kitchen.

Surprised at his admission, but pleasantly, I recalled only a few months ago when Pa wanted me to run away from being sheriff. It was not in my future, he'd said over and over. He'd tried to talk me out of it, citing all sorts of dire predictions, but I hadn't listened. Being sheriff was something I wanted and *had* to do.

"Want to go to church with me?" Pa held my coat.

"It'd probably do me good, but I gotta get to the office." I gave Pa a raised eyebrow.

"Maybe next week."

We closed the front door, stepped into cool air pummeled by agonizingly bright sunshine. At the end of our walkway, we stopped, enjoying being what family we had left. He gave me another hug. "Go get 'em, sheriff."

He buttoned his coat, flashed a lopsided grin, then sauntered up the street as if he'd had twelve hours of sleep, the bounce in his step enviable.

I buttoned the coat, although I barely noticed the temperature, and strode down Main, hoping, praying Rudolfo still breathed.

It took a good ten minutes as Doc Monroe's office was six blocks away and up a side street. Plus, about a hundred and fifty million men and women stopped me along the way to ask about last night's big event. It was the talk of the town.

A bell tinkled when I opened the door. I stepped into the reception room only to find Seth standing there, hat in hand, talking to Doc's wife, Wilma, who was also his nurse. Both turned as I walked in.

"Glad you're here, Maud." Seth extended his arm so I could get hugged again. I accepted his closeness as I studied Wilma's face. She made the ideal nurse. Hair pulled back into a tight bun, sympathetic eyes over a turned-up nose. Wire spectacles tended to slide almost to the end of the upturn, which she pushed back up to the bridge of her nose. They'd slide, she'd push. It was a constant, subconscious dance.

"How's Rudolfo doing? And the other fella?" I wanted to know, needed to know, but didn't want to know. I looked from Seth to Wilma.

"Mr. Ritchie should heal up fine." Wilma said. "That

bullet missed a major artery, so it's now a matter of time and exercise."

"This Mr. Ritchie have a front name or is that it?" I asked.

"Bertram," Seth said. "Bertram Ritchie. Fairly new in town from what I've been told. I talked to the customers after you left to go find Rudolfo's wife and they told me."

Bertram Ritchie. I mulled the name over in my head. I wondered if that was his real name. So many names changed when people moved west, it was hard to keep track. I'd have to search the wanted posters that had pictures. Name sounded familiar, but I wasn't sure. Then it struck me. I had to arrest Mr. Ritchie right now for killing Fred. As soon as he could be moved, I'd march him to jail. Mentally, I checked the circuit judge's schedule, then pictured my own calendar. He wouldn't be in town for a good three weeks. I knew I sighed out loud because both Wilma and Seth looked at me.

"And Rudolfo?" I turned to Seth, who raised one shoulder.

"The doc can tell you more than we can." Wilma pointed over her shoulder. "Mr. Garcia's still alive, which is a good thing."

"Can I see both of them?"

Wilma stepped from behind the desk. "I believe they're both asleep. Doc gave them a good dose of laudanum." She turned toward a closed door. "Follow me."

Seth and I rushed to keep up as she marched down a long hallway, open doors on both sides. I vaguely remembered this layout from one time I'd burned my hand on the stove. Ma had brought me in and I wasn't thinking too clearly even before the laudanum.

We stopped at one door and peered in. Odors of alcohol wafted across my nose. My eyes burned as I squinted into the dim room. Rudolfo lay still, eyes closed, his chest rising and lowering in tiny spurts. Doc stood on the other side of the bed, screwing on the top to a bottle.

"How is he?" The words shot out of my mouth before I could be sure they were soft.

Doc Monroe glanced down at his patient and then up at all three of us. "Touch and go. If he lives for the next twenty-four hours, he's got a fighting chance. Bullet was in deep, but I got it out." He glanced down again. "No infection so far."

"Should I go tell his wife?" Seth asked.

"Already been in this morning." Doc flapped his hands for us to move as he came around the bed. "Said she'll be back later. After she gets the kids ready for church."

"Mr. Ritchie?" I said.

Doc pushed past us and marched off. He crooked a finger toward a room down the hall.

We stopped two doors down. The room was dark, scant light coming from a lantern turned low. Bertram Ritchie lay there, snoring. Part of me wanted to snicker, the other half wanted to beat him senseless.

Doc stood to one side of the door. "He'll live to dance another day."

"Won't dance while he's in jail." I stepped in and studied the room. As soon as I could, I'd have to officially arrest him, which meant he needed to be in handcuffs—which were back at the office. What could I lash him to where he wouldn't escape before I hauled him off to jail? Probably his wrist to the bedframe. "How soon can he be moved?"

Doc lowered his voice. "You gonna arrest him, Maud?"

"Right now." I had no sympathy for this man who'd shot an innocent person. And tried to murder another man. I thought back to his comments, calling Rudolfo a 'greaser'. At least he'd get what's coming to him when the judge came to town. Maybe if I got a telegram off to Sacramento today, they'd get the judge to come sooner.

I'd arrested only a handful of people since being sheriff. My first were two women who ended up fighting in my office. It was a catfight of epic proportions and even now when I look back on it, I laugh. One was getting married to the husband of the second woman. I learned language I'd never heard before.

Right now was as good as any to arrest this man. Not sure exactly how to word it, I started out simple. "Mr. Bertram Ritchie, you're under arrest for the murder of Fred..." I looked at Seth hoping he knew the last name. He shrugged, but I continued undaunted, picking up steam along the way. "Fred and attempted murder of Rudolfo Garcia." I paused for effect and carried on. "You'll remain in jail without bail until the judge holds a trial."

I'm sure my badge sparkled and gleamed right then as I stood straighter. Maybe there would be justice for Rudolfo and Fred after all. I vowed to make sure.

* * *

I SECURED MR. RITCHIE—HEARING those iron handcuffs *click* was incredibly satisfying—and promised to check in later on Rudolfo then headed for the undertakers. Truthfully, I'd never been inside and when I opened the door, my skin prickled. Some sort of acrid smell, I assumed embalming fluid, inundated my entire being. I was sure my clothes would reek of it for years.

Mr. Marconi, the undertaker, greeted me in the middle of the main room. Three wooden caskets leaned against the walls while one of finer wood, probably mahogany, sat open on the floor. It was lined with silk or some shiny fabric. A small pillow, covered with similar material, sat at the end. I pushed down a shiver.

He stuck out a hand. "Good to see you again, Sheriff. It's been way too long."

"Yes, sir, it has." I struggled trying to remember when last we'd met. A party the bank threw to woo investors about three years ago, had to have been it.

Not one to spend time on casual conversation, he pointed behind him. "Come in about Fred?"

I nodded, unsure why exactly I was here. There was

nothing I could do to change the outcome. "I witnessed it last night. Can't stop seeing it in my mind, wishing I could do something. Should've done something."

Lowering his voice to a velvety tone I'm sure he reserved for grieving widows and befuddled sheriffs, he said, "Don't second guess yourself. Does no good. I'll make sure he's buried proper. We'll give him a good send-off."

I considered. A send-off. Maybe we should. We'd hold it at the Tin Pan. I'd buy a round and see if anybody else would join me. We'd hoist a cold one to a man shot down in the prime of his life.

"Sheriff?"

Mr. Marconi's voice snapped me out of my planning. "Sorry."

"Was asking if you knew Fred's next of kin. Some place I can send his belongings or someone here in town."

"I don't even know his last name." With those words, tears filled my eyes, the inside of the room blurred.

He patted my shoulder, quick. "Full name's Federico Gaspioni. Good Italian name."

No wonder they just used "Fred." I swiped at one lone tear rolling down my cheek. "I didn't know him, but some of the men at the saloon do. I'll check with them."

I said good-bye and thanked him for his help. He assured me again everything would be fine.

Except for Rudolfo and Fred, I thought as I walked down Main. All right, I mentally composed myself and consulted my list. Arrest the killer. Check. Make sure Rudolfo was still alive. Check. Fred was being taken care of. Check. The items on the list grew, spreading out like roots of a tree. They went everywhere. First, I wanted to find Emily and give her an eye-witness account for the newspaper, which hopefully would squash rumors and untruths that I'm sure by now raged around town. Then find Fred's family, more interviews with witnesses and, oh joy, the paperwork. A note to the judge, finding someone to watch Mr. Ritchie at night in jail...

I slid to a stop. How could one person do all this? My part-time deputy was full-time busy. I couldn't think of anyone else who could or would help. If screaming helped, I'd be doing so right now.

But everything on the list had to be done by someone of the law. Officially. I continued my trip to see Emily at the paper, my gaze sweeping the boardwalk. Emily had set up an office not far from mine, so I aimed my feet that way.

"Maud? Maud! Wait up."

I stopped again, searching for the familiar voice. Behind me, trotting across the dirt street, hopping over road apples, came my Knight in Shining Armor.

Aldridge bounded over to me, smothering me in his arms and cuddly body. "I'm so thankful you weren't hurt. I just heard." He leaned down, planting his soft lips on my forehead.

"I'm fine," I lied. "Really."

Holding me at arm's length, his scrutiny roved from shoes to bonnet, landing on my face. "You're sure? Look kinda tired."

"I'm sure. Late night." Maybe in a year or two I'd be fine. Maybe by then I'd be able to sleep. Or... if I cuddled with him one night, I'd probably relax and sleep. I pushed the warmth-inducing images away.

"Wanna get coffee? Maybe strudel?" He pointed over his shoulder and gave me that Cheshire cat grin I'd come to love.

"I'd love to, but I've gotta find Emily, talk to her." I flashed my own coy smile. "Then maybe coffee." Strudel sounded good, but not now. I doubted I'd lost any taste for it, but my stomach wasn't ready for eating quite yet.

His eyebrows angled upward. "Then you're in luck. Emily's over at the Tin Pan interviewing Sam and other witnesses. That's how I knew you were there last night."

As much as I wanted to know why he was in a saloon at this hour of the morning, I couldn't think about that now. Later. Maybe over coffee.

We walked toward the saloon having to stop about every ten feet to answer questions. Seems as if everyone had their opinion of what actually happened, and I tried hard to set them straight. Maybe an interview with Emily would cement the story once and for all with important facts.

I paused at the batwing doors.

"You all right? Lost all the color in your face, Maud." Aldridge stood close. "And you're shaking."

All of a sudden, I wasn't sure I could go inside. I forced air in and out of my lungs, but I couldn't breathe. My world turned gray, cold and clammy. Tears dripped over my cheeks. Aldridge's arm around my shoulders pulled me into his chest.

I sobbed.

CHAPTER TWENTY-FIVE

TOUCHED BY ANGELS...

FATE HAD AN ODD WAY OF PRESENTING ITSELF. After I'd dried what was left of my tears, composing myself enough to actually step foot into the Tin Pan, Emily, notepad in hand, stepped out. We located three chairs, others were stretched up and down Main, lining the boardwalk. Not an ideal place to talk, as town folk would stop and listen, a few giving their own opinions, but it was close enough to the crime scene and yet not *inside*.

Aldridge, bless him, remained quiet, yet attentive, by my side the whole time. Once or twice, he'd touch my arm, possibly as a reminder he was there or, maybe to keep me from running away. Between shaky deep breaths, I recalled the gunfight and its subsequent outcome in detail, leaving nothing out, except my feelings. Those had no place in an article like this.

A half hour later, we were done.

Emily stood, pulled her skirt out from under her shoe, checked her notes then turned tired, blue eyes on me. "Thank you, Maud, for doing this. I know it was hard."

I'd thought about this for hours, and while I was all about free speech, I was also all about getting the facts correct. "Would you have a problem with me reading your article for accuracy before it goes to print?"

Although her eyes were fatigued, hints of red against the white, they shone as her shoulders arched. "Problem?" Her mouth curved up at one end. "No, none at all. In fact, I welcome it. Make sure I didn't misquote you."

All my worries drained. All on their own, my eyes looked heavenward, thanking whoever was in charge up there that someone in such an influential position as Emily's, had the right morals.

"I'll have it shortly after the mid-day meal." Emily stepped off the boardwalk into Main street, looked right and left then back at me. "Stop by my office then and I'll have you approve it."

All of a sudden, my agenda seemed shorter and the sun a bit brighter.

Aldridge realigned his chair to where it rested against the wall. "Coffee now?" His tongue played with the end of his mustache. "Peach strudel today. At least that's what I think I've been smelling."

Peach? Oh yes. Then reality hit. "I've got to send a telegram to the circuit Judge Andrew Richfield in Sacramento. Hope he can swing by here sooner than three weeks from now."

Mr. Hero's handsomely sculpted lips rose on one end, his hunky eyes smiling at me. "Fine. I'll go with you and *then* coffee?"

Slipping an arm into his crooked elbow, I nudged his arm with my shoulder. "Only if you'll let me buy. It's my turn."

He pushed back. "I like a woman who takes control... and pays."

* * *

STOMACHS full of Hilda's to-die-for peach strudel, accentuated with bits of cinnamon hidden inside, Aldridge and I stood on the boardwalk enjoying the sun. While it was close to what I'd call cold, the sun more than made up for the lack of temperature. Aldridge's closeness had nothing to do with my warm cheeks, I was sure.

My mind returned to business. "I was thinking about giving an official send-off for Fred."

"Like a party?"

I considered. "Sort of. Thought we'd have it at the Tin Pan, if I can ever go inside again."

I cringed, hopefully not enough Aldridge would notice. "I'll buy a round, say a couple of words, maybe his friends would too."

Mr. Amazing grinned. "Like a good, old-fashioned Irish wake. Been to one or two of those. All those whooperups. They'll send the poor fella off with song and dance."

Envisioning a bunch of loud, drunk Paddys, it seemed like the way to go with Fred, except he was Italian. Irish, Italian... a party was a party. He wouldn't know the difference and Sam would recoup some of his lost revenue.

"Then it's settled." Despite the reason for the send-off, I was excited. More so than having a dance for the town biddies. "I'll talk to Sam and then the undertaker."

Aldridge turned to face me directly. "Tell you what. Let me make the arrangements and announce it." His head cocked to one side. "You've got enough to do, and I feel like I should help."

Bless him. My angel. Another weight lifted from my shoulders. Were those birds singing? I couldn't nod fast enough. "Absolutely, yes. And thank you!" A hug was not near enough payment for his kindness, but here out in public, it would have to do. "The sooner the better. Maybe Friday night?"

This was Sunday, giving him five days to pull it off. I figured, however, when it came to free beer, we wouldn't have any problem finding men to toast Fred's passing. Why was I all of a sudden looking forward to this?

After saying goodbye, Aldridge turned right heading up toward the Tin Pan, I wandered left toward my office and that ever-so-delightful paperwork. Plus, I had to be sure the cell was ready for occupancy. When was the last time Pokey or I had shaken out the mattress? I was sure months ago, if ever, and the cotton in there needed fluffing as well as tiny livestock nestled inside needed relocating.

I walked, grumbling about fluffing. Where did it say a sheriff had to fluff? And how about dusting and washing windows? And *sweeping*, for Pete's sake? None of that had anything to do with keeping the peace. I slowed. Maybe it did. Neat house, neat town. All right, I'd fluff and sweep and dust. But I didn't have to like it.

A tingling sensation ran down my spine as I passed the big office window, which needed washing again thanks to rain last week. Was someone in there? I couldn't be sure through the mud splatters.

Something wasn't right, and by the time I opened the office door and stepped in, I knew. Standing like ruffled peahens, the three town councilors huffed and mumbled, having stuffed themselves into the office. They took up all of its air.

Turning in unison, their faces resembled rabid wolves—lips snarling, eyes glowing, fangs dripping. I froze and, along with my body, any breath I had.

"What the devil's *wrong* with you, Maud?" Harvey Weinberg's bulbous nose glowed, much like he'd been drinking. His muddy-brown eyes widened then narrowed. He pointed a skinny finger in my direction. "You've got the entire town stirred up. And it's your fault."

"What he's sayin' t'is God's honest truth." Ian MacKinney, his brogue so thick right now, I had to guess at what he was ranting. "How can ye, in awl good consciousness, sleep a' night?"

I turned to Slim for interpretation. Of the town's leaders, I could usually count on him to be in my corner. Him and Seth. Slim raised a shoulder, maybe to indicate he didn't understand either, or to say he sided with them. I was on my own.

Harvey crept forward, as if hunting a ferocious beast. A

glance back told me the door was still open and I could escape. Run out into the cold air, hollering and flapping my arms. Would help arrive in time? But, on second, more rational thought, this was my office and I'd stand my ground. No amount of tiresome windbags would drive me away.

I pulled in air, stood straight and glared back. Hoping my fingers weren't shaking, I untied my bonnet, hung it on the hook near the door, all the while staring at the three wolves. Should I unbuckle my holster? Would I need a gun handy? Probably not, but maybe I looked a bit more menacing with a six-shooter rig around my waist. I'd keep it on.

Harvey stopped as I inched forward and I briefly wondered why he'd done so. Then I realized while considering whether or not to unbuckle my holster, I'd been tapping the butt of my gun with my index finger. A habit I'd been trying to break. Guess I appeared more of a threat than I'd imagined.

I kept tapping as I made my way to the desk. Standing behind it always made me feel protected. It was a shield against the crazies in the world. "If you'd all calm down, take a seat, we can figure this out." Of course I had no idea what we had to figure out, but eventually, they'd get around to it.

Slim was first to find a chair and pull it up near the desk. He planted both feet on the wooden floor, leaned forward and back, steepled his hands. Slim stared at his entwined digits like they held the answers to the universe.

Easing down into a chair, I spied a new pile of mail on the desk. Would it never end? Fortunately, in this bizarre twist, something more pressing had arrived and the stack would have to wait.

Keeping a close eye on me, both Ian and Harvey screeched chairs across the floor, stopping near Slim. We studied each other. My gaze trailed across the men's faces, not quite so menacing as earlier, then landed on Slim. "What's the problem?"

Harvey stretched forward, his curls bobbing. "You know what the 'problem' is, Sheriff." He sniffed. "It's you and your conjured ideas. First a woman runnin' for mayor, then a dance and now... now a shootin'."

"Your fault." Ian sat tall, stretching as much of his squatness as possible. Even so, he barely could see over the desk. He pointed a crooked finger at me, waved it in my face. "Wouldn't be havin' deese problems if ye were man."

I'm sure part of that was true, and I would've laughed if I hadn't been so angry myself. Before Slim could come to the rescue, which I didn't need from him right then, I fought the urge to clear leather and shoot. Not that I would try to hit them on purpose, but it would be quite satisfying. And I'd get their attention. But maybe I'd hit the window and glass would go everywhere inside and out and I've have to clean it up and they'd really be angry and I'd have to pay to replace it and—

"Maud, we've been concerned about the image Dry Creek is giving to other towns." Slim's voice, usually loud and a tad abrasive, turned soft and smooth, soothing. "Women running for mayor is a queer idea, not to mention a school for Chinese children *not* run by the Orientals."

"And businesses run by women now." Ian eyed Harvey, nodded and continued. "T'is not done. Not in polite society. Women's place is to run a home, not newspaper or... bakery."

A gasp escaped over my outrage. I swear the men licked their lips. From what I'd heard, these three airbags were some of Hilda's finest customers. However, the big event, the shooting, hadn't come up yet. I wondered how I would be blamed for that.

And then like clockwork, it came.

Harvey groaned up to his feet, placed both hands on the desk and leaned into me. From here, he was close enough to either kiss if I leaned in, too, or punch in the nose. My vote was for the latter.

"That shooting last night," Harvey said. "What were you

doing in the Tin Pan, drinking, having a fancy time and setting those three men on each other? Arguing over your affections."

"What?" I stood so fast, the chair fell back, and Harvey did, too. "What exactly are you accusing me of? The three of you?" My stomach clenched, bells rang in my head, my hands fisted. "You think I had something to do with that? How dare you."

I yelled instead of remaining under control. "I was doing my job. Checking on the businesses, even yours Ian." I turned my attention back to Harvey. "And yours. I wasn't drinking, cavorting." I glared at Slim. "I was making sure all was safe in *your* saloon."

For the first time in a while, I was furious. More than furious. I continued to yell. "Don't ever, for one second, come in here again and accuse me of not doing my job." I pointed toward the Tin Pan. "Hell, I didn't shoot those men. They shot each other."

I froze. I'd said 'hell,' a word verboten to proper women. It was a word I'd only thought before but never, ever uttered. One my ma would have absolutely washed my mouth out over. But I was in a man's world right now and they'd backed me into a corner. I could say more, but apparently didn't need to.

They stopped dead, like being encased in a block of ice. All three stared, mouths open, flapping like grounded trout.

If I'd known one little swear word would have shut them up, I'd have used it long ago. But I'd never been so outraged before. First to melt, I pointed toward the door. "You all need to leave right now. Before I throw you in jail. Locked up and key tossed out."

Slim inched his way up out of the chair. "Sorry, Maud." His voice, sounding more like a squeezed puppy than a pudgy saloon owner, raised both shoulders. "We'd been told—"

"You were told wrong." My words turned to steel. Right then I didn't like Slim at all and the other two, well, they were hanging somewhere between loathed and downright despised. I paused for effect. "Now. Get out."

Like scolded choirboys, they hung their heads, mumbled apologies and trailed out the door, their tails between their legs. That sight, an image ingrained in my head, gave me a tad bit of pleasure. I wondered how soon they'd be back to collect their egos.

Energy flushed through my face, down my body and drained out my feet. I actually looked down to see where it had puddled. Exhausted, tired, angry, hungry. What else was I feeling? Betrayed? By Slim? Indeed. Why didn't he stand up for me? Pouring a cup of hot coffee, thanks in part to Pokey who kept it going all day when he could, I returned to the chair and sighed. I'd much rather be home, feet up, drinking a cup of Pa's coffee, but that wasn't about to happen.

I pushed aside new wanted posters, glancing at faces and names, not seeing anybody I recognized. One, near the bottom, caught my attention. Face matched the fella who'd been shot in the leg. This poster named him Brent Richman, but no mistaking that face. There, staring back, was Bertram Ritchie. No doubt.

Reading the fine print, said he was wanted in three states and one territory, for bank robbing and murder. Now, I could add another count of murder. The reward took my breath. One thousand dollars. Just as quickly, I realized even though I was an officer of the law, taking the reward wasn't good public relations. The town paid me enough. But how about the money going to either Rudolfo or the town? Either could put that money to good use. I'd apply for it and immediately give it away.

Maybe the town could use the reward money to pay for Ritchie's meals for three weeks. Serve them right. The councilors never got the chance to grouse about what it would cost to have Ritchie as a guest of the town for several days. Two meals a day for three weeks would add up. I'd make sure he got the cheapest food from the restaurant. Maybe "old sock broth," or perhaps "last week's beans." Maybe "bottom of the pan slumgullion." A smile rose on one side of my face.

Before any more bad news could come waltzing into the office, I finished off the cold coffee, tied my bonnet, wrapped my coat around me, and headed outside. Wintry air nipped at my cheeks and nose, but it felt good. Invigorated, I needed to visit the doc, the newspaper and then go home. This would probably be my last night in my own bed for a bit, unless Pokey could stay nights guarding the prisoner. When I found him today, I'd ask.

Since the newspaper office was close by, I headed there, perhaps a bit early, but I tended to be optimistic. Maybe Emily would have it written.

Sure enough, she'd just finished when I scooted in, closing the door against a sudden gust of icy wind. I read the paper she handed me, nodded in the right places, cringed in others as I relived the shooting, and admired her writing style. We'd found a winner in her.

"Think it'll be all right, Maud?" Emily peered over my shoulder as I finished the last sentence.

"Yes, ma'am." I handed it back and caught my hands trembling. Would I ever get over that feeling? Of disbelief, of total horror, of not being able to stop it? I prayed I would but knew deep in my heart, it would always be there, just below the surface. I'd have to work to keep those feelings, those images at bay. No way would I allow myself to be led by "what could'ves" and "what should'ves". No way.

I thanked Emily who said the paper's first edition would be out early tomorrow morning. In many ways a reason to celebrate. She also mentioned Aldridge had already stopped by to take out an ad about Fred's send-off.

So maybe good *can* come out of something terrible. I thanked Emily, who I placed in the *angel* category, then girded myself for going outside and, with a deep breath, plunged into cold.

News and rumors about last night's shooting were

subsiding as I was stopped by only a handful of interested citizens. Making my way to the doc's in less than half an hour, I stepped in and was pleasantly surprised to see Mrs. Garcia smiling. She stood in the reception area, her youngest folded in next to her, clutching her hand, both eyes on me. I smiled down at the boy, but like a terrified chick, he dug his face into his ma's skirt. So much for charming children.

Since she was smiling, I figured it would be all right to ask about Rudolfo.

"*Sí*," she nodded. "He is much better. Doc Morgan is a blessed lifesaver."

Without thinking, I hugged her. And to my relief and surprise, she hugged back. At least *she* wasn't angry with me for going into that saloon. Or if she was, that would come later.

Wilma, followed by the doc, appeared like the cherubs they were. Materializing in the room without me noticing the door opening and closing, simply added to the mystique.

"Glad you're here, Sheriff." Doc Morgan pointed over his shoulder. "Mr. Ritchie should be able to be moved tomorrow. Leg's coming along nicely."

"I'll stop by in the morning, take him off your hands." I didn't really want him in the jail, but that's what I got paid to do. "And Mr. Garcia?"

Doc raised a stiff eyebrow, which I thought an odd thing for a medicine man to do. They were generally skilled at hiding their true feelings. "Got a long recovery ahead of him but should be fit by Christmas."

Christmas was a ways off, but at least he'd have a Christmas, unlike poor Fred. With Doc's permission, I made my way to Ritchie's room, make sure he was still handcuffed.

CHAPTER TWENTY-SIX
FIRST UP...THEN DOWN...

THE LOCK'S *click* RESONATED AGAINST THE WALLS, bouncing around the room like a marble in a tin can. From inside his new home, Bertram Ritchie grabbed the cell bars, wedged his head in between, and hollered.

"This any way to treat a man? Huh? Hurt so bad can't even stand?" He paused. "Huh?"

He was lucky I didn't coldcock him with the revolver. I'd like to show him how he should be treated. But I didn't. I kept the gun in its holster and the mumblings under wrap.

Ritchie raised his voice as if I was deaf. "Hey, Sheriff? Sheriff? I oughta be back at doc's. I been shot." He pulled his head from between the bars, squeezed his shoulder in. His eyes bulged. "You got no right to put me in here. I'm sick."

I shook my head as if I didn't understand. Having eye witnessed the shooting, I had no doubt he was guilty. I'd seen him. Also, I had no doubt he'd killed other men and more than likely robbed a bank. I'd put money on the notion he'd committed other crimes that weren't listed on the wanted poster.

And I definitely didn't care he was in pain. Too bad. He deserved it.

I held the door near the lock, pushed and pulled the iron bars, rattling the cage so to speak, but making sure locked was locked. I'd get fired for sure if a murderer escaped the jail. If I had to sit in front of the cell every day and night until the judge showed up, that man would stay behind bars until he was convicted of murder and hauled off to state prison.

He'd be gone soon, I hoped, but there was a sliver of doubt worming its way around in my brain. I brushed it aside, gave the bars one last tug, glared at the prisoner, then marched off, key in hand, slamming the door to the cells. Normally, I'd leave the wooden door open so I could keep an eye on the troublemaker, but I didn't want to look at him. Not right then.

I poured a second, possibly third, cup of coffee, sprawled into the chair, held the cup in hand and considered. Life was odd. A series of ups and downs, a lot of sideways, a couple backtracks, but mainly, mostly simply going forward.

The door squeaked open. A gust of cold air swept into my office, Pokey behind it. He pushed the door closed, blew on his ungloved hands, nodded in my direction, and headed to the coffee pot. He poured the brew clear up to the rim, sipped and slurped, his hands cradling the tin cup.

After thawing, Pokey turned his famous grin on me, and sighed. "Thought I'd about freeze to death, Maud. Why's it so cold?" He took his usual seat across from me at the desk, sipped again.

A rhetorical question, I let it slide and sipped my own coffee. I wondered why he wasn't quite so bubbly this morning. Maybe he'd had a late night. I wouldn't pry, but curiosity was about to kill me. I wanted juicy details. Of gossip quality. How could I wheedle it out of him?

He leaned back, placed one ankle on a knee, sipped and stared at a spot above me. As much as I wanted to turn around and look up over my shoulder, I knew he saw images that weren't there. I'd let him stew on whatever he'd had for breakfast this morning and be quiet. Which was hard. But I distracted myself with paperwork. Lovely paperwork.

Before I got down to finding a blank piece of paper and a pen to write a report, my mental list spread itself out. Was the newspaper printed yet? Was Fred's send-off ready? And how about Pearl and her campaign for mayor? I hadn't heard much about it recently. Penelope and her fire department? I'd need to talk to her about the fella wanting to sell fire insurance. Had he actually set up shop? Bigger, more aggressive worms of doubt and alarm went off in my brain. Something wasn't right about him, Nathaniel Ford if I remembered his name correctly.

Had I even seen him around town lately? Maybe. The downside of being sheriff was that everything seemed to be of vital importance and before I could get one crisis resolved, something else would take its place. It was more vexing than pulling weeds after a rainstorm. Yank one out and by the next day, three more have taken its place.

Another sip brought my attention back to Pokey. Something flickered far back in those walnut-colored eyes as he brought his gaze to me. We made quite a pair, each sitting there, staring at unseen images above each other's heads.

"How's Mae—"

"Did you—"

We spoke together.

"You go first, Pokey. I'm sure what you've got to say is much more interesting than mine."

Nodding, he pointed his cup toward town. "I figured when Mae and Mr. Armstrong decided to start a school, I'd still see her all the time. But she's always with *him*, planning." He narrowed his eyes. "It's like she doesn't even know I'm there anymore. It's 'our school' this and 'our school' that. I mean, we still see each other, but she's not with me. In her mind, she's with him and that stupid school."

Well, I had never seen that side of Pokey before. A

jealous side. Of course, I'd never seen him in love before. More ups and downs of life.

"Come to think on it, I haven't seen much of Aldridge, either. A little bit here and there, but he's busy, too." However, he always seemed to be there when I needed him. Cocking my head, I pursed my lips.

Pokey shot me a quizzical glance. "You're not worried are ya, Maud?" A semblance of a grin started its way up one side of his face, pushing part of his thin mustache. "I mean, it's just business." The grin stopped. "Right?"

"Right." The tin cup thumped to the desk. Maybe we should take a walk around town, see what we could find. After all, Pokey was a part-time deputy and had the right to investigate. Maybe we'd find Mae and my Mr. Amazing embroiled in a tangled web of arms and legs, melding to each other like glue. I shook those images out of my head, citing momentary insanity. I opened my mouth to offer an official stroll, but he finished his coffee, wiped his mouth with his coat sleeve.

"Gotta go. Mail time then what needs doin' at the store." Pokey uncrossed his legs, eased up to his feet. "I'm doin' more than sweeping now. Mr. Otis has me stocking shelves and such. Fact is, he said he give me a raise on account of him doing so much business with the distillers."

Ah! That was it. Mystery solved. Must be quite a few distillers. I congratulated him on the big win and thanked him for telling me.

Before he left, we decided he could stay overnight tonight to guard the prisoner. He'd come right after he returned from his mail run. I was sure within a few hours the entire town would know Bertram Ritchie was locked up in jail. It wouldn't be surprising if one or two wanted to take it upon themselves to drag him out of the cell and have a necktie party at the cottonwood down by the river. 'Vigilante justice' some called it. I called it illegal.

Pokey closed the door, leaving me standing at the potbelly stove, cup in hand, thoughts of Aldridge and Mae...

* * *

CROWDS outside the newspaper office told me what I'd walked over to find out. The first edition of the *Dry Creek Courier* was written, printed and distributed. People stood in the street, on the boardwalk, sat on their horses, gathered in twos, flipping the pages back and forth. Murmurs, lips silently reading, children pulling down the pages to see better, filled the area.

I pushed through the throng, elbowing my way inside the office. Way over in the corner on the opposite side of the door, stood Emily Penderton, editor. Parts of her hair, always pulled tight back into a bun, had sprung loose and hung around her face like light brown rivulets. Black ink smudges accentuated her normally light pink cheeks. Her blooming smile would fade as someone hollered at her and would instantly return upon a handshake or pat on the shoulder. From this distance and, with the number of men and women crammed into the office, I couldn't hear what was being said, but she appeared to be pleased.

Someone handed me the paper. I threaded my way to an unoccupied wall, leaned and glanced at the front page. I'd been afraid she'd start off with the shooting in bold type across the front, but no, she'd led with a story of the new fire department. In skimming through it, there was a quote from Penelope. Farther down the front, Emily had written about the upcoming dance and women's reactions.

On page two, halfway down, I found the story I'd been dreading. So afraid she'd gone back on her word and sensationalized something as horrific as a senseless killing, I almost didn't want to look. But there was the story. I scanned it once, then read more carefully word for word. Just the facts, no drama, simply what happened. I wondered if she'd run reactions to the shooting in next week's paper.

Down at the bottom of the page I spotted an ad, its message set off with a border of flames. Intrigued, I read it.

Nathaniel Ford, Insurance salesman. It went on to say one never knew when one's property would be affected, "better to have insurance now, than to have regrets later."

All right. I needed to investigate this jasper more thoroughly. Something about him I didn't trust. So engrossed in the newspaper inspection, I failed to notice Emily wending her way over to me until she nudged my shoulder.

"What d'ya think?" Emily nodded toward the paper in her hand, cradling it like Ma cuddling her newborn.

"Terrific first edition!" And I meant it. I was so relieved I'm sure my smile lit up the room. "Keep up the good work. It's everything I imagined. You'll make a go of this, I'm sure."

Giving her a quick hug, I folded the pages and surveyed the room. Seth took up one corner intently listening to a couple bending his ear about something mightily important. He glanced up at me and raised his chin and eyebrows.

I said good-bye to Emily and squeezed my way outside. The crisp air brought my shoulders back and one hand into the coat pocket. I stepped into the street, peered left then right. Mr. Ford's ad hadn't said anything about an office, which meant I had to find him. Today. Now. But where to start? Normally, I'd head for the saloon, where everybody knows everything, but I couldn't bring myself to go into the Tin Pan, nor any of the other four for that matter.

Turning my attention to the bank, figuring Ford would need money to start this supposed insurance business, I beelined for Pa.

Nope. Nathaniel Ford hadn't been in asking for a loan. Hadn't opened up a business account or even a personal checking account. No one had seen Mystery Man.

Back on the street I went. Maybe over coffee and Hilda's strudel I'd find someone who knew. As I hurried, I realized it was a good excuse to eat something sweet. Something Hilda and Ester made. Something heavenly and something I didn't make.

I opened the door, enjoying the bell's tinkling, stepped in out of the cold and stopped short. Seated at a table in the back of the room was my Mr. Wonderful and that... man, Nathaniel Ford. All the air escaped my lungs. Pictures on the walls grew fuzzy and gray. I zeroed in on those two while shock invaded my brain, taking up all the room I had for forming words.

Standing like a store dummy, I couldn't move my feet. I couldn't go forward or backward, out the door into the street pretending I'd not seen them together. This was worse than seeing him with another woman. Worse than—

A customer bumped my shoulder pushing past me to get to the door. "Excuse me, Sheriff."

I awakened from my stupor as Hilda swept past with a plate of baked apples drizzled with syrup and a plate of sliced stollen, precisely dotted with powdered sugar. The aroma sailed under my nose, awakening me much like the prince's kiss did Snow White.

There had to be an explanation. They obviously knew each other, so why hadn't Aldridge mentioned knowing him? What were they hiding? I hated to think like that, I blamed it again on my badge, but there they were. The two of them. In cahoots. Up to no good, I was sure.

Taking a deep breath, pulling in all sorts of wonderful smells, I held my shoulders erect and picked my way over to their table. Aldridge smiled as he looked up at me, then stood.

"Maud." He cleared his throat. "Sheriff. What a pleasant surprise. Please, come join us." He pulled out an empty chair and pushed it back in when I sat.

"So, we meet again." Mr. Ford offered his hand. As much as I didn't want to touch the man, we shook, then I wiped my hand on my skirt, under the table.

I'm sure Aldridge felt the need to explain their meeting as his words were rushed, tinged with a hint of guilt. I listened carefully, taking mental notes and hating myself for doubting him.

Ford, I was sure, was a miscreant of the highest sort.

Aldridge nodded toward Mr. Ford who had picked up his coffee cup. "Turns out, we're staying at the same boarding house, Maud. Got to talking at breakfast yesterday, talking about this and that, discovered we'd been in San Francisco around the same time and then Sacramento. What a coincidence. This morning, decided we'd have a bite here."

Uh huh. Sounded more like conspiracy to me. But I'd give him the benefit of the doubt. Ford, not so much.

The same young waitress, freckles splattered across her cheeks and nose, slid a cup of steaming coffee in front of me. I guessed being sheriff had its up sides, and this was one of them. I thanked her, blew across the cup and eyed Ford and Aldridge. Maybe I was making too much out of a chance meeting. But was it honestly 'chance' or something much more sinister?

Figuring I'd take the high road, I started out innocently enough. "So, Mr. Ford. Still enjoying Dry Creek?" I hoped he'd say no, he hated it, was leaving and never, ever, not in a hundred thousand years, coming back. Mentally, I crossed both sets of fingers and my toes.

"Love it here, Sheriff. Fine town you've got." He flashed a smile exhibiting a full set of teeth—an oddity around here. "Fact is, Aldridge and I were sitting here formulating a plan to scout a location for my new office. Hope to open next week."

Dang and double dang. Curses raced through my head, a few threatening to escape through my mouth. I reeled them in. "Next week?" Had I said that out loud?

"Wish it could be sooner," Ford said. "But I hate to rush things and make mistakes."

"Besides." Aldridge added a dollop of honey to his coffee, then stirred. "I told Nate you and the other town officials welcome new businesses. That's what keeps Dry Creek afloat and so... vibrant."

Vibrant? Dry Creek? Obviously they weren't looking at the same town I was. But my man was right. The town council encouraged businesses, at least ones that weren't owned by women.

I had to dig deeper into Ford's background, but right now all I could do was ask questions. "What sort of insurance will you be offering? You said you specialize in fire."

Ford put down his cup, turned his full attention on me. I wanted to shrink back, like being cornered by a cougar, but I held my cup between us. It made a poor shield, but it was all I had.

"Fire, yes. My company promotes, and sells, peace of mind, Sheriff." Like a serpent out of the Bible, instead of a forked tongue, Ford flicked a smile my way. "And it happens to come with a price tag. Small, but necessary, I assure you."

Aldridge raised one eyebrow, started to lean in as the waitress brought more coffee. He waited for everyone's cup to be refreshed, nodded to her, then leaned in toward Ford. "A small price tag? For what, exactly? Seems to me, if people set up their own fire fund, they'd be able to rebuild whatever burns themselves. Tell me, Nate, I'm curious. What exactly do people get for this 'small price tag?' What benefit do they get by paying you instead of putting money in the bank?"

I also wanted to know and was grateful Aldridge had asked instead of me. Again, he became my hero.

Ford ran a soft finger across his mustache, smoothing it as he went. Blinking more than I thought he should, finally, he canted his head sideways just a bit, and gave a slight nod. "I hear that argument often, Al."

Al? Who was Al? For a moment, I was lost trying to figure out who exactly, he was talking to. Well, Heaven's sake! He was addressing my Mr. Wonderful. I'd never consider, not for one measly second, calling him 'Al'. It didn't fit. And why, after knowing each other only a day or so, would they call each other by such familiar names? Nate? Al? Even among men, not done so soon. Doubt crept into my stomach and knotted there.

"Your question, Al deserves an explanation." He glanced

at me, then returned his attention to Aldridge. "What would it cost, say to rebuild this restaurant? From the ground up?"

Aldridge peered around the room like he was assessing it for decorations. I could almost see the pencil flying across the paper, numbers adding up in his head. He gave it some thought. "I'd say five thousand, complete with tables, chairs, lost wages for employees."

Lost wages? I'd never have thought of that. He *was* amazing.

"That's about what I'd estimate." Ford's head bobbed up and down like on a spring. "Five thousand." He turned full attention on me. "How long would it take you to save up that kind of money dedicated to a fire fund?"

He had me there. So far, I'd managed to save about a hundred and I didn't have the expenses of rent or food. Pa and the county paid for those. "A few years at least," I said honestly.

"Uh huh." Ford raised one shoulder and softened his voice. "My point is, few, if any person has saved enough to rebuild in case of calamity. Fire, flood or whatever God throws our way."

Somewhere in the back of my brain, I remembered Ford sitting in Seth's office giving parameters to what they covered and what they didn't. But now didn't feel like the time for details. I drank the coffee, trying every scenario I could to make insurance a waste of money.

But he had a point.

And I hated him for it.

Ford gave us a moment to ruminate on his words, then fished around in his vest pocket pulling out a small wad of cash. He counted two bills and put them on the table. Standing, he nodded to us both. "Need to go meet a potential client. Sorry for leaving such fine company, but duty calls."

Aldridge and I stood. Mr. Wonderful shook hands with Ford while I kept my own occupied with cup and cloth napkin.

He left and Aldridge and I retook our seats. I wasn't ready yet to face the world and besides, I had questions about the Chinese school as well as Ford and Aldridge's connection. I flagged down the waitress and asked for a menu. This would be a long conversation.

CHAPTER TWENTY-SEVEN
BEST "MAN" FOR THE JOB...

ALDRIDGE AND I RELAXED IN OUR CHAIRS, ordered two ham sandwiches and glasses of milk. Before I bit into my sandwich, a man and woman I'd seen around town, stopped at the table.

"We hear that killer is locked up in your jail, Sheriff." The man, bowler hat in hand, wide mustache covering his upper lip, stood at my shoulder and glared down.

I scrunched around in the chair looking up at him. I considered standing, but my sandwich called and my laziness was intact right then. "He is. Judge'll be here any day." Or so I hoped.

Sliding a protective arm around the woman's shoulders, the man eyed Aldridge and spoke to him more than me. "That... that... murderer ever get out of jail, I'll hunt him down myself. Kill 'im. Man like that don't deserve to be locked up. Too good for him. No sir. String 'im up right here and now is what I say."

All right, that did it. I sprung to my feet, feeling my skirt caught under a shoe. I couldn't stand as tall as I wanted. "Sir. He's entitled to a fair trial and that's what he'll get." Squaring my shoulders, I moved in closer hoping he'd back up. He did.

"My tax dollars—"

"Your tax dollars are hard at work protecting the fine people of Dry Creek. Mr. Ritchie will not escape and he *will* stand trial." I watched the woman's face soften and his harden. His cheeks reddened and for a moment I thought we'd have a tussle right here in the restaurant. Instead, the man took another step back, relaxed his shoulders and removed his arm from around the woman.

He glanced at her, then Aldridge, and finally me. "Fair enough." Aiming for the door, he pushed her in front of him. He stopped, looked back. "I'll be at that trial, Sheriff. He better be found guilty, if you know what's good for you."

With that, he and the woman marched out of the restaurant while I sank to the chair. The sandwich lost its appeal. Bile had risen to my throat.

Aldridge placed a wide hand on my arm. "It'll be all right. But there's more like him. Want me to guard the prisoner today? I'm supposed to talk with Mae about the school, but we can do that in your office."

All doubts about Mr. Fantastic washed away with his words. How could I have ever questioned him? He was almost too good to be true. I'd have pinched myself if I could have unclenched my hands.

"I would appreciate it, Aldridge. And you're right, I'm afraid. Men might decide to act on impulse and what they think of 'right,' instead of simply threatening me."

He bit into his sandwich, pieces of ham peeking out from between slices of sourdough bread. Suddenly, I was starved.

* * *

ALDRIDGE ASSURED me everything was in place for Friday night's big 'send-off' of poor Fred. The Tin Pan would buy the first round of whiskey, not beer. Whiskey was cheaper Mr. Amazing told me in a whisper. In fact, two of the distillers each had donated one of their batches, as apparently Fred had been a regular customer of theirs.

He hinted of music being provided, more than the tinny

piano, which played non-stop Friday and Saturday nights. I could hear it at my house several blocks away. Perhaps a fiddle player or two would stop into the saloon, resin up their bows, and put smiles on men's faces.

And there was always a chance a few patrons would stomp and cheer, sending Fred off properly.

To my surprise, I had high hopes for a send-off-wake-funeral this town wouldn't soon forget.

I gave My Honey the key, said our goodbyes, then his long legs took him toward my office where he promised he'd stay until I returned. Between Pokey, Aldridge and me, that prisoner had no chance of either escaping or being broken out of jail. They'd have to come over us to get to Mr. Ritchie. I prayed it wouldn't come to that.

I wandered up Main to the telegraph office, which also housed our postal office, hoping the judge had sent word. Inside the room, one half reserved for mail and newspapers, the other half taken up with a wooden counter for the tele-graph portion, I spotted a head full of light red hair bent over the telegraph key machine.

The telegrapher, Mr. Rune Maguire, a wild Scotsman if one ever existed, was way too old to have that much hair. The head looked up and I recognized Seamus Maguire, grandson.

"Howdy, Sheriff." Seamus beamed, all of his thirteen years crowding onto his wide face. "Good seein' you again." He extended a hand.

"You, too." We shook and this time I didn't wipe my hand on my skirt. "Working for your grandpa?" But why wasn't he in school? He wasn't quite old enough to have graduated yet.

"Sure am!" His shoulders pulled back and he cocked his head. His eyebrows seemed to have pointed up a bit more, too. "In charge of everything today."

"Everything, huh?" With no one else in the office, I figured we had time to chat. One arm propped on the counter, I relaxed. "Your grandpa feeling all right?"

Seamus dropped both shoulders. "No, ma'am. Grandpa's a bit poorly today. And Ma's got the baby cryin', the twins are in school same as my other two sisters, Pa's off huntin' somewhere and—"

"You're the best man for the job." I stifled a laugh at Seamus's sudden upright posture, his green eyes, the color of ferns, shining. Even though he was the *only* man left for the job, possibly he hadn't thought about that. My compliment got his attention and he flashed a sincere smile.

I continued. "Since you're the important man in this office, did I get a telegram from anybody? In particular a judge?"

He pushed aside papers, checked under the counter, moved an ink blotter, even looked under his grandpa's cold coffee mug. He eyeballed the entire room. Finally, Seamus wagged his head. "No, Sheriff. Sorry. Nothing here. But I'll make sure you get it first thing when it comes in."

"Thanks. It's important. And tell your grandpa I hope he gets to feeling better real soon."

"Yes, ma'am." Seamus moved more papers, searching a second time.

I left Seamus to continue his hunt and stepped into the street. The church now doubling as the school wasn't far, and since I was in the neighborhood, so to speak, I'd stop by. While I walked, I thought about the fact there was not much I could do about Mr. Ritchie until the judge was in town and, I couldn't do anything else until I knew when, exactly. Frustrating. Why couldn't we have our own judge? Guess the county didn't have enough people. Nothing I could do about that either.

I spotted Pearl McIntyre, school marm, outside the church, watching the children at recess. Memories of those days brought a grin to my face and warmth to my chest. I'd always loved school. And playing outside after a long morning of working inside was such a treat. I'd run with the girls, playing "horse" or "tea party" and then the boys would chase us, sometimes with frogs in their hands. We'd squeal, of course, which delighted the fellas. And then at some point, us girls would ignore the boys, I suppose being tired of running, and continue the "tea party." The boys would wander off throwing rocks at each other, wrestling in the dirt or whatever it was they did.

Pearl waved to me. I guessed that meant we were still friends even though at times we'd been sworn enemies, vying for the same boyfriend—Seth Critoli, mayor, real estate broker and eligible bachelor. Besides his good looks, he'd make a great catch. He was smart, not wealthy but not poor, either. Came from a strong, Italian family. I wasn't completely sure he was husband material, but he was a good kisser. Not as sensational as Aldridge the Astonishing, but still the kind of kisser who could bring tingles to my toes.

Pearl and I met at the picket fence in front of the church. While still chilly, the recent winds had died, and the sun worked hard to warm the world. It was winning, and for that, I was grateful.

We spent a moment or two on pleasantries and then I got down to business. "You still plan on running for mayor?"

Her mouth flapped open, eyes widened, hands fisted to her hips. "I absolutely *still* am! Why would you think otherwise?" She moved in closer to where her flat stomach, which I envied, leaned into the wooden fence. "Did those three city... three wind... three town councilors say anything to you? Are they trying to get me to quit? Did they send you after me? Try to talk me into—"

"Whoa, Pearl." I held up a hand. "Nobody sent me. I hadn't heard much about your campaign yet and well, the election's less than a month away. I was wondering if you'd changed your mind." I knew things would be a lot easier if she withdrew, but I figured, with my luck, she'd decide to run for Governor.

Or President.

Jabbing a pointed finger toward the center of town, she gritted her teeth and lowered her voice into something resembling a snarl. "Those three jackasses don't want me for mayor. Think I can't do a good job. Think it's only a man's world." She turned her narrowed eyes on me, as if I was the enemy. "Women can do anything a man can. And better. I'm running a full-page ad in next week's paper and I'm having fliers printed. Got a speech prepared in my head that I'll write down soon."

All right, I was duly impressed, not so much at the intensity of her conviction, but at her swearing. Even I didn't have the nerve to call the town councilors 'jackasses' out loud. Maybe I was rubbing off on her. "I'm in your corner, you know that. But what about some of the issues? You ready to address those?"

"Like what?"

Suddenly, I had my doubts about supporting Pearl. Why was I the one to list issues? Shouldn't she have already thought of them? But I would help her along right now. "Building a school, is the obvious." Did I even have three or four ideas? Dry Creek seemed to run itself relatively well. I stretched for other issues. "And how about attracting more women-driven businesses?"

"Like what?"

She had me there. We already had a fire department, bakery, charm school, soon-to-be-Chinese school and newspaper. Did we need anything else? "How about a clothing store just for women? Or just for men? With all the latest fashions?"

"Huh." She actually snorted. "How about a new blacksmith shop? Or... I know." Her eyes went wide. "A construction company? Where they build houses and stores? Instead of relying on friends and neighbors to come help, this business could build houses."

While that sounded like an interesting idea, Dry Creek was way too small to make that business go. And I didn't like her idea of another blacksmith shop. The one we had was fine.

Behind Pearl, kids ran around the yard, one boy tugging

a girl's pigtails, two boys chucking rocks as far as they could, hitting the fence. *Ping... ping... ping*.

Pearl seemed preoccupied, oblivious to all this. Maybe if I saw it all day, every day, I'd be oblivious, too. I wondered how much longer they'd be in the glorious sun when she shook her head, sighed and called to the youngsters.

"Recess is over, children. Time to go in." She turned to me. "I'd like to sit down and talk to you, Maud. You've got good, progressive ideas. Just what Dry Creek needs."

A compliment in the highest order. Nobody had ever accused me of having 'progressive ideas'. They'd accused me of much more than that.

We agreed to meet Friday, but then I remembered Fred's send-off. We decided the weekend would work better.

CHAPTER TWENTY-EIGHT
A SEND-OFF TO REMEMBER...

I WOKE WITH A START. SOMETHING CAUSED ME TO bolt upright, heart pounding, mouth hanging open. I clutched the quilt like a soft barrier, hoping it would protect me. But from what? A dream? No, the ones I generally had were about as exciting as pulling weeds out of my garden. A long, blurry survey of my bedroom revealed no burglar riffling through my drawer, no rooster perched at the foot of my bed, no Pa saying he'd see me tonight before he left for work. Nothing but early-morning light worming its way into my bedroom.

I listened harder. Outside chickens clucked in the neighbor's backyard and farther, a horse clip-clopped toward town. Should I go explore?

That danged sun beamed harder, as if urging me to get up and get going. There was much to do today and time was wasting. Blast the happy sunshine. I pulled the quilt over my head and burrowed back into my nest for more much-deserved sleep.

Sinking into the sanctuary of my oh-so-comfortable mattress, my eyes closed, body relaxed and visions of black swept over me. A firm hand grasped my shoulder and gently rocked it back and forth.

"What?" I ripped the cover from my shoulders and sat

up. Pa stood, half a smile on his face. I must've looked a sight. My hair sticking out, eyes rolling and blinking. His face returned to serious. I mumbled an apology for my abrupt greeting, which he ignored.

"You heard knocking on the front door?" Pa tipped his head toward the living room. "Few minutes ago?"

I nodded, my mouth not ready for words yet.

"And ignored it?"

A shrug.

Pa's bushy eyebrows shot up, close to his hairline. "You need to come see." His outstretched arm waved. "I don't like it."

Tingling cold filled my chest. I didn't like it when he said 'don't like it.' This couldn't be good.

I barefooted into the living room, carefully opening the door as if the boogeyman would jump out and get me. Instead, I stared at a folded piece of paper tacked to it. Pa pulled it down, ripping part as he did and unfolded it. His lips moved as he read, then silently handed it to me.

"Watch out" written in red, scrawled across the page. Someone used lipstick instead of ink. To throw us off their trail? Whose trail? Watch out for what? And was this for me? Or Pa? Had to be for me, but since I hadn't told Pa about the other notes, I decided not to let on now. Both of us looked at each other, the paper, then at each other.

Right on cue, we stepped back into the house, closing the door.

"I'll make coffee," Pa said, heading for the kitchen.

I thought that was a great idea until I remembered the taste of what passed for his coffee. It hovered somewhere between dandelion bitter and so weak I could see the bottom of the cup. "I'll do it. You get dressed."

While he shaved, not humming as he usually did, I put the coffee on, scrambled eggs and fried up four pieces of bacon. Sliced sourdough bread went in the oven for much-needed toast. All the while I stewed over the note. At the least, it was a coward's way of talking about an issue. A cold familiar knot turned my stomach as I thought. I'd already been warned—more than once. Why wasn't I listening?

The list of recent people and places and conversations and discussions ran through my brain while I set the table. Seth? Nope. Penelope? Nope. Bakery ladies? Nope and nope. Pearl? I stopped at that one. Could it be her? And what did "watch out" mean? I continued my search. Aldridge? Absolutely not. Nathaniel Ford? Oh, *there* was a possibility. The three blowhards? Probably not, plus they would never hesitate to march into my office and confront me. I crossed them off my list. Who else? Pokey and Mae were instantly disqualified. The newspaper lady? Possibly, but not likely.

"Smells good."

I jumped, whirling around, fork and knife in hand. Pa stood, buttoning the top button of his shirt. He smelled like Bay Rum aftershave. My favorite. How long had I been standing there?

Without waiting, he pulled out a chair for me knowing I'd take it when I was done serving, then took his own, tucked the napkin under his chin. There was nothing in front of him, but he patiently sat, knowing that like a miracle, food would appear.

I poured coffee then served breakfast. I sat, mentally examined the note. We bantered speculations, neither of us coming up with answers. All we had were questions. Part of me felt bad about not telling him about the other notes, the other part not wanting to worry him. Until now, I had felt mildly threatened, more confused.

Pa patted his mouth wiping a renegade piece of egg off his neatly trimmed mustache. "I still can't think of anyone angry enough with the bank to threaten us like this." He stood, folded his napkin and laid it by his empty plate. "I'll pay more attention today. It *could* be me."

I chose to remain quiet since this was apparently escalating. I'd try to figure it out today. In front of the living room mirror, he ran his hands over his already smooth hair, fitted his bowler just so, thumbed his mustache, then nodded at an imagine he approved of. He threaded his arms into a well-fitted coat and wrapped me in a much-needed hug. "See you tonight."

He stepped out and then I remembered this was Friday. Big doings tonight. I called after him. "You coming to Fred's send-off at the saloon?"

Stopping, he turned around on the dirt walkway. "I doubt it. Didn't know him, and you know I'm not much for drinking and carousing anymore." His lips pursed. "Too old." He turned back around continuing his walk. "See you when you get home. Have a good time, but be careful, Maud." A wave, then he paraded through the gate, pivoted right and I'm sure his thoughts instantly turned to banking business, images of the note left far behind.

I stepped inside, closing the door. What did the warning mean? After cleaning up the kitchen, hoping Mrs. Tran would be pleasantly surprised, I changed into a plain brown skirt, topped by a blouse with tiny pink flowers that matched the skirt. After slipping the note into my skirt pocket, I pinned up my hair, slapped on a bonnet, buckled my rig around my waist and checked the gun to see if I still had a bullet in it. Satisfied I was ready, I shrugged into my coat and headed out the door.

I locked it extra carefully.

By the time I reached the office door, I was somewhat lathered up. Why had I ignored the other warning signs? All right, I hadn't totally ignored them, but obviously I hadn't treated them as seriously as I should have. And coming to my house was taking things too far. What would "they" do next? Pin it to my forehead?

Lines of scared bumps covered my arms as I sucked in my breath. Visions of me, lying in bed, a nail through my forehead knocked me into a cocked hat. Then more thoughts struck me. Something would happen tonight at Fred's send-off. It made total sense. Interfering with his wake would indeed make an impact, not only on me, but the entire town. Whoever was behind this, would show his face. I'd have to be extra ready.

I opened the office door and spied Pokey leaned back in a chair behind the desk. He stretched his arms and produced a canyon-sized yawn. "'Mornin' Maud." He tilted his head toward the closed door leading to the two cells. "Prisoner's already been to the privy and fed. Complained the whole time. Wish I could buffalo him just once. He'd be more grateful for grub after that."

I hung up my coat, bonnet, and gun, then poured water into the coffee pot. "You can't knock somebody senseless with your gun just because—"

"I know." Pokey rose to his feet, his arms stretched out again, another yawn. "Sure would feel good, though." He held out my key. "Aldridge said to give this to you."

I pocketed the key, added coffee grounds to the pot, lit the kindling and set the pot on the stove. I plopped into the chair enjoying the warmth left from Pokey's rear end.

He thumbed over his shoulder. "Gotta do the mail run this morning." His meaty legs took him to the door, then hand on handle, he turned back. "I'm thinking I'll stay here tonight and maybe Aldridge or maybe another fella ought to stay here during Fred's big send-off. Maybe a few of those ol' boys'll get jingled and come over here to break him out. Try to give our prisoner a necktie party before the judge comes."

Pokey had sure done some thinking overnight. And I was grateful. "Great idea. Aldridge is organizing the 'do' tonight, but maybe he'd rather be here. Should I get a third man?" My stomach knotted thinking of possible scenarios. Jail escape. Lynch mob. Guns blasting. "You know, just in case?" The note this morning added a notch to my tightly strung nerves. I decided not to tell him about it.

Ideas flitted across his furrowed forehead. He didn't think like this often, but when he did, it was serious. "Wouldn't be a bad idea, Maud. Maybe that fella helping out Mr. Swensen in the livery. He's muscled up well."

He was at that. Images of Jackson Powell popped into my head. Taller than most men in town, his shoulders were as wide as the door. Almost. And his skin. A lovely bronzy ebony that seemed to glow. The couple of times I'd spotted him without a hat, his curly black hair showed no signs of gray, so his age was a mystery. But no doubt he would do wonders keeping the peace.

"Thanks for the suggestion, Pokey. I'll stop by this morning." The aroma of boiled coffee brought me to my feet. I was in need of coffee and right now. And then it dawned on me. If I had to leave the office, I still had a prisoner to be watched. How could I be in two places at once? This having a prisoner was a novel idea, one that took a lot of planning.

Pokey opened the door. "Might have time to see Mae before I leave." His eyes took on a golden glow. He was in love, that much was plain.

"Before you go, do me a favor." I figured he'd have to forego Mae this one time. "See if Aldridge can come stay here this morning."

He looked at me through a hank of hair hanging in his eyes. He brushed it back. "This keeping prisoners sure puts a damper on life, don't it?"

"For a fact." I matched his half smile. "Have a safe run and I'll see you tonight."

"I'll see if I can find him and send him your way." A wave over his shoulder and he was gone. Before I sat sipping coffee and going through new wanted posters, I checked the prisoner. That proved to be a bad idea since during my chat with Pokey, Ritchie had been quiet. But once he saw me, he jumped off the cot and limped side to side, like a caged cougar.

"Can't keep me in here like this." He pointed to his leg. "Need a doc. It's painin' me something fierce."

I'd like to shoot his other leg, but reluctantly thought better of it. "If you stay off it, Mr. Ritchie, leg'll heal up just fine." I turned to go, already tired of his whining.

"Need the privy, Sheriff."

"You already went today."

"Some things can't be regulated. When I gotta go, I gotta go." He gripped the bars of his cell door, cocked his head. "I'm 'bout to piss myself somethin' fierce. And you'd have to clean it up!" Fits of laughter doubled him over. "Clean it up..."

Without response and not wanting to call his bluff, just in case, I returned with cell keys.

Before turning the key, I leveled my gun at him. "One wrong move. One." I hoped my voice was deep and deadly, but I doubted it. "Or you won't live to see the judge."

"That a threat?" His lips twisted slightly.

"A promise." I sucked in air trying to keep my hand from shaking and my heart pounding. I *really* wasn't good at being menacing.

He hobbled down the hall, my gun at his back. We went out to the alley where I waited for him at the privy's door. He took his time until at long last he stepped out and buttoned his fly as we returned to jail. I didn't relax until that cell door clicked and the key turned. Locked nice and tight.

I closed and locked the door to the cells behind me, poured coffee and plopped into the chair. Ritchie hollered a time or two, but when I didn't respond, he finally stopped. More than likely wore himself out.

The note on my door this morning rattled me more than I'd liked to admit. That piece of paper with red lipstick and two words felt much more threatening than I'm sure I looked with gun drawn, marching my prisoner to the outhouse.

As I sipped, I mulled over "Watch out." For what? Or who? Probably not a where or when. I considered the other three notes I'd received in the past few weeks. Pulling out my top desk drawer, I moved various scribbled reminders, copies of citations I'd issued, which turned out to be two, a crinkled wanted poster, extra bullets and at the bottom, the folded notes.

I pulled them out, straightened my shoulders and reread. Two "Bak offs," "Your next," and now "watch out" was chicken scratched across the papers. None were written in red, but with what looked like typical India ink. Handwriting could've been the same, but hard to tell with slightly smeared lipstick. And knowing 'your' and 'back' were misspelled didn't ignite any sense of doom and gloom. Until this morning, I'd figured it was one of Pearl's students playing tricks. Now I wasn't so sure.

Fact was, I was real sure I had a problem.

* * *

ALDRIDGE SHOWED up an hour after Pokey left, which had given me plenty of time to flip through wanted posters and sweep the office. I was on my third cup of coffee when Mr. Hero tapped on the door. He kissed me lightly, which sent tingles clear to my toes, then gave me a sound hug. He set me back on my feet. I didn't want to be released and it must have shown on my face.

"Wouldn't do for someone to come in and see the sheriff kissing one of the citizens," he said. "At least not while on duty." His sensitive dove-gray eyes melted me.

I sighed, possibly from the kiss but more likely from knowing that the badge burning into my chest never came off. "I'm *always* on duty."

"I beg to differ." He waggled a gorgeously soft finger toward my face. "I remember a time or two—"

"That was different."

We stood in silence for a moment. I couldn't tell what he was thinking, but I knew what *I* was. And my thoughts were not too sheriff-like or too lady-like. I smiled at his lightly pink cheeks. We must've had the same ideas.

"Any more of that coffee?" He pointed at the potbelly stove in the corner, then managed to unstick his boots from the floor and walk toward the aroma.

"Help yourself." Since Pokey hadn't had any, there

should be a cup or so left. My legs didn't want to move, but they sensed Aldridge had left, so they followed. I sat behind the desk while Mr. Wonderful took a seat across and sipped his black brew.

"How long you need me here?" He cocked his head toward the Tin Pan Saloon. "Still have a couple things to finish up before tonight's send-off."

"Shouldn't take more than an hour. Two at the most." I stared at the Adonis-of-my-dreams. He was gorgeous and I was so incredibly lucky.

"... agreed to play his bagpipes tonight. Who knew he brought them over with him." Aldridge shrugged. "Amazing the background of people."

Refusing to admit I hadn't been paying attention, I agreed, then changed the subject. "As you know, there's talk of breaking Mr. Ritchie out of jail and stringing him up. If the men get too much of that tonsil varnish tonight, they're liable to head over here and take the law into their own hands."

Aldridge ran a hand over his freshly shaved cheeks, smoothing his recently trimmed mustache. "That's a good possibility. Who's guarding the henhouse?"

"Hoping you, Pokey and Jackson Powell from the livery." I'd absolutely die if anything happened to any of these men. "I hoped after you get things going tonight, you could come over and guard. I'll keep an eye on the saloon."

"I could do that. And Powell? I've met him. He's one gigantic muscle."

My thoughts exactly. "I'll go ask him soon as I leave here. I'll find money to pay the two of you for babysitting. Pokey gets paid since he's already a part-time deputy."

And then it struck me. I had the right to deputize Aldridge and Mr. Powell. Then their presence guarding the prisoner would be legitimate. I ran the idea by my sweetheart.

"Me? Deputy?" Aldridge sat mouth open, holding his cup halfway to it. And then he chuckled, which grew into a full-blown laugh. "Never ever thought, ever considered I'd be a deputy, especially to a female sheriff. Oh, that's rich." He plopped the cup on my desk.

I wasn't sure whether to be delighted or offended. I chose delighted but guarded. "You have a problem being my deputy?" Maybe I'd come on a little too strong, but it turned out I was more offended than I'd thought.

His mirth faded as he considered. "You gotta admit it's unusual having a woman as a law officer. Especially one so beautiful." He leaned forward. "It's been a stretch for me to believe you're a sheriff, but I've seen you in action. I respect you for taking on such a job."

"And?"

His face blossomed. "I'd be honored to be a part-time, temporary deputy sheriff." He winked at me. "Especially for you."

If I hadn't been sitting, I would've melted into one gigantic puddle. As it was, I struggled to keep the smile from hurting my face. We held hands across the desk. "Thank you."

After finishing my coffee, I couldn't think of a good reason to stay. Assuring him I'd be gone only a while and that the prisoner had already gone to the privy twice this morning, there shouldn't be any problems.

I slipped into my coat, fastened the gun belt around my waist, pulled open the top drawer where I kept my gun. I froze. Underneath lay the notes. Should I tell Aldridge? Most of me screamed yes, but the logical, cautious part warned me off. While I deeply, honestly liked this man, how much about him did I really know? This time, I listened to my level head and kept quiet.

I tied my bonnet, stepped into a frosty morning. If I turned around to wave, I'd go back inside. So, determined to get things done, I aimed for Swensen's livery and black-smith shop. Swensen's was one of two liveries, but the only blacksmith around for miles. He did a tremendous business, I'd heard.

As usual, it took longer to get to the end of town than it should because so many people stopped to either simply chat or ask about the prisoner, the trial, tonight's send-off, or to jaw about their past experiences with miscreants. At last I broke free and entered the shop.

The aroma of fresh hay and oats collided with the odor of horse sweat and heated coals. In one corner, hunched over an anvil, stood owner Swede Swensen, a burly but sweet older black man. He put down his iron hammer and smiled at me.

"Howdy, Miss Maud. Good ta see ya again." He pulled off a thick glove and held out a callused hand. We shook.

We talked about his business, how it was booming with the town acquiring new residents now and then. I asked about Jackson Powell since I didn't see him around the livery stable or blacksmith shop.

Swede shook his head. "Sent him out ta Dirkson's farm dis mornin'. I bought deir ol' buggy. Gonna fix it up and plan ta sell it. Might make myself some money off it."

"He'll be back today?" My hopes for three deputies tonight faded.

"Lordy, I hep so. Why, Miss Maud, if he ain't back by dinner time, I be mighty surprised."

My hopes blossomed. I explained my temporary part-time deputy idea and Swede agreed.

"You're always thinkin', Miss Maud." Swede shook my hand again. "Yessiree, always thinkin'."

I wondered once more how this man, obviously of African descent, had acquired the name of Swede Swensen. I'd asked once and he'd simply laughed and said it was a long story. Maybe some other time he'd tell.

"Would you have him come over to the office the minute he gets in?"

"I will, Miss Maud." Swede tugged on his gloves, picked up his hammer and waved.

* * *

To admit I was nervous, anxious, close to panicky, would be an understatement. It for sure wasn't the wake itself that sent my heart pounding whenever I thought of it. If we'd planned a send-off only, I would've been able to eat supper. But with the added concern of a lynch mob applying frontier justice their own way, I was a wreck.

I breathed a huge sigh of relief when Pokey showed up at the office at dusk. We went over where the rifles were—I'd moved them from their rack in the front of the office just in case. Pokey had both cell keys, the ones to the cell itself and the one to the inner wooden door, in his pocket.

Jackson Powell walked in on time and I swore him in. I'd managed to find two extra badges, which I'd assumed were from the previous sheriff's days. Jackson snapped to attention and stood straight as an oak while saluting. When I pinned on the star, his broad shoulders grew even wider, if that was possible. I saluted back and he dropped his arm and relaxed.

I figured the town councilors wouldn't approve of spending money on these deputies, but I'd worry about that later. Right now, I needed three deputies, and that's what I would have.

Pokey and Jackson roamed the office, checking their weapons, the windows, even the full coffee pot. I'd made fresh in case they needed some tonight. I opened the door allowing cold air to rush inside while tinny piano music wafted in with it. Although cold, it was refreshing. A couple of cowboys sauntered down the street toward the festivities. I hoped the send-off would be well attended, and I realized, again, this was the right thing to do for Fred.

The Regulator on the wall showed six, straight up. Hopefully, within the hour Aldridge would come in and I could head over to the doings. From what I could tell, it would be a fine Irish wake, one that might live in Dry Creek infamy.

The three of us paced, sat, slurped coffee, told stories and grew quiet. I nearly jumped out of the chair when the door squeaked open. My Mr. Honey stood there surveying the room and then closed the door. He hung up his coat and pinned on his new badge.

"Are we ready for this?" Aldridge shook hands with Jackson and Pokey while I eyed the three of them now standing close together.

Nodding, a swell of pride made me stand up taller. Things would be fine tonight. These men would see to it nobody, but nobody, would break Mr. Ritchie out of jail.

My gaze trailed over Pokey, his eyes wider than usual. Jackson pursed his lips and nodded. Aldridge winked at me. Maybe I should stay here and help guard. Dragging my feet to the door, I wrapped myself in my coat. I turned back. "Thank you again for being willing to do this. The whole town owes you a big thanks."

Aldridge held the door open for me. He waved toward the saloon. "Go send off Fred. It's already quite the party. We'll be fine here. Don't worry."

I wanted to hug and kiss him, but instead I smiled and nodded.

The Tin Pan Saloon was about as noisy as I'd ever heard. And crowded. Men from all walks of life stuffed themselves into the room. The piano player's fingers raced across the keys while several men and two women attempted to sing along. Faro, normally in the back of the room, was being dealt up front. I didn't spot any poker games, but that was sure to come.

Men appeared congenial, happy, boisterous even, but not rowdy. I elbowed my way up to the bar and stood, glass in hand, watching the celebration. I'd about decided to keep a low profile right where I was when, lo and behold, Rudolfo Garcia hobbled in. Locating me, he immediately made his way over.

"Shouldn't you still be in bed?" For crying out loud, he'd been shot, almost killed, less than a week ago.

"Had to come." Rudolfo leaned against the bar where Sam pushed a beer mug in front of him. "Pay my respects."

I wanted to ask if his wife had agreed to his hobbling over here, but thought better of it. "One beer, then promise to go home?" Boy, howdy, did I sound like a mother hen. But I worried about him.

He nodded over his beer.

"Speech! Speech!" The crowd chanted and grew louder with each passing 'speech.' I knew then I couldn't keep a low profile. In fact, I mused, my job and badge preceded me wherever I went. There *was* no such thing as going unnoticed.

Beer mug placed on the bar, I held up both hands for quiet, then wended my way through the happy revelers until I stood near the piano. Thankfully, he stopped playing and my ears quit ringing. I hadn't planned on anything other than "so sorry," which made me wish I'd thought this through a little better.

The hundred or so men shushed each other while a drunken voice in the back yelled for quiet. "Thank you," I said. "We all want to pay our respects to Fred Gaspioni, who lost his life right here in this saloon. I'm hoping he's in a happy place now." I raised an imaginary mug until someone shoved a real one in my hand. "Here's to Fred."

Right on cue, a bagpipe droned from the back of the room. Strains of Amazing Grace wailed and the room grew quiet. Heads turned to locate Paddy O'Dougal, cheeks puffing as he blew into the straw-like mouthpiece and played. His fingers ran up and down the pipe, the sound creating a soulful resonance. A plaid bag perched under his right arm flapping up and down, pumped air into what I assumed was the main pipe. I'd never seen one up close.

A few sniffles punctured the music. My chest swelled and eyes teared as I fought to keep my composure.

By the time he finished, there wasn't a dry eye in the room. I held up a mug once more. "To Fred."

"Here, here." The crowd raised their mugs, some clanking with others.

"Last round of whiskey on the house," I told the group.

Somber mood shattered, men stampeded toward the bar, and I wished I hadn't said it so loudly. By the time I got through the crowd, Rudolfo was gone, which was good. I enjoyed the pats on the back and words of 'did the right thing' from various men. A sweep around the room and I decided that yes, indeed, it was a grand idea. The men were behaving themselves, which frankly, surprised me.

I relaxed, but only a bit, knowing that in a few hours, this would be a memory.

Clang! Clang! Clang!

Did I hear right? The fire bell—again? I pushed my way outside, joined by half the men.

Unquestionably the fire bell. And then I spotted it. Halfway down Main and two blocks over, red played off the underside of clouds. Fiery orange hovered over the town like the devil himself. And then I smelled it. Smoke.

All sorts of questions along with bad words filled my head. "Somebody find Penelope.

Let's go!" But I didn't have to say that. Men and the few women emptied out of the saloon, running full out toward the flames. Some grabbed water buckets, which sat next to watering troughs. Men yelled orders. Everyone ran. Knowing it wasn't my house, which was the other way, I remembered only private houses sat in that part of town. But whose?

I skidded to a stop in front of my office. Pokey met me at the door.

"Nice and quiet here, Maud. What's going on?"

"Fire. Make sure you're on your toes. This could get ugly."

He nodded, closed and locked the door. I prayed the fire wasn't meant as a distraction to break out Ritchie. Skirt held high enough to see my ankles, I rushed toward the fire, joining the throng already there.

Although it was dark, I immediately recognized the house. Mrs. Anna Simpson, a widow, and her grown daughter who was a bit 'touched in the head' as they said, stood in the road watching flames lick their two-story house. They clung to each other while the bucket brigade filled, tossed, and doused. I spotted Penelope Plunkett right up front, giving orders and taking charge as she should.

By the time the fire was under control, it looked to me like the entire structure was lost.

Fortunately, houses on both sides had escaped flames, but I was sure they'd smell like smoke for weeks.

A woman slid her arm around the widow, regarded the daughter, then led them off. I presumed they'd go some place to rest and figure out what to do next. The idea of having fire insurance smacked me in the face. If Mrs. Simpson had insurance, she'd recoup at least part of what it would cost to rebuild. Then it smacked me even harder. What if Nathaniel Ford set this fire to make an example? That had to be it. Ford at his worst.

And what about the note? Was this the 'watch out' it threatened? Had to be. It all made sense now.

If I could find Ford tonight, I would arrest him on suspicion of arson, even though the cause of the fire hadn't been determined. That would come in the next few days.

But still. I clenched both hands. I *would* arrest him.

CHAPTER TWENTY-NINE
TO PROTECT AND...

THE EXHAUSTED PART OF ME AIMED FOR MY HOUSE and bed. I'd deal with Nathaniel Ford, the arsonist, tomorrow. Visions of cool water erasing the smoke and grime from my face pushed me onward. The thought of a wet, soapy cloth running up and down my arms and legs, removing the smell of my soot-encrusted body, propelled me even faster. After my spit-bath, I'd then have a long drink of water and slide into bed.

The sheriff part of me nixed the whole idea. What sort of law person was I if I simply went home and didn't at least stop to check on my men? I smiled at that image as I turned around and headed for the office. *My* men. Sounded good. So sheriff-like. But I had to know the deputies were safe and the prisoner still behind bars. *Then* I could sleep well.

Stepping up onto the boardwalk in front of the office, I straightened my hat and wiped my eyes, still stinging. I sniffled in more smoke, rubbed my face and opened the door.

Darkness greeted me. Why had I failed to notice no light in the window as I walked by? Heavy breathing, followed by a groan or two sailed from the room. I took a few steps and stumbled over a body. It grunted.

"Aldridge?" I called out.

No answer.

"Pokey?"

Groans from across the room told me where a second man lay. "Mr. Powell?"

Silence. Afraid to move to keep from falling over someone, I called again, panic gripping my breath and filling my chest. More groans, this time off to the right. Gunpowder aroma wafted under my nose. Knowing I couldn't stand here until daylight, I edged around the body at my feet, slogged through papers and what felt like a wooden chair splintered on the floor and at last located the lantern on a table by the desk. I fished around for a lucifer, struck it on the wooden wall and lit the wick. Golden light filled the room.

A nightmare beyond anything I'd ever encountered, screamed at me.

Even in the soft glow, I made out Jackson near the door, the man I'd toed as I'd entered. Aldridge lay near the open door to the cells and Pokey sagged against the wall under the window. He raised a hand and let it fall back onto his lap.

I picked my way through the debris and knelt by Pokey. "You all right? You shot? What happened? Who did this?" The questions poured out over my stunned heart. I had more, but they wouldn't come.

Pokey raised a limp arm again and whispered, his voice gravely. "They took Ritchie. Men with hoods."

"But are you shot?"

He wagged his head.

"Rest here. I'll be back." I found Aldridge sprawled face down, blood pooling under his arm. Shaking his shoulder, I hoped, prayed he was still alive. What had I done? I should've let the mob take Ritchie, then nobody, except the prisoner, would've been hurt.

"Aldridge?" I placed my hand on his back and felt breathing. A silent *thank you* sailed upward.

As much as I wanted to focus on My Man, My Hero, I

rushed to Jackson Powell. He lay a foot from the front door and from the way he was angled, I thought maybe he'd chased someone outside. He was on his side, so I checked for breathing. Alive.

I stood and sent monumental sighs and *thanks* skyward.

What I knew I'd find, but didn't want to see, was an empty cell. Did they take him alive or hang him right here? Neither option appealed. As soon as I knew the answer to this mess, I'd find Doc Monroe and rush him here.

A glance into the slate gray hallway revealed no body swinging from the ceiling. And no body lying dead on a cot. In fact, both cells were empty. For that, I was grateful. On the other hand, now I had to ride off to find the prisoner before he got himself killed.

I told Pokey I was going to get the doc, assuring him things were all right. He didn't appear to be shot, but more than likely Jackson and Aldridge were. Sprinting up Main Street, I thought about my deputies. They were lucky to be alive. How could I have let these men be deputies knowing I had put them in harm's way? I scolded myself all the way up the street and over a block. By the time I arrived at Doc's door, I was beyond fuming at myself. How could I?

I banged on the door until a light bloomed from the front room. A sleepy Mrs. Wilma Monroe answered the door. I explained what had happened, my words rushed and breathless. It was then I realized tears clouded my vision.

"He'll be right over, Maud. Give him two minutes." Her voice, reassuring and confident, relaxed me.

I nodded, turned and sprinted back, hoping they were all still alive. When I opened the office door, Aldridge sat leaning against the wall and Jackson sat on the floor, propped against the desk.

Within minutes, Doc Monroe yanked open the door, marched into the room and immediately took control. I couldn't remember being so glad to see someone as I was then. He would be the savior to fix my men. I pointed out the three and speculated as to their wounds.

All three were now conscious—*awake* would be a stretch —and mumbling, Pokey assuring me he was fine. He didn't look fine with blood caking on the left side of his head and, even in the dim light, a fist-sized bruise forming on his right jaw. I helped him over to a chair, which I up righted, made sure he could sit without falling over. Patting his shoulder and grimacing at more emerging bumps and bruises, I left him to nurse his aches. I knelt by Doc at Aldridge's side. Doc's voice was low but conclusive.

"... shoulder's gonna need surgery to get that bullet out."

My injured Super-Hero mumbled a response, something I thought sounded like bad language. Really, genuinely bad language. I'd give him this one. Knowing Aldridge was sort of in one piece, I turned my attention to Jackson.

Still collapsed against the desk, his chest heaved up and down like the steam engines I'd seen in Sacramento. Eyes squeezed shut, he jerked when he moved a leg.

"Stay quiet now." I tried my finest doctoring voice and found it lacking. I hadn't had much practice. "Doc Monroe is here, and he'll take care of you."

"Tried... to stop 'em." Jackson's voice, warped by pain, came out flat, expressionless. "Sorry... tried..."

Guilt froze my throat and squeezed. It was my fault. All this, my fault. I patted Jackson's arm, then stood. Knowing I had to make a plan and do it alone, I reached for the three rifles and one double-barrel shotgun I'd hidden in a back storage room. Gone. All gone.

Not only were the men who'd absconded with Ritchie successful, but they were now heavily armed and plenty riled up. Probably even liquored up. A disastrous combination. I shoved my shaking hands into my skirt pockets, fisted and unfisted them. As the saying went, this had been a 'bag of nails' day, for sure.

I stood for a moment, lantern glow reaching as far as my feet. A couple of deep breaths, I relaxed my hands and stepped back into better light.

Doc glanced up from Jackson. "He'll be fine, Maud. Grazed, dazed and bruised, but otherwise all right."

I sent another *thank you* upward. Whoever was in charge in Heaven must've been digging out from under the barrage of *thanks* right now. I considered smiling at the image but couldn't bring my mouth to form even a grin.

"Let's get 'em to my office, Maud." Doc gripped Jackson under the arms lifting him to his feet. I helped Aldridge stand while Pokey managed on his own.

Stopping often, Doc and I managed to walk Pokey, Aldridge and Jackson to his office where Doc's wife met us at the door. The waiting room was ablaze with many lanterns and down the hall, light spilled out from doorways. Wilma gripped Pokey's upper arm and led him away.

My Sweetheart gripped his arm, clenched his teeth and swallowed what I was sure was agony. Having a bullet in your shoulder must hurt worse than Lucifer's fire. As much as I wanted to hug him, kiss him, I wanted him to get patched up even more. Before I could tell him how much I cared, Wilma appeared and led Aldridge down the hall. I'd tell him later.

Doc helped Jackson navigate the hallway down to the end room. I followed, not really helping much. There was not enough room for three abreast.

"I'm going after the men who did this, Doc."

He looked back, frowned and opened his mouth I'm sure to tell me not to go, to let someone else handle this, to let it be.

"I'll be careful. And I'll be back." My voice brimmed with conviction. I *would* be careful, I *would* return and dang it, I *would* get those men.

As I rushed back to the office, it dawned on me mayor Seth and town councilor Slim Higginbotham had helped me before and would probably step up again. As much as my bravado demanded I do this alone, my intelligent self begged to differ. I needed help. And now.

I reversed course and headed for Seth's house, figuring he'd already be in bed by now. But maybe not. I'd seen him at the fire, so maybe he was in the Tin Pan. Changing course again, I aimed for Slim's house. I hadn't seen him tonight, even though he owned the saloon in which the send-off took place.

I knocked on his door, loudly, the wood echoing alarm. His darkened front room suddenly lit, and he opened with the third pounding.

"Maud? What's going on?" He blinked, yawned and frowned at the same time.

"Jail break. Some men took Bertram Ritchie, plan to hang him, I'm sure."

"That the fella killed Fred?"

I nodded. "Pokey, Aldridge and Jackson Powell were standing guard."

"Any of them hurt?" Slim's eyes narrowed, his lips a tight line.

"Aldridge... shot in the shoulder. Other two got beaten. Doc says they'll recover." I realized my voice quavered, but I forced myself to stand tall. "I need help. Couple men to go with me. Gotta find the lynch mob before they hang Ritchie."

To my relief, Slim nodded. "I'll meet you in the office in ten minutes. Gotta get dressed first."

I backed off the porch and then stopped. "And you should know... they took all my rifles and shotgun."

Slim muttered under his breath as he closed the door. I figured it was words similar to Aldridge's.

Luck holding, I located Seth coming out of the Tin Pan. I told him about the situation, and he also agreed to help. Bless them both.

* * *

WE MET IN MY OFFICE. I'd righted all the chairs and pushed aside other debris. Both Slim and Seth inspected the empty cell, which I took to mean they didn't trust that indeed, Ritchie was gone. I pushed down outrage remembering they'd come in the middle of the night to help me.

"Clean gone." Seth nodded as he looked into the cell, the door wide open.

"Sure is." Slim looked over Seth's shoulder then turned to me. "When'd this happen?"

"During the fire. I was thinking it was set by Nathaniel Ford for his insurance business, but now I'm thinking it was to keep us all busy while they grabbed the prisoner." Voicing my thoughts like that confused me. Maybe it wasn't Ford, after all. But it probably was.

Before leaving, we checked ammunition. My revolver revealed a full load, Seth and Slim nodded they were loaded as well. I locked the outside door, aware of the cold seeping under my coat, but there was nothing I could do about it. I chose to ignore the light wind bringing even colder temperature. And then I remembered I didn't have a horse. I needed to run back home, saddle up Pa's mean-tempered nag. I'd probably get bitten in the process.

I let out two loud swearwords, which brought both men to a halt. I spoke through gritted teeth. "Gotta rent a horse before I go. Not taking Pa's." How could I be so stupid? What was I thinking?

"Don't worry." Slim pointed to the hitch rail in front of the office. "Brought you one."

I could've kissed him, or hugged him, but I felt too foolish. "Thanks," I managed to squeak out.

Mounting with a long skirt on wasn't easy, but I remembered soon how to do it. One foot in the left stirrup, a boost from Seth and I was on. They swung up into their saddles while I adjusted my weight and slipped my shoe into the right stirrup.

"Pokey said he thought someone said they'd go to that stand of cottonwoods down by the river." I regarded both men and sent another note skyward, this time one of good luck. "Think we should head there."

Without a word, the three of us galloped south out of town, then turned east toward the river. A partial moon toyed with our path. I could make out the road, the nearby trees, but nothing much else. We stayed silent, the beating of hooves the only sound in the forest. We traveled at least three miles, maybe four.

And then a noise in the distance. Voices? We reined to a stop and sat. Yep. Voices. Men's orders. Another voice pleading.

I wanted to ride in, shooting, doing sheriffing actions, saving Ritchie, but my logical mind said to dismount and walk in. "Let's stop here," I whispered. "And like hunters, sneak in."

"How many you think there are?" Seth eased from his saddle, looped the reins around a tree branch.

"Sounds like six, seven, maybe." Slim tied his horse while, reluctantly, I dismounted, gathered my skirt and tied off my horse, too.

"Sounds like they've been drinking." Seth kept his voice extra low. "Use it to our advantage."

I considered the options quickly. A pleading voice, higher this time, rolled our way. Drunken laughter cut the darkness.

"Let's go together," I said. "Seth, you get Ritchie. Slim, you and I'll distract them." My heart pounded one second then quit the next. Breath caught in my chest. "Shoot over their heads.

Shoot to kill only if absolutely necessary. Stay safe."

We zigzagged through the trees and stopped when we could make out the men. I counted six, two holding torches, giving us just enough light to see men with raised bottles saluting the endeavor.

Under a towering cottonwood, a terrified Ritchie, hands bound behind him, sat on a horse. One man looped a noose around his neck while the other tossed the end over a thick branch, one hand up to catch the rope. Another man held the horse's reins.

Using the one man's attention on catching the rope, Ritchie kicked out, connecting with his chest.

The man I didn't recognize clutched it and staggered back. The other man reached up, grabbed Ritchie by the shirtfront pulling him sideways, and smashed his fist into Ritchie's face. Bloodlust was at a fevered pitch, and I knew we had seconds to save his life.

Gun drawn and cocked, I stepped into the light. "Hold it right there." I shot into the air, Ritchie's horse backed, but the man gripped the reins and held him. Bits of tree rained on our heads. "Let him go."

"You heard the sheriff, fellas." Slim's voice to my left, echoed tough, decisive.

To my right, Seth's boots pushed aside fallen leaves. His gun cocked, giving off a metallic warning of impending death.

"Don't tell us what to do." Jim Bob Buchanan, a man I recognized from church, held up a torch and stepped toward me. "Gonna hang this bastard right here, right now."

"Back off." Pointing my gun at Buchanan's chest, I cocked it and stepped toward him. "You're not lynching this man tonight, or any night." I waved the Colt across the men frozen and tensed, as if waiting to pounce on us. "You're all under arrest."

Buchanan, eyes glowing in the torchlight, took a step backward. I moved forward.

Seth edged his way over to Ritchie, the men around him easing backward. "Get 'em up." Seth waved the gun.

One man raised his empty hands shoulder high, but the other refused. A fella I'd seen around town, but didn't know, brought his gun up, pulled the trigger.

Bang!

I jerked and Seth lurched sideways, falling against the horse, skittered sideways, dislodging its rider. Ritchie whumped to the ground, laid still, the noose looped around his neck, the rest of the rope snaking across him.

Trying to figure out what had just happened, I glanced at

Slim who shot over heads. Several of his *bang, bang, bangs* zinged across the river. I aimed toward the men and then shot upward. Like the drunken cowards they were, all turned and ran for their horses. They swung up in one fluid motion, kicking their mounts into full-out runs.

"You're all under arrest!" I yelled at the receding marauders, like they would all stop and come back. Down to a man, they galloped off, bent over the horses' necks, determined to put distance between them and us.

When it became clear I'd arrest no one tonight, I let down the hammer on my gun, holstered it and turned my attention to Seth. He sat on the ground gripping his left arm. I knelt next to him, his brown eyes trailing up to me. My words came out ragged. "You all right? You shot?"

He regarded his shoulder, then tugged at his coat sleeve. A tear, part of the material burned, showed a bullet's path. "Gonna need a good seamstress, Maud." Seth patted his arm and shoulder, then grinned. "Seem to be in one piece."

Sighing out loud, I kissed him on the temple. "Think you can stand?"

He nodded, getting to his feet before I could.

With Seth relatively unscathed, I checked on Ritchie, still lying on the ground with Slim kneeling over him.

"What d'you think? He all right?"

Slim nodded then turned his eyes to me. "Wind got knocked out. He'll be fine."

"Good." Deep down, body-numbing fatigue enveloped me. Could I lie right here in the forest, sleep until tomorrow? Maybe through next week?

Taking the noose off Ritchie's neck, Slim pulled him to his feet. "Taking you back to jail. Behave yourself." He patted the butt of his gun. "Would hate to have to shoot you."

While Slim helped the prisoner onto his horse, Seth slid an arm around my sagging shoulders. "You done good, Maud. Damn good." He hugged tighter.

I needed to hear those words. I needed to know something went right. A weight lifted from my entire body.

Seth pulled me in close, kissed my forehead. "When're you going after the arsonist? I hear you're looking for Nathaniel Ford."

Yep, I was right—*always* on duty.

CHAPTER THIRTY
THE NEED FOR COFFEE...

I'D HATED LIKE THE DEVIL TO ASK SETH TO STAY guarding the prisoner overnight, but I just *had* to get home for much-needed sleep. As it was, the Regulator was striking three when I let myself in the front door. Pa's snores rolled down the hall, fluttering the curtains. Not exactly that bad, but enough I was afraid I wouldn't get any rest.

Turned out, I slept like a rock. An exhausted rock.

Sunlight radiated into the bedroom accosting my eyes. I blinked awake, angry at that danged cheerful sunbeam until I stumbled into the living room only to discover the Regulator had struck nine a quarter hour ago. Letting out a string of curse words then realizing I needed to stop doing that, cursing not being ladylike, I padded back to the bedroom. I dressed in record time, pinned my hair up with only a strand or two coming loose and headed for the kitchen. This being Saturday, Mrs. Tran didn't come in until noon. Maybe Pa had made coffee.

But I didn't smell any. And just as I suspected, a cold, empty pot sat on the stove, waiting for water and ground up beans to be added. I did, however, find a note from Pa stating he'd get breakfast down at the Café and not to bring him any. I started to curse Pa, then reversed my thinking. If

I stopped at Hilda's, I could get good coffee *and* strudel. Maybe she would have apples to go on that confectionary delight along with a dash of cinnamon on top. I licked my lips.

So, today wouldn't be so bad after all.

Hilda not only had extra apples for the strudel, but she brought a brimming plate of scrambled eggs and two slabs of bacon that overflowed rim to rim. I ate like I'd been nearly starved to death and then realized that was close to the truth. As I stuffed myself, I thought about my last meal and couldn't figure out when it was, exactly. Yesterday? Maybe.

As much as I wanted to spend the entire day bathed in scrumptious smells and delicious coffee, I had people to see and things to do. Wiping my mouth one last time, I pushed back and waddled to my feet. I pulled out coins for a tip knowing the town picked up my main meals. Part of the perks, being sheriff.

On my agenda was checking in at Doc's to see how the three deputies were doing. But first was going to the office, relieving Seth and seeing how the remainder of the night had gone. Feeling especially lazy this morning, I gave Hilda extra coins and asked her to send over two cups of coffee every couple of hours. That way it would be hot and fresh and most importantly—I didn't have to make it.

The bounce in my step was obvious as I headed for the office. Citizens of this fine community waved and nodded as I passed. A few called out "Good morning!" which I agreed with. Even though it was on the nippy side, the air was surprisingly warm and the sun especially bright, no clouds blocking its efforts.

I pushed open the door and froze. Four male faces turned in unison and stared at me. My stomach clenched and breakfast stuck in my throat. Ian MacKinney, Harvey Weinberg, Slim Higginbotham and Seth Critoli stood in my office, taking up all the space and most of the air. Judging by the dark circles under both Slim's and Seth's eyes, their cheeks in need of a fresh shave, I guessed both had stayed up all night. All of a sudden guilt hit me. I should have stayed.

Smiling, I unfroze. "Gentlemen. Good morning." I tried a chipper attitude hoping they were here simply to congratulate me. "What brings you out on this beautiful Saturday morning?" I hung up my bonnet and coat but kept the rig buckled around my waist, demonstrating, I hoped, I was indeed of sheriff quality. It was obvious word had gotten around about last night—I had a gun and wasn't afraid to use it.

Harvey pushed his way closer to me. "Maud. We heard what you did last night." His curls bounced against his temples. "First the wake, then the fire and *then* the lynching. *Oy vey!*"

"*Near* lynching," I corrected. My chest puffed a bit knowing I'd done my job well and, of course, there was a commendation forthcoming.

"'Tis all well and gud." Ian elbowed Harvey out of the way. "But what is the circuit judge goin' ta see when he gets here?" He looked behind him for what I assumed was support and raised his eyebrows. Ian pointed a stubby finger at me. "I'll tell ye what. He'll see a fire company, businesses, candidate for mayor... all run by womens. Womens I tell ye. We canna let that happen, Maud. We simply canna."

At least I'd had two cups of coffee before this, so I was fully awake. But not prepared. Deflated, I angled toward the desk hoping to use it as a shield against these crazy men.

"And we all know," Harvey followed my trajectory. "A woman's place is in the home. Not running around putting up signs or putting out fires. That's for men to do."

"'Tis correct, he is." Pocket-sized Ian seemed to stretch as he nodded at Harvey. "'Tis sinful, is whut it 'tis."

Now safely behind the desk, I stood, arms folded, wondering why Slim was here and why Seth so quiet. They knew what was going on, I supposed. As much as I vowed not to get into a shouting match, I lowered my voice and pointed toward the window. "And what about last night—saving the other houses around Widow Simpson's? If Penelope hadn't been right there, the entire block would've gone up in flames. And what's wrong with a woman being mayor?" I figured I was pushing that one, but now I was mad. How dare they barge in here and bring this up.

Again.

Before I could continue, Seth stepped out of the group. "I gotta go, Maud. Slim and I both stayed last night and right now I could use breakfast and sleep." He nodded to Slim, wagged his head at the other two, then was gone before I could thank him.

"All this trouble, Maud." Harvey scooted a chair across the wooden planking of the office floor, grunted into it. "All because of females. If you and your kind had stayed home, stayed out of business, we wouldn't have the troubles right now."

My fuse was lit. These men had stomped all over on what had promised to be a terrific day and now I'd stomp on theirs. Screaming and hollering would do no good, so I calmly gathered my skirt and, in my top ladylike fashion, sat. I interlaced fingers, placed hands on the desktop, pulled in two chestfuls of air. Vowing they wouldn't get me rattled this time, I raised both eyebrows. "What, exactly, is the problem, gentlemen? What, exactly, do you expect me to do?"

"Well... uh, well," Ian sputtered. "Looks like you're a-leadin' the female pack. If ye back down, those she-wolves will too."

"You'd like me to resign?" It took all the power I possessed to push down the rising bile indignation produced. Heat radiated up the back of my head, but I refused to play their game. "I think not. You see, I was elected properly, and the people of this town deserve someone who follows through with promises."

Harvey rapped his fist on my desk. "Now see here, Maud. Your time has come and now it's gone. Kaput."

Untwining my fingers, I placed both hands palm down on the desk and pushed to my feet. "You'll have to excuse me gentlemen. I have to see to the prisoner, then continue my duties."

I glanced at Slim, who grinned and nodded.

"You canna—"

"Good day now, gentlemen. Thanks for stopping by." I opened the door, ushered out a flapping Ian and fuming Harvey. Once I closed it, a slow half-grin crawled up my face.

Slim stood clapping. "You're amazing, Maud. Look how you backed down those two." He hugged me tighter than I'd wanted, but I enjoyed it anyway. "Proud of you."

He let go and I'm sure I blushed, my face warming more than the inside temperature.

"You and Seth both stayed last night? There a reason?"

"We talked about who would stay, then decided that lynch mob might come back." He shrugged. "Wanted to be ready, just in case."

Taken aback, I'd never considered that. Again, what had I been thinking? "But they didn't, right?"

"Right." Slim thumbed over his shoulder toward the cell. "Ritchie's already had breakfast, been to the privy. Don't let him tell you otherwise."

I nodded, then asked, "Would you be able to stay a few more minutes? I gotta go to the Doc's, check on the deputies." Especially My Honey Hero. "Shouldn't be long."

"Sure." Slim stepped behind the desk, pulled out the chair and eased into it. He lifted a leg to set his boot on the top of the desk, glanced up at me, then thought better of it and set it back down. "On one condition, though."

I tilted my head. No telling what he wanted.

"Bring back some coffee. Please." Slim held up two fingers. "Maybe two cups?"

* * *

I OPENED Doc's door and stepped into a surprise. Pokey sat upright and awake in a chair in the waiting room. Dark purple splotches dotted his swollen face, his split lower lip protruding like a duck's bill. Next to him, holding his hand, sat Mae.

Leaning over, I nodded to Mae and studied Pokey. Those bruises, some inky black, others deep purple, one crimson surrounded by purple, made me wish I'd shot, or at least wounded, one of the lynch party men. They deserved a bit of hurt.

"Feeling better, I see." What I meant was at least he was up, awake and not groaning.

He nodded, patted his split lip, one corner of which rose. Grimacing, he mumbled something. I dipped an eyebrow, leaned in closer.

"He say 'better', Ms. Sheriff." Even with Mae's accent, while hard to understand at times, that particular word came out clearer than Pokey's. She patted the hand she was holding and gently leaned into his shoulder.

Pokey's eyes closed, a soft, sappy, relaxed look on his face replacing the hard, trying-not-to-wince look. He opened his eyes, which trailed up to me.

"I'll make sure you get extra pay. You deserve it." I already knew the town would pick up the medical bills for all three men. Envisioning the rant I would get from two of the three windbags when they got the bill rather delighted me.

"And," I realized with a start, "I'll find a relief driver for you for at least a week. You'll stay here, heal up, and in about ten days make that mail run again." The mail had been the last thing on my mind, but now I had to find a driver by Sunday evening. Pokey's run was Mondays, Wednesdays, Fridays like clockwork. Everyone counted on him.

I stood up straight and laid a hand on his shoulder. "You'll be dancing at the upcoming gala before you know it." I smiled at Mae knowing she was the greatest medicine in the world. "Be sure to make him go. I'll bet he's a good dancer."

Mae's smile transformed her face into sheer sunshine. She bobbed her head. "I think, too."

Yep, Pokey found a keeper. I was beyond happy for him, but what about my own Mr. Amazing? Was he in good shape, too? I flashed a grin at both then tiptoed down the hall, searching for the right room. Doc's wife stepped into the hall, pointed to the right.

"He's awake, but resting. Doing fine."

Relief melted my entire body. I wanted to jump up and down, shouting "hallelujah," but I didn't. Instead, I smiled. "Good to hear. And Mr. Powell?"

Wilma shrugged. "Left this morning. Feeling well enough his wife took him home."

That piece of good news knocked me back a step. While it was great, I had not been expecting him to be released so soon. I'd have to stop by his house today, make sure my temporary deputy was being taken care of.

Turning my attention to Aldridge, I nodded to Wilma and stepped into a room lit by one brass oil lamp, its wick turned down. Golden light spread across the room. Except for the smell of iodine disinfectant, it was almost homey.

His face, swollen and bruised, broke my heart. How could I have allowed these men, especially my man, to almost get killed? For some no-good killer who'd end up lynched anyway? I stood beside Aldridge, looking at, admiring him. Reaching for his hand, I then pulled back. I'd hate to disturb his rest. Before I eased away, he opened his eyes.

Tears blurred my vision. I sniffed and took his hand. "Doc says you're doing fine."

He reached up managing to swipe the single tear tracking down my cheek. "Quit worrying. Getting shot isn't so bad."

I swiped at an additional tear. "How's that?"

He pulled up the blanket until it covered his chest. "I get

to lie around all day. Have people bring me food and water whenever I ask. And..." he pushed his bottom lip forward as if in thought. "The world's prettiest gal is right beside me."

The room turned into a furnace and I'm sure my face showed it. I couldn't smile wide enough. I kissed him gently, afraid I guess, of breaking his lips.

Using his one good arm, he brought it around my waist pulling me into him. It was more than likely awkward looking, but I didn't care. I lay my head on his chest, listening to the *thrum thrum thrumming* of life itself. Never had a moment been more wonderful.

"Oh, excuse me."

Doc's voice behind me made me jump. Why couldn't he have waited five minutes? Or ten? Better yet, an hour? I released Mr. Awesome and turned to Doc Monroe now busy uncoiling a stethoscope from around his neck.

"Wilma tells me he'll be up in no time." Tucking in the back of my blouse, which had pulled loose from the waistband, I made sure my demeanor was upbeat but professional.

Doc listened to Aldridge's heart, chest, then straightened and spoke to me. "He'll be fine. Fact is, I want to keep him overnight and tomorrow, he can go home." He turned to Aldridge, I guess remembering he was in the room. "That all right with you?"

"Long as my beautiful nurse here is available." He winked at me. My heart melted faster than butter on a hot stove.

"Of course I am." But I wasn't, and we all knew that. However, for the moment, I meant it. One way or another, I'd take care of him. And not just until his shoulder healed. Until... well, I hadn't honestly thought that far ahead.

Doc flicked a smile my way and patted Aldridge's leg. "Go easy on that laudanum.

Already had quite a bit." And then he was gone, flitting out the door and disappearing into another patient's room across the hall.

"I gotta go." I thumbed over my shoulder. "Slim's watching the store for me, and I've still got things to do."

His eyes closed as he nodded, mumbling something I firmly believed sounded like "love you." Of course I couldn't be sure as I mulled it over on my way to Jackson Powell's house. But the farther I walked, the more sure I was. Maybe it was the pain killer and maybe not. I chose *not*.

Mr. Powell's wife met me at the door and reported he was resting. Although he was sore and bruised, he'd already eaten a light breakfast, drank coffee and, otherwise, all right.

I assured her he'd get an extra something in his pay, then stepped off the porch and waved good-bye. Jackson's house was on the north edge of town, back where all the "colored folk" lived. As I headed for my office, I considered the town's layout. On one end we had colored. On the other, up on a hill, were the Celestials. The Irish banded together in their own enclave of houses and shanties on the west, the Italians on the east and everyone else, including me, closer to the middle.

Whack, whack, whack interrupted my deep thoughts. Finding myself on Main, I stopped, turned in a circle, searching for the noise. Sounded like a hammer. Another *whack* and I located it. Down at the end of the block, in front of Seth's office, stood Pearl, hammer in hand, busy tacking up a poster on the message board.

Before I could catch up with her, she marched across the street, posters under one arm, hammer swinging in the other. I met her at the Tin Pan Saloon just as she pushed on the door and stepped in.

"Hi, Pearl." I called to her and she stopped. "Putting up signs?" Now that was a stupid question. Of course she was.

She waited for me to join her, both of us just inside the door. Pearl handed me a poster. "Stopped by your office and Slim said I could tack one up over there by the bar."

I studied it. A realistic sepia toned tintype featured a

serious-looking Pearl in the middle. Above it, words proclaimed:

Pearl McIntyre for Mayor!

And below:

A Vote for Pearl is a Vote for Democracy!

"Who took the picture?" Was that all I could say? I mean, after all, Pearl was brazen enough to possibly change history, and here I was asking about a photo.

She looked over my shoulder at her image. "You like it? Went all the way to Sacramento to one of those portraiture palaces to get it done." Pearl nudged me a bit. "Cost a whole bunch, too, but figured it was worth it. You can't go cheap when you're running for office."

"It's a fine likeness of you."

"Had the picture copied onto these posters. There's a good printing shop not far from that palace." She raised her chin and brought her shoulders back. "Printer said I was the prettiest politician he'd ever seen. Said I was sure to win."

I applauded her confidence. "But even if you don't, you'll have a good portrait. Hang it in your front room."

Pearl leaned close and dropped her voice into an icy, snarling growl. "Think I won't win? Do you? Thought you were on my side."

I held up a hand. "I never said that. I think you've got a fair chance, especially now since you're putting up posters."

"Damn right I'm putting up posters." Not apologizing for the profanity, Pearl snatched it from my hand and tromped over to the bulletin board near the bar. She ripped down a few employment notices, a page from the *Sacramento Bee* tacked at the top, and from what I'd been able to read, before she wadded it, a legal notice about a business opening.

"I'll show 'em." Pearl held up the poster against the

board, placed a short nail above her picture, and *whack*, her image stared at all the patrons, as if her eyes followed their every move. She stepped back admiring her work. "There."

I followed her outside and noticed that already, several fine citizens of Dry Creek gathered around the posters lining Main Street. A few laughed loud enough to be heard this far, but that didn't seem to faze Pearl. She and her self-possession marched across the street to a farm supply store, owned by Penelope's grandpa. Without a word, she *whacked* up another poster, stood back admiring, then headed down toward my office.

When she skidded to a stop eyeing the board to the right of my office door, I managed to catch up. "Sorry. Only official law-like notices go there, Pearl. You know... bank robber wanted posters, town ordinances. That sort of stuff."

She whirled around and to my surprise, stamped her foot. "Dammit, Maud. You're my campaign manager. I can put this here!"

I'm sure my mouth opened and shut three times before words escaped. "Campaign...? Wait. I said I'd help, but—"

"But nothing." Pearl was on a roll. A determined roll. "If you're not going to help, tell me."

"Said I would, but I shouldn't get that involved in elections." I backed up a hasty half-step. "I'm sheriff and shouldn't—"

"Fine. Fine. I get it." Pearl studied the notice board. "Uh huh. This fella," she pointed at Wild Bart Reinhart, wanted for horse stealing. "He's been caught and hanged already. Last year." She ripped down the paper, released it, sending the announcement fluttering down the street.

"And this one." She squinted at the fine print. "The last sheriff put this one up and everybody knows you can't shoot firearms inside the church. Don't have to post something like that. Ridiculous." Her indignation and logic brought red to her cheeks.

Before I could disagree, she glanced at the two remaining notices, yanked those down and *whacked* her poster up there for the world to see. She held up her hammer. "Got two more places. Wanna come?"

Slim opened the office door and stepped out. "What's all this noise?" He spotted me standing there shaking my head. "Oh, it's you, Sheriff." He came around and read the poster. "Huh."

"What d'you think, Slim?" Pearl stood next to it. "Think it's a good picture?"

"Sure looks like you." Slim eased backward toward the door. "Sheriff, you here to stay? Got things I gotta do, too."

"Me, too." Pearl patted the posters under her arm. "Two more places, then Maud, I'll stop by and we can strategize. Like we'd planned." She marched off, head high, chest out— a woman on a mission.

Slim wagged his head. "Never thought I'd see the day."

About time I wanted to yell at him and the world. But I didn't. Instead, I asked a neutral question. "You get your coffee?"

His face lit up. "Sure did. Hit the spot, too. Funny thing, though. Ended up with four cups." He nudged my shoulder with his. "Saved you two."

Back in the office now and with Slim gone, I located both cups, one cold the other lukewarm. Slim had placed them on the desk where I sank into the chair and released a long, pent-up *ahhhh*. I still didn't know when the circuit judge was coming, I didn't know who had started last night's fire or the school fire for that matter. I didn't know who would drive the mail run next week, and I definitely did not know where Aldridge would stay while recovering. It couldn't be in the boarding house. Not the hotel. Positively, absolutely not my house. That would never do. Then it hit me. Seth. He lived alone. With some rearranging, two men could live there. At least for a couple of weeks.

I made a mental note to seek out Seth while finishing the cold coffee. After pushing more papers around, I stretched up to my feet and checked on the prisoner. There he sat, on his cot, leaning against the rock wall, reading. Reading?

First of all, he reads? Second, where'd he get the dime novel? Had to have been Slim. He carried a Beadle & Adams novel at all times.

Ritchie looked up, moving nothing but his eyes.

"Good story?" I appreciated that he'd been quiet while I worked at the desk. I'd have to get more of those yellow backs as I'd heard them called. Maybe those would keep my prisoner entertained until the trial.

His eyes returned to the story. Which was fine by me. Supper wasn't until four, and it was now around noon. Hopefully he was a slow reader.

Closing the wooden door to the cells, I stood, my gaze trailing over the office. One chair lay in pieces in the corner, but it looked as if Slim had cleaned up the rest of the room. I think he'd even swept. I'd have to remember to thank him.

The second coffee cup in hand, I turned at the door squeaking open. In stepped Mayor Seth Critoli, dark circles hanging under his eyes. Guess he hadn't found his bed yet. In fact, his clothes were a bit rumpled, something he never allowed.

He extracted the cup from my hand, drank it empty, plopped it on the desk. "Better." He ran a hand across a face that needed shaving. "How's Mr. Belligerent?" He nodded toward the cell.

"Quiet. He's reading."

"Really? Guess he wore himself out from last night and this morning." Seth pulled a chair up to the front of the desk, sat and waited for me to take mine. "You know, Pearl's putting up posters all over town. She's making a big deal out of this election."

"It's important to her."

"We've still got, what, two weeks before voting?" He leaned back and then forward. "Still time for her to pull out. Call it quits. She's no match for me."

Instantly, my hackles raised. "No match for you? What exactly have you done that's so special? And why *not* Pearl?" I could have gone on, but I started to stutter and stammer.

It was his turn to stutter and stammer. "Why? She's a girl, for starters. And besides, she doesn't have any experience."

"You didn't either, if I remember right. And, in addition, you're a boy."

"A boy?" His mouth tweaked at one end. "Don't you mean a *man*?"

"Not if she's a 'girl'." I could tell some of the wind had been taken out of his sails because his shoulders rose with a slight grunt. Maybe because he was so tired, or because he was so confident he'd win. I'd put my money on his exhaustion.

He picked up the empty cup, stared into it, I guess hoping coffee would miraculously appear, or wondering what happened to the coffee, then set it down. "I like being mayor, Maud. A lot. I plan to keep my office and hope you're behind me on this." Seth glanced at the wall behind me, raised both eyebrows and leaned over the desk.

As much as he'd made me mad, thrown the gauntlet a bit, I felt sorry for him. He looked so tired. If I had made coffee, I'd let him have the entire pot.

He placed his right leg on his left knee and ran a finger over the side of his boot, tracing the stitching that held the sole to the upper part. I watched for a few seconds, but I hated wasting time like that. He interrupted my impatience. "You're good at campaigning, Maud. I remember in July when you ran for Sheriff. You brought out ideas and—"

"The debate was ruined by a drunk man, remember?"

"Followed by one helluva brawl." Seth smiled full out. "Excuse my language."

I ignored the apology. "Wouldn't want that happening again, but I do think a public debate, out in the open, would be a good idea. That way you and Pearl could explain your vision for the town."

"Vision?" Seth hunched his shoulders. "I don't have a vision."

I stood, adjusted my skirt, which I'd just stepped on.

"You need to get one. Pearl does, and she's going to win unless you do some thinking."

He studied the floor, the window, the wall, his head rotating back and forth, up and down. At last, he stretched up to his feet. "Maud." He walked around my desk and hugged me, whispering in my ear. "You know... you're really good at shaking hands and always saying the right thing." Seth kissed my cheek. "With your help, I'll absolutely win. Guaranteed."

I wiggled out of the hug. "I don't think—"

"Would you be my campaign manager?"

I let out a low groan. I needed coffee.

CHAPTER THIRTY-ONE
BRILLIANT!...

SO FAR ON THIS FINE LATE SUNDAY MORNING, nobody had demanded to know what I had found while investigating the fire at the Widow's house. In truth, I hadn't even had time to look and, thank goodness for Penelope. In a few minutes we'd go over there together, hopefully figure it out. Could it be something as obvious as kids playing with matches? Or maybe the Widow's retarded daughter had left the stove burning? I crossed my fingers it was something that simple. And accidental.

Sitting at the desk, pushing the endless mounds of papers around, my stomach growled. Penelope should be here any minute, which meant we could grab a mid-day meal and then search through the ashes. In a perverse sort of way, I was excited to do that. Finding the answer reminded me of playing hide-and-seek as a child. It was there, the answer. I simply had to uncover it. I sent a sign upward to let us find matches, but at the same time, doubted my use of "simply." I had learned in the past few months, that with a sheriff's job, nothing is simple.

I supposed, technically, I shouldn't leave a prisoner alone, but I was out of deputies. With Ritchie busy reading, I felt relatively comfortable slipping out for a bit. More than likely, the lynch mob wouldn't strike during the day, cowards that they were. However, I'd keep an ear aimed toward the office.

Right on time, Penelope opened the door, stepped in with a sack under one arm. "Brought dinner."

My hero! I made sure the door to the cell was closed, although I could see it was. And while checking, I realized what a silly thing that was to do. I could see it closed, I knew it was, and yet, I made sure as if a spirit had come in and, behind my back, opened the door. Shaking my head, I pointed to a chair in front of the desk. "Sit. We'll eat here, then go."

Penelope set the canvas bag on the table, extracted two sandwiches along with two apples. She held them up. "From our orchard." She sat, opened the waxed paper from one sandwich.

"Such a treat!" And I meant it. Nothing better than a recently plucked apple. I dug into the meal reveling in the freshly baked sourdough bread slices, pieces of ham setting off the flavor. I could have eaten all day.

Penelope swallowed. "I've been over to the house already." She sipped a cup of water, all I had to offer. "Found something interesting."

"What?" My curiosity was not only piqued, but it also full out galloped.

"Could be matches. Found two burnt lucifers at the back corner near the door. From the way the house burned, I think the fire started there." She bit into her sandwich much like a coyote attacking a chicken, wrestling it into submission.

We munched and sipped, mulling over possibilities. Finished, we folded the waxed papers, slipped them back into the sack, tossed the apple cores into the potbelly stove and headed for the door. I tied my bonnet and thought about checking on Ritchie. After all, he'd been darn quiet all day. Of course, by now he'd be getting grumpy.

Why chance a good thing? I buckled my rig around my waist, pulled out my gun checking it was loaded, and slid it back into the holster feeling like I was one of those beady-eyed gunslingers from the dime novels. The dastardly outlaws ride into town, romance the beautiful harlot with the heart of gold, then rob the bank, skedaddle with the money and break her heart when she's left behind.

Doorknob in hand, I screeched to a halt. Most of that had happened to me, except I wasn't a harlot. Recently, though. Eli J. Goodman, my first true love, had left me alone for five years, trotted back into town, robbed the bank. He undeniably broke my heart. But I'd managed to find him and his gang, arrest them all. Yes, he crushed me, but he was now sitting in prison somewhere thinking about what a bad idea that had been.

So, turns out, there *is* justice in the world.

Penelope tapped my arm. "You coming?"

Pulled back into the now, I shook off memory's cobwebs and joined her on the sidewalk. I closed the door tight, locked it, then rattled the knob. I considered again what a dumb thing that was—if locked, no need to twist the handle. Habit, I guess.

Along the way to the Widow's house, I felt like the Pied Piper of lore. Men, women and a few children dogged our steps bombarding us with questions and threats.

"You checking on the arson?"

"Got him in jail yet, Sheriff?"

"It's gettin' to be unsafe to go out anymore. How come you're not protecting us, Sheriff?"

"We should get a *real* sheriff."

"If I was in charge, I'd—"

"You don't even carry a gun, Bill."

"Who did it, Penelope?"

On and on until my ears rang. Penelope and I picked up speed and almost ran to the Widow's. By the time we arrived, I counted twelve folks right behind, more undoubtedly on the way.

I turned to the throng and held up both hands. "Please. We're investigating the scene and need to keep it just like it is. So, don't come any closer." I waited to get most of their attention. "Please? Stay back."

"Sure, Sheriff."

"Tell us what you find. We'll wait here."

"I tell ya, Jenny Sue, it's an arsonist. Pure and simple. Hired man to set fires."

"I agree. Bet my money on it."

"Think he's from around these parts?"

"Brought in a professional, I heard."

"There such a thing as professional arsonist?"

"Hey Maud! There's part of the roof over there. Look under that."

"She won't find anything there, Claude. She's gotta search..."

I ignored the crowd, focusing instead on finding matches, kerosene buckets, more cloth under fallen timber like at the school, anything pointing to what happened. After we figured out exactly what, we could hopefully figure out who.

"What's all this ruckus? What're you all doing out here?"

I straightened up at that voice. Harvey Weinberg. Good grief, not him, too. Immediately, I turned my back, took a knee at the bottom of an upright four-by-four. At least most of the house still stood, which made combing through debris a bit easier. From this position, I hoped Harvey wouldn't recognize me, but unfortunately, a couple helpful citizens pointed me out.

He stood next to me to where I had to squint up, shielding my eyes against the sun. As I glanced down again, I spotted it. A can with pieces of burnt material sticking out. I shot to my feet as if I'd been poked.

"Penelope. Found something." Had I actually discovered the source?

An audible gasp from the crowd brought them surging forward. Harvey held up a handand, like he'd put up an invisible wall, they stopped.

Harvey, Penelope and I studied the can before touching it. Like candle wicks, wads of singed material, much like I'd seen at the school, stuck out of the can which was pressed against the base of the house. The material, muslin I figured, had burned down to the top of the can and then went out. But apparently, enough had burned, leaning against the side of the house, to catch the wall on fire. It hadn't rained in a while, so things were dry. Penelope picked up the can, holding it close enough for the three of us to inspect.

"Gotta be." Penelope turned it back and forth before sniffing. She yanked it from her nose. "Kerosene. This is it."

"And look." I brushed a small pile of what could have been straw before it burned.

A cheer rose from the crowd and before I could stop them, they rushed forward, some even stomping through what was left of Widow Simpson's house.

"I hear that insurance office just opened," someone said.

"I'm goin' over there right now. Get me some insurance so if this happens to me..."

"Wait for me, Martha!"

The words were lost in the crowd doing an about-face and rushing toward downtown. I knew where they were headed and within moments, I'd be right behind them. That NathanielFord character would be leaving town tonight, his pockets full of money. I was sure of it.

* * *

BY THE TIME I made it to Ford's new office, which happened to be directly in the middle of Main Street, a line snaked out the door and down past the mercantile. Looked like his business was beyond booming, but I was convinced he'd started that fire to get his business off to a roaring good start. On the one hand, I contemplated while I stood there, his strategy was brilliant. Create a need and then fill that need. Good business.

On the other hand, he'd burned down at least one woman's house, and I hadn't fully decided he'd set fire to the school. But it made sense. My theory, which I'd run past Penelope after Harvey had stalked off, was Ford had sneaked into town, possibly in disguise, set the school on fire, scurried out of town like a weasel. Then a few weeks later rides into town all innocent-like. And that too, was brilliant.

What I couldn't put together was Ford's relationship with my Mr. Wonderful. My Mr. Injured-But-Wonderful. Please, please, please, I sent a message skyward, which was already jam-packed with my requests, let it be an innocent, chance encounter. In the boarding house as they'd said. Please, I asked one more time.

A woman and her husband I recognized from church elbowed their way out of Ford's office. Before anybody else could squeeze in, I jostled my way to the door, stepped in and closed it.

There sat Ford the Fraud, hiding behind a stack of official-looking papers piled on his desk. He stood.

"Sheriff." He extended a slimy hand. "Good to see you again." He pointed toward a chair near his desk after realizing I wasn't about to shake with him. "I understand you found the incendiary device that instigated the dreadful event of the previous evening."

His fancy, big-city words did nothing to dissuade me from accusing him. I remained standing, hoping to intimidate him, even a tiny bit. "Have some questions for you, Mr. Ford." I produced my deepest sheriff tone, dipped my eyebrows and stared into his deceitful eyes.

Ford pointed again toward the chair. "Here. Please sit. I'll be delighted to explain my recent activities." His arm swept the room. "New workplace. Enchanting town. I'm so fortunateto have chosen to seek my fortune here. Ask me anything. My life and whereabouts are not shrouded in secrecy."

That, for me, was the sure sign he, indeed, had something to hide. Why else would he say that? I remained on my feet. "Where were you last night between six and seven?"

Ford leaned back in his chair, steepled his fingers, and stared up at the ceiling. "Let me remember... last night at six?" His eyes flashed to me. "My answer is rather mundane, I'm afraid. Supping at the Shoo Fly Restaurant, enjoying a lovely repast of roast beef, potatoes and scrumptious rolls." He cocked his head. "Apple pie for dessert. With coffee."

Despite wanting to lick my lips, I pressed on, not convinced of his honesty. "How long were you there? And can anyone vouch for you?"

A slow rumble shook his shoulders. "Absolutely, besides the waitress and ten or twelve other patrons. I was fortunate enough to share my table with a woman and her husband." His eyes roamed the ceiling again. "Mr. and Mrs. Henry Apertife... no, Apertide. Yes, Apertide. Lovely young couple. Henry and Cecilia. We exchanged stories most of the evening."

Their names didn't sound at all familiar, and I knew most everyone in Dry Creek. "Where do they live at? Did you ask?"

Something of a sly smile inched its way up his conniving face. "Not from around here, I'm afraid. Said they'd purchased a ranch in Oregon. Heading there right now, just as we're speaking. Stayed overnight at the hotel and have already left on today's stage."

Dang and double dang. I would have to check at the hotel and the restaurant, which thinking on it, a quick bite of that apple pie would help keep the rest of the afternoon on the right path. One more question. "What time did you leave the restaurant?"

He turned his soft, pudgy hands palm up. "We heard the fire bell, saw people running, so we quickly paid the fare and left the fine establishment to ascertain the situation." He pointed toward the Widow's house. "When I realized my help was not necessary, I said farewell to the Apertife's...

sorry, *Apertides*, and returned to the boarding house. Must have been..." he paused as if in thought, but I doubted the thinking part. "Half past eight."

Uh huh. And I'm the queen of England. I didn't buy it for a second. He was up to something. I couldn't quite yet put my finger on it, but I vowed to have him in jail sooner than later. Maybe the circuit judge could try him in addition to Ritchie. Which reminded me, I needed to stop by the telegraph office. Hopefully I'd have an answer.

With my hand on the doorknob, I turned to Ford. "Don't try leaving town. I've got deputies watching you." I was smart enough not to tell him he was my number one suspect or the fact my deputies were busy recovering instead of watching. But he didn't need to know that.

Ford found his feet while a smile crawled to his lips and curved itself like a snake. "Absolutely, Sheriff Overstreet." He sauntered toward the door. "I'm not going anywhere. I have a business to run."

I stared at him, inches from his face. "I'll be in touch." With that, I opened the door, which smacked a man on the shoulder. Wagging my head, I waded through the crowd and strode west toward the Shoo Fly Restaurant. Memories of apple pie perched on my tongue. My stomach growled.

Just one piece. And coffee. After all, I had things to do, people to see.

CHAPTER THIRTY-TWO
I'M WARNING YOU...

I WADDLED MY WAY UP THE STREET. SO, TURNED out, one piece of heavenly apple pie wasn't enough. I couldn't decide which I liked most, the slice of sharp cheddar cheese slightly melted on top, the incredibly flaky crust, or the thinly sliced apples laced with a hint of expensive cinnamon and a dash of nutmeg which melted in my mouth. So, to be fair, I had to sample another. And two was too many. At least I was fortified for the remainder of the afternoon. As full as I was, supper would have to be nothing more than carrots, for the sake of my too-tight waistband. While there, I'd arranged for yet another tray of food for the prisoner to be brought over within the hour. At a dollar a day, Ritchie was getting expensive. I'm sure the Three Windbags would point that out—loudly.

The trek back to the office took longer than I liked, but many of the townspeople stopped me, asking about the Widow's house, what I had found, who I had arrested, and on and on.

Turned out, everyone had heard something different about what I'd actually uncovered, and they all presented varying theories. No one knew exactly who had set the fire, but they would know him when they saw him. Of course I appreciated their concern and interest, and I assured each and every one I'd take their suggestions under advisement.

Ears still ringing, I stuck the key into the office door. *Click*, but something about it was off. Simply didn't sound right. Then again, with all the conversations rattling around in my head, it was quite possible I hadn't heard correctly. Still, first, I'd check on Ritchie, make sure he was there.

I closed the door behind me quietly. Why, I wasn't sure, but it seemed the right thing to do. No telling if some miscreant was still in the office doing who knows what. A quick sweep of the room revealed nothing out of place, until my gaze trailed to the desk. Shivers bolted up then down my back, covering it like an icy cold sheet.

In the middle of the desk stood what looked like an old Bowie knife, handle up, stuck into the wooden top. Without a doubt, I hadn't left it there and, on top of that, I didn't even own one. Fear, like the quick hot touch of the devil, shot through me. Heart fisting in my chest, I swallowed and yanked open the door to the cells. There stood Ritchie, huddled back in the far corner. I gripped the iron bars and stared at him. As close as we were, he looked to be in one piece.

"You all right?" As much as I wanted to see justice served this man, I didn't want him dead in the jail. Penned up the way he was, he had no fighting chance.

"Afraid that mob had come to break me out again." He pointed toward the office. "Heard couple men's voices, some sorta loud *thump*, louder mumbled threats and curses, then nothing 'til you came in."

"How long ago?"

Ritchie sank to his cot. "Maybe ten, fifteen minutes. Not long." He shook his head. "Kinda glad to see you, Sheriff. Thought for sure they'd break me out and lynch me. This time they'd succeed."

"You didn't see them?"

"Nah. Just heard two different voices. Both men."

Half of me was glad I hadn't walked in on them, the

other half wishing I had. Either way, I'd get this figured out once and for all, chiding myself for that extra piece of pie. Shouldn't have left him alone so long. I couldn't let it happen again. But at least Ritchie was still there and in one piece. I left the door between the cells and my office open.

And just as I figured, a note was pinned under the knife.

Soon. Real Soon.

Not in red lipstick this time. Looked more like pencil. I yanked the knife blade out, picked up the paper. Wrinkled like it was, seemed like it had been wadded and then taken out of a trashcan, almost as an afterthought. Was it? Or simply using old paper? And then I turned it over. It was a wanted poster I had tossed earlier this morning. So, they couldn't even bring their own paper.

Then it hit me. I shivered again. Maybe they hadn't meant to leave a note. Maybe they'd planned to threaten me in person. Maybe... I decided I was lucky I hadn't been at the desk when they walked in. But now I had to watch my back. All the time.

I spent time thinking—had they used a key to get in the front? Who had a key besides me and Pokey? Was it Pokey? I found that impossible to believe. But there had been *two* voices. And did someone have a key from the old sheriff days? I pushed those thoughts around while searching the rest of the office, the storage room and even the back door to the alley that led to the privy. The thick wooden door had been locked and from what I could tell, no one had tried to pry it. Those men had walked in the front, bold as blazes. I counted myself doubly lucky not to have been here. But, what would I do if they came back?

Keeping an eye on both doors, I set coffee on to boil, double and triple checked the rifles, which Seth and I retrieved from the attempted lynching. Surprisingly, the men had dropped them when I'd said, "drop it", and hadn't bothered to pick them back up. I shook a box of shotgun shells and pushed them into the chamber, then added cartridges to the revolver. All weapons now loaded, hopefully, I'd never have to use them. But lately, I couldn't guarantee that.

Pouring myself a cup of strong brew, I poured one for the prisoner. While I didn't like the man, I was glad he was still alive. Or at least still behind bars. Either way, I was glad. After presenting him with his own cup, I took a seat at the desk and thought. And thought.

Nothing made sense. Who was doing this and why? Similar to the fires, as soon as I figured out who, I could find out why. I added the threats to the others:

Soon. Real soon. Watch out! Or else. Your next.

Numb, almost paralyzed, I chanted like the gypsies and card readers I'd seen in Sacramento. *Be rational, be rational. Breathe. Deep breath.* What did the notes mean? Or did they actually mean anything? Like a crazy person, I turned the paper sideways, then upside down, then upright again and re-read. Threats were all I came up with and even then, threat for what? What was I doing, or not doing, that they wanted changed? And who were *they*?

A light knock at the door and then the squeak of it opening shot me to my feet. Heart thudding, I brushed the butt of the revolver before recognizing the teenager from the restaurant, a tray of delicious-smelling food in his hands.

"Did I startle ya, Sheriff?" He pushed the door closed with his foot. "Sorry. Didn't mean to. Brought this here tray of food for Mr. Ritchie. Hope he likes it. Cooked up some of it myself. Mr. Bromburg, you know he's the owner, well, he lets his wife cook and sometimes she lets me do..."

He rattled on. I pointed toward the cell but that was a needless gesture. He knew where Ritchie was since he'd been the one to deliver every meal. I followed the young man, barely of shaving age, and stood guard while he slid the tray under the locked iron door. The prisoner was allowed coffee and a nutritious meal plus a spoon. No fork or knife. This evening he had pot roast, boiled potatoes, a sourdough biscuit along with a scoop of apple pie for dessert. Plenty enough for any jailed person.

Eyeing the supper, I wondered if I could get a tray delivered to me. However, I wasn't quite hungry yet, but I would be. It was simply a matter of time. And unless one of the deputies miraculously recovered, I had no one to relieve me.

We stepped back into the office and I followed him to the door. At last I gave in.

"Would you bring me a plate like that in about an hour?" I lowered my voice to right above a whisper. "Don't have any deputies and I gotta stay here."

The youngster brightened. "Sure, Sheriff. I'll be glad ta!" His volume matched mine as he dropped his voice. "Won't tell no one you're all alone. No, siree. Not a soul. Mum's the word. Why, I'll even—"

"Tell you what." I fished around in my skirt pocket for a nickel. "First off, tell me your name again?"

"Hoyt. Just like my grandpa. He was—"

"Besides bringing me my own supper, Hoyt," I held out the coin. "I need you to go ask Mr. Higginbotham, over at the Tin Pan Saloon, to come see me. Soon's he can. All right?"

Hoyt's cookie-brown eyes, which matched his hair, opened wide. He couldn't nod fast enough. "Right away, Sheriff. He'll be over here in two flashes. Just like a lightning bolt. Yes siree, Sheriff. Right away."

I pushed open the door, holding it until his long, gangly legs and arms, spinning like windmills, gallumped toward the saloon. I closed the door, considered locking it, but thought better. Honest citizens had the right to come in without having to knock. Then again, honest citizens wouldn't mind.

The *click* allowed my shoulders to droop for the first time in an hour. I pocketed the key, checked the back door—just in case—and sank to the chair, tin coffee cup in hand. Hopefully, after I told Slim about the notes, he and I could figure out who was behind them and exactly what they had in mind.

Did they want my badge? My money? That thought gave me pause. A sheriff's salary?

What *were* they threatening?

Ritchie called for more coffee and a trip to the privy. Too lost in thought to argue, I unlocked his cell and marched him out back to the alley. While he was occupied, I scanned the alley both ways, even the roofs, figuring I'd spot a gunman, or at the least his shadow. Nothing but a pigeon roosted up there. A pigeon and the blue sky.

It seemed as if Ritchie took days in there. I opened my mouth to urge him along.

"Good God, there you are!"

I jumped, spun and pulled the gun without thinking. Heart in my throat, I spotted a shadow at the end of the alley. It held up its hands.

"Maud? It's only me, Seth. Don't shoot!"

I squinted. Seth came into focus. "Sorry." I holstered the revolver. "Ritchie's in there, taking his time."

Seth eased toward me as he lowered his arms. "Tried the front door. You know it's locked?"

I nodded.

"Thought you were in trouble, so I came around here."

Hands still shaking and a bit sweaty, I wiped them on my skirt. "We had unwelcome visitors today." I thumped on the privy door. "Let's go Ritchie. Been in there long enough."

Ritchie stepped out, allowing the door to bang shut.

"Don't like the idea of you out here in the open." I pointed toward the back door. "Let's get you inside."

After Ritchie was again locked behind sturdy iron bars, I closed the door between the cells and my office and ushered in Seth.

"Thought I'd stop by so we can strategize about the campaign." Seth poured himself coffee and filled the cup on my desk. "But looks like you need some help."

I explained the notes, the recent visit to the office, and discovered I was more unnerved than I'd let myself realize. My hands still shook and breath became harder to pull in. I also mentioned that Slim would hopefully be coming by soon. Maybe between the three of us, we could come up with answers. I wasn't holding out much hope, but at that moment, it was all I had.

"By the way," I decided to change the topic and my thoughts. "Aldridge will be discharged from the doc's tomorrow morning and needs a better place to stay for a few days. I was wondering—"

"If he could stay with me." Seth rubbed his chin, desperately in need of a shave. "How long you think?"

I shrugged. "A week?"

"Maybe." Seth's eyebrows dipped as his gaze roamed around the room. He nodded. "All right. He deserves it, I guess." He pointed a long finger at me. "Just understand, I'm no doctor *or* nurse. I'll make sure he gets fed, but—"

"Thanks." If I hadn't been so tired, I'd have gotten up and given him a kiss, but instead, I flashed my virtuous smile. "I'm sure he'll appreciate it."

By the time Slim arrived, Seth and I had gone over all the ways I'd thought about campaigning—for both him and Pearl. How did I get myself in these messes, anyway? I'd also talked him into having visions of Dry Creek—he opted for promising to build a new schoolhouse and creating a group of townspeople who would schedule socials, dances and such, on a regular basis. We decided that strategy would bring in the women's vote, even though they couldn't mark a ballot. But they had their men's ears and that was usually enough.

Hunching over the desk, Slim, Seth and I then mulled over the notes I'd received in the past month. We arranged them, rearranged them, picked them up, Slim even held one up against the window light. I expounded on the various handwritings, where the notes appeared. Judging by the furrowed foreheads, downturned mouths and narrowed eyes, I decided they were concerned. Maybe worried—real worried.

The more we talked, the more uneasy I became. Why hadn't I told them sooner? Based on the notes, and the one thing Slim and Seth agreed on, was I needed to watch my back every second.

Banging on the outside door made us all jump. I shot to my feet sure those men were back with a bigger knife, before realizing someone simply desired to come inside. Knowing both Seth and Slim stood behind me, I unlocked the door, eased it open. A kid, maybe ten, stood frozen, eyes round and mouth open, a piece of paper gripped in his hand.

"Sorry for the locked door." I waved him in. "Can I help you?"

"Ain't never been inside a jailhouse before. You're the sheriff, right?"

I nodded.

He took one hesitant step in then flapped the paper at me. "Mr. McGuire, down at the telegraph, said for me to come give this to you quick." His eyes flicked from Seth to Slim and back to me. "Said it was im-por-tant."

I opened the note and sure enough, to my major relief, it was a telegram from Circuit Judge Andrew Richfield. He'd be in town tomorrow. Tomorrow? Hallelujah! I felt like dancing right then and there, but instead, dug out another nickel from my pocket, handed the coin to the messenger, thanked him and closed the door, careful to lock it.

"Tomorrow!" I about burst into song as I turned to the men. "Judge comes tomorrow.

Stage gets in at what, ten?"

"Supposed to." Seth pulled out his pocket watch.

"Maybe we can have the trial by eleven." I ran quick mental calculations. We'd need a lawyer for Ritchie and a place to hold the trial. And witnesses to find. "On second thought, maybe by one." I definitely, in no way, was going to wait longer than one. Could I make it 'til then? And was it

Ritchie the notes were about? No, some had come before he killed Fred Gasipioni.

The three of us retook our seats after pouring more coffee. I leaned back then forward and glanced at the closed door leading to the cells. I lowered my voice. "We're going to have to keep it quiet about the judge. If those fellas who took Ritchie last time find out about tomorrow, they might try to break him out tonight."

Slim rubbed his chin, his gaze scanning the desktop. "Guess I can stay here tonight, Maud."

"Me, too." Seth plopped his cup onto the desk. "Haven't had much sleep in the past two days. What's another night?"

I looked at these two men. True heroes to my thinking. "Thanks, but I can't ask you to—"

"I know." Slim stretched up to his feet. "But it gets kinda lonely at my place, and I don't mind passing an evening here." His face bubbled into a smile. "Long as it ain't very often."

Seth stood also and turned to Slim. "If memory serves, you owe me a game of checkers. Or was it poker?"

The sun's orange-gold rays slid across the east wall. Within an hour it would be candlelight time. An unwelcomed shiver hitched my shoulders. Company tonight would make the hours go faster.

CHAPTER THIRTY-THREE
TRIALS AND TRIBULATIONS...

SETH AND SLIM PROMISED TO RETURN WITHIN THE hour. Both wanted supper, Seth promising to get some for me and bring it back, even though I had a plate coming soon. I figured between the three of us, it wouldn't go to waste. Slim said he'd supply extra blankets. While waiting, I set up a canvas cot in the supply room and would sleep there when I couldn't fight fatigue any longer. Unquestionably that would be more comfortable than trying to sleep slouched in a chair.

I lit every lantern in the room, trimming the wicks to half. I'd have to save some for another evening, but it would've been nice to see every corner in the room. While there was a curtain on the window, I'd never pulled it closed. Should I do it now? And what was the point? So people couldn't see in? Wasn't that the idea? If I left it open, they could see someone was in here.

Standing there at the window, I changed my mind and decided to close it when a light tapping at the door made me cringe, then jump.

"Yes?" My voice was shaky and too high for a sheriff.

"It's us."

Right. I recognized Seth's voice. I unlocked the door, they stepped in, then I shut the door with a foot. I turned to look at my compatriots. Instead of Seth and Slim, there stood two men I recognized from the lynch mob. Names didn't come, but at that moment names weren't important.

"Sorry, gentlemen." I pushed down panic, my hand brushing the butt of the gun. "We're not open right now."

One man, his knee-length duster hanging on his slim frame, held up a hand. "Just come to see if'n the little law lady needs help."

"That's right. You're just a girl playin' grown up." The other man turned to his friend.

"She's a right comely thing, too."

"Comely? Don't you mean *homely*?"

He doubled over, slapped his knee. "You're right. Meant homely." He glanced at his friend. "Looks like she fell outta the ugly tree and hit every branch on the way down."

They laughed too loud, too long. I pointed toward the door. "You men need to leave."

"We hear the judge's in town tomorrow." The other man, taller and wide shouldered, stepped toward me. "Thought we'd come by, save the judge time."

The second man straightened. "And while we're at it, we're fixin' ta take over your office. After all, it's a man's job. Ya should be at home bakin' pies."

Without thinking, I backed up a step, then remembered I was sheriff, no matter what they said. I was still in charge and these men wouldn't get to Ritchie unless they climbed over me. "Sorry, men." I inched toward the door to the cells. "The prisoner stays right here until I walk him to the court-room tomorrow."

Both men, bigger and most likely stronger than me, sidled toward the closed door. Their creeping brought them within a foot of where I stood. I swallowed alarm and pulled the gun. Aiming at the one closest, I spoke over the cold panic enveloping me. "You need to turn around and go home. You're not getting Mr. Ritchie tonight. Or any night. And you sure as hell aren't taking my badge."

"Oh, lookee there. She cusses. Ain't very lady-like." The

taller of the two, with a face like granite, same color as his eyes, produced a short-barreled shotgun hidden under his duster.

He pointed it at my chest. "Move. Or die." He raised one shaggy eyebrow. "Your choice."

The other man nodded at me. "Y'all look like ya got yourselves a Mexican standoff." He smoothed his thick black mustache. "Now put away your peashooter, little lady. My friend here don't miss. 'Specially up this close."

His Southern accent rang a bell. This haughty man with craggy features had been a deacon of the church when I first moved to town. And look at him now.

I eased over to the closed door, standing within inches of it. Would I have to shoot? Possibly kill a man? Probably, if they wouldn't listen to reason. "Back off, men. I don't want to shoot you, but I will." Did that sound like the threat it was meant to be?

"Oh, listen to you." The shotgun holder thumbed back the hammer. The metal on metal sound echoed around the room. "You talk like you mean it. Like a real sheriff. But sister, you ain't gonna pull that trigger. You ain't got the *cojones*."

To my surprise, I aimed just above his right shoulder, cocked the gun and fired.

Bang!

The bullet zinged into the wall above the desk. We all flinched. Without thinking it through, I dove for the man's legs and took him down to the floor. He landed flat on his back with me on top. The gun flew out of my hand and slid across the floor.

Boom!

The shotgun fired and I wasn't sure where the buckshot went. I just knew it wasn't in me. As it was, my ears rang. Under me, the man heaved and pushed me off while the other man grabbed my shoulders. I sailed across the floor and rolled toward the desk.

Bang! Bang!

"Hold it right there! Drop it!" Two men's voices I recognized for real flew around my head.

Vision a bit fuzzy, I located Slim and Seth, guns drawn, marching toward the men.

"Push the shotgun away." Seth pointed at the man still lying on the floor. "Nice and easy."

"I'll take that." Slim plucked the gun from the other man, now standing with both hands shoulder high. Slim slipped the Colt into his waistband.

I scrambled to my feet, rearranged the skirt now firmly wound around my legs, then picked up the gun on the way. Nodding to Slim and Seth, I turned attention to the two men. "Take off your dusters. That all your weapons?"

Seth, without being asked, patted both men top to bottom. "That's it, Sheriff. They're clean."

Waving the gun toward the cells, I wasn't sure how having these two locked up next to Ritchie was going to work. But, I had only two places for prisoners. We'd keep the wooden door open and the three of us would take turns guarding. "Let's go, men. Time to see how you like being behind bars."

Slim followed on my heels. "Good thing Judge's coming tomorrow. We can get all three tried in an hour."

The bigger one growled as he looked over his shoulder. "This ain't over yet, Missy."

"It is for you." I swung open the iron door and made sure they stepped in. "Make yourselves comfortable. Judge starts the trial at one." The *slam* of the door shutting, the *click* of the lock brought a smile to my face. I jerked on the door. Yep, closed tight.

I stepped back glaring at the men. "How's it feel to be locked up by a woman?"

"Hey, Sheriff!" Ritchie hollered from the far side of his cell. "You can't do that. They're tryin' to kill me."

"Stay where you are, you'll be fine. They can't reach you from there."

"But Sheriff..."

Seth, Slim and I returned to the office, the inner door wide open. Hands still shaking, I pulled in several deep breaths and felt stronger. We located one bullet, mine, in the wall above the desk. Above the front door, we found six buckshot embedded in the wall.

Slim pointed at the holes. "You're a lucky lady, Maud. You know what they say about buckshot?"

I shrugged.

"Buckshot means buryin' every time."

Forcing down fear, I nodded. "Thank goodness for small favors." The two from Slim and Seth had plunged into the ceiling. With all the lead flying around, it was a wonder no one had been hit.

Seth stepped outside and brought in two sacks, mouth-watering smells wafting from both. I locked the door while he held them up. "Brought all of us supper. Left it outside when we saw what was going on."

"How'd you know?" I opened a sack and spotted a pail of what I assumed was stew.

"Heard what we thought was a shot. Couldn't be sure cause Silas' piano playin' brought people to yellin'." Slim pointed toward the front window. "Saw you and those fellas when we walked past."

Part of a smile lifted his mustache. "You were rolling around on the floor on top of that man, but didn't appear you were enjoying his affections."

Thank goodness I hadn't pulled that curtain all the way.

While we unpacked supper, which indeed, was mutton stew, along with fresh sourdough biscuits, corn and boysenberry pie, we talked about the upcoming trial. Tomorrow morning I'd have to write up a report on those two would-be lynch men, find a lawyer for them and Ritchie, and meet the stage.

But tonight, it was all about friends and food.

* * *

Dawn arrived at long last, pink driving out gray light. I yawned and stretched, having taken the cot sometime in the middle of the night. Since I hadn't been jerked awake by shouting or more gunfire, I assumed the prisoners had found peace and Slim and Seth had finished their poker game.

I stood, smoothed my hair and skirt, yawned and stretched again. After a trip to the privy and a strong cup of coffee, I'd have an over-due chat with the newest prisoners. I presumed they were the note writers, actually *hoping* they were, but I needed to know why.

A quick trip outside, I then joined Seth and Slim who were sitting around my desk. Seth behind it, Slim at the end, both holding cards. Seth looked up and grinned. "Sleep good?"

"Right as rain." Part of that was bravado, but I'd had more sleep than they had. "Who's winning?"

Slim frowned up at me. "Let's just say Seth gets free drinks at the Tin Pan 'til he's an old man."

"That bad, huh?" I poured myself coffee, stood by the stove sipping the tepid brew. Apparently, they hadn't made fresh overnight. "Prisoners give you any trouble?"

"Nah." Seth splayed his cards on the desk. "Two pairs, aces and tens."

Slim folded his hand, tossing them toward Seth. "A really old man."

Stomach grumbling, I thought back to last night's suppers. That restaurant truly fixed a mean stew. And when the kid had brought the tray, I doubted we would touch it, but I was wrong. All remnants were gone. I wouldn't mind having seconds about now. But bacon and eggs sounded good, too. After not much persuasion, Seth agreed to find us something to eat and bring it back while Slim and I chatted with the prisoners.

I stepped into the holding area, and, like monkeys, the three prisoners sprang to their feet and grabbed the iron bars.

"Get us outta here." The newest prisoner, the man with gray eyes, rattled the bars. "We don't deserve to be locked up."

I held up a hand and ticked off on each finger. "I'm charging you both with attempted murder on a peace officer. Threatening a peace officer. Breaking and entering—that was from yesterday morning. Resisting arrest."

"Attempted murder?" He pushed his arm between the bars, reaching for my badge, I guessed. "Lady, if I had 'attempted' for real, you'd be dead."

Another wave, this time more like icy snakes, slithered across my back. I shrugged, hoping to dislodge my anxiety. I kept my voice calm and controlled. "After I talk to the judge, I'll see what other charges will be filed against you and your friend." Now I needed to get down to basics. "What's your name?" I glared at both men.

The one who hadn't pulled a gun, mumbled, his accent strong. "Benton. Charles Benton." He narrowed his eyes at his cellmate. "Told ya not ta come back. Told ya. Told ya we'd be pushing it a might too far."

"Shut up, Chuck!" The man pulled in his arm and used it to push Benton, who stepped back a foot.

"Name?" I was losing patience and wanted to go in the cell to twist his arm, but immediately thought better of it. They'd more than likely get the drop on me, and then Slim would have to come charging in to the rescue, and it would be *so* embarrassing...

Benton filled in the silence. "Theodore Philmont." He cocked his head toward his partner. "Everybody calls him Ted."

Now we were getting somewhere. Finally. Slim stood in the doorway, leaning against it, watching the interrogation. I breathed easier knowing he was close.

"Before the trial gets under way, I need to know a few things." I stared at Philmont, then turned to Benton. "Did you both write all those notes? Or just one of you?"

Philmont huffed, folded his arms and turned to face the wall. "Ain't talkin' to no female law dog without my lawyer."

"Ah will, Sheriff." Benton's copper-brown gaze settled on me.

"Shut up!" Philmont shook a finger at Benton. "Shut your yap and quit talkin'."

"Ah ain't gonna swing." Benton regarded Philmont, stepped back a bit, his eyes locked on his partner. "Ah ain't done nothin'. Was all your idea."

I trained my gun on Philmont. "Let him talk."

Benton cocked his head toward Philmont. "Ted don't care much for women, especially law types. He only wanted ta scare ya into quittin'. Ya see, he wanted ta be sheriff. Real bad. So, he started sendin' ya notes, hopin' he'd drive ya out. An' when ya arrested Ritchie, well Ted figured ta take credit for his hangin'."

"What's your involvement in all this?" I wanted to shout for joy now that I knew about the warnings.

Benton's shoulders rose and fell while he glanced at Philmont. "We been ridin' together a good long while. Ah found religion when Ah moved here, but he didn't. Ah became a church deacon, then Ted made me leave with him. Just came back maybe a month ago. Ted grew all het up with bein' sheriff. Hell, even made himself a badge. Show her, Ted."

"Shut up, you little weasel!" Philmont lurched toward Benton, then wrapped his hands around Benton's neck. "Just shut the hell up!" He squeezed tighter. Benton's face bloomed into purple red.

Afraid they'd kill each other, I fumbled for the cell key in my pocket, inserted it. The door flew open and Slim swooshed in. Within seconds, he had both men pulled apart, one gripped in each hand.

I pulled the revolver, eased into the cell, now crowded with four people, and pointed the weapon at Philmont. "Let him go, Slim. I'll shoot if he moves." I cocked the .44 to make a point.

Slim released Philmont's shirt front and pushed. "Over there. Don't move. I guarantee she'll shoot you." He stepped closer to him. "And if she don't, I will."

Apparently, Slim's words had an effect because Philmont slunk down to the cot, alternating his glares between me and Slim. I didn't think it was a good idea to have Philmont and Benton in the same cell anymore.

"Benton, you come on out. Slim, lock Philmont up nice and tight." I eased down the hammer on the gun and waved it toward the outer office.

It took a bit to find handcuffs in my somewhat-organized desk, but finally I secured Benton to a wooden shelf in the supply room. He'd have to pull down the wood braces and drag the pieces off before escaping. I figured one of us would notice.

I plopped into the chair, swiped a hand across my forehead. Slim poured me the remaining coffee. I looked up at him and nodded.

Over my final sip, Seth came in, food bag in hand. "Good news." He smiled. "First time ever, stage was early. Judge just got into town. Says he'll be over directly."

CHAPTER THIRTY-FOUR
JUDGMENT DAY...

"GUILTY AS CHARGED!" JUDGE RICHFIELD BANGED the gavel, and within moments, Ritchie was escorted out of the Tin Pan Saloon by deputy Federal marshals who traveled with the judge.

I leaned back against the chair and whispered to Slim. "Guilty? Did I hear right? Life in federal prison?"

He held up a thumb and presented a wide smile. Ritchie's trial had lasted less than half an hour.

While Seth, Slim and I marched across Main to retrieve Benton and Philmont from the office, *tap tap tapping* and voices calling from a few blocks away slowed us. I stopped on the boardwalk, cocked my head as if that would clear up the sound.

A wagon loaded with lumber and three husky men on top rumbled behind us. I turned and there sat Penelope, reins in hand, her brother, pa and another fella perched on the rough-sawn boards. Penelope pulled the team to a stop.

She leaned toward us, pointing south. "Gonna help rebuild the Widow's house. Wanna come?"

I stepped back into the street, knowing I was due back in court within moments. But standing out here with the fire chief for a minute or two wouldn't hurt. I turned to Slim and Seth. "Go ahead. I'll be there directly." They nodded and continued on.

"What's going on, Maud?"

"Trials. I'll tell you later. What's this about helping the Widow?"

Penelope glanced behind at the men in the wagon. "We all decided she needed help rebuilding. Half the town's already there." She picked up the reins. "You comin'?"

"Can't right now. But I'll stop by soon's I can. No telling how long this trial'll last." I wondered why I hadn't heard about this town effort, but I'd been busy and focused on my prisoners. I'd check with Seth. Being mayor, he seemed to know everything.

She clucked at the horses and nodded. "See ya then."

And with that, she and the wagon trotted off, leaving behind the air of going on a picnic instead of building a house. The end of the wagon disappeared onto a side street while I refocused my thinking back to being sheriff. It would be wonderful, now that Ritchie's gone, not having to worry about food and privy. But what about Philmont and Benton? Theirs might not be quite the open and shut case I figured. And although I'd had some dealings with Judge Richfield beforehand, no way could I second-guess his decisions.

I joined Seth and Slim at the office door. Slim kept a tight grip on Philmont and Seth on Benton. I locked the door behind them and then marched out front, my gaze flitting up and down Main. No telling what a crazed lynch party mob might do. And who may come to rescue these men?

While we walked, Philmont complained, threatened and whined the entire time. Benton remained quiet.

Judge Andrew Richfield banged the gavel once we had our prisoners seated. I got up and explained the situation, Philmont disagreeing—at peak volume.

Richfield pointed at Philmont. "That outburst just cost you thirty days." He glared over his frameless spectacles. "Another'll cost you a year."

I fought rolling my eyes. Terrific. Philmont in my custody for a month. Great! Just what I wanted.

Seth, Slim and I presented our case, explaining in detail what had happened. Finished, I sat, hoping, praying the judge would see fit to send Philmont to prison for a long, long time.

Philmont had his turn to speak, finally. "And Judge," he sneered over his shoulder at me, "No female has the right to be a law man. Hell, judge." He froze at Richfield's glare but continued on. "They can't vote. Buy property. Hold an office. But she's holding this one. And look at all the trouble she's caused. She's a menace to society. *She's* the one oughta be locked up. Not me."

Richfield looked at Benton. "What's your role in all this?"

Benton visibly gulped and stood. He stared at me, then Slim, then Seth, then Philmont who narrowed his eyes and glared.

"Well, sir. Ah figured 'bout the same as Ted, but then been watchin' th' sheriff in action. She fights fires, helps people, even faced down a lynch party who was tryin' to hang Ritchie. When we broke into her office, Ted wrote the note, but Ah used my knife to tack it on the desk." He turned around to face me. "An' those things Ah said last night, 'bout you bein' ugly?"

I bristled and squirmed. While I knew it was simply posturing, at some level it hurt. I wasn't the prettiest girl in town—far from it—and knew it. But, being told to my face stung.

Benton hung his head, his gaze sweeping the floor. "It weren't true. Ah don't think you're ugly or homely. Fact is, if you weren't sheriff, you'd be rather handsome."

I found myself smiling. He wasn't such a bad sort, after all. I hoped Richfield would go light on him.

Benton turned back to the Judge. "Ah'm greatly sorry for what Ah did, your honor. An' after Ah serve my time, Ah plan to return to bein' a deacon of the church. Just like before."

"You may be seated." Judge Richfield scanned all of us in the front. "I'll take a ten minute recess to make my decision." He pointed at me. "Have your deputies watch the men. I need you in my chambers."

Panic clutched my chest like it was *me* about to be sentenced. As if in a dream, I stood, pulled part of my skirt from under my shoe, nodded to Slim and Seth, and followed Richfield into Slim's office.

He shut the door and pinned me with his wise eyes, watchful, missing nothing. "What do you think? Did you feel threatened?"

I spent half a minute or more contemplating. "Not at first. But the note on the door at home scared me, and then yesterday with the knife..."

"Based on their attacking you alone, I could sentence them to hang, or the very least, life in prison." He took the chair behind Slim's desk.

More thinking, weighing the crime with the punishment. I stood staring at Slim's shelves, most holding jars, papers and two books. Thankfully, the judge gave me time to gather my thoughts. Things came together.

"Ted Philmont could be dangerous. After all, he did ride with the lynch mob, and he did attack me. His thinking keeps escalating his actions." I stopped with that sentence. I'd never really thought about his actions in such a way before, but I was right. Next thing he'd do would probably be awful. Someone would get hurt.

"I agree." Richfield leaned back and stretched. "I'm inclined to toss him into Federal prison for five years. I'll add the thirty days for contempt. All that time'll give him a chance to reconsider."

I couldn't nod fast enough. "Benton, on the other hand, seems relatively harmless."

Visions of him in jail ratting out Philmont made me

smile. "If I were in charge, Judge, I'd give him probation. Order him to help rebuild the Widow's house and help build the school when we get to that point. Otherwise, I remember him from the church. Seemed to do well enough then."

Richfield's face lit up like he'd just won a prize. "You're a smart woman, Sheriff." He pushed up to his feet. "I agree with you on both cases."

We walked to the door where he placed a hand on my shoulder and rocked it. "I better be careful. Could be one of these days you'll take my job." He winked at me, not flirting, but friendly. "You'd make a heckuva judge."

I bet he only *walked* back to the bench, which was a board over two kegs, but I *floated* into the courtroom. With a vague sense of reality, I watched as first Philmont and then Benton stood, the judge pointing the gavel at each and pronouncing sentences. Still on my heavenly cloud, the judge's words ringing in my ears, the world wrapped itself in gauze. Words turned muffled, foreign.

One Federal deputy, his chest the size of a whiskey barrel, grabbed Philmont's upper arm and hauled him out the door. Philmont stared back over his shoulder, daggers of hatred aimed my way. Benton smiled wide and long then came over to shake my hand.

"Thank you, Sheriff. Thank you." He clasped my hand like a lifeline. "Ah won't let you down. Ah've learned my lesson."

I extracted the hand, fairly sure he was serious. "I'm sure you'll do fine. Just be careful who you partner up with next time." He started to step away, but another thought hit me. I pinned him with my best stare. "Keep in mind, I've got my eyes on you. No more trouble." My shoulders sprung back. I'd sounded like the law. I beamed.

He flashed another smile, tipped his hat to the judge, Slim and Seth, then scurried out the door.

The two remaining deputies, along with the judge, tipped their hats to me and like phantoms, disappeared. I figured they went to Slim's office, and then escaped through the back door.

Seth slid an arm around my shoulders. "Tell you what, Maud. Soon's this place opens for *real* business, how about I buy you a beer?"

That sounded almost as good as being a judge.

* * *

A COLD BEER relaxed my body clear down to my toes. I passed up the offer of a second as I was anxious to visit My Mr. Honey. He and Seth had already worked out housing arrangements and, much to my pleasant surprise, at this moment he was at Seth's house. A small, three-room cottage fit Seth fine. But two bachelors? I wasn't sure it would work, but being only temporary, maybe they wouldn't kill each other right away.

I tapped on the front door, its wood gray with tiny cracks running up and down. Movement inside relaxed me more than the beer. My Honey was up. Within moments the door swung inward and there stood Mr. Astonishing, my hero, my man. Here he was in one piece, upright and smiling. Mr. Miracle. He gave me a halfhearted squeeze and let go.

While I'd envisioned a much greater, warmer, even passionate greeting, still I was more than pleased he was mobile so soon after being wounded. He backed up, I stepped inside. Over Aldridge's shoulder I spotted Mae, standing like she'd been caught with her hand in the proverbial candy jar. Eyes wide on her flawless oval face, her mouth shrunk to a prune. Her hand, long fingers splaying across her heart, trembled.

I took it all in, jumped to judgment, despite what the Good Book said, and froze like a rabbit spotted by a fox. That rabbit and I both hoped we were wrong in our thinking. My eyelashes fluttered for their lives while I listened to Aldridge and then Mae sputter and stammer.

Aldridge, my not-so-wonderful man, turned sideways to

Mae, then swiveled back to me. "I know how this looks, Maud. I know." Using his one good arm, the other resting in a sling, he guided me into the front room, big enough for a dark brown pinstriped settee, its arms stuffed, a round mahogany table and one brocade wingback chair. "We were talking about the Chinese school for girls."

Mae bent slightly at the waist. "We hope to open next week."

I didn't know whether to return the bow, ignore her or shake her hand. Instead, Aldridge deposited me at the end of the two-seater. He eased down beside me as Mae, who seemed relieved I didn't flatten her with a one-two punch, settled into the remaining available chair. Her slanted eyes flitted from me to my clenched hands to Aldridge and back to me. She plastered a hint of a smile on her face, a flicker rising to the edge of her mouth, which only served to make her look more guilty.

Of what, I wasn't a hundred percent sure. Maybe it was nothing. But then again, maybe it was a clandestine romance that Pokey and I were oblivious to. Maybe, just maybe, these two had been lovers in Sacramento and came here to rendezvous. Or, better yet, maybe they were married in secret—an Anglo and Celestial never made a good combination, despite what I told Pokey—and had a child or two. Maybe—

"Maud?" Aldridge shook my upper arm. "You all right? Got that look on your face again."

What look? I had a 'look'? I wiggled on the soft seat and rearranged my skirt, which once again, seemed to find its way under my shoe. "Fine, thank you."

Aldridge half-turned in his seat and addressed both of us. "Mae came over to finalize plans for the school. Maud, it's incredibly exciting." His face turned into an invitation to shared happiness. No way could I resist those gleaming eyes.

Shoving doubts, along with a few disgusting theories aside, I allowed excitement to creep into my chest. After all, this school would help the community, maybe bring everyone closer.

"So, tell me all about it. Where's it gonna be?"

Mae scooted her petite body forward to where she teetered on the edge of the seat. With her being so tiny, that chair swallowed her. "To start, we use uncle's store. Back storage room. We clear out, bring in chairs, two tables."

"What store?"

Aldridge jumped in. "Tai Pan owns a small mercantile, dealing mostly in rice and bai jui. Both, of course, imported."

Memories of too much baijiu roared around my head sending my stomach into waves of nausea. I swallowed down that night, the mortification, and focused on the future. Never again would I drink that much. Probably.

"My uncle sweep floor, let us use... free." Mae flashed a sincere smile twinkling her ink-black eyes.

For the first time I noticed her eyes were slightly crossed, like she was looking at the end of her nose. On her, that feature enhanced her already-beautiful face. No wonder Pokey found her irresistible.

I hated to broach this subject, but after all, it was the core of this project. "Do you have any girls signed up? How'd the men react to this?"

Mae's gaze traveled across the floor then up to Aldridge. "Men not too happy, but wives say yes. In America, they say, need education. Fathers let daughters go."

Amazing. Maybe there was hope yet. "What about a teacher or two?" I couldn't help but wonder who in China-town would be willing to teach girls.

"I am." Aldridge sat up straighter. "Mae will be my assistant. With my teaching experience, figured I'd be the man for the job since Miss McIntyre is busy teaching other students." He took a quick breath and continued. "I'm hoping that maybe, possibly next year we'll be able to combine our classes. That way, we can learn about each other's cultures. Wouldn't that be wonderful?"

It would, but I didn't think it would happen. Prejudices seemed deep set and changing people's minds about topics such as religion, politics or race was an uphill battle. But the younger generation would be the appropriate place to begin.

"Maud? You all right?" Aldridge tapped my arm again. "There's that look on your face."

I wagged my head. "I think what you two are doing is noble and a terrific idea. I hope it works." My stomach growled. Supper time was yet an hour or so away and now that I didn't have to worry about feeding a prisoner or two, I was free to eat where I wanted. Not rushing back to the office felt good.

Hating to leave the soft cushions behind, but knowing I still had things to do, I rose to my feet, followed immediately by Aldridge and Mae. I leveled my eyes on both. "If I can do anything to help, I will. Just let me know."

Aldridge glanced at Mae who glanced back. I caught the look in the pit of my stomach. Was something amiss? For real? Aldridge cocked his head toward his bandaged shoulder, the arm in the sling. "The dance that's coming up?"

I wasn't sure where this was going and wasn't sure I'd like it. I silently nodded.

"It'll be hard for me to dance with you like this." He lifted his white sling. "So, Mae and I were thinking about fund raising for the school at the dance. We could sell lemonade. Or have a booth selling good luck charms. Or..."

Mae glanced up at Aldridge. "Love potions."

Love potions? I didn't really want to know what that involved right now. I still hadn't decided if their relationship was on the up and up or not. Taking my time considering, I didn't see much of a problem with that. People got thirsty and in addition to the punch bowl that mysteriously got spiked, there wasn't much else to drink. But love potions? I raised a shoulder. "Sounds like it'll work."

I stepped toward the door, thoughts bounding back to the unspoken relationship between My Honey and Pokey's Honey. Something didn't feel right.

Aldridge stood in the doorway and tried to hug me. His sling made it awkward along with the grimace when my head got too close to his shoulder. He'd taken a bullet only a few days before, and I knew he was still in pain.

"Think you and Mae will be ready by next Saturday? We'll have elections all day and then a dance that night. Got Pete Dempsey to play fiddle and he's bringing some of his boys to back him up." I could almost hear the fiddle sawing and washtub bass plunking away at Scottish reels or *Little Brown Jug*. My feet tapped.

"Plenty time." Mae bowed and this time, I returned it.

Aldridge followed me to the edge of the porch. "You're my favorite girl, and I'm disappointed we won't be dancing. But... next time." He bent, his lips lightly pressing against mine. They were surprisingly soft and seductive. I wanted more. Right there, right then.

He withdrew, straightened. His gaze traveled up and down my tingling body, and I felt his thoughts. They were mine, too. We stood for a moment, transfixed by possibilities.

Without warning, his shoulders sagged, and he took an unsteady step back. His suntanned face turned ashen. I grabbed his good arm, turned him around and guided him inside. Mae jumped up from the settee.

I pointed toward the bedroom. "Got to get him in bed." While that somehow didn't sound innocent, at that particular moment I didn't care. Mae could think what she wanted. I led him through the front room into Seth's bedroom. Aldridge sank into the bed, and I covered him with a quilt I found on the chest.

My Honey's eyes closed, his breathing grew rhythmic and solid. I tiptoed to the other room.

Mae, still standing, eyes worried, looked down. "Too much for one day."

"I agree." I looked behind me wondering if I should stay or just let him sleep.

"I stay. Watch." Mae tilted her head enough that her shoulder-length hair hung into her eyes. "All right?"

"Fine." I aimed for the door. "I'll bring supper by after a while."

She closed the door behind me. I tramped down the street wondering what would happen next. Would she share his bed? Share his meal? Sit in the front room and continue planning for the school? Brew some tea? And what about Pokey? Why wasn't she with him? Were Aldridge and Mae planning to run away? Take Pokey's and my hearts with them? And what would Pokey do when he found out? Would I be the one to tell him? And where was he right now, anyway?

I reversed course.

CHAPTER THIRTY-FIVE
DEBATE THIS!...

I SPENT THE REST OF THE DAY ARRANGING FOR A notice about the dance to be included in the *Dry Creek Courier's* next edition. The front page would also carry information about the upcoming election scheduled for the same day as the dance. My thinking was people would come in from outlying ranches and farms to dance, why not have them vote too? Emily noted she'd have to interview both Seth and Pearl to be sure her story was fair. Our little town was booming and part of that was due to the presence of the newspaper. We were indeed, shining things up, and I was honored to be part of it.

With the promise of the dance being on the front page of this Friday's paper, Emily Penderton, pen in hand, nodded as I shut the door behind me. I had told her the town councilors would pay for the ad, which brought a sly smile to her face. And mine.

I sauntered down the street stopping to pass time with various people. Most wanted to know about the trial and then about Pokey, Aldridge and Mr. Powell. Only two chewed their words about the mayor's race, wondering—at top volume—how in tarnation did Pearl have the right to run? She couldn't even vote, so how could she run? I explained that I had faced the same predicament and yet, here I was. That shut them up, but they grumbled and mumbled as they stormed off.

Pokey slept in the back of Otis' Mercantile, in a small room that was cozy, functional and reeked of maleness. No pictures on the wall or beside the bed, a plain quilt covering it. A rag rug covered part of the floor and, against the wall, opposite his bed, a two-drawer dresser held whatever clothes he owned. On top, a ceramic washbowl with pitcher and shaving implements crowded the space. He had only one window and it was curtained with calico fabric that must have been left over from someone's skirt. But, he was happy here.

Door half open, I rapped on the jamb and let myself in. Pokey rolled onto his side, opened his eyes.

"Wanted to see how you're doing." I stood by his bedside. "Door was open. Hope you don't mind." Kneeling, I figured, would work better than sitting on the bed or standing over him, hovering like a mother hen. Although at this point, he probably needed a mother. I started for the floor.

"Sit. Here." He pushed up with an elbow, grimacing and trying valiantly not to. Once he was sitting up, I plumped the pillow behind him.

Even though the mattress was narrow, there was room for me. It was probably more comfortable than the floor, anyway. I scooted around until I was sure I wouldn't fall off and studied his face. The black ringing his eyes and cascading down his cheeks was now more purple than black, a bruise on his chin mustard yellow. Soon, he'd be every color of the rainbow.

I handed him a cup of water I found on the floor near his head. The slight tremble in his hands worried me, but he was strong and would recover soon. He sipped twice, then handed the cup back. "Thanks."

"How're you feeling?" While I knew that was a dumb

question, I couldn't think of a better one. Maybe he'd tell me honestly or not.

"Been better. But not as bad as I thought I'd be. That fella had a fist like a ten-pound hammer."

We passed an hour discussing the trial, the outcome, the dance, the election but mostly about Mae. He knew she'd been to see Aldridge and had given his blessing.

"I wanted to sleep and Aldridge was keen on getting the school started. So was Mae, for that matter." Pokey's eyes closed for a moment.

Not knowing exactly where he was injured, I touched his forearm and pushed up to my feet. "Gotta go. Get plenty of rest. I'll check in later."

I pulled the quilt up to his chin, being the mother-hen-nosey-parker I was, but he was already snoring. I ever-so-quietly let myself out.

Pearl McIntyre met me at the front of Otis' Mercantile as I stepped onto the boardwalk.

"A week and three days, Maud." Pearl shielded her eyes from the late afternoon sun. "I'll be the new mayor. Won't that be grand?"

"How're your posters doing? Getting much response from them?"

"Absolutely! That's all anyone's talking about. How they're going to vote for me." Pearl waved her arm up and down Main. "They've all said I would be good for Dry Creek. All of them!"

"We need a debate, Pearl. Between you and Seth." I considered possible dates. "How about this Saturday? Three days from now? Should be plenty of time for you and Seth to get ready. Come up with your strategy and what exactly you want to say."

Pearl stepped off the boardwalk, into the street. "Wonderful! Great! I'll run down to the newspaper office and let her know."

"And I'll tell Seth. How about two o'clock, right here in

front of Otis's?" I figured most Saturday shoppers would be here anyway.

Pearl flashed a winner's grin, turned and walked off mumbling to herself. I couldn't wait to give Seth the good news.

* * *

"YOU WANT ME TO DO *what*?" Seth stomped from his desk to the window where he turned and glared at me. "Debate Pearl? Come on, Maud. Don't you think this's gone far enough? I mean... I mean... it's pointless. I'm gonna win." His arms flew out from his sides. He *pfffed*. "Anybody in their right mind will vote for me. Not some... some school teacher *woman*."

He pronounced 'woman' like it was a bad thing. I moved in close and pointed my finger at the window and toward the street. I kept my anger to a soft boil. "It's only fair to have a woman run. What's wrong with us running government? We already do things men can't... or won't."

"Such as?"

"Such as?" He was so frustrating. Why did I have to spell it out? I counted on one hand. "Cooking. Cleaning. Running a home. Raising children. Giving birth." I eyed him on that one and he gulped. I held up the other hand and ticked off on my fingers. "Gardening, doctoring, teaching, secretary-ing."

He held up both hands, his eyes wide, while I grabbed a breath. But I was on a roll and continued. "Why not in busi-ness and government, too? We can be a fireman... fire-woman... run a bakery, a charm school, a newspaper and... and... be mayor." It had made sense in my head and I hoped the list came out that way.

Seth's arms flew out again as he stepped in closer. "Maud, you just can't let Pearl run. You got the wrong horse by the tail. She and I... *used* to be... well, you know. She's gonna lose and it'll hurt her. I hate to see that happen. But

I'm gonna fix this flint for good." Seth leaned in so close I smelled Bay Rum aftershave. He growled, "Set the date."

Righteous indignation straightened my shoulders. "Already have. It's this coming Saturday, three days from now. Voting is the following Saturday. Same day as the dance."

Seth ran a hand across his dark, oiled hair. His Italian-fused passion sparked his copper eyes where tiny flecks of green danced in the iris. Although fuming at his lack of respect for women, I leaned back, noticing for the first time his lightly wrinkled eyelids. But his eyelashes remained as I remembered—dark and dense. My heart did a quick two-step until I remembered Aldridge. But still, there was some-thing about Seth, even when he was angry, confused and full of himself, like now, that seduced me. His Italian-ness roared at times, and right now it was howling.

I pictured his pa at this age, ranting and pacing around his store in Verona. While Seth calmed, I thought about his family, the hardships and bravery it took to pack up every-thing, kin and kith, and move halfway around the world. Seth had been a toddler, possibly two when he made the voyage. Maybe someday I could chat with his ma about her experiences.

While Seth poured himself a glass of water, swallowing his outrage, I took my idea one step further. Why not ask Mrs. Critoli to come speak at the school? Or better yet, at the charm school? Students should know how different cultures work and, where better than at a charm school?

I smiled, not totally to myself. I was brilliant. Hopefully, she'd be honored and willing to come talk. I'd check with her tomorrow. Maybe she'd even invite me to supper. Her spaghetti, smothered by big chunks of spiced tomatoes, was legendary. She added oregano, dried basil and what I was sure were secret ingredients. My stomach grumbled. Right now, however, I needed to get her little boy to understand the finer points of debate.

"I'll stop by later this afternoon, maybe around five, and

we can go over some strategies." I hoped he'd lassoed his indignation by then and would be reasonable.

"Fine." He plopped into the wooden chair behind his desk, clutched papers that had been laying there and pretended to read. Lines snaked across his forehead as he focused on the papers.

"Fine." I hoisted my skirt while making my way across the room. I'd let myself out, then have a good, long laugh. With my hand on the doorknob, I glanced over my shoulder. Our eyes met.

"Fine," he huffed a second time.

* * *

ALL THE IMAGES of Mrs. Critoli's mouth-watering spaghetti turned into the task of bringing supper to Aldridge. Should I bring enough for four—Seth, Mr. Amazing, Mae and me? Or just two? Mae and Seth being on their own. As I sauntered up Main on my way to the restaurant, I passed the bakery and slid to a halt. If she was still open, I'd snag something delicious for dessert. I tried the handle and to my total joy, the door sailed open.

Only one customer stood at the counter, the upturned chairs balanced on the tables. I'd stopped by just in time. Aromas of cinnamon, nutmeg, baking crusts and other delicious ingredients lingered in the store. If I was smart, I would move my office to next door. That way, I'd smell this heaven all day.

I nodded to AnnaBeth Orlandi as she clutched a boxed pie on her way out. She had a brood of five children, another on the way, and a lumberjack husband. One pie probably wasn't enough, but they'd make do, I was sure.

"Howdy, Hilda!" I produced a wide smile and thumbed over my shoulder. "See you're about to close." My gaze swept the empty case where mouthwatering goodies usually stood, waiting to be eaten by hungry people, their sweet tooth screaming to be satisfied. One pie stood alone, waiting for just the right person to come along and savor it. And I was that person.

"Ya. No more pie. No strudel." Her sad eyes filled with tears. "No more pastries."

A dumpling-sized knot filled my chest. "What do you mean, 'no more'?" My focus now on Hilda.

She glanced left then right as if someone scary skulked around the corner listening in, her German accent in full force. "I must to raise prices *next week*. Then they be too high. People will... no buy."

"Why? What's going on?" No way did I want her and Ester going out of business. I vowed the Dry Creek Sweet Shop would live. Oftentimes, it was only her strudels that got me through the day.

Voice lowered to a whisper, her gaze swept along the entire counter. "We buy insurance. Have to. We were so afraid... our store would burn up." Her eyebrows lowered. "We don't want to be like the widow. Left with nothing." She flailed her arms. "Kaput!"

I patted her hand. "I understand. But how high is the insurance?"

Her eyes trailed up to meet mine. "Mr. Ford charges much. We can't bake enough to cover costs without raising prices. Customers will pay two times. Looks like we must close the bakery."

"What? You can't." The panic wasn't just for myself, although I had to admit a good part of it was. I scrambled for a solution. "Tell you what. I'll talk to the town council. Try to get to the bottom of this. It's not right or fair."

Swiping her sleeve across her eyes, she sniffed and tried a half smile. "*Danka*. Here, take this last pie. Canned peaches and fresh apples." She pulled it out from under the glass-fronted counter, found a box and presented it to me like I had just won a prize.

I handed her a dollar, which she pushed back.

"No charge, Sheriff."

While I hated taking a pie for free under these circumstances, her set mouth told me not to argue. I'd find another way to pay.

My indignant stomach and I marched down the street toward Seth's house to see how Mr. Wonderful was doing. It dawned on me as I stomped, I needed to bring supper, too. While it was fine with me to have only pie as a meal, Aldridge tended to want meat and potatoes first. Seth did too. And Pa. What was it with these men, anyway?

I passed Seth's office, slid to a stop, turned and knocked on his door. I let myself in and found him right where I'd left him—at his desk, reading. However, this time, his feet were up on his desk, holding down a stack of papers. He glanced up as I closed the door behind me.

"We need to talk." I set the boxed pie on one corner of the desk, then took a chair in front of it. "That insurance man. That Nathaniel Ford." I growled as involuntarily, my entire hand, one finger pointed, waved toward the street. "We gotta do something."

He swung his legs up off his desk, swiveled, and plopped his shoes on the floor. His elbows anchored the desk. "What're you talking about?"

I hadn't actually thought about this on the trek along Main, but it would work. "Insurance can be a good idea, right?"

He nodded grudgingly.

"Let's have you and Pearl debate the pros and cons of insurance on Saturday. If people are convinced it's necessary, I think we should bring in some competition. And..." I leaned forward, a thread of cinnamon apple whiffling under my nose. "We should bring in another insurance business. That would help keep the premiums low. Good, old-fashioned competition."

"I'll ask again. What're you talking about?"

I explained the travesty Mr. Ford was doing to Dry Creek, how the bakery may be shutting down, and how the increase in costs would raise all the business's prices. After what probably had been a five-minute diatribe, I leaned back, straightened my skirt, and took a breath.

He steepled his fingers, inspected them like they were new, stared out the window, blew out air, then turned his eyes on me. "Pie smells delicious! Where do we start?"

CHAPTER THIRTY-SIX
THE LADY WITH THE GREEN DRESS...

"ONCE MORE." I HANDED PEARL A REFILLED CUP OF tea as she sat on the edge of the two-seater, its brocade stripes glinting in the fading afternoon sun. My living room always perked up this time of day, its windows mainly facing west. I waited for her to take a good, long sip, then continued. "Give me two good reasons Dry Creek should have an insurance company."

Her blue-jay colored eyes rolled up toward the ceiling. She set the cup and saucer on the end table, sighed loud and long. "You know I don't like the idea of insurance. Seems to me we'd all be better off if we just saved enough money to replace our property. Why give our hard-won money to some shyster who'll just take it and keep it? Why let him make interest on our funds? Why not us?"

While I had to agree with her on pieces of her logic, begrudgingly I'd reached the conclusion insurance was a necessary evil. "For the sake of argument and for the debate, give me *one* reason to have it. Remember what we said earlier?"

She eased to her feet, rubbed her lower back and looked toward the front door. "I think I'm ready for the debate and yes, I remember what we said."

"We should practice some more."

Pearl turned her round eyes on me, her mouth set in a tight line. "Seth is the one should do more practicing. He doesn't know what he's talking about and he's going to regret not practicing when he loses the election Saturday."

I stood also, knowing we were done for the day. "The debate is tomorrow. Two o'clock. What're you going to wear?"

Pearl straightened her shoulders and flashed a wide smile. "Bought a new dress for the occasion. And I'll also use it when I'm sworn in." She held out her brown skirt. "It's so much better than this. It's blue calico with bows at the bottom. The top is a slight scoop neck, little pearl buttons down the front and sleeves with a bow at the wrist. It's *so* lovely!"

"Can't wait to see." And I couldn't. I loved new dresses, especially mine, but with Pearl's slim figure and blond hair, I'd bet she was stunning. And I'd bet she'd paid a hefty price for the honor. I hoped it was worth it.

We stood on the porch enjoying the unusual warmth early winter ushered in. Before she started down the steps, Seth strode up the pathway, his long legs eating up the yards. One step up on the stoop, he stood, frozen. Pearl, also frozen, stared down at him. That moment had to be the definition of awkward. I'd about forgotten Seth had planned to stop by for last-minute advice before the big day and, seeing him walk up like that, I leaned back hoping Pearl's claws would stay sheathed long enough for him to get inside.

Instead of claws, Pearl stuck out a dainty hand. "Mayor Critoli. Good to see you again." Syrupy sweetness dripped off each word. "I see you're in need of advice. Too late."

Seth blinked in butterfly fashion, swallowed, then took her hand. "Miss McIntyre." He held it up like he was going to kiss it, but didn't. He clasped it long enough to make a point, then releasing it, bounded up the two remaining steps and disappeared inside my house. I had to admit that move was classy.

Pearl turned and spoke over my shoulder, aimed at Seth's receding form. "After next week, after I win, I plan to redecorate the mayor's office, so might as well start packing now —*Seth*." She hollered more than simply threatened, but she'd made a point and started down the steps.

Seth appeared in the doorway making me pirouette like a ballerina I'd seen on stage in Sacramento.

"Oh, yeah, Miss School Marm?" Seth now stood at my shoulder, his outstretched arm pointed at Pearl. "Don't know why you think you'll win. Don't know anything about running a town." He lowered his voice to a purr. "Leave it to the professionals."

Pearl spun around like she'd been kicked, bounded up the two steps ending up right in Seth's face. They were close enough to kiss if they'd been in a different frame of mind.

"Don't know...? Running...?" Pearl's cheeks flared crimson, her hands fisted. "I run a school. Teach children who'd rather be outside playing. I instruct them on good manners —which you clearly missed—reading, writing, ciphering. Also on sharing, learning to work with others. I run my classroom with discipline and *re-spect*." She popped the *p*, pulled in a worldful of air and dropped her voice to a whisper. Her narrowed eyes pierced him like porcupine quills. "How do you run *your* town, *Mr.* Mayor?"

For once, Seth and I were speechless. Maybe she would win if her debate tomorrow came with the same fire, grit and brimstone I'd seen on the porch. I stood, wondering, watching who I figured to be the next mayor of Dry Creek nod to me, glare at Seth, turn with grace personified, skip down the steps and march out to the street. She disappeared into the setting sun.

Seth thawed as he stared after her. "My God. Did you see that, Maud?" He turned to me. "Think I'm in love."

* * *

THE BIG DAY—DEBATE day—dawned bright and sunny, a crisp chill in the air, but nothing a light coat couldn't handle. I sat at my office desk, coffee cup in hand, enjoying two things: the warmth from the potbelly stove and, more importantly, the quiet. Although it was early, barely before eight, no town councilor or two or three had marched in demanding I put a stop to the debate. No group of women had insisted on having the dance tonight instead of next week. And nobody had been shot, beaten or robbed. Nor any chickens reported missing.

This would be a grand day.

I finished the coffee, pushed papers around, tacked up a new wanted poster on the bulletin board, swept the floor and at last admitted to a bit of unease tightening my muscles. I wasn't used to this... this solace.

The office, now neat and clean, grew quiet. Real quiet. After rinsing out the coffee cup, I tied on my bonnet, slipped into my coat, wrapped the rig around my waist, checked to be sure a cartridge or two were in the gun's cylinders, and headed out the door. I rattled the knob. Good and locked. I wasn't too keen on any new surprises like last time.

It was almost eleven, so I figured I'd step into the bakery for a bite of strudel. After all, this was Saturday, and I always treated myself to strudel on Saturday. And if Hilda wasn't open, I'd head down to the restaurant where their flapjacks on a chilly Saturday would warm anyone. Maybe I'd stop at both.

It had become second nature scanning both sides of Main as I walked, looking for people I knew as well as people recently arrived. I waved to a couple on the other side of the street, then turned my attention to ahead of me. A tall man and a woman whose top of her head came up to his shoulders, walked half a block down, their backs to me. Something about them seemed familiar. Could I recognize people from their backs and the way they walked? Was I that good?

No. Not at all. But I recognized her dress and his bowler. Both unusual being her skirt was an emerald green—not one I'd seen often around town. And his bowler had a wider brim than normal. I'd seen them before, but where?

I couldn't help myself, my sheriffing senses in full force. I followed them, matching their stride. We made our way up Main toward the hotel. Were they new in town staying there? I kept them in sight and walked faster.

Insurance seller Nathaniel Ford stood on the sidewalk in front of his office and caught my arm. "Howdy, Sheriff! It's quite the big day, I understand."

Yanked to a stop, I pulled out of his grip trying to stay focused on the couple. "Sorry, Mr. Ford. I can't chat right now."

He held my upper arm again. "Oh, I apologize for interfering with official endeavors. It's merely you seemed to be enjoying this fine weather, and I thought we could sit and have civil discourse about insurance for your office." He rushed his words. "Or your private residence."

In the moment it took to wrench my arm out of his grasp and glance at him, when I looked back down the street, the couple was gone. Disappeared into thin air.

Drat and double drat! Now I'd have to hunt them down. I'd start with the hotel. "Excuse me, Mr. Ford. I really do need to go."

Ungraciously, he maneuvered in front of me and it took a bit of a dance to get around him. Was his obstruction intentional? I'd have to think it was.

He called after me. "Maybe tomorrow?"

Ignoring him, I aimed for the hotel. But what would I say, exactly? Maybe it would come out like I was stalking them. Whatever I was doing, it was official business. My badge allowed me to stalk.

Within sight of the hotel in the next block, I crossed the street and then it dawned on me.

I'd seen them a month or two ago as they went inside

this hotel. And, they could have been the people who'd been seen sitting with Mr. Ford at dinner one evening—right after the widow's fire. He said they'd taken the stage up to Oregon Territory the next morning. Was that them? The more I thought about it, the more I was convinced they were one and the same. And it all seemed fishy. Besides, they were strangers and part of my duty was to "welcome" them.

Maybe my imagination was stampeding itself over a cliff. Maybe I was right. Maybe they were arsonists, in cahoots with Ford. Or maybe, just maybe, they were an innocent couple who happened to be wearing clothes I'd seen before.

I tried to tell myself that was it, it was merely the clothes, but little bells tinkled in the back of my head. I followed the bells.

I checked the hotel. Before inquiring, I stretched my memory for names. Finally... Henry and Cecilia Apertide. That's what Ford had said.

The desk clerk wagged his head as I read down the register of recent customers. My finger passed Clark Weinstein, Wm. H. Alvery, Mr. and Mrs. A. Tideman, Mr. Wadsworth C.... I went back to Tideman. That was sort of close to Apertide.

I spun the register back around and drilled the name with a pointed finger. "This one right here. Says they signed in yesterday. What d'they look like?"

The clerk, who I didn't recall ever seeing in church, squinted at the finger, adjusted his thin spectacles and gave a nose whistle. "I'm sorry, Sheriff. Our guests' names are privileged. I'm not at liberty—"

I leaned over the counter and grabbed him by his vest—a move surprising both of us. "I'm not asking." I tugged harder. "I'm telling. It's a matter of utmost importance."

Released, he stepped back, adjusted his vest and string tie. "I see." He cleared his throat, glanced left then right. "If you must know, this is the third time they've stayed with us. First was a few months ago, maybe around September, then two, possibly three weeks ago. They arrived yesterday. Delightful guests they are. Quiet. Well mannered. Always tip our help."

"They sign in under the same names?"

I wanted to shout "whoo hoo" when he nodded, but instead, cocked my head a bit to the right. Like snowflakes, pieces of the puzzle floated to the ground, connecting themselves to make a bigger picture. "He wearing an oversized bowler? She in a dark green skirt?"

He gulped so hard his Adam's apple bobbed. Blinking, he nodded ever so slightly.

Something began to smell and it wasn't supper. It was rotten and had Nathaniel Ford's name all over it. I prayed Aldridge's wasn't. "Are they here now? I thought I saw them come in a moment ago."

Shaking his head hard, the clerk's eyes grew wide. "No ma'am. I've been right here, right behind this desk since seven this morning. I've seen them leave but not come back. No ma'am."

"What room are they in?"

He backed up until he slammed against the mail and key sorter cubby. "Oh no, I'm real sorry, Sheriff. I sincerely am. I can't tell you that. It's against company—"

"Get me the owner or manager." I wasn't playing and obviously he knew it.

He scurried from behind the counter. "Yes, ma'am. Right away."

Within moments, J.R. Potter appeared at my elbow. "Miss Overstreet. Sheriff. A pleasure." He extended a hand. "I understand you're looking for a guest of mine."

"Utmost importance." I glanced up the stairwell at a man coming down. Not my quarry.

"Well, unfortunately," Potter said, "we don't give out guests' room numbers. Not forany reason."

Tired of this game, I leaned in close, dropped my voice.

"I can arrest you for harboring criminal fugitives. I can shut you down. And will."

Where did this come from all of a sudden? I didn't spend much time thinking about it, but I was enjoying my new-found confidence. It felt good—as if I'd suddenly genuinely become sheriff. A lady of the law.

Potter held up one hand, tiny beads of sweat glistening on his forehead. "Fugitives? Arrest? Shut down? No need for all that." He turned to the clerk who held up ten fingers. "Uh, they're in room ten. Upstairs, second door on your right."

I didn't plan to search their room right away, figuring to bring Penelope Plunkett with me. Not that I knew exactly what to look for, she probably didn't either, but she would know more about arson than I would. Besides, two pairs of eyes would be better. And if things went cockeyed, she could back me up.

I thanked Mr. Potter, took a final glance up the stairs as the Regulator's bell on the hotel's wall announced noon. Plenty of time to find Penelope, then get ready for the debate in two hours. I headed out the door.

First things first. I needed to see Penelope but didn't have time to walk out to her farm. I decided to pay a kid to go fetch her and found gangly teenaged Raymond Gilman leaning on a post in front of Otis's Mercantile. His slouching alternated between being bored and peering across the street at a saloon. While he wasn't old enough to drink legally, that never stopped the bartenders from serving men with coin.

Raymond would be ideal. He said his ma was inside buying material, but it would be another hour or two before he'd have to walk her home. After telling him what I needed, he agreed readily, his mouth curving into a delighted smile and his wide-brimmed hat shading sparkling eyes. He and his long legs took off the moment that nickel hit the palm of his hand.

Next. Platforms and chairs for the candidates. I took two wooden chairs from behind Otis's desk in his office and placed them on the boardwalk to the side of his doors. After much searching, I found two almost-empty wooden boxes of pistols. Made of oak, these boxes would be sturdy enough for Pearl and Seth to stand on when they spoke. With the help of Pokey, who was at last up and about, although slow and careful in his movements, we emptied the crates, careful to lay the weapons in another crate, and carted them outside.

Newspaper editor Emily hung a banner behind the chairs declaring today's debate. I stood out in the street and admired our handiwork. My stomach fluttered with hopes everything would go well. No big fistfights like earlier this year when Pokey and I both ran for Sheriff. Our debate had deteriorated before it even got off the ground.

I had higher hopes for this one.

With everything set and waiting for Penelope, I offered to buy Pokey a sandwich at Dry Creek's Cafe.

"Would love to Maud." Pokey spoke over still-swollen jaws. "Can't really chew right now." He stared across Main to the Palace Saloon. "But I can drink. How about you buy me a beer?"

At least up at the bar, they offered pickles, hard boiled eggs and pickled pigs' feet for two cents each, so I wouldn't starve. "On me." We crossed the street, careful to avoid buggies, horses and road apples.

From there, standing at the pine bar, which until a few months ago visiting it would have been unthinkable on my part, I watched for signs of Raymond and Penelope and also Seth and Pearl. It wouldn't do for my candidates to skip the debate.

We finished one entire mug each, two eggs and shared a pickle before I spotted Penelope glance inside the mercantile. On her heels stood Raymond. "Sorry, Pokey. Gotta go." I ordered him another beer, dropped a dime on the bar and headed outside.

"Penelope!" I waved as she turned at her name. We

stood under the overhang while I explained the situation. She understood immediately what I suspected and agreed they looked suspicious, only because they'd been seen with Ford. We decided the minute the debate was over, we'd visit Room Number Ten.

CHAPTER THIRTY-SEVEN
FIGHTING FIRE WITH FIRE...

SETH SHOWED UP FIRST, THEN FIVE MINUTES later, Pearl, her new calico dress reflecting the blue sky, shimmering in the sunlight. She had selected well—it was spectacular. Parts of me screamed jealousy. Other parts accepted the fact I'd never, ever, look like that. I was way too tall, a bit too rounded on the edges and my eyes, as well as my hair, were a boring, normal shade of light brown. Nothing special about me.

I wallowed around in self-pity for a good minute until shaking loose. This was not the time to make life all about me. I had a debate to conduct and if the stars aligned correctly, nothing would keep us from a half hour or so of high-spirited discussion of the future of Dry Creek.

Precisely at two, I stepped up onto one of the overturned boxes and waited for a crowd to gather closer. Several curious citizens milled around, gradually gravitating toward the two mayoral candidates. I peered over heads and estimated a good fifty people, including several youngsters, standing, waiting for someone to say something brilliant. Maybe they thought they'd be entertained, or possibly, decide which mayoral contender would be the better choice.

For an introduction, I chose my words carefully. Seth and Pearl were friends of mine and since I was campaign manager of both parties, I'd have to be doubly impartial. Plus, I was sheriff and it wouldn't do to show favoritism.

Within a minute the crowd quieted, hushed whispers floating in the back. I drew in a long breath, let it out inch by inch. "Welcome to Dry Creek's Mayoral Debate." I spotted the three town councilors standing in the far back, arms folded across their chests like petulant children refusing to eat something healthy. Why were they glaring at me? This hadn't been *my* idea. Well, all right. The debate was, but the election was something the town founders had decided on a decade ago. Absolutely not my fault.

"Before I introduce the two candidates who need no introduction, I'd like to state two rules to guide this debate." I paused, hoping no one would heckle me. No one did. "First. Each candidate will be allowed to speak for five minutes. After each is allowed their time, I'll ask questions, giving each one a chance to answer."

Heads bobbed and people mumbled what I hoped was approval. I marched on. "Second. No throwing anything— vegetables, rocks or bullets." I hoped I'd get at least a snicker, but I didn't. "This isn't the place to practice your pitching." That received two head wags and one guffaw.

I opened my mouth to continue, but a fella from the crowd beat me to it. "Let 'em talk, Maud. Want ta hear what they've gotta say."

I held up a hand knowing I'd pushed the endurance limit for waiting. "On my right is Miss Pearl McIntyre, our school marm." A slight smattering of clapping broke the silence. "After spending time in San Francisco, she had the good sense to move here. She's been teaching our children here in Dry Creek for the past several years." I surveyed the crowd. "Fact is, some of you were probably her students."

More heads nodded, people mumbled to each other.

"On my left, Mayor Seth Critoli is no stranger to anyone. He's been your mayor for the past four years and when he's not out kissing babies and shaking hands, he runs a successful real estate business right here in town." I looked at him as the crowd applauded.

Waiting for the clapping to settle, I wondered if this was such a good idea. And then I thought again. Absolutely. It was a great idea.

"As you know," I addressed the gathering, "I've asked each candidate to speak about what they see being mayor should be, and also to address the insurance question. They've agreed to speak candidly about their feelings on this and other topics." I glanced at Pearl who straightened her shoulders, pushed out her chest and stood as tall as possible. "Our first candidate to speak is Miss Pearl McIntyre."

Polite applause.

Pearl stepped onto the oak box, raising her a good twenty inches off the ground. Her hat, sitting at a jaunty angle, matched her new dress and set off her heart-shaped face. Now I was doubly jealous.

"Thank you, Sheriff for that lovely introduction." Pearl didn't look over at me as she began. Instead, she focused her attention on the people standing in front of her, much as I'd guess she did in the classroom.

I removed myself to the shadows. Seth stood near, his attention on Pearl. It dawned on me right then and there how much he wanted to win and what being mayor meant to him. I'd never seen such a look of determination on his face.

As Pearl spoke, I scanned the crowd to be sure no one would do anything to hurt either candidate or the debate itself. So far, no drunks had come staggering out of any of the five saloons and no one hollered disagreements at Pearl. So far.

I checked Seth's pocket watch. One more minute, then Pearl would have to move over. I tuned into her closing remarks.

"... run this town as I run the schoolhouse. Passion, caring and respect are the doctrines in my classroom. With respect, which I'll employ when I'm mayor, we can—"

Clang! Clang! Clang!

I jerked around. The fire bell. Say it wasn't so! Tell me someone was playing a trick. The crowd turned and twisted, their thoughts probably the same as mine. And then a man pointed north.

"Smoke!" He shook his arm as he stared into the sky. "Smoke! Looks like the livery's on fire!"

Penelope led the mob while I ran somewhere in the middle. My legs weren't as long as hers and my skirt kept bunching around them. I shouted instructions lost to the wind. No one needed to be reminded to get the fire buckets that were set out on the boardwalks. No one needed to be reminded to form a bucket line, but still, I hollered.

I followed the crowd and smoke up around a corner and over three blocks. Sure enough, flames engulfed Monahan's Livery Stable. Horses snorted, rearing in absolute panic. I swear I heard one roar, but I'd assumed only cats did that. As I got closer, the sound without doubt came from a horse.

Pete Monahan ran back and forth, tossing buckets of water on the flames. His face, black lines running down his cheeks, was one of absolute panic. His eyes were almost as big as his horses' eyes.

Bless her heart, Penelope directed the group's efforts. First order of business was to save the animals. Men, including Swede Swensen owner of the other stable, led them away from the burning barn and into a pasture behind the building. Flames now covered the roof, cascading down the wood timbers holding it up.

The building creaked, its wood rafters groaning as if a giant sat on them.

A bucket brigade formed immediately with women toting wooden buckets full of water from Dry Creek, then handing them to men who threw the water on the flames. In the melee, I spotted Seth, Pearl, the three town councilors and surprisingly, Nathaniel Ford, all hoisting buckets.

A fella I recognized trotted up to Penelope and me. "That's all the horses. Got 'em all out. No one hurt."

Relief relaxed my shoulders. While we would for sure lose the building, we wouldn't lose an animal. *Be grateful for small favors*, my mother used to say. And I was.

Penelope coughed and then hollered at the crowd as loudly she could despite the smoke. "That's it. Pour water around the stable. Building's a total loss."

The urgency dissipated as the flames ate the business. My heart hurt for him. Within moments, everything Pete Monahan had worked years to build, now lay in smoldering ruins. I briefly wondered if he had insurance.

One by one, the men and women wandered off, shaking their heads, wiping soot and smoke from their faces and discussing what had happened. I searched for Mr. Ford, but not surprisingly, he had vanished.

I stood next to Penelope, Seth and Pearl watching the roof groan to the ground, sparks flying from it. The stench of burned leather from the buggies and harnesses crinkled my nose. I held my hand over it hoping to breathe better.

Thoroughly defeated, shoulders drooping, a shuffling in his gait, Mr. Monahan stepped over to me. His sad, reddened eyes looked at Penelope and then me. Between his strong Southern accent and smoke-clouded throat, he managed to croak out a full sentence. "This was no accident, Sheriff. No accident *atall*."

* * *

DEBATE FORGOTTEN, Penelope and I marched toward Nathaniel Ford's insurance office. I was certain he had something to do with the fire and while I walked, contemplated what charges to arrest him on. Unfortunately, watching a fire was no crime. Nothing else came to mind, but I was confident, given time, I'd find something. He'd spend the next hundred years in jail if I had my way.

A familiar line snaked out the door as Penelope and I rounded the corner onto Main.

"Hard way to drive up business," I muttered to our fire marshal.

She ran a sooty hand under her sooty nose. She sniffed. "I'll bet he has eyewitnesses who put him right here when it started. They'll swear to it."

"Sure you're right. Saw him at the fire." I dropped my voice as we neared the first couple in line. "No way he's innocent, though. No way."

We elbowed through the door and into his office. An older couple sat in front of his desk, paper and pen in hand.

He looked up, face contorting into a Cheshire grin. "Be right with you ladies." Ford pointed to chairs lining the opposite wall. "Need to finish up with this couple first."

Penelope and I looked at each other. While I didn't have much, if anything, to go on, I was sure Ford was guilty. In fact, he was Suspect Number One. The couple I couldn't find would be Suspects Number Two. As much as I didn't want to sit and wait, that's what we had to do. Since I didn't have proof positive Ford was the arsonist, I had to behave myself.

The Fire Marshal and I plopped into the hard, wooden chairs and squirmed. Fifteen minutes later, the older couple I vaguely recognized as having a farm north of town, stood, shook hands with Ford, handed him cash and left.

Pleasantries and good-mannered conversation pushed aside, I accosted Ford before the door closed. "I need to know where you were during the debate. Right before the fire started."

"You were spotted watching the fire, Mr. Ford." Penelope wiped a smudge of something black off her hand. "We know you were there."

Easing to his feet, his face hardened into granite, losing any semblance of polite decorum.

"Of course I was there." He shrugged. "It affects my business, after all. Plus, half the town was too." He shook his head. "No crime in that."

Ford was not about to distract me from my questions.

"I'll ask again, Mr. Ford. Where were you?" I leaned over the desk. "Make it good."

He leaned forward, so close I could see his shave line from this morning. "I don't have to explain my whereabouts to you or anyone. You're not my mother *or* my wife, and I'm not under arrest. You have no right interfering with me conducting business."

Penelope's shoulder touched mine as she also leaned. "Answer the sheriff's question then we'll leave. Let you *do* business."

Huffing out disgusted air, his upper lip rose into a sneer. "Right here. I was at this very desk, if you must know." He leaned back a bit. "Heard the fire bell, noticed people running, so naturally, I followed."

"Anybody here with you?" I knew he was lying, but couldn't catch it.

He raised one bushy eyebrow. "Nobody here, for a change. I was busy pushing papers. Signing, dotting, and filing." His steely eyes narrowed in on me. "I do that sometimes, you know."

I shook off his rudeness. "Anybody see you come out of this office?"

That sneer returned to his face. "Only person saw me leave here was a gentleman I bumped in to. He growled at me but continued rushing toward the fire." His smugness grew more obnoxious. "And no, I don't know who he was."

There was no way I'd find whoever that was, even if it was true. Nathaniel Ford was guilty of arson, or at least planning arson, and I'd get to the bottom of this mess. I vowed to see him behind bars within a day. Might take two, but I'd put him there.

"Anyone else, Mr. Ford?" I glanced toward the door, noticing eager faces peering in through the window. "You speak to anyone along the way?"

Shaking his head, he shrugged again, this time with a dramatic flair. His performance face reappeared. The face he gave potential clients. "Don't recall any such conversations,

Sheriff." He pointed toward the door. "Now, if you fine ladies have no further questions for me, I'm afraid the delightful citizens of Dry Creek are seeking my assistance." He stepped from behind his desk and moved for the door. "You'll have to excuse me."

I wasn't going to "excuse" him, but for now I'd leave. Penelope and I pushed through the growing throng and headed for the hotel, questions for the desk clerk already forming in my head.

No, he hadn't seen them since I'd asked a couple of hours ago. Yes, he'd send a boy to find me the minute they came in. He turned his back when Penelope and I started up the stairs. I guessed that was too much for him. At least he could honestly say he wasn't a witness to our illicit undertakings, although he'd given us the key.

Half an hour later, we found nothing in their room implying they were arsonists. No half-burned lucifers, no jars of alcohol with wads of cotton stuffed into the tops, nothing suspicious. Penelope eased to the bed, its tick mattress sagging. Not uncommon. I sat on the other side, which didn't sag as much. I didn't think much about the difference until Penelope pointed it out.

We hoisted the mattress, flipping it onto its side—no easy feat. Pieces of cotton ticking floated out dropping to the floor. I sneezed. And then we spotted it at the same time. A poorly sewn seam near the end of the mattress.

All sorts of tingles and tickles covered my body. Hallelujah. We were on to something. I just knew it. "Should we?" I asked Penelope.

"Oh, let's."

Together we opened up the seam and, like a surprised prairie dog, out popped cash. Not just a bill or two, but hundreds. We pulled and tugged until all we got was cotton. Piling the money on the floor, I counted one thousand, nine hundred and seventy-five dollars. Quite a haul.

We scooped it up, righted the mattress and traipsed downstairs with the loot. They'd need to answer to this, and it had better be good. We returned the key to a grateful clerk, left a note for the A. Tidemans—if that was their real name—to come to the Sheriff's Office immediately. While the clerk scanned the note, his thin mustache, which looked to have been drawn on with India ink, gyrated like the wheels of a steam locomotive. He then folded the paper and slid it in the appropriate slot under their room key.

Now we'd wait.

On the street, I turned to Penelope who had tucked the bills inside her blousy shirt. "Let's go by the bank, put this money some place safe."

She cocked her head while half of her mouth rose into a smile. "Never thought this much money would make me itch."

Glad my pa was still at the bank, I gave vague answers when he questioned where I got the cash. He knew enough not to ask. We deposited the stash in his vault, thanked him and offered to take him for a mid-afternoon snack. "I believe Hilda is still open," I teased. "Ooohhh... apple strudel."

Pa shook his head, slowly. "Can't. There's a board meeting in half an hour and I need to finish up here."

Penelope and I stood at the door. We both raised noses toward the street. "Yum... smells like cinnamon," I said.

"Are those peaches I smell?" Penelope winked.

Pa shooed us out and closed the door.

CHAPTER THIRTY-EIGHT
DIVIDE AND CONQUER?...

"THINK WE SHOULD FOLLOW FORD? SEE WHERE HE goes to?" I spoke after my final bite of peach strudel, its flaky heaven now a memory. I hated to see it end.

Penelope, fork halfway to mouth, held it there as she brought her eyes up to mine. "Thinking the same thing. It's a good idea. But who?"

We bantered names back and forth. Not either of us, for sure. Aldridge? No. As much as I hated to admit, there was an off chance he was in on the scheme, although I was certain he wasn't. Pokey? Maybe. Seth? No. Pa? We stopped at that one. Would Pa be willing? Maybe not trail Ford, exactly, but ask him to supper. See what he could find out. Or Pearl?

Ah. That was it. Pearl wanted to be mayor, thought she could handle the job and this would test her mettle. We scraped every last crumb of our scrumptious mid-afternoon dessert, promised Hilda we'd be back soon, and went in search of Pearl.

She wasn't hard to find. First place we looked was her classroom in the back of the church and, there she was. Glasses perched on the end of her nose, she sat deeply engrossed in a book. She jumped when we closed the door.

Pearl whipped off the glasses, tossed them onto her desk.

"That was sure one helluva debate, Maud!" Crimson flared on her cheeks. "What the hell happened? I mean... a fire? Who started...? Why...?" She took a breath, her blue eyes reaching for the ceiling. "*Again?*"

I'd not seen her this rattled, I believe *ever*. Her day, destined to be stressful to begin with, had been shot all to smithereens. Her cursing was about to become legendary. That was twice this month. And now here she sat, her lovely new dress dotted with soot. I wasn't sure how she'd clean it without turning the bodice a streaky black.

Before Penelope and I could find the right words, Pearl sniffed in what I was sure were tears.

"Dang it! I'm never gonna get to be mayor, now." Pearl searched her top drawer and pulled out a handkerchief. She wiped her eyes then her nose. "I mean, there was so much I wanted to say. So much!" She looked up at me. "And I'd even practiced!"

I nodded.

She blew into the handkerchief. "I mean... what's happening around here?"

Penelope and I moved to either side of her. I slid an arm around her shoulders before she could stand. It wasn't the end of the world, far from it, but in her mind, the fire had more than likely burned away all her dreams of winning.

She took a moment to compose herself, gave one final sniff, then stood, bringing us with her. "You got who did it? Right?" She balled both hands. "When I get—"

"Got away." Penelope raised an eyebrow and pursed her lips.

"But..." I employed my happy voice. "We think we know who's doing it."

"You do?" Pearl's reddened eyes trailed up to mine.

Penelope pointed outside. "Fairly sure. A couple from out of town." She glanced at me. "And Nathaniel Ford. Just gotta find 'em now."

Pearl straightened her skirt, brushing at soot, the action mushing the black into the fabric. "Let me help. I can help."

She looked at me then Penelope, her mouth set in a tight line. "I wanna help."

I knew, simply *knew*, we'd catch these people soon. And then I'd see Ford behind bars. Glory days were indeed ahead.

The three of us plotted and planned how Pearl could either follow the couple or even possibly befriend them. At the very least, the two women could compare skirts.

"Better yet. I'll go talk to Mr. Ford. Right now." Pearl marched to the door, fitted her new hat, now a bit smoky, and tossed a cape around her shoulders. "I'll pretend I'm interested in buying insurance." She moved with the hard grace of a woman scorned. "He won't know what hit 'im."

We closed the door after stepping into the late afternoon blue. A wispy cloud here and there marred the otherwise flawless sky. No breeze ushered in cold. Weather-wise, the day was as close to ideal as possible. Too bad I had to spend the remainder of it chasing criminals.

With Pearl hunting Ford, Penelope and I went in search of the mysterious couple. We ducked inside the Dry Creek Café, our town's newest eatery, only to find two single men at opposite tables, shoveling in steak and potatoes. A quick check with the waitress and she reported no such couple coming in today. Hadn't seen them at all, in fact.

Back on the street, we stood, gazing left and right. A handful of men were still out and about, but no women. I assumed they were all home cooking supper. My stomach rumbled. Supper would be good about now.

"Suppose they're at your office?" Penelope raised one shoulder. "Think they'd have the guts to come into a law office and demand their money back?"

I hated playing devil's advocate, but I couldn't help myself. "What if that was say, inheritance money we took? What if it's completely legal?"

"So, why didn't they put it in the bank in the first place?"

Good question. I started toward my office, thinking

out loud, Penelope in tow. "Maybe they don't trust banks. Maybe they were simply staying one night. Maybe—"

"'Maybe' my foot, Maud." She gripped my arm tugging me to a sudden stop. "Nobody keeps that kind of money in a mattress—except outlaws in those Beadle and Adams dime novels. Nobody in real life does."

She had a point, so why make excuses for the money? As we walked, we tried to examine the money from every side, always coming up with the same conclusion—it was either stolen or hush money from Nathaniel Ford. I preferred the latter.

I unlocked the door and found no note slipped underneath demanding the return of almost two thousand dollars. Penelope did a quick sweep of the rooms, including the cells, while I hung up my coat and bonnet. A fire in the potbelly stove would warm the place and we could get coffee going.

It didn't take long and we sat, mulling over not only the day's events, but possible beaus for Penelope and me—in case Aldridge didn't work out. She had her eye on a fella who was foreman on a ranch south of town, Brent something she'd said.

"Comes into town but once a month, picks up supplies, has his horses shoed." Her eyebrows arched over eager eyes. "He's got muscles like this." She held up hands forming a circle at least twelve inches across.

I sipped my coffee and thought of Aldridge, my Adonis. Life had been so busy lately and with him hurt, I hadn't seen him much.

We sat in silence for a bit, slurping and thinking. The door squeaked open making both of us jump.

"Sheriff?" A man I recognized by his wide brimmed bowler, held the door for a woman in an emerald green skirt. My mysterious couple.

I stood, mentally cursing my boring brown skirt now firmly wrapped around one leg.

Pulling it loose, I nodded. "Come in. We've been expecting you."

Both eased inside and then shut the door after a beat. My guess was they had discussed leaving the cash behind or coming up with a story of how it rightfully belonged to them. This would be good.

Penelope brought over two chairs usually occupied by irritated town councilors. I pointed. "Have a seat." I looked from face to face. "See you got my note."

The woman lowered herself to the edge of the chair while he remained standing.

"Please sit, Mr. Tideman." I pointed again. "This could take a while."

Instead of sitting, he placed one hand, palm down on the desk and leaned in. "I don't mean to sound disrespectful, Sheriff. But I believe you came into our room, searched it, and stole something that belongs to us. The desk clerk told us." His hawklike features were both frightening and elegant. A well-clipped mustache hid his upper lip. "I don't see how any of this is legal."

"It is when I'm conducting an arson investigation." Like a snake slithering up a tree, I stood, eyes narrowing in on him. "Sit down, Mr. Tideman."

The woman gasped. "Arson?"

Tideman took his seat, then her hand and patted it. "There, there, Annabelle. It's some mistake, I'm sure. They can't accuse us of arson when they have no proof."

"And we weren't even in town." Tears watered her eyes.

Penelope crossed her arms. "Where were you then? Before today's fire, around two?"

Tideman pointed north. "Inspecting a string of horses at the Bar X Ranch. You know where it is?"

I nodded. Everyone knew. North of town on several hundred acres of rolling grassy land, the most top-notch grazing area around.

"We're looking to improve our stock," he said. "Maybe even race one or two." His gaze traveled from Penelope to me. "Racing is quite popular these days. Nothing illegal about buying horses."

"No, there isn't, long as you have papers to prove owner-ship." Penelope dropped her arms. "You got 'em?"

Tideman jumped to his feet like he'd been poked. "Haven't bought 'em yet." He glared at me. "Seems someone stole my money."

His wife tugged on his arm, urging him to sit. "It's all a misunderstanding, Abernathy. Sit back down." Her voice turned soft. "I'm sure they'll return the money and then we can buy those horses."

It all made sense. I hated it. And then I had an idea. Would it work? I couldn't take Penelope aside to explain my strategy, but she was smart and would most likely pick up on it quickly.

I pushed back my chair and stood. "It'll take a bit to get your money out of the bank, they don't open again until Monday morning. In the meantime, I'm wondering Mrs. Tideman, if you could walk over with me to the mercantile. I love your skirt and I'd appreciate you helping me pick out good material."

Her eyes lit up like fireworks. "I'd love to!" She stood and spun to her husband. "If you don't mind."

"I'll go with you." He rose.

Penelope held up a hand. "Mr. Tideman, since you're an expert at judging horse flesh, I was wondering if you could stay here and give me some pointers. See, besides being fire marshal, I own a ranch and I'm looking to buy good breeding stock."

Tideman's head swiveled from Penelope to Annabelle, his gaze finally resting on his wife. "If you don't mind, Annabelle, I'd much rather talk horses than fabric." He turned to me. "I want that money when you come back."

I tossed a smile his way. "You'll get what's coming to you, don't worry." I buttoned my coat.

As Annabelle and I aimed for Otis's Mercantile, I hoped Penelope would get what she needed and Pearl hers. I was sure, together, we'd fit all the puzzle pieces into one big picture.

The bell tinkled when I pushed on the door. Gunnar Otis looked up from behind the counter greeting us like long-lost friends.

"Sheriff! Good to see you here." He scurried over. "What can I help you with?" Otis regarded Annabelle. "Good to see you again, Ms. Apertide. Need more of that muslin? The end pieces? Don't worry. I got a new bolt in this afternoon. Plenty of fabric."

Alarms went off in my head and I'm sure my stomach did the Virginia reel. Apertide. Puzzle piece number one set in place. Muslin? Where did that belong?

"No, thank you Mr. Otis." Annabelle pointed at me. "The sheriff's interested in skirt material, like mine." She held out part of the green fabric.

"Of course. Dry goods're right this way." He led us to the far side of the store. Ten, possibly as many as fifteen, bolts of fabric lined the wall. "I don't close for another hour, ladies. So take your time." Otis returned to his counter.

In an odd sort of way, material shopping was fun. New skirt possibilities were endless and I might even end up with fabric. But I forced my mind back on the woman standing next to me. I couldn't resist asking. "So, why'd he refer to you as Mrs. Apertide? Isn't it Tideman?"

The slightest hint of blush pinked her cheeks. "It's similar sounding, isn't it? Probably just mixed up is all." She held out dark blue material, the color of sky at sunset. "Been called that before."

I ran my hand across the blue, watching Annabelle's face for any hint. "Really? Seems 'Tideman' and 'Apertide' are very different."

"I know. Guess people don't listen." She picked up another bolt, this one of bright pink and yellow flowers over a white background. "I just love fiery colors, don't you?"

The hues reminded me of a sizzling sunrise, with a few clouds thrown in for reflection. It was lovely, and I could see it as a dress, scoop neck, pinched in at the waist, full ruffled skirt. Just right for dancing the night away with Aldridge.

"Like fireworks," she gushed.

Annabelle jarred me back into the present. I had no business daydreaming when there was work to do. I examined the material. "This is good cotton. What do you do with muslin?"

With her nose close to being buried in fabric, she mumbled. I couldn't understand what she said so repeated my question. She turned her face to me. "Sorry. Said I make a pattern for my dresses out of muslin. Much cheaper than silk or even this cotton."

"Go out much, do you?" What I hoped she'd say was that yes, she and her husband went to all the Arsonists' Society events. I'm sure they featured bonfires with a red-hot string band and... I wiped the beginnings of a smile off my face.

"I make sure. Every chance we get." Annabelle moved to another bolt then rejected it. "Sometimes we go to dances, sometimes socials with cake walks, and of course the Fourth of July fireworks! That's my favorite."

"Why is that?" Now the conversation was where I wanted.

She turned to me, her stature reminding me of a little wet bird. "Why? Don't you absolutely adore blowing things up? Seeing all the bright colors?"

What felt like an earthquake hit my stomach. "I like the sparkles in fireworks." I held the material between us. "You like seeing things explode?"

"No, not explode." She shrugged, her narrow shoulders rising then falling. "I don't like the noise, but I'm crazy about reds, oranges, yellows... sparkles." Without provocation, Annabelle's coffin-shaped face contorted with rage. She dropped the material bolt and moved within inches of my face. "You think I'm the arsonist, don't you? Don't you?"

I stuttered something like *no... no.*

She fisted her thin hands onto her hips. Although her

voice was a bit tinny, she snarled—loud enough to make my ears ring. "Well I'm not. Neither of us are." She shook a pointed finger near my nose. "You got no right accusing us of that. No right!"

Her shouts brought Mr. Otis scuttling over. "Everything all right, ladies?"

"Fine, Mr. Otis. Just having a discussion." I couldn't arrest her for anything and didn't want him to think I was harassing her. Above all, I wanted to figure out how she fit into this mystery.

"You're a liar, Sheriff. An outright liar!" Annabelle eased toward Mr. Otis. "She's accusing me of... of—"

"Sorry if I offended you, Annabelle." I reached to pat her arm but thought better of it.

"Got no right to blame anything on me." She marched for the door, shouting over her shoulder. "Pick out your own cheap material."

She stormed past Mr. Otis who stepped aside before he was trampled. He eased to the front of the store where a customer was craning his neck to witness the ruckus.

I followed her out, running to keep up. For someone so small, she sure could walk fast. At this point, I didn't think I was any further ahead with my investigation than before, except for the last name. I'd have to ask Mr. Otis about that.

Annabelle reached the office a good ten paces ahead of me. She swung the door inward not bothering to shut it. I reached it in time to see Tideman jump to his feet, glare at me.

"Where's my money, Sheriff?" Mr. Tideman held out a hand. "I'm ready to buy horses and I need my cash."

Using my foot to push the door closed, I wagged my head. "I apologize. Like I said, bank doesn't open until Monday morning. Nine sharp."

Annabelle threw off her cape, tossed it over a chair. She narrowed her mousy-brown eyes at me and pointed. "She thinks we're arsonists, Abernathy. Imagine. Us?"

Tideman gripped her upper arm, pulled her behind him

and moved in close to me. "What gives you the right? Told you before, I'm a horse buyer." Red and purple flushed his cheeks. His voice tightened. "You're the criminal here, Sheriff. You and your fire marshal." He glanced back at Penelope. "You're both scoundrels of the worst kind."

I'd been called names before, but 'scoundrel' wasn't one of them. I took it personally and wanted to say "nah uh," but that sounded too schoolyard-ish.

The door squeaked open, ushering in the first burst of cold air today. We all jerked our heads up. In stepped Pearl, her face pinked. Seeing everyone, she did a quick intake of breath like someone about to jump into icy water.

I rushed to close the door and escort her in. She stood as if glued to the wall. My nudges brought her over to the desk.

"Pearl, meet Mr. and Mrs. Tideman. Pearl's our school marm." I looked at Penelope who kept an eagle eye on the strange couple.

Pearl thawed, nodded to Abernathy and Annabelle, then spoke softly to me. "Sheriff, I need to see you... outside. Something's come up."

She and I stepped into the biting early evening air, shutting the door firmly. Pearl turned her back to the door. "He's gone, Maud."

"Ford? Nathaniel Ford?" I stared down the street.

She pursed her lips and nodded. "Made a nine in his tail and took off. Gone."

"Took off? What d'you mean *gone*?" Astonishment squeezed my chest. I couldn't breathe.

Shrugging, she pointed toward town. "Gone. As in office cleaned out. Not in the restaurant, saloons, boarding house." She raised both shoulders. "Gone."

CHAPTER THIRTY-NINE
HERE AND GONE...

PEARL, PENELOPE, ALDRIDGE, SETH AND I STOOD in the middle of the former insurance seller's office, all turning, listing sideways like broken tops. As if the blank walls and floors would yield clues, I studied each. We'd all searched through the empty desk drawers, pulling out all three, even turning them over in hopes of discovering a secret message tacked under one of them. Out of frustration, I crawled under the desk—nothing but dust.

Seth picked up the desk chair, examined under the seat then set it back down with ease, like he did that with all the furniture. Penelope looked under the other two wooden chairs with the same luck.

Pokey stepped in from the back door. "Sorry. Nothing." He wagged his head. "No sign he was ever here. Simply vanished."

Spinning one last time, my shoulders collapsed. "What the hell's going on?" Pearl's bad language obviously infected me. But right now, cursing felt justified. "And where do the Tidemans, Apertides... whoever they are... where do they fit in? I *know* they're in on it."

"Unless they're simply odd, or even crazy, like a loco bedbug." Penelope leaned against the wall next to where My Mr. Amazing leaned. "One thing's for sure. Mr. Tideman knows his horse flesh. In that respect, he ain't crazy. I'd say he's legitimate."

That wasn't what I wanted to hear. "But—"

"And since he's a champion for horses," Penelope continued. "I can't see him setting fire to a stable. He wouldn't have done something like that. Those horses could've burned to death."

I shuddered.

Aldridge pushed off from the wall. "Unless we missed anything, we're done here." He thumbed over his shoulder. "Maud, how 'bout you and I go talk to Mr. Otis?" He pulled out a pocket watch, frowned, then snapped it back into his vest pocket.

"He's closed, isn't he?" It was well after six, I knew. "Then we'll have to go find him. He's probably at home enjoying his wife's good cooking." Instead of the meat and potatoes I was sure he was eating, visions of Hilda and Ester's strudel, stollen and apple kuchen danced across my eyes. My stomach rumbled. It was past suppertime and I briefly wondered if I'd get any tonight. Maybe a sandwich at the café later. They stayed open until well after dark but closed earlier if no one was eating.

Our group stepped into the night, congregating on the boardwalk. By this time of year, daylight ended much too early for me. I preferred eating supper when I could see it. But someone needed to lead this investigation, and that someone would be me. I formed quick assignments. "Pokey, would you check with the hotel's desk clerk? Since you're an official deputy, you can ask questions. See if the Tidemans are still there and see what you can find."

Pokey saluted, his still-swollen hand coming to rest against his still-blue and purple cheek. "Yes, ma'am. Will do." He limped off toward the hotel.

I turned to Seth, but before I opened my mouth, he held up a hand.

"I know. I get the distinct pleasure of telling the town councilors." Seth pried off his bowler, ran long fingers through his hair, and reset the hat. "They're not going to be happy."

Blowing out frustrated air, I stared down the deserted street. "I know. But we've got to figure out if he's really gone."

"With their money." Pearl kicked at a loose board on the walkway. She regarded each of us. "How do you tell people Ford absconded with their money? How do you look into the faces of say... Mr. and Mrs. Emery who have only a little money? They couldn't really afford his prices, but she told me they couldn't afford *not* to." Pearl stepped away, turned and stood. "How do you tell them?"

Silence wrapped us in thought. Dark thoughts. Pearl's question was one I'd hate to try to answer. But at some point, word would get out and the town would be abuzz with irate citizens. And I couldn't blame them at all. I'd come close to buying insurance, but fortune smiled on me, this time.

We stood like a group of perplexed Army scouts not sure which way to go. After each of us gathered information, we'd know more. I hoped for the citizens' sake, we'd find Ford. And soon.

"Let's meet back at my office when you find out anything." My gaze passed over each person involved with running this town. Good people, each and every one. A touch of pride swelled my chest but deflated when I considered the consequences of not finding Ford, and to a lesser extent, the person... or persons... who set the fires.

We split up, each going our separate ways. Aldridge walked beside me, slower than usual, but at least he was upright. A day resting at Seth's had brought color back into his cheeks. Within a few days, I knew, just *knew*, he'd be back to normal.

The two of us sauntered down a side street, turned right, two more blocks and stopped in front of Gunnar Otis's house. I'd been by once or twice, but since it was on the opposite side of town from my house, I didn't have much reason to come this way. Situated on the edge of town, it was close to what was becoming Dry Creek's China Town. Slightly rolling hills from here on east made dividing the town ethnically easy.

Mrs. Otis answered our knock and right behind her appeared Gunnar. Aromas of pot roast seasoned with rosemary rolled outside. My mouth watered.

He stepped onto the veranda while she disappeared back into the house. "What can I do for you, Sheriff?" Gunnar nodded to Aldridge. "Evening."

We both returned his nod and got down to business. "Earlier this afternoon, Mr. Otis, I came into your store with a woman in an emerald skirt. You called her by name. Mrs. Apertide."

"That's right. How can I forget?" A half-smile crawled up his round, boyish face, wrinkles jutting out from his owl-like eyes. His spectacles enlarged his small eyes making them look big. While I didn't consider him short, he wasn't much taller than me.

"Quite a scene she made of herself. No?" Traces of a long-forgotten German upbringing colored his words.

I nodded. "Sure did. But how do you know her, if you don't mind my asking." I glanced at Aldridge, hoping, praying there was nothing on his face implying he knew anything about the arsonist. Nothing there. I relaxed.

Gunnar peered over my shoulder toward the street. "I first met her in Sacramento, maybe five years ago. I've seen her there from time to time. I went on a buying trip where she and her husband were also buying."

"Buying?" My interest riveted on his story. "Buying what?"

He flapped a plump hand. "Oh, you know. Items for my store. The usual." His gaze trailed up toward the sky. "Flour, axes, a plow Mr. Sniderman ordered, candy and bolts of fabric." He looked at me. "Mrs. Apertide loves fabric."

"She introduced herself as Apertide?" I knew I was on to something. "And she liked fabric?"

Aldridge shifted his weight and I couldn't tell if he was nervous, tired or impatient. My Honey pulled in air as he asked, "Did you know Mr. Apertide?"

"Not really. He was there in that warehouse but let her do most of the buying."

"And she bought...?"

Gunnar stood still and thought. Finally, he wrinkled his forehead. "Funny you should ask. I remember thinking it was a strange combination. She bought muslin, some bottles of... whiskey." He turned first to Aldridge and then to me. "Yep, out of the ordinary."

That was indeed a strange combination. But nothing illegal.

Aldridge snapped his fingers. "Got it!" His words danced as she spoke. "Don't you see? She pours out the whiskey and adds kerosene to the bottles. Tears off strips of muslin and lights it on fire. Makes great colors and they'll explode if you throw them!"

Holy smokes. Why hadn't I put two and two together before?

Gunnar nodded. "Of course." He dropped his voice. "But why?"

"I got this one." Proud of myself for paying attention, I explained. "She likes colors. The brighter the better. Fires are full of different colors—reds, oranges, yellows, blues." I spun toward the street. "Makes sense."

Aldridge turned me back around. "What about Mr. Apertide? Tideman? Where does he fit in?"

The three of us grew quiet, I supposed thinking, but I smelled that pot roast again. My stomach reminded me it was time to eat. The polite thing to do was let Gunnar get back to that roast. The even politer thing was being invited in to join them. But I had a job to do and needed to get back to the office. So, I decided, while standing there, that even if she offered us supper, I'd have to decline.

"How can we prove she did it?" Aldridge's voice brought me back to reality, although my stomach grumbled.

We looked at each other again until Gunnar shrugged. "Maybe tomorrow I go to the stable and find what happened."

A smile filled my face, my cheeks stretching. "We'll all go, Mr. Otis."

We agreed on a time and Aldridge and I strode back the way we'd come, discussing what we'd learned. Was it possible Mrs. Apertide or Tideman, was the arsonist? I couldn't wait to see what the others had dug up.

Aldridge and I didn't sit in the office alone for long. Pearl came in, a sack of something wafting mouth-watering aromas, in hand. She set it on top of a stack of wanted posters I'd ignored. My desk was a handy place to hold everything except paperwork.

"Thought you'd be hungry." Pearl pulled out a waxed paper-wrapped sandwich. "I know I am." She handed one to Aldridge, then me and took another one for herself.

We sat munching, going over today's events, talking with our mouths full. This roast beef sandwich was about the finest I'd ever had. The sourdough was baked to perfection, the beef cooked but not overdone and the lettuce on it crisp. I hoped she'd brought at least two for each of us.

Before my sandwich was halfway gone, Seth appeared, selected a sandwich as if he'd been invited to, sat and munched. Two big bites later, he glanced up. "I shared the good news with the three councilors." He stared at me. "Brace yourself. They're mighty upset."

"We all are." I talked around the roast beef. "But I think we're closer to solving it."

Seth sat straight up. "You are?"

I opened my mouth to begin my recitation about the conversation with Gunnar Otis right as Pokey stepped in.

"Talked to the hotel desk clerk, Maud." He headed for my desk, selected a sandwich, unwrapped and bit before continuing. "He wasn't willing to talk until I showed him my badge."

"And?" I couldn't stand the suspense anymore.

"And the Tidemans are still there. He said they'd gone up to their room and as far as he knew, they haven't come down." He took another bite. "Said he'd be on duty 'til eleven and he'd keep an eye out for them. Send a kid over here if they leave."

"Nice." Butterflies stomped around in my stomach, kicking aside the roast beef. "Tomorrow, in the light, I'm going to the livery stable, see what I can find."

We sat back in our respective chairs, mulling over the day when Penelope waltzed in, small piece of paper in hand. She waved it.

"Got it, Maud. Got it." Penelope eyed the sack on my desk, then fluttered the paper at everyone. "I wired a stable owner I know in Sacramento. He's also a deputy sheriff. Said he knew Abernathy Tideman as a horse buyer and breeder. Good man. He'd vouch for him."

I was on the edge of my seat. Even the air seemed to be holding its breath. Penelope's eyes glowed and I knew, just *knew* there was more to the note.

"He also said..." she paused, "Mrs. Tideman was under suspicion for arson. Seems fires kept erupting for no reason. No more fires once she left."

"I knew it." I pushed back from my chair, jumping to my feet.

"There's more." Penelope held up a hand. The room soaked up the anticipation. "My friend said," she waved the paper. "He said Nathaniel Ford is actually... Nathaniel Ford Tideman. Her uncle."

"What?" Had I screamed that out loud? "Her uncle?" It all crashed together. Ford paid her to set fires. His business would explode, he gave her kickbacks. Mr. Tideman used that money to buy horses. Was he in on it? Undoubtedly had to be.

Penelope shouted to be heard. "I sent a reply asking if he could prove it and why wasn't she locked up?"

When we quieted a bit, I hated to ask the next question.

"Where do you suppose Ford went to? We need to get that money back."

Pearl folded her sandwich wrapper. "I asked at the boarding house earlier today and they said he'd simply taken his one case, thanked the owner, and left. Gave no forwarding address, no hint as to where he was going. Simply left."

"We'll find him." I hoped I'd said that with an air of certainty I didn't feel. This was big country and people could get lost easily. And quickly. Probably already too late. I sat again, swallowed the last bite of supper and mentally prepared myself for putting together a posse at first light. I'd ask Pokey to keep an eye on the Tidemans and Penelope and Aldridge to go with Gunnar Otis to sift through the livery's remains. Pearl and Seth could keep an eye on the town and continue their stumping.

I'd make sure my revolver was loaded.

CHAPTER FORTY
SURPRISE...SURPRISE...

SWEDE SWENSEN AT THE OTHER LIVERY STABLE saddled a horse for me while I stroked her long nose, a white star making her nose look even longer. Her bay coat shone against the rising sun. As much as I was in a tearing hurry, I knew spending a minute or two with her would come in handy later on when I was riding, and she'd be gentle. Hopefully, she remembered me. Maybelle and I had a history, going back a good four or five months. She and I had pursued bank robbers together and, more than likely, she took some of the credit for the bandits' capture when she and her stablemates got together to compare adventures.

I smiled at the vision of a bunch of horses standing around neighing to each other, one trying to top the others with tales of derring-do.

Early morning sun spread warming fingers of light across the barn, the stable and the bottom of houses. Soon, it would be light enough to see where I was going and to follow Ford's tracks. Assuming he'd left some. Mr. Swensen had reported no horses rented yesterday afternoon and, all livestock was accounted for. Maybe he'd taken a horse from the torched stable—the ones in the pasture. But no doubt,

Nathaniel Ford was gone. Out of town. Vanished. Like a ghost.

"All set, Sheriff." Mr. Swensen patted Maybelle's shoulder, then tugged on the cinch strap. He wove his fingers together making a seat of sorts. "Here ya go. Give you a boost up."

My heart pounded as I raised my left leg, skirt bunching around it. He was too much of a gentleman to move the fabric, so I pulled it free of my shoe. Undoubtedly, he'd seen my ankle, or at the least the top of the lace-up shoes, but I wasn't a real modest type of woman, especially since I was sheriff. If men saw the top of my shoes, so be it.

I stepped into his cupped hands, pushed off with my right leg and he catapulted me up, almost completely over the horse's back. My right leg wrapped itself tight against Maybelle's ribs while I grabbed the saddle horn, managing to right myself with a hint of dignity still intact.

He handed over the reins and stared up at me. "Remember, she's mighty tame, and I think she knows you, but she don't like being kicked in the sides. Jest say 'Giddy up' and she'll do fine."

Maybelle and I walked out of the stable and onto the street. At this hour, we were the only traffic. Seth and Pokey had assured me last night they'd round up a posse. So far, looked like they'd had no takers.

But again, I was wrong. A lone rider trotted toward me and I immediately recognized the shadowed outline, Slim Higginbotham, one-third of the town councilors. Would he be coming along? After all, he'd ridden with me last time I'd formed a posse. And a great help he'd been.

We reined up at the same time in front of my office. Legs shaky, I dismounted and held onto the saddle's skirt until I knew I could walk without embarrassing myself.

"Need some company?" Slim wrapped the reins around the rail, took mine and wrapped them, too. "Ford's a slippery devil. Might take the whole town to find that scoundrel."

"Might at that." I unlocked the office, where Slim followed me in. "Anybody else coming?"

Slim's shoulders rose then fell under his thick, sheepskin coat. He pulled off wool-lined gloves and blew on his hands while I shoved kindling into the potbelly stove. Within minutes, the office was toasty.

We both stood, hands over the heat, wishing for a cup of coffee. But I didn't want to take time to boil it, or to drink it. Five minutes of chit chat and hand warming later, I shoved my thawing digits into gloves I'd found in my coat pocket.

"Looks like nobody else's coming." While disappointed, I wasn't surprised. It was cold, overcast and most people weren't yet aware of what Ford had done. Also, maybe it was a good idea if two of us searched—less chance of disturbing evidence. If there was any.

Slim and I stood outside while I fumbled with the key. Locking the door with cold, gloved hands was harder than I'd imagined.

"Here, Maud, no need."

I jumped at the voice in my ear. Pokey stood at my shoulder like he'd been there all along.

Pokey cocked his head toward the hotel at the end of the block. "Thought I'd spend some time in here so's I can keep an eye on the Tidemans. If they go anywhere, I'll follow them. And if they do anything suspicious, I'll arrest them 'til you get back."

Brilliant! Pokey had brains back in there somewhere.

I handed him the key. "All yours. But don't you have to work today? Over at the mercantile?"

A smile crept up Pokey's face. "Mr. Otis gave me the day off. And I'll be driving the stage again starting Friday."

Slim shook hands with Pokey. "Glad you're feeling up to it. You had us worried there for a bit."

"And I'm sorry about that." Pokey hung his head. "Sure didn't expect to get whooped like that."

I unwrapped the reins and stood next to Maybelle. The

stirrup was high and my trying to get a left foot in it was tough. Pokey held out two clasped hands like Mr. Swensen had done. He boosted me up, waiting until I settled in the saddle.

"Wait, Sheriff." Pokey dug around in his vest pocket, hidden under a heavy coat. He pulled out something gripped in his hand. "Been meaning to do this, but I think now's the right time."

He held out a jade stone, a rawhide necklace attached.

"It's beautiful." I immediately fell in love with it but wondered why he was showing the talisman to me. Unquestionably, Mae would cherish the gift.

"For you." Pokey stretched the necklace waiting for me to remove my bonnet. He put the jade amulet over my head. "And see... there's Chinese writing on it. Says it awards you luck. And love." His cheeks pinked.

Admiring the good luck piece, its green reminding me of leaves in early spring, I leaned down as far as I dared and gave him a tight hug. "Thank you. I'll treasure it always." Releasing him, I "giddy upped" Maybelle into the street, then pulled rein. I spoke over my shoulder. "Pokey, let's hope I won't need this token, but I really, really adore it."

I tucked it under my coat. Slim and I waved as we trotted off down the road, me holding onto the saddle horn, Slim doing the same.

One road ran east-west becoming our Main Street. Roads that were more akin to paths, ran north-south. It hadn't rained lately which made finding tracks impossible to spot in the dirt and leaves.

We circled the town, hoping hoofprints or even footprints led away, off into the forest where we'd find Ford waiting for us. I knew that wouldn't happen, so concentrated on looking down, studying every marking in the dirt. Once, we followed a set of prints up a hill, checked on a cabin which was empty, then lost the trail, disappearing into the woods.

Turning over every rock, so to speak, we circled the entire town, which took until the sun stood overhead. Nothing. No clue.

Defeated and downcast, my vote was to head back to town and call Ford officially gone. My stomach rumbled. One of the café's sandwiches, roast beef maybe, would taste great about now. Of course, Hilda's strudel called. Dessert. Yum.

"Let's look south one more time." Slim buttoned the top of his coat, wind bringing pink to his cheeks. "Then if we find more of nothing, we'll go back."

I agreed, reined Maybelle south over a hill which last year had been cleared of boxelder maple trees, and headed toward disappointment.

Past the clearing and over the next hill, which had not been cleared, we rode in silence, searching, wishing, hoping. I headed east toward a clutch of bushes.

"Hold it, Maud. Got something over here." Slim urged his mount toward a thicket of blackberry bushes.

"What?" I turned around as Slim dismounted and pushed into the undergrowth.

He stumbled back, hand over his mouth and nose.

I swung off Maybelle, tied off then joined Slim. "What you got?" I had a suspicion it was someone dead, but the who baffled me.

Slim pointed over his shoulder. "Ford. Dead."

Chest filling with shock, breathing became difficult. This wasn't at all what I'd expected. At the very least, I figured by now he'd be in Dutch Flats having a late breakfast. Not dead. "You sure it's him?"

Slim nodded. "Looks like he'd been shot at close range. Don't look. It's stomach-turning."

As much as I didn't want to, I had to. My job demanded it. I pulled in air, studied the ground, then pushed aside the brush. One look and I knew it was Nathaniel Ford.

I stepped back. "You see any satchel or money bags or

some such?" I glanced at Slim who shook his head. "Who'd do this?"

But that was a ridiculous question. I knew. One of the Tidemans. It couldn't have been a disgruntled client because no one knew he'd absconded with their money. No one except the Tidemans.

Untying the reins then, without help, I swung up into the saddle. "Let's fetch the undertaker and the Tidemans."

We galloped to town, lost in thoughts and gruesome images hard to erase. Slim pulled up in front of the undertaker's while I headed to the office.

Thank goodness Pokey was still there. With heavy breathing, I filled him in.

Pokey wagged his head. "Last I checked, which was about twenty minutes ago, they were still in their room. Desk clerk said they hadn't come out yet."

"Doesn't add up. Not even for breakfast?"

He shrugged. "Maybe they're not hungry."

A sinking feeling, like a ship floundering in a storm, enveloped my entire body, stem to stern. "Or not there."

I bolted out the door, Pokey on my heels. We made the three blocks in record time and skidded into the lobby. The same desk clerk stood behind the register, his eyes widening as we charged in.

"Room ten. Tidemans," I gasped. "You seen them today?"

"No, ma'am. Ain't seen 'em since yesterday evening." The clerk glanced left then right.

"An' that's the truth. I swear."

The key and message cubby labeled 10, sat empty. Keys on either side poked out of their slot, but not 10. It would appear the Tidemans were still in their room.

"Let's go Pokey." I pointed up the upstairs. "We'll pay a visit to our guests."

"But you can't—"

A glare at the clerk silenced him. Pokey and I bounded

upstairs, knocked on 10 and when hearing nothing, Pokey put shoulder to the door. One bang and it slammed open.

We marched in, my hand on the revolver nestled in the holster. I prayed I wouldn't have to use it.

Just as I'd suspected, the room stood vacant. No clothing, no bags, no people. Nothing but an empty hotel room.

CHAPTER FORTY-ONE
THE QUESTION...

BY MIDAFTERNOON, SLIM AND I HAD AGREED there was no need to search for the Tidemans, Apertides or whatever they called themselves. Since we'd already spent hours searching for Ford, nothing we'd come across had implied which way our arsonists-murderers had skedaddled. We knew it had been dumb luck finding Ford. So, we left it at that. The Tidemans were gone. And so was the money Ford had taken.

However, we still had the cash taken from Tideman's bed. Without doubt, that would cover some of what the citizens had lost.

Besides writing a short article for our new *Dry Creek Courier relating* the events and describing the Tidemans, I wired as many sheriffs and marshals as I could within a hundred-mile radius to warn them about this villainous couple. I suggested the lawmen not be taken in by her looks or his money, which I was certain they had quite a bit of. And I mentioned the different names. Hopefully, someone would spot them.

I sat at my desk realizing I'd done everything I could. Reverend Josiah Jenkins thought having a funeral would help the town heal, but I wasn't so sure. For once I agreed with the Town Councilors—bury the man quietly or no telling what would happen. Word had gotten out within minutes of bringing him back to town, and his name had been dragged through the mud.

We buried immediately with no fanfare, just the Reverend saying a few words over him. I concluded that was a sad ending for a human being.

But here at my desk, I wondered. Should we have done more? Done things differently?

Many townspeople had praised Slim and me for discovering Ford, and Slim even bought me a beer at his Tin Pan Saloon. I was sorry Ford was killed, but if anyone deserved it... No, I decided. Nobody deserved to die.

* * *

THREE DAYS PASSED without much town drama—for which I was grateful. This morning, I sat behind the desk, third cup of coffee in hand and shuffled papers. In the last two days they'd seemed to multiply as fast as dandelions after a rain. I sipped while mulling over the upcoming election and dance.

Tired of paperwork, I set down my coffee cup, leaned back and stretched. It seemed as if all my friends were busy and couldn't simply "drop in" for a visit. In fact, I'd had to eat my mid-day meal alone—twice.

I played with the amulet Pokey had given me and while I didn't believe in good luck tokens, or bad luck tokens for that matter, I did have a bit of faith in this one. And, at the very least, it was a beautiful piece of jewelry.

I stretched, twisted again, pushed up to my feet when the door squeaked open. And praise be to the good luck charm, in walked My Adoring Man, My Aldridge. He and Mae had spent the past several days registering girls for school now that they had a place, and Mae's uncle had the back room in his store ready to go. This past week, I'd missed My Hunky Man, more than I should have. Was I in love?

My feet, with springs on them I was certain, bounced me over to where My Honey stood. He waited for me, probably thinking if he rushed forward, we'd smack together like two dueling rams. We'd both end up with aching heads and stagger around like drunken sailors. He wrapped me in his arms while I breathed in his scent. Perhaps a touch of bay rum aftershave added to the aroma. Whatever it was, it was heavenly. We stood, embraced, slightly swaying, enjoying each other's touch. I never wanted to release him.

Giving me a tight squeeze, he let go and stepped back. "All done." His smile lit up the office. I swear it glimmered off the window. "School's ready to open tomorrow."

"Tomorrow?" I did quick calculations. "But tomorrow's Thursday. Isn't that an odd day to start?"

Aldridge eyed the coffee pot then me. "Thought we'd get a couple of days to shake off the cobwebs, then by Monday be ready to start full swing." He crooked his head toward the stove. "Got any more?

I did. I always did. I poured him a cup, refilled mine, then, shoulder to shoulder, we stood looking out the window. Main Street came alive, awash with people hurrying about, horses clip clopping, a dog chasing a wagon. Business as usual.

My Favorite Man slipped his arm around me. "It's been a rough week or two, hasn't it?"

I nodded, wondering where he was going with this line of questioning.

"Maybe it'll calm down." He sipped then used his cup to point outside. "I mean, looks like the arsonists are gone—"

"And half the people's money."

"That, too." He sighed and glanced at me. "But that wasn't your fault. Nobody could've seen that coming. I mean... you mentioned the school burning, what, two months ago?"

I nodded.

"I'll bet you the farm it was the Tidemans. They were testing the water, so to speak."

I instantly saw where he was going. "I'm sure now, too."
I wagged my head remembering

I'd seen them in town around then, remembering her
sky-blue skirt attracting my attention.

"Can't believe people would do that." A deep sadness
drilled to my core. Generally, I believed in people's good
will, but now I wasn't so sure. I couldn't trust anybody
anymore.

Aldridge slid his arm from around my waist, turning me
toward him. The kiss was magical. My toes tingled.

"How about I buy you dinner? To celebrate." He took my
cup and placed both of ours on the desk.

My stomach did its grumbling thing, reminding me I
hadn't bothered with breakfast this morning. A mid-day
meal would be perfect.

As we walked, Aldridge discussed the school. Excitement peppered each word until I was as enthused as him.
We halted at the front of the restaurant. He raised both
eyebrows at me.

"I've been waiting for the right time. And now with the
school about to start, wanted to ask you something. Something important." His eyes melted into mine. "Hope you say
yes."

My stomach flip-flopped into my throat. Of course, I'd
say yes! This was the question I'd been waiting for my
entire life. Even longer.

He held both my arms while a hint of a smile raised
his smooth cheeks. His words came out soft, smooth.
"Mae and I have talked. We were wondering, if you're
available that is, if you'd cut the ribbon on the school
tomorrow."

I stood stock still, waiting. When he didn't add anything
else, I blinked until my eyelashes hurt. That was it? While I
couldn't see myself, I knew disappointment showed. My
shoulders drooped, my gaze dropped to the ground, pressure built behind my eyes. There was nothing to say,
besides, words wouldn't form.

"You all right? Maud?" Aldridge moved in close. Real close. "You've lost color there. Feeling all right?"

I nodded, totally deflated.

"Good." Aldridge spoke a bit louder. "I'll ask again. Would you be willing to join us tomorrow in opening the school? I mean, you were a big part of it." His mouth formed into a sexy grin, one I'd seen just for me.

"Fine." Other words refused me.

CHAPTER FORTY-TWO
AND THE WINNER IS...

THEY'D RUN A CRIMSON RIBBON ACROSS THE DOOR to the schoolroom and I cut it. Cheers and polite applause behind me brought a smile to my face. Turned out, that was fun. My chest ballooned realizing I was involved in true progress of a town that needed progress.

Once the ribbon barricade was removed, Aldridge and Mae ushered in what looked to be fifteen bright, shiny Chinese faces on some of the smallest little girls I'd seen. My heart melted as they quietly took their desks, two to a bench.

Aldridge, Mae and I stood in the front of the room while Pokey, parents, grandparents and newspaper editor Emily Penderton, waited in the back. Mary Beth and Sadie who ran the Saturday Charm School were there. Excitement and anticipation squeezed the air out of the room. I looked around for a window to open, but no such luck. I guessed there was no need for windows in a storage room when the store was built.

"Zǎo shàng hǎo." Aldridge tilted his head toward the children then flashed a quick grin at me. "Good morning, young ladies."

Mae beamed. The girls as well as the parents answered politely.

I scanned the attentive faces. It dawned on me that almost without exception, the children looked alike. Their slanted eyes, black like ravens' wings, radiated a hesitant sparkle. Their slim bodies sat up straight, their slender fingers intertwined and placed on top of their desks, hanging on to every word both Aldridge and Mae said.

After a couple of short introductions and then instructions, school for the day was dismissed. The children lined up to greet Aldridge, Mae and me. I bent way down and shook hands with the girls. As I met them, I gave each one a name I could pronounce. As I did, they would twitter and nod.

"You're Petunia," I said to the tallest.

"Pe-tune-ya." She tried out her new name producing a smile with a million-dollar shine.

"Marigold." I pointed to another. "And Rose, Ivy, Iris, Lily." Each gave me a slight bow, tested their new names and ran giggling to their parents.

"Daisy, Jonquil, Jasmine, Zinnia, Fern..." I was on a roll and delighted the girls were happy with their names. Of course, I'd never remember who was who, but hopefully they would and tell me when they introduced themselves. I finished naming each and turned to Mae. "You should be Mayflower. That's a lovely name, don't you think?"

She gave a slight bow and smiled. "Thank you. I will be Mayflower from here on." We both turned to Aldridge who held up a hand.

"I'm not gonna be named after some girl flower. My given name is fine."

And it was fine, even though he hadn't come through with the right question yesterday. Maybe in time, he would. But darn, it was hard to wait.

Once all the students and guests left, Mae, Pokey, Aldridge and I headed to the Shoo Fly Restaurant to celebrate. Mae announced she had promised her ma to help doing something mighty important, so would not be joining us. Pokey offered to stay and help, too.

The Shoo Fly was a great restaurant, but I wondered if they would have allowed Mae in when she was with us. My feet took flight as we traipsed down Main. My stomach grumbled when I envisioned their roast beef sandwich on sourdough bread.

My Loving Man and I entered, sat, and within a minute after placing our order, Harvey Weinberg and Ian MacKinney waltzed in making a beeline for our table.

My stomach clenched. Based on the looks on their faces, this visit would be just as unpleasant as usual. They hovered near Aldridge at the end of the table.

"Saw ye in here, Sheriff." MacKinney's thick brogue was understandable, so far. "Went by yer office, but ye wasn't in."

"Aldridge and Mae officially opened their Chinese school this morning." Why did I feel the need to explain? I was sure the town councilors knew all about it. And I realized right then, none of the three were at the ribbon cutting.

Weinberg, curls bouncing on the sides of his head, leaned in. "It's the election on Saturday. And the dance. What were you thinking when you scheduled them for the same day? It's gonna be disastrous and mighty confusing."

MacKinney pointed outside. "People banjaxed, runnin' up and down the street, fistfights over votin', horses and dogs tryin' not to run over dem, women cryin' 'cause no one will dance with dem—"

"What?" I stood, my skirt catching under a shoe. I pulled the material loose and put one hand on my hip. "You're talking bedlam and I'm thinking nice and orderly. People will be in town to shop, eat, vote and then dance. It brings business to the hotel, the two eateries, the unburned livery, even your saloons. And our fine citizens will have an enjoyable evening."

Aldridge, bless him, looked up directly into MacKinney's face. "What's wrong with some fun?"

"It's not *fun* we're having trouble with." Weinberg lowered his voice a notch. "It's doing both at once. Can't sell whiskey until voting is over. So this election is not good for our pockets, after all."

Aldridge pushed his chair back easing up to his feet like a bear defending cubs and stood nose to nose with Weinberg. My Hero glanced way down at MacKinney then up to Weinberg. "The election and dance *will* happen Saturday, gentlemen. Miss Overstreet here has put a lot of thought and effort into both, and I'm sure people will be on their finest behavior."

The waitress, a plate in each hand, appeared at our table. Aldridge took the opportunity to extend an olive branch. He pointed to the food. "If you'd care to join us, Councilors, we'd be glad to pull up more chairs."

I wouldn't have been nearly as gracious. Fact was, I'd been thinking a million unladylike thoughts about then.

While Weinberg stood mouth open, MacKinney answered for them. "Nah, thankee, kindly." They turned to leave then MacKinney turned back. "Be warned, Sheriff. It's gonna be a hooley night with ever'one actin' the maggot." He gave a sharp bow. "Mark me words."

"Don't worry, Mister MacKinney. My deputy and I have it covered." While I wasn't exactly sure what he foretold, I hoped my words sounded more sure than I felt. Up until this point, I hadn't thought anything more than a disgruntled suitor would pick a fight.

Without warning, my appetite disappeared. I studied my sandwich. I hoped the councilors were wrong. Real wrong.

* * *

SATURDAY AT LONG LAST DAWNED. The church was set up as a polling place, which we had thought was close to ideal. Who in their right mind would start a fight in a church? By the time sun was full up, more than a dozen people had voted. I stopped in on my way to the office, made sure things were going well. I wished with all my heart women could vote. Why not? We had heads, thoughts, feelings. Like men, only better. I snickered at the idea. Maybe after this election, some of the women would start pushing for voting rights. I'd be right behind them.

Three of the women from the Town Temperance Society had volunteered to run the election. One to take names, one to assist if help was needed in reading the ballot, and one to take the marked paper. She then folded it and put it in a box. I offered to help count ballots at five, when the poll closed.

Walking up the street to my office, I nodded at and stopped to chat with more people than usual. Dry Creek's early-bird citizens were out in full force today. Several women thanked me for setting up the dance while the men glanced skyward.

I stepped into Otis's Mercantile to check on Pokey and make sure he had run the mail coach without problems yesterday. I spotted him near the tools and before I could talk to him, a woman I knew to be on the dance committee touched my arm.

"Maud," she beamed. "Just wanted to let you know we got a prime act for the dance tonight. It's going to inspire everyone to get out and let loose."

"What kind of act?" While I was sure it was innocent, lately I'd had my doubts about nearly everyone.

A smile blossomed on her face. "Why the Dancing Grannies, of course."

"Who?" I smiled with her, but the vision of tottering old women trying to strut their stuff gave me pause.

"Dancing Grannies." She patted my arm. "I'm sure you've heard of them, dear. Coming all the way from Dutch Flats. Six or seven gals—older gals. Like us. Might even do the Polka or Five-Step Waltz. Imagine."

Us? Older gals? She lumped me into that category. Was I? I'd have to circle back on that thought in a bit. But right now I couldn't imagine Dancing Grannies doing anything but tottering around, but I didn't tell her. Instead, I gave her a half-hearted grin. "I'm sure they'll be the talk of the evening."

"I'm certain they will." She waved. "Have a wagon load of things to do. See you tonight."

Fortunately, the remainder of the day was peaceful. No fights, no confrontations, no horses racing down Main. And Pokey's run had been uneventful. Nothing of any significance—exactly the way I hoped.

Shortly before five, I wandered down to the church to declare the election officially closed. Two men stood marking their ballots, but otherwise, the church held only the three voting officials and me.

Pearl, the officials reported, had stopped by to see if things were running smoothly. And Seth had come by twice, once to vote and once just to chat. I wasn't sure he could do that, but on the other hand, I wasn't sure he couldn't.

After the two men marked their ballots and left, I closed the church doors. The women and I spread the papers around on a makeshift desk. One called out a name, the other stood over her shoulder watching, the third used a blank ballot to tally. I watched.

Within half an hour and with over two hundred ballots marked, it was clear Seth had won. Pearl had given him a run for the money with over thirty percent of the vote, but it was definite who would be mayor.

Now... to tell them. The committee tied a ribbon around the ballots, placed the bundle in the box, closed the top and handed it to me. I agreed to lock it up in the office safe for a while, bringing it out in case of an argument. One of the women wrote Seth's name proclaiming him the winner on paper then tacked it to the church's front door. I needed to see Seth and Pearl before word got out.

* * *

SETH EMBRACED me like a long-lost cousin. "Thanks, Maud! I knew I'd win, just knew!" His arms flew out at his sides while he surveyed his office. "They like me. See. The people of Dry Creek like me."

"What's not to like?" I didn't dare answer my own question because I *did* have answers.

What I didn't have was time and the right mood. "Gotta go tell Pearl the news." I headed for the door. "You going to the dance tonight?"

"Maybe." He escorted me to the door. "If I do, can I have a dance?"

Me? Dance? How many toes could I step on? But I nodded anyway. "I'll save the waltz for you."

He pecked my cheek, hugged me tight and closed the door on my backside.

On my way to Pearl's house, I mulled over what I would say. Should I come out and tell her she lost, or tell her she almost won? No, that was a lie. Seth won seventy percent of the vote.

I collided with Pearl on the boardwalk in front of Otis' Mercantile. She was looking down at a bundle of something in her arms, while I was looking right. We bounced back, managed to stay upright, and then recognizing each other, smiled.

"So sorry, Maud. I don't know where my head is at." Pearl pinched her lower lip with her teeth. Light from the oil lamps hanging on the uprights glowed orange on her face.

I took a deep breath. "I'm sorry, Pearl." My words, one at a time, revealed the outcome. "The election—didn't go your way."

Her shoulders dropped, her gaze swept the boardwalk, now mottled with lamplight.

"How bad?"

Not about to tell her, I shrugged. "Doesn't matter. But there's always next time."

She adjusted her packages and stared down the street. "This country's not ready for women in office. Not going to be a next time." She brought her eyes up to mine. "Figured I wouldn't win, so been doing a lot of thinking."

I was happy she'd taken the news so well. I thought she'd be in tears by now, maybe even blaming me for her loss.

Pearl sighed. "Not much money in teaching school and it looks like no knight in shining armor is coming to rescue me." Her eyebrows raised. "So, I'm considering opening a business."

"What kind?"

She looked down the nearly empty boardwalk. "Either another saloon or insurance."

I stepped back, the shock knocking me almost into the street. "What?"

She nodded. "Saloons here are busy and Dry Creek's growing. We could use another one. We have only five. And while I hate the idea of insurance, I think it's necessary."

I sure hadn't seen any of that coming. Maybe Pearl needed a good luck charm necklace, too. I'd ask Pokey about getting her one.

"You know, Pearl." Would I wish I'd never said this? "I might want to be a silent partner with you. In the saloon, I mean. Not insurance."

It was Pearl's turn to step back, her eyes wide. "Really? You would? Silent partner?" She flicked a grin my way. "Let's sit and talk soon. I won't have time to get it going until after school's out for the summer. But that'll give us what, eight months to figure things out."

"Howdy, Maud!" Aldridge's voice startled me. "I was hoping to have supper with you before the dance." He turned to Pearl. "Heard about the election results. I'm sorry."

She held up her packages, cocked her head. "Me, too." Pearl straightened her shoulders.

"I've got other things to think about, though." She raised one eyebrow at me. "We'll talk soon."

After saying goodbye to Pearl, My Handsome Man and I sauntered down the boardwalk toward the restaurant while she headed the other way, home.

We took seats across from each other at a table near the back, nice and quiet. After ordering, Aldridge reached out and took my hand. An odd mingling of wariness and amusement danced in his eyes. "Need to ask you something, Maud."

My good luck charm burned against my chest. Maybe it really did work. Excitement took my breath and just as quickly extinguished it. I wasn't getting any hopes up. Been down that hill before. First was Eli, my obsession for five years who left me quite alone and then robbed the bank. I'd arrested him, sent him to trial and ultimately prison in San Quentin. And now... Aldridge, had stolen my heart even stronger than Eli had done. Would My Perfect Man squash my feelings, run over them like a buffalo stampede? Or did he have another ribbon needing cutting? I sat silent, waiting, girding myself for the question.

"So, Maud." Aldridge rubbed the top of my hand with his thumb. "I need to go to San Francisco to pick up something. Shouldn't be gone more'n two, three weeks."

My curiosity piqued. "Pick up what?"

His gaze sailed around the room, then out the door. Words started and stopped, then started again. "Frankly, I'd rather not say at this point."

"Why not?" Was it something wonderful for me? The list of possibilities ran rampant. Of course it was for me. Otherwise, he'd be more forthcoming. "So, when *will* you tell me?" I wasn't about to let this drop.

He studied something over my shoulder, but I refused to turn around. Instead, I stared at our hands and then his face.

Aldridge lowered his voice. "When I get back, I'm hoping things will change. For us. I know they will for me."

"You're coming back? For sure?" The crushing weight on my chest lifted. But he still hadn't answered my question.

"Of course. If you'll let me."

Absolutely, I'd let him. I nodded rather than speaking, sure my voice would crack.

"Tonight, at the dance." Aldridge stuttered. "I'd like to announce..." He rubbed my hand hard. "Announce our betrothal. If you say yes."

Words failed me. Probably due to lack of air in my chest or numbness in my entire body. "Ask the question and I'll give you an answer." Did those words actually come out of my mouth?

His head cocked slightly. "Maud," his voice so soft I strained to hear. "Would you do me the honor of marrying me?"

Everything in my body screamed yes! Yes! And double yes! Before my mouth managed to form the word and get it out, my brain interrupted. Instead of committing, it instructed me—I had concerns and questions. Lots of them.

"What about—"

"A place to live?" Aldridge's eyes danced. "We'll rent a house in town and then, I figure, in a year after the school is going well, we'll move to Sacramento, open our own." He covered my hand with his. It trembled. "Please say yes."

Move? Sacramento? "What about my job?"

His mouth turned down while his eyebrows dipped. "Your job? As sheriff?" He released my hand and struggled with another breath. "I... I assumed you'd give it up. No need for you to work. I've recently come into a goodly sum of money, enough to support you and... children."

That exact picture was what I'd envisioned as long as I could remember. But... did I want it now?

Our eyes met and, in that instant, it was clear. I was sheriff. I liked being sheriff. Heck, I was a lady of the law.

A LOOK AT: TRAIL TO
TIN TOWN
THE COLTON BROTHERS SAGA

The exciting action and adventure western series from award-winning author Melody Groves and starring the Colton Brothers continues!

Despite battling a frenzied horse, poisoned water, aggravated Apache, a fanatical Army officer, along with other life-threatening trials, the four Colton Brothers—Trace, James, Luke, and Andy—refuse to turn their three thousand longhorns around and head back to Mesilla, New Mexico.

Determined to deliver the contracted beeves to Tin Town, California, on time, James Colton drives men and cattle as hard and as fast as he can. The brothers hope to celebrate the end of the Civil War and the cattle drive by hoisting a beer in Tin Town.

But Whid MacGilvry has other ideas. Killing James is not enough to exact his revenge for incorrectly perceived injustices. Destroying the entire Colton family will have to do. And where better than out on the range?

AVAILABLE NOW

ABOUT THE AUTHOR

Melody Groves is author of NM Press Women's Zia Award-winning *She Was Sheriff*, set in 1872 northern California, prequel to *Lady of the Law*. She also penned the Colton Brothers Saga: *Border Ambush*, *Sonoran Rage*, *Arizona War*, *Kansas Bleeds*, *Black Range Revenge*, and *Trail to Tin Town*.

Her non-fiction books include: the New Mexico Book Award winner, *Hoist a Cold One! Historic Bars of the Southwest*. Also, Zia finalist *Butterfield's Byways: The First Stagecoach Line and Overland Mail Route Across America* and *Ropes, Reins, and Rawhide: All About Rodeo*, *When Outlaws Wore Badges*, and recently, *Before Billy the Kid: The Boy Behind the Legendary Outlaw*.

Melody writes for national magazines. She won the prestigious National Press Women's Award for her article in *True West Magazine*.

When not writing, she plays rhythm guitar with the Jammy Time Band.